BJ SWANN   **ELIZABETH BEDLAM**

The Dark Ones öf Darkñess

Temperance Holocaust

+

Black Metal Jesus

Temperaṅce Hölöcaust

Chapter 1: Soiled Purity

The following is an excerpt from an interview between Jon Vertigo, editor of *Soiled Purity* extreme metal fanzine, and Sister Blood Cunt Christ Fucker, often simply known as Sister Blood, lead guitarist and self-proclaimed spiritual leader of the underground Christian black metal band Temperance Holocaust. The interview took place in 1998, just months before the strange and bloody events that would catapult the band to international stardom – and eternal infamy.

Jon Vertigo: So, you say you've actually met Jesus?

Sister Blood: Black Metal Jesus!

JV: Right, Black Metal Jesus. You've met him?

SB: Of course I've met him! I met him in the flesh. I was his bride, you know? At the convent. He came for me, to claim my cunt. He broke my hymen. He gave me Communion. I drank his blood, his cum. I ate his skin. He gave me his Word.

JV: His Word?

SB: The gospel of Black Metal Jesus!

JV: Right... And what did he say?

SB: He said to drink booze, take drugs, and fuck all night long. To sleep in the day and live by the dark. To spill blood and set things on fire. To smash all the rules and leave this retarded society in rubble! Only by hating humanity and doing whatever the fuck you want can you appease *Him*. But you must also cause destruction and chaos, too. Humanity has failed, you see. They are disgusting, and must therefore suck bitter death from the teats of oblivion! This is the twilight of the cunts. Pure fucking armageddon! It's time for all the little pigs and shit eaters to drown in their own blood. It's time for the world to burn. We're here to light the match, in His name.

JV: So you hate society and want to destroy the world, and you propose a philosophy of total hedonism...

SB: We must fuck like at Sodom and Gomorrah!

JV: Some people say your philosophy is exactly like that of the Satanic black metal bands that you profess to hate. What do you say to that?

SB: (spits on the floor) Satan? Fuck Satan! Satan is a faggot bitch. The Black Metal Messiah fucks him in the ass and makes him squeal like Dani Filth. Satanic black metal is for wimps and posers. Satanic black metal fans worship nothing more than an asshole.

JV: An asshole...?

SB: Yes! An asshole, that is correct. One with maggots and shit seeping out of it. They lick it because they are the asslickers! We swear eternal revenge on them.

JV: You're in conflict with them?

SB: An Eternal Conflict! It has been raging for over four months now. But we, the true believers of the Black Dragon, shall prevail! However, Satan's flock will not be so lucky (laughs). For they shall be slaughtered and cast down like their shit-eating master. You just wait...

JV: I heard you will be on tour with some Satanic black metal bands this summer, including Flagermus, the Danish Satanic band. They are very vocal in their hatred of you.

SB: It is good that they hate us. They are our arch-nemesis in the Eternal Conflict! We will watch them die.

JV: You're saying you're going to kill them?

SB: I said we will watch them die. They will be smote down by Black Metal Jesus for being the blasphemous heretics they are. But who knows, perhaps we will help make them die? Maybe we will poison them and set them on fire.

JV: Aren't you worried about going to jail?

SB: We are brides of Black Metal Jesus. We are not afraid to be martyrs for the cause. I don't care about going to jail for killing someone. If I hate them enough, it will be worth it. I don't give a fuck!

Chapter 2: Fans

"You mean they really were nuns?" asked Katie, her voice raised above the clamor of the crowd.

"They sure were," said Patrick. "They all came from Hollóhegy Convent in Hungary. It was some sort of prison for dangerous nuns."

"I heard it was an asylum for insane nuns," said Benny.

"Whatever," said Patrick. "It's hard to find out for sure. The whole place burned to the ground in nineteen-ninety-six. They say Sister Blood and the others set fire to it at night, roasting the rest of the nuns to death while they were sleeping."

"No way," said Katie. "They would have been arrested for sur."

"They fled the country, went to Rome. After that, they went to Norway to record."

"They went to Rome?"

"To get a sanction from the pope, to preach the Word of Black Metal Jesus. The Holy Father met them in a sealed session. No one knows what went on in there, but they say the Sisters fucked his withered old brains out in a filthy orgy. Since then he's been a huge fan, and he's used the power of the Vatican to protect them. That's why they've never been extradited to Hungary for arson and mass murder. That's why they got away with all that stuff in Norway too."

"What stuff?" Katie's eyes sparkled with interest. She was feeling increasingly fascinated by these black metal nuns, whom she'd barely even heard about before this afternoon. She'd mostly come to the Dark Ones of Darkness festival to see Pig Molester, a grindcore band featuring two former members of the infamous Hoghead outfit.

Word is they stabbed some Satanists in Oslo," said

Patrick. "And burned down a record store. Also, they mutilated cattle and desecrated graves. Plus, they were involved in an opium trafficking ring..."

Katie laughed. "No way. You shouldn't believe all these crazy rumors."

"It's true!" said Patrick. "They're the real deal."

His face was deadly earnest. So was the face of his friend Benny. They both had long hair and thick corpsepaint on their faces, even though it was 96 degrees. Their denim jackets were covered with Temperance Holocaust patches and nothing else. Darker spots on the denim, less faded than the rest, told the story of other band patches recently removed and discarded to make way for a singular obsession. Underneath their jackets the boys wore Temperance Holocaust T-Shirts, with the weird distressed logo and the title of the band's first and only studio album – Dawning of the Death Gash. Between the titles was a photo of naked feminine thighs spread wide to reveal not the model's cunt, but a slice of raw beef scored with a cross dripping beads of blood.

"Wow," said Katie, impressed by their devotion. "You really believe in these chicks, huh? Does that mean you're, like, black metal Christians or some shit?"

They stared at her without a shred of humor.

"That's right," said Patrick. "I used to be a Satanist –"

"I used to be a nihilist," said Benny.

"Right, but we both saw the black light when we started listening to the Sisters. Black Metal Jesus is where it's at. There's nothing more dark, more brutal. All that Satanic stuff is just wussy and gay in comparison."

Katie peered at them quizzically. From what she could tell, this black metal Christianity thing was pretty fucking weird. Still, as far as Christians went they seemed pretty cool. They were definitely cooler than those Jehova's Witness assholes who always came round on a Sunday, hammering on her door and trying to give her their stupid pamphlets and magazines.

"So what do you..."

Katie's voice trailed off as a cheer rose up from the crowd. She turned to see the curtains on the stage slowly parting. The sound check had finished; Temperance Holocaust were about to go live.

Patrick and Benny glanced at the stage, then at each other. They let out an ear-splitting roar, which was echoed by only a few other members of the crowd. Temperance Holocaust were not well known, which was why they were the first act on the bill, way before the headlining nu metal bands Noose and Jizz Biscuit, even before Flagermus, the Danish satanic black metal band whose members had supposedly burned down a MacDonalds in Copenhagen because they'd been too drunk and lazy to find the nearest church.

The curtain spread wider, revealing a huge bank of speakers and amplifiers, as well as a banner with the band's logo emblazoned above a cross. Katie stared at the logo in amusement. She'd never seen a cross at a metal gig that wasn't upside down before. The sight almost made her laugh.

A few people screamed and whistled as the curtains drew fully back, but the crowd was still relatively sedate. Most people seemed vaguely curious at best, rather than excited. Patrick and Benny, for their part, seemed oblivious to the lukewarm atmosphere surrounding them. Their eyes were wide with excitement. Their pupils bulged massively, obscuring their irises with blackness. Katie wasn't sure if they'd done some speed when she wasn't watching, or if they were just really, really excited to see their favorite band play live for the very first time.

"They're coming out!" shouted Patrick.

Five young women in nuns' habits filed out from behind the black banner and took up their positions on stage. The first was tall, pale, and willowy, dressed only in a skimpy black leather dress. A selection of knives was duct-taped to her torso, ready to be used. Her bare arms and legs were covered in scars, scabs, and poorly-healed lacerations. Her face was covered in corpsepaint that made her features look skeletal and sunken. Katie looked at her and felt a chill move down her spine. There was something eerie about the woman's expression - something intense, cold, and remote, as though she were not of this earth, but a visitor from some alien landscape of sorrow and perpetual winter.

"That's The Hand of Glory," said Patrick. "But most people call her HOG."

Katie thought "The Hand of Glory" was a silly name for a person, but she was too spooked to say anything. The scarred woman picked up a microphone, staring intensely at the crowd.

Another woman came and stood next to her. A distressed cross was painted on her face in black over white. She was dressed like a nun, except that her skirt was cut short and ragged, baring her pale tattooed legs. She picked up a guitar and strummed it once, unleashing a rusty explosion of sound from the speaker banks behind.

"That's Sister Blood!" said Benny. "She writes all the lyrics!"

Another black metal nun came and picked up a bass guitar. She was dressed like a fetish model or a dominatrix, with lots of tight latex and leather. Nordic runes like thunderbolts were painted on her cheeks in black over white. She had a serious case of resting bitch face.

"That's Sister Leper Licker," said Patrick. "She plays bass."

A short woman hurried into position behind the drum kit. She had corpsepaint and a habit like the others, but otherwise her clothes were casual, consisting of cut-off black jeans and a T-Shirt with holes in it. She spun her sticks in the air, her whole body throbbing with manic energy.

"That's Sister Whoreface," said Patrick. "The fastest fucking drummer in the world!"

Another woman came and stood behind a keyboard, but she was largely obscured from Katie's view by the curtains.

"Who's that?" asked Katie.

Patrick and Benny both shrugged.

"No idea!" said Patrick.

All three of them stared at the stage as Sister HOG raised the microphone to her black-painted lips.

"Only by sin can you be saved. Sin all Fucking Day!"

She pointed at the crowd as she spoke, and as the last syllable left her lips the music began. Whoreface hammered the drums in a frenzy. A wave of brutal percussion rolled out from the speakers, freakishly fast, loud, and monotonous. Sister Blood and Leper Licker strummed their guitars, unleashing rusty chainsaw sounds. HOG's voice hit the air, brutal, guttural, but terribly clear. To Katie, she sounded like that possessed kid in *The Exorcist*.

As the aural onslaught rolled out over the crowd, a change began to take place. The atmosphere shifted, dominated by the music. Something dark and unearthly was being unleashed; Katie could feel it in her shuddering bones. She watched as frat boys who'd come for the nu metal headliners began to retreat from the stage, unable to withstand the band's dark brutality.

Pussies, thought Katie with a grin.

Others began to draw closer. Many of them were grindcore fans like her, or devotees of thrash and death. Their instinct to mosh had been awakened.

"We've gotta get in there!" shouted Patrick. "Right up front!"

"There's no way!" screamed Katie.

Surely, she thought, they were too far back, and the crowd towards the front was getting too dense. But the boys didn't seem to care. They were intent on getting close to their idols.

"We'll get in there!" roared Patrick, with the certainty of a religious maniac. "You coming?"

He held out his hand to Katie. She hesitated a moment. She barely knew these guys, and had only met them while standing in line to get into the festival. But they seemed cool enough. With a smile and a shrug she took Patrick's hand, and he led her into the mosh. Benny, the bigger of the two, took up position at the vanguard, rudely thrusting his way through the crowd. Plastic beer cups went flying. People cursed at him, and a few pushed back, but most shied away from his painted face and six-foot frame as he barrelled through them like a tractor through wheat. Following in his wake, Katie and Patrick were soon deep in the mosh pit, where the ceaseless drumbeat reverberated through the ground like the beginnings of an earthquake, and the dirty, screaming sound of vocals and guitars tore through the air like the claws of some terrible ghost seeking to rip through the flesh of reality itself. Katie couldn't make out many of the lyrics, only the chorus —

Sin All Night
Drink, Fuck, Fight
Fornicate your life

Katie felt the music throbbing through her body, waves of sound bashing her bones, caressing her internal organs. Her heart began to hammer fast as adrenaline exploded in her veins, aroused by the excitement of the music and the mayhem of the mosh-pit, where bodies thrashed and leapt all around her. The tunes were just to her liking – fast and brutal. And yet, there was more to it than that. There was a feel to the music, an atmosphere, something transcendental. It wasn't skilled music, it wasn't beautiful music. It was crude, chaotic, even nasty. But it filled her with a sense of something primordial. She wanted to punch someone in the face. She wanted to fuck. She wanted to drink hot blood.

"These guys are wicked!" she said as she leapt into the mosh with abandon, shoulder-smashing everyone around her, bouncing back and forth between the larger frames of young men and boys. She was a slight thing, and knew she could be easily crushed by any one of them. The danger was part of the fun.

Patrick and Benny moshed beside her, shouldering and bludgeoning their way to the absolute front of the pit. Soon they were looking up at the Sisters, who unleashed another song – "Tortured Whores of Gehenna." Katie lost herself in the thundering thrum of buzz-saw guitars and never-ending drum beats. The stench of spilled beer and body odor filled her nostrils, completing the experience. She closed her eyes, savoring the moment –

Then felt something warm and wet hit her face. She opened her eyes, touched her cheek, and drew back fingers red with blood. Looking up she saw a young man clutching a busted-open mouth. His lips were torn and a tooth was hanging between his fingers on a thread of raw nerve. He was wearing a Flagermus T-Shirt. Groaning in pain, he pushed past Katie towards the rear of the crowd. As he left, Benny caught Katie's eye and shot her a wink. There was blood on his elbow.

Katie froze for a moment, before being knocked forward by someone behind her. She steadied herself against Patrick, then started jumping around once again. You had to keep moving in the mosh, or you'd go down.

Katie looked up at the stage, and saw even more blood. Sister HOG had removed one of the knives from its duct tape sheath, and was slicing into the flesh of her left arm, leaving shallow lacerations that dripped bright blood all over the front of the stage. She shrieked in otherworldly tones as she cut herself, then flailed her arms, flinging the blood into the crowd. Katie closed her eyes and mouth as panicked thoughts of Hep C and HIV flashed through her mind. She wiped her face and opened her eyes to see Patrick and Benny splattered with the blood, their mouths open, their tongues roving across their lips and painted cheeks to lap up the redness.

The song ended and another began, erupting like a bomb blast following a split-second pause. Sister HOG screamed out the name of the track – "Rot my cunt."

Less than a minute into the song a vile stench filled the air. At first Katie thought someone in the mosh might have shat their pants, but the scent was more acrid, more biting. It felt wet in her nostrils, like a physical presence, as if a slimy specter was picking her nose. She gagged, then looked up and saw the source of the stink. Sister Leper Licker was holding up a black trash bag in front of HOG's face. HOG reached in and removed a dead rat. The thing was in a state of vile putrefaction, bloated, discolored, flesh sloughing off, maggots oozing out of its disintegrating hide.

As it emerged into the air the stench got worse. HOG breathed in the stink with such emphasis it looked like she was snorting a line of invisible cocaine. She touched the dead rat, coating her fingers with slime, then traced them along her wounds, mingling the putrescence with her own blood. Then she slipped her fingers between her legs, and sang –

Angel of decay
Rot my cunt
Angel of decay
Heal my heart

Katie's eyes went wide. She couldn't believe this shit. These bitches were crazy!

Chaos spread through the mosh pit, as if the madness on stage was affecting the audience below. Fights broke out in patches. Katie saw two shirtless skinheads openly punching a death metal fan in the face. It's always fucking skinheads, she thought. But it wasn't just skinheads. She saw Patrick and Benny take out another Flagermus fan with almost surgical brutality. First they flanked the poor guy, then simultaneously shoulder-slammed him, crushing him between them. As he slumped, winded, Benny turned and kneed him in the balls. He sank to his knees and Patrick swung wildly, elbowing his face and knocking him prone. As he slumped into the dirt, both Patrick and Benny started jumping up and down on his legs. When some concerned metalheads dragged the guy to his feet, Patrick and Benny backed off, pretending the whole thing had just been an accident. In the heat of the moment, Katie wasn't sure what to think. It was shocking – but also kind of cool. And it almost felt right somehow, especially as the next track – "Call of the Bone Smasher" – came blasting from the stage.

The song was the heaviest, wildest yet. As it began, HOG threw the dead rat into the crowd. It bounced off a skinhead's bald dome and landed near Katie's feet. She looked down and saw that its tiny rat feet had been impaled with nails, like some rodent Christ crucified by hardware store Romans. She kicked it away, feeling a spark of sick excitement as her boots made contact with the corpse.

More dead bodies rained down, a dozen varieties of roadkill – raccoons, foxes, feral cats, even a dog with its collar still on, emblazoned with the name "Tiddlywinks." The air reeked of death so profound it drowned out the iron tang of HOG's blood along with the stink of sweat and beer. One guy threw up, while others fled from the mosh. Katie kept her gorge down and stayed right where she was. Disgusted though she might be, she couldn't pull away. The frenzy of the music intensified. HOG, her hands crawling with maggots, gestured to the crowd, beckoning them closer.

Metalheads began mounting the stage and leaping off into the mosh, surfing the sea of bodies. Katie reached up to support their weight, helping them pass overhead towards the rear of the pit. Then Patrick grabbed her hand and dragged her to the stage. A flurry of excitement and fear fluttered through her guts as she realized she was about to share the same space with those death-sniffing, self-mutilating maniacs.

Patrick climbed up after Benny, then dragged Katie up after him. Benny threw up the horns, then leapt straight back into the mayhem. Patrick was about to follow suit, when Sister Blood grabbed him by the wrist.

Katie watched, frozen with wonder, as the lead guitarist pushed Patrick down to his knees in front of her. The music slowed to an eerie, ritualistic crawl. The madness of the mosh diminished as all eyes fixed on the spectacle.

"It is time," roared HOG, "Time for Cuntunion!"

Cuntunion? thought Katie. What the fuck is —

Sister Blood raised her tattered dress. She wasn't wearing any underwear. Her pubes and thighs were smeared with gore, and a thick string of menstrual blood was slowly oozing from her cunt. She grabbed Patrick's long hair and thrust his face between her legs. Eagerly he dove in and began lapping at the gore.

I guess that's what Cuntunion is, thought Katie, as a burly security guard took her by the arm and dragged her to the edge of the stage.

It was time for her to dive. She leapt into the crowd and found herself carried away, watching the shapes of Patrick and the Sisters get smaller and smaller, until she was deposited on the outer edge of the pit, like flotsam carried by the cruel sea to a deserted island. There she was trapped until the set finished five minutes later.

"All Hail!" shouted HOG, making the sign of the cross instead of flipping the horns. She dropped the mic, and the Sisters departed the stage to the sound of patchy applause. Some people were clapping and screaming like mad, while others just stared, shocked and perhaps even appalled by what they'd just witnessed. Katie stood by herself, rooted to the spot, her heart still hammering fast in her chest. A few minutes later Patrick and Benny came walking towards her. Patrick's face was covered in menses. Most people gave him a wide berth, as though scared of the blood. Benny looked at him enviously.

"I'm never washing this off," said Patrick, pointing at his bloody mouth. "Never. Fucking. Washing it!"

They paused when they saw Katie, smiling at her. Even Patrick's teeth were red.

"So," he said. "What did you think of Temperance Holocaust?"

Katie beamed. After today, she knew she'd be a fan for life.

Chapter 3: The Hand of Glory

"HOG? Are you eating?"

The Hand of Glory knew a voice was trying to convey a message to her, but it wasn't the message - or the voice - she desired. All around her the sheep wandered about in their people skin. This wasn't the place she wanted to be. Everyone was dripping with black leather, indulging in earthly delights. They were just so...*alive*. It disgusted her.

"I said *are you eating*?"

"I'm fasting," said HOG, glancing up at Whoreface, the tiny drummer. HOG's voice was more like the croaking exhalation of a corpse than the sound of a young, living woman - which was just how she liked it.

"At least have some water," said Whoreface. "Come on, I'll get you some. It's hotter than a whore in church out here. You need to drink."

Whoreface took HOG's hand. Her sweat mingled with the singer's drying blood.

HOG allowed herself to be led through the hordes of pretenders. She saw no use in arguing, no point trying to explain how she didn't actually need food or drink anymore. She was beyond all that, and had been for quite some time. On one level she was already dead, yet she continued to linger on the fringes of life, awaiting the day when the Black Dragon, her one true love, her spirit husband, decided she was worthy to come to Him. Until then, she would atone.

HOG scratched her prominent ribs. The Florida heat, combined with the hairshirt she wore beneath her habit, made her skin itch even more than usual, irritating the wounds she suffered from the three cilice garters she wore at all times. Homemade from wire hangers and razorblades, the garters made sure she was always bleeding, and that every movement resulted in at least some modicum of agony. HOG did all these things to mortify her flesh, and yet it never seemed enough. No matter how much she tortured herself or abstained from the pleasures of the world, the disdain HOG felt for her disgusting body, her sinful cunt, weighed on her day after day, year after year. But HOG knew she had no choice but to continue to scar her skin and defile her gash, until He called her home.

"Sit down and drink this," said Whoreface, pushing HOG down into a chair and placing a styrofoam cup of water in front of her.

For a moment HOG ignored the cup and observed her surroundings. The shadows cast over the food tent by the cheery yellow canvas above did little to stifle the humidity of the Florida day. The air reeked of sweat and fries. And yet, the weather alone was not painful enough. HOG turned to Whoreface and held out her hand.

"Salt," she demanded.

"Just drink the water, Sister," said Whoreface.

HOG stared at Whoreface. As devoted as the drummer seemed, HOG knew she lacked the true passion needed to ascend beyond the level of a mediocre musician to something more. She could never possibly understand HOG's devotion.

"Salt," the singer repeated, her words stern.

"Here," said Leper Licker, tossing her a handful of salt packets. She smirked as HOG ripped open two of the sachets, dumping the contents into a wide cut on her forearm, smearing the crystals into the wound.

"How's that feel?" Leper Licker asked.

"It burn*sss*," HOG hissed, feeling the stinging caress of her Jesus. *He* saw her sacrifice, and she knew how aroused it made him. Only He was capable of squeezing a drop of wet desire from between her thighs.

"No shit it burns," said Sister Blood as she popped open a soda can and drank.

HOG eyed her, noting silently that she hadn't prayed before consuming the beverage. HOG expected such carelessness from anyone else, but to see it coming from Blood shocked and sickened her. Once her Sister of the Veil had been as devoted as she. Both had heard the Word of the Black Metal God early - HOG as an anchoress, Blood as an inmate of the convent. But since those early days it seemed as if their paths had begun to veer in different directions. HOG could see it more clearly every day - Sister Blood was starting to worship the music before God.

Having prayed through an act of salty self-sacrifice, HOG felt she could now drink her water. "Tastes like it was stored in the bladder of a pig," she remarked, though she took a second gulp nevertheless. Some dribbled down her chin, but she couldn't be bothered wiping it away. Oh, how she wished for the water to be not water, but of *Him*. Her holy husband. How she ached for his purifying blood on her skin. His hot iron scepter between her thighs. His holy white purity swimming in her guts. His -

"What do you think?"

One of them was trying to talk to her again, ruining yet another vision. HOG didn't respond, but with her reverie broken, she had no choice now but to sit, drink her tepid water, and listen to her Sisters bicker about the concert, heavy metal culture, and other bands on the tour, all meaningless earthly problems that meant nothing to HOG. Sometimes she didn't even know who these nuns were anymore.

HOG's Sisters all agreed: the first show had gone worse than any of them could ever have anticipated. No one had been hospitalized, and the fights had been juvenile at best, with minimum blood spillage.

The crowd had cheered too loudly. Their desperate enthusiasm was pathetic. And to top it all off, just after the set, the Sisters had been threatened with dismissal from the tour if they used roadkill in their act again.

"It's a health risk, surely you understand," said the faceless assistant tour manager whose name HOG could not remember.

"What of the dove?" she asked, holding up a Cheeto bag that stank of decay.

"Uh...sure," came the manager's mumbled reply. "Just the one. Keep it, um, in the bag though, okay?" he added before hurrying off.

HOG had found the dove at the airport while she and her Sisters were waiting for the bus. It was the first beautiful thing she'd seen since arriving in America. The bird looked as if it had been crushed by a speeding car, then left to rot in the 90 degree heat all day. HOG scraped it off the pavement with her fingers.

"Give me that bag," she said to Sister Leper Licker.

"Are you serious? It still has -"

"This is an omen. I need to preserve it!"

Leper Licker sighed, shrugged, then emptied the bag of Cheetos she'd just purchased into the pocket of her tunic.

"Here, fucking take it," she said, handing the bag to HOG.

The rest of the band watched as HOG dumped the mangled and bloated remains of the dove into the bag. She scraped up bits of bones and dry entrails, then tossed them in too, where they mingled with the cheesy dust coating the bag's shimmering lining.

"So what's it mean?" Leper Licker finally asked. "This omen?"

HOG didn't answer. She spent the rest of the night meditating on the meaning of the divine message. Finally she received a vision, which she recorded in the back of her hand-written Bible, using her blood for ink as she so often did. The entry, titled "Dove Rot Prophecy," contained ragged sketches of the images she'd seen —

Alligators bathing in blood.

Headless cockroaches dancing with miniature canes and tap-dancing shoes.

Nine turds arranged on a throne of gold, being worshiped like the Golden Calf.

A two-headed serpent biting itself.

A crimson she-ape riding on a pig with four heads and four heinous erections.

Mannequins bursting into flames and melting into a pool of sticky red syrup.

A castle exploding.

HOG's own face withering, transforming into the image of a skull.

What a glorious vision it had been, what delightful clues it offered for events yet to come. HOG let it replay through her mind over and over, until she was once again distracted, brought back to the present by the chatter of her Sisters.

"I can't eat this shit," Whoreface said, shoving her tray of food aside so violently it flew off the table and landed on a guy's foot. The man was wearing a backwards baseball cap. As the food soiled his shit-colored Timberland boots, his previously vapid expression grew angry.

"What?" snapped Whoreface, staring at him insolently. "Do you have something to say?"

The man who was dressed like a teenage boy glared at her for a second, then shuffled on, mumbling under his breath.

"That's what I fucking thought," hissed Whoreface. "Pretender!" She scoffed, then turned to her Sisters. "What the fuck is wrong with these people? I thought

Americans loved to fight. I haven't seen one fucking gun since we got here."

Whoreface was obviously disappointed. All her life she'd heard about the incredible violence, mayhem, and wonderful churches of the American south. She'd been sure she would fit right in. But so far everyone was fat, their mouths dripping with trash. This was not the land of her dreams.

HOG shifted her focus from Whoreface's disappointment to the obvious ego clash occurring between Leper Licker and Sister Blood.

"We need to do more interviews," said Leper Licker. "Did you see all the horns at that show? What the fuck was that? No one knows what we're even about. I think -"

"We have already done too many interviews," said Sister Blood, interrupting the other. The tension had been mounting between her and Leper Licker for a while now, and the band's arrival in the States had only made it worse. "We do not play to get popular," she added. "We don't waste time doing stupid interviews. Those worthy of the Word will find us, and that is how we'll spread the holy Dragon's message, not through endless streams of propaganda bullshit. We just need to play his gospels. That is all."

"Fuck that!" said Leper Licker. "We've done a single interview, Blood. One! Do you suddenly speak for us all? Are you so special that Jesus made you His one and only mouthpiece?!"

HOG could tell Sister Blood was annoyed. This exact same argument had come up so many times before - at rehearsal, during confessional, before mass, even during the Orgy of Holy Sin. It seemed neverending.

"You know that is not what I'm saying," snapped Sister Blood. "This expectation, this rod of popularity you seek, I break it over my knee. No more!"

"What are you talking about?" said Leper Lick-
er, laughing theatrically. "Ha! I will speak the truth as it
was given onto *me*! I will expose the frauds, and bring
forth the darkness of the Black Metal Messiah down
onto the masses!"

As Sister Blood and Leper Licker continued to yell
at each other, Whoreface placed a hand on HOG's.

"I think you might need a few stitches this time,
Sister," she said, eyeing HOG's self-inflicted wounds.
"That one looks deep."

"No," said HOG. Her voice was firm. How could her
Sister even suggest such a blasphemous thing? They
had all taken a vow to give themselves to Black Metal
Jesus. Pain and mutilation came with the territory. And
yet it was only HOG who truly embraced it. Only she
loved Him enough to truly revel in self-destruction, to
court death with each cruel devotion. A little deeper, a
little harder next time with her knife, and she'd be lying
with her Black Dragon King in Heaven, instead of sitting here amidst the stench of deep fried potatoes, listening to her bandmates quibble about interviews.

Sister Blood and Leper Licker were still arguing. HOG eyed them in disgust as they alternated between shouting at each other and cramming greasy
french fries into their mouths. Clearly they were enrap-
tured not by Jesus, but by worldly delights such as saturated fats and the mindless adoration of the masses. They were drifting away from the sweet, dark kiss
of their Savior, while only HOG continued to dive deeper into Black Metal Salvation, seeking the raw, bloody
bite of repentance. Only *she* sought the bottomless
pit in which her soul truly lay. It was a path with only
one outcome: glorious martyrdom. But the others? A
time would come, HOG knew, when she might have to
choose between her bandmates and salvation. And if

that day came, she knew she'd have no choice but to leave them behind. And that would be their own damn fault.

Whoreface filled up HOG's styrofoam cup with more water, and urged her to drink again. "You look horrible," she said.

"I am fine," said HOG. She pushed the water aside and nodded toward the bickering guitar players. "Will this shit ever end? Make them be quiet."

"You know it'll only get worse if I say something," said Whoreface.

"Where is that girl who plays the organ? Make her do it then," HOG said. She and Whoreface looked around, but the keyboardist was missing as usual.

They turned their attention back to the table as Sister Leper shoved her chair back and rose to her feet. "I can't take this fucking heat!" she snapped. "How can anyone live in this hellhole!? I need a shower - and a priest. Is that okay with you? Or do I need your permission to take a shower and suck off a seminarian, *Sister*?"

She glared at Blood, but Blood didn't answer; her attention had been caught by something in the distance, far behind Leper licker.

The rest of the Sisters turned to see what she was looking at, then scowled as they caught sight of Flagermus, the notorious Danish Satanic Black Metal band, entering the food tent.

"How did they even get out of their shitty country?" asked Leper Licker. "When I saw them on the bill I thought for sure it was a mistake. But it looks like they'll let anyone join the tour. Even cunty, blasphemous heretics!" She raised her voice so the Danes could hear, but they either didn't notice, or didn't care.

Leper Licker's nostrils flared like those of an angry sow. She strode towards the Satanists, raring for blood. Blood and Whoreface hurried after.

"Come on," Whoreface said, tugging HOG to her feet and dragging her along.

"Where the fuck is that useless keyboarist?" Blood muttered, following after Leper Licker as the latter shoved through the crowd towards the Satanic trio.

"Move!" Leper Licker shouted, shoving a guy in a boiler suit aside.

Leper Licker seemed determined to finally get her hands on those sinful Danish worms. The rivalry between Temperance Holocaust and Flagermus was intense, and yet, despite having been locked in The Eternal Conflict for almost four months, the two bands had never met in person. Temperance Holocaust were banned from Denmark because of a legal dispute, and Flagermus weren't allowed in Norway due to an incident involving an underage girl and fifty feet of fishing line.

Thus it was that the two feuding bands had been forced to wage war by more subtle means, including a series of disparaging remarks in black metal fanzines and a campaign of prank international phone calls. Through such dastardly measures the intensity of the conflict had ratcheted up to a boiling point. HOG had hoped that by coming to America, she and her Sisters would be granted a reprieve from this neverending blood feud. Yet here the enemy was, looming and stinking before them, like a Baphomet statue made from human excrement.

"Ladies - I mean *Sisters* - your show was so...*cute*," said the lead singer of Flagermus, Jokum Panzer. "A little preachy for my taste, but good nonetheless."

"Stay here," Whoreface said as she left HOG's side, slipping a straight razor from her boot, with the obvious intention of cutting the stinking smirk off Panzer's face. She clearly didn't care that he was six feet five inches compared to her four feet nine inches. She often assaulted people who were taller than her.

HOG wondered briefly if she should stop the petite drummer. A murder could result in them being jailed and deported. But what if it was His will? She placed her hands together and prayed for guidance, while the ruckus continued around her.

"Hail Satan!" yelled a member of Flagermus in a tight fishnet shirt and spiked dog collar. He threw up the horns like a declaration of war. By this time many of the other bands were beginning to gather around the confrontation, some merely spectating, others choosing sides.

"Fuck the filthy sinners up, Sister Whoreface!" shouted Lady Arc, lead singer of Bible Licker, a Texas-based Christian thrash band.

Whoreface lurched forward, ready to carve a cross into Jokum Panzer's forehead.

"Yeah, do it, Whoreface!" shouted Arc, as several of her bandmates cheered.

"Quiet, pretender!" shouted HOG, shocking and silencing them all. She had received His instructions, and was ready to speak. "Blood spilled soaks into the ground and is wasted. Yet blood of truth spilt on parchment is pure, in that it is the true Word of the Lord, the Black Dragon, having nothing to do with the body of the flesh. All hail!"

The musicians stood for a moment in awkward silence. Neither the Sisters, Flagermus, nor anyone else seemed to comprehend the divine truth HOG was offering.

"So I *can't* stab 'em?" asked Whoreface, holding her blade questioningly.

HOG said nothing; she felt she had made her point quite clear.

"No, Sister, you can not," Sister Blood said, taking

control of the situation. "Not now, anyway." She added in a sinister whisper, "There are too many witnesses."

Sister Leper Licker fondled the knife taped to the inside of her thigh. "Seriously?" she said. "Let's spill some blood for -"

"No!" snapped Sister Blood. "Let's go. HOG is right." Blood gave a stern look that neither Leper Licker nor Whoreface dared to challenge.

Departing the food tent, the Sisters emerged into the sickening sunshine. The haughty laughter of Danish worms followed them.

"Those subhumanoid creeps," hissed Leper Licker. "I can't believe -"

"Relax, Sister,' said HOG, her croaking voice full of serenity. "Relax, and be joyful. For I have seen the future in the guts of the dove, and I know that death is coming to this Festival sooner or later - death, bloodshed, and purifying flame. In the meantime, we must preach the Word!"

Chapter 4: Whoreface

The music from the main stage blared so loudly Whoreface could hear it from inside the stuffy tour bus. Unfortunately it wasn't loud enough to drown out the sound of her two Sisters, Blood and Leper Licker, who were still fighting about whether the band should do more interviews.

"Fuck this shit!" screamed Leper Licker as she smashed a bottle of gin and stormed out of the bus.

"You want to be a leader, but you are not a leader!" Blood shouted as Leper slammed the door. "Cunt!"

Blood hissed even more curses under her breath, then fled to the back of the bus where a makeshift chapel had been constructed for daily devotionals to the Black Metal Messiah.

Whoreface sighed and turned to the singer.

"Hey HOG, want to check out some of the other bands? They're total shit, but I need to get out of here."

HOG didn't answer. Picking at her teeth with her switchblade, Whoreface excavated a large chunk of meat from a cavity in one of her molars, briefly inspecting it before flicking it in HOG's direction. It landed on HOG's cheek, but still the singer did not respond. She was too busy staring at the sky in a trance. When she got this catatonic, almost nothing could get through to her - but that didn't stop Whoreface from trying.

"Come on!" shouted Whoreface. "We can go find someone to fuck up, or find some smack, or *something*. Anything. Hey!"

Whoreface leaned across the table and stabbed HOG in her lower arm. HOG didn't flinch.

Whoreface sighed. "Fine, catch you later," she said, rising from the seat and pulling the blade from the singer's arm. Blood glistened on the tip of the stiletto. Whoreface licked it clean before resetting the blade and stashing it in the back pocket of her ragged jeans. "If Leper comes back," she said, "don't let her and Blood kill each other. That's something I don't want to miss."

HOG remained silent.

"Right, fuck off then. Later."

Whoreface pushed out into the evening. It was like entering a jungle. The air was humid and sticky, buzzing with mosquitoes and the noises of the festival. The bands seemed to play louder at night. The crowds, drunk and obnoxious, became more destructive. Whoreface headed in the direction of the mainstage, the sound of screaming fans growing louder as she approached.

The foul creatures that made up the headlining band, Noose, were banging on steel trash cans while the singer rapped over the tap of the incessant metal clanging. Soon two guitarists and three bass players joined in, along with a DJ and a keyboardist, causing the people down in the pit to lose their fucking minds. Whoreface counted four percussionists in total. "What a waste, just get one good one." Her observation was mostly drowned out by the scratching of records from their subpar DJ. She figured it was a good thing they were the headlining band and made actual money, because splitting a hundred bucks twelve ways would suck.

As Whoreface continued to stare, not even her thick corpsepaint could hide the obvious look of disgust and annoyance that sat on her sour little face.

"I can see you think they fucking suck, too. Can't believe we had to open for those fucking fairies. What kind of bullshit is that? Fucking gay assholes, I tell ya..."

Whoreface looked to see where the voice in her ear had come from, and immediately wished she hadn't. It was the man-child in the baseball cap and baggy cargo shorts from the food tent, Ted Découché. His little patch of chin hair annoyed her. She wanted to slice it off and make him eat it. Instead, she turned back to the stage, where the singer was trying to play an acoustic guitar while the crowd held up lighters. She tried to decide which was worse - watching Noose stumble around half-blinded by their masks, or talking to this homophobic motherfucker Ted Découché.

She thought maybe if she didn't look at him he might go away. It didn't work. He lingered in her peripheral vision, talking...talking...still fucking talking. Beginning to feel desperate, she glanced past him, looking for a way out.

"Hey, you like this?" came his whispered voice in her ear, even more humid and disgusting than the Florida air.

She felt a heavy, sweaty hand grasp her wrist. It took her a second to realize it was Ted Découché guiding her hand towards his crotch. Overcome by a shameful curiosity, she briefly fondled the man - and burst out laughing. What a pathetic worm! More like a baby finger than a cock! What would she even do with such a thing? She couldn't imagine. Whoreface yanked her hand away and walked off.

"Don't follow me!" she screamed.

(twenty minutes later)

"...so we smeared it all on a cracker, then each took a bite. And that's how we got the name Jizz Biscuit, you know? You follow...? Huh? Cool, right? Yeah, I know. Just talking about it makes me speechless sometimes."

Whoreface stared at him, finding it hard to believe he was *still* talking. She'd moved from one side of the stage to another multiple times, trying to lose him in the crowd, but he just kept reappearing, ignoring her threats, and spilling verbal diarrhea in her ear. She needed him to stop talking, RIGHT NOW, or she was going to lose it.

"...So by exposing their tits it's meant to be like, librating for the woman. I mean, what bitch wouldn't want to show 'em off and get paid for it? If I had 'em I sure as shit would. I'd be flashing my tits *allll* over the place. Ha-ha! But fucking politics right? I mean, you get it. Censorship and bullshit. The government has been trying to repress artists since the beginning. I mean, you totally get it. The public cares if two fags can't get service at a bakery, but no one gives a fuck about artists. Ya know? You got homos over there in like, um...where you from? I don't know, all those countries are like, the same - COLD! Ha-ha!" He cleared his throat, " But uh....Norway, right? Yeah, we toured there. Lots of *cool* chicks, ha- ha!" He didn't seem to notice Whoreface wasn't laughing. "Too bad we can't get more of you guys to immigrate over here, instead we get people from all these shit hole countries ruining the system for *real* Americans. Ya know? You guys got problems with foreigners too?"

Whoreface turned and walked toward the wide grassy field behind the stage. She figured she could lose him in the crowds on her way back to the bus. She really didn't want to be stuck on the bus, listening to Blood praying frantically, or HOG rambling in a trance, or Leper Licker talking about sucking off seminarians or that Nazi bullshit she sometimes went on about. But fuck it, Whoreface would deal with it. Anything would be better than being talked at by Ted Découché. She zigged and she zagged among the throngs of metal zombies and their beers.

"....I know, it pisses me off too. You get it, yeah? Fuck yeah you do..."

Somehow, no matter how much she zigged

and zagged, he was *STILL* right there beside her, TALKING. Was there no end to her misery? Why had she thought it was a good idea to leave the bus?!?

Chapter 5: Ted Découché

After an hour spent warming the little nun up, she was finally leading him away from the crowds, probably toward some semi-private place where she could swallow his load.

Well, if you insist, thought Ted. He was never one to turn down a tight cunt or willing mouth. No matter how smelly or grungy a chick was, you'd have to be a total queer to pass on anything with tits. And this bitch was really doing it for him. That nun head scarf thingy, that smeared make-up, it was driving him crazy. He bet this little one gave a killer blowjob.

He wasn't sure how good her English was, so he'd tried to convey his message of love in other ways. Mostly by using his sharp wit and brain. Chicks like her were always turned on when he talked about the road, politics, and his three Grammy awards. He knew his suave routine was working when, less than five minutes into their meeting, he caught her checking out his cock. She quickly turned away and tried to pretend she was watching the stage, but he knew.

Usually he intimidated bitches with his size. "Hey, you like this?" He asked her, taking her hand and placing it over the crotch of his cargo shorts. She giggled, then playfully sped away, yelling something like "follow me!"

Oh, she liked to be chased. He was cool with that.

Here, kitty cunt, he thought, sniffing her out. It took him fifteen minutes to find her huddled behind a stack of amps. After seducing her with his genius mind he could tell her thighs were ready to open. She gave him the *come hither* look and hurried off again, this time towards the grassy area behind the stage, where the tour buses were parked amidst faded beer cans and ancient condoms filled with desiccated sperm. He followed, barely able to keep up as she dodged between couples and jumped over cords. Damn, this bitch was dripping for him!

"So where did they park your bus? Ours is right over there with the headliners and stuff. Cool right? Hey, want to come on over? We got some killer bud and -"

Chapter 6: Whoreface

Whoreface stopped abruptly, turning to regard the unending horror that was Ted Découché. Her head only came up to his chest, but she could still make out the feebleminded look on his face. The guy was a fucking idiot, that much was obvious.

"Enough!" she shouted. "I don't know *why* you're talking to me, but I can't take it anymore! Just shut the fuck up already! Or I'll -"

She paused, thinking - could she really? She'd certainly be doing the world a favor. But her Sisters would be so pissed off! Assuming they found out, that is. But... What they didn't know, they couldn't get upset about...

"Or you'll what?" said Ted, even though he already knew the answer. He knew she was warning him that if he didn't stop arousing her right now with his charming conversation, she'd lose her mind and try to suck his cock right in front of everyone. That sort of thing happened to him all the time. It was his smile, his body, his fame, it got him more pussy than a toilet seat. Why should a nun be any different? They were women too. They had needs. Probably more needs than anyone else, since they were all spinsters and virgins and shit.

"Hold on," he said. "Before this goes any further, how old are you? Because there was this one time with this girl in Montana, and..."

Chapter 8: Whoreface

Whoreface scanned the parking lot, trying to find someplace private. She couldn't take Ted Découché back to the bus. And she certainly couldn't go back to his bus either. Unfortunately the whole lot was infested with roaches posing as people. She began to despair of finding anywhere to do the deed, until her gaze stopped on a row of plastic blue porta-potties. It was the one place nearby no one would be able to stumble into.

Meanwhile, Ted was still talking.

"...her parents were cool with it as long as I paid for the abortion and, oh shit! That's right, you're Catholic. Um..."

"Come with me, Douche," Whoreface said.

"Ha-ha! It's Dé-cou-*ché*. It's French. Hey, where are you from, again? You never answered. Like, Sweden or Finland right? Are you friends with those Satanic Dutch guys? They seem cool."

Whoreface wanted to open his throat for that remark alone, but instead pulled him into the blue shitter at the farthest end of the row. Their bodies pressed tightly together in the cramped, smelly interior.

"Oh-*kay*," he said. "Whoa...in here, huh? That's cool with me. Yeah, sweet!"

Whoreface pushed him so he was sitting down over the open shithole.

"So you want to suck it or ride it, Sister?" Ted asked, before he launched into yet another tangent. "So you nuns and priests really have orgies? Ha-ha! I could get down with that. You want to kiss my ring?"

Whoreface ignored his verbal diarrhea. The time was at hand. She plucked the stiletto from the back pocket of her jeans, flipped out the blade, and poised it for the thrust.

"For you my Black Dragon, my holy husband, except this sacrifice!" she screamed.

"Huh?" said Ted.

Whoreface plunged her blade in and out of the man's fleshy side, just below the ribs. The jabs were so swift he didn't even have time to drop his dick. A wet choke escaped his lips, probably the smartest thing he'd said that evening. A foul stench rose up as his bladder and bowels began to malfunction. He lifted a hand to try and stop the killer nun, but his strength was already ebbing. Whoreface shoved his feeble arm aside and watched the life bleed from him. When Ted became still, Whoreface closed her eyes and began to pray.

"Jesus, my Black Metal Messiah," she whispered, "I thought for sure you hated me, that I was cursed. But now I see - *I SEE!* Your plan, for him and for me, has now become clear. You honor me with this task of delivering such a foul sinner into the arms of the Devil! I pray that he shall have his larynx ripped from his throat and devoured over and over for all eternity! No more talking, *ever*! No more perverting the silence of the ignorant masses and retarding their brains with his bullshit blasphemy! NO MORE! With you guiding my hand, *we* have made way for YOUR WORD to be spread. Surely they will need a band to fill the empty space that this -" she hated to even utter such a stupid name, yet she forced it to pass her lips, " - this Jizz Biscuit once filled, and it shall be Temperance Holocaust. I know it! I am blessed by your darkness -"

"Hey, you almost done in there?" cried a voice from outside the toilet. "I gotta shit real bad. I ate, like, eighteen burritos."

Whoreface cringed. These Florida men were disgusting. She quickly prayed for fire to rain down and devour the entire state before an earthquake sent it crumbling into the ocean.

"In Your name, Amen," she said, finishing the prayer. Then, shoving the door open, she smacked the waiting man in the face and ran off into the crowd.

Chapter 9: Kyle

"Damn, what the hell? You broke my nose, man!"

Through a haze of fresh tears, Kyle could just make out the sight of a diminutive figure dashing from the port-a-potty and out into the Florida night.

"Fucking asshole," he muttered, pulling open the door.

"What the fuck!" he shouted as he laid eyes on the figure within. "Ted Découché! Is that really you, man?! Hey! Hey! I'm Kyle, I fucking love Jizz Biscuit! It's like my favorite band of all time. I fucking worship you guys. Hey, you like meth? I got some good shit here and....Ted?"

Kyle shoved himself inside and bolted the door behind him, inspecting the body of his idol. Ted didn't twitch.

"Oh, shit man...did some guy do that to you? OH! Ted, you're totally bleeding out, dude. Uh..."

Kyle thought about making a run for it, but then other ideas began to flood into his mind. Ted was his fucking hero. This had to be destiny.

"Man, we could do so much cool shit together," said Kyle. "Just, um...here, let's tuck your dick back in your pants... and I just got this wicked Noose shirt, so we can slip that on, and Bam! We're good to go. Ready to party, right Ted? Ha, yeah..."

It was a challenging for one man to dress another in the tight space of the porta-potty, but there was no way Kyle was leaving without Ted fucking Découché.

"Uh, yeah, come on," Kyle grunted. "...let's just..."

"Hey bro, you almost done in there?" asked someone outside.

"Fuck off!" Kyle shouted through the door. "Come on, Ted, let's get that zipper shut, and..."

"Fucking fags," hissed the man outside. "Can't you

find somewhere else to blow each other? I need to take a piss!"

"Fuck you!" shouted Kyle as he buttoned Ted's cargo shorts. Sweat was pouring down his face. He used Ted's old shirt to wipe up most of the blood, then shoved the soiled mess down the toilet. Then he took his gas station sunglasses off and stuck them on Ted's face. They sat slightly crooked, but looked wicked cool anyway.

"There, good as new," said Kyle. "Come on, bro, let's get you the hell out of here. I told Brandon I'd give him a ride home, but ha! Fuck him!"

Kyle kicked the door open and leaned all of Ted's weight against him, like one might do for a friend who was drunk and passed-out. Moving sideways, he managed to drag him from the shitter.

"What the hell?" said a passerby. "Is that Ted Découché?! Oh man, fuck, it is!"

Ignoring the rubbernecker, Kyle dragged the corpse as fast as he could toward his dented burgundy minivan.

"Here, we'll just stick you right in the front seat," said Kyle, propping Ted against the side of the vehicle while he searched his jeans for his keys. Once the door was open, he set about getting Ted into the passenger side. Ten exhausting minutes later, Ted was buckled in and ready to go.

"Damn it's hot in here," said Kyle. "Sorry Ted. The air should kick in soon, once we get going."

As he pulled out of the lot, Kyle glanced over to his passenger, just to confirm, just to make sure, that yeah, it was him, Ted fucking Découché, in his motherfucking van.

"This is the best day ever," said Kyle as he sped down the road, away from the Dark Ones of Darkness Festival, and toward the face of destiny.

Chapter 10: Leper Licker

"Fucking bitches," hissed Leper Licker as she stomped into the parking lot. Her bandmates were driving her crazy. She had to get the fuck out of there, blow off some steam, get herself some carnal relief.

She scanned the parked vehicles. None of them were hers. She'd never owned a car in any country she'd ever lived in. Nor had she ever borrowed one. And yet, she never worried about finding any wheels.

"There you are, you little whore," she said with a smile as she caught sight of a beige Ford Fiesta.

She trudged across the lot toward the battered hatchback, kicking up gravel with her black platform boots. The Florida night was sticky and oppressive, making her feel almost feverishly hot. Her sweaty hair was plastered to her scalp beneath her ill-fitting headdress. Her PVC fetish gear, which clung to her body in criss-crossing strips, was equally damp with perspiration.

"I hope this thing has working AC," she said.

Her pulse quickened as she sidled up to the car. An intoxicating feeling spread through her body, starting in her guts, one part excitement, one part nausea, one part anxiety – the delicious cocktail of adrenaline. There was no one in the parking lot, but the fear of being caught still made this fun.

Leper Licker dug into her purse and pulled out a length of plastic packing tape, the type used to bind stacks of newspapers and music magazines. Folding it carefully, she slipped it through the thin gap between the driver's side window and the doorframe. Once it was inside, she angled it down and slipped it over the bulbous tip of the locking pin. With a deft movement she jerked the pin upwards, and the door lock opened with a CLICK that echoed in the car's hollow metal compartments.

"Still got it," she said, smiling to herself.

Stealing cars was one of the many skills she'd picked up during her teen years in Vienna. One of the many infractions against society which had sent her down her current path in life, landing her first in juvenile prison, then in a convent, then in that wretched Hungarian hovel, and finally here, in the world's best – and only – black metal band made up of renegade nuns.

Leper Licker slipped the packing tape loose from the locking pin's neck, shoved it back in her purse, then opened the door and quickly sat down behind the steering wheel.

The car's interior was stiflingly hot and reeked of a fat man's ass. The leather upholstery felt disgustingly fleshy against the bare strips of her skin. For a second she thought about stealing another car, but she couldn't be bothered. She was in too much of a rush. Visions of sexually anguished seminarians were already crowding her brain.

She went into her purse for her second tool: a popsicle stick. When someone had first told her you could steal a car with one of these, she'd laughed, thinking they were joking. But it wasn't a joke. Some of these cars were like nymphomaniac whores: you could stick anything up them, and they'd always get turned on.

"Sort of like Sister Blood, that slut," said Leper Licker as she slipped the thin piece of wood into the ignition and turned it gently.

The engine coughed like a diseased old man, the lights glared on, and music started playing. Leper Licker grimaced as she heard the sound of delta blues careening from the speakers.

"Filthy negro music," she said, ejecting the CD and throwing it over her shoulder into the gloomy back seat. She took a CD from her purse and placed it in the player. A moment later, the dreadful noise of Burzum's *Filosofem* began to fill the air.

"That's more like it," said Leper Licker.

She threw the grumbling hatchback into reverse and escaped the parking lot. As she drove out onto the road she fiddled with the AC.

"Fuck!"

It didn't work. She wound down the window, opening the car to the Florida night. A stream of humid air blew in to displace the humid air of the car's interior. The change was negligible. Leper Licker sighed and punched the gas, sending herself and the hatchback hurtling down the road.

"Stinky American nigger weather," she said.

She sped past murky palm trees shrouded by evening. From the distance she fancied she could hear the sound of alligators crunching the bones of inbred white trash murder victims. The thought brought a smile to her face, which quickly faded as her thoughts flitted back to her prevailing irritations.

"Those fucking bitches," she hissed.

She was so sick of them all. Sister Blood was always so arrogant, always telling everyone else what to do, always dominating the band's creative direction. Sister HOG was always off in space, lost in her psychotic daydreams of death and oblivion. And Whoreface was just a violent thug. None of them took Leper Licker seriously. None of them showed her the respect she so obviously deserved. Just because she was only a bass player! But she had more talent than that. She could play lead too, and drums. She could even sing. Just like her beloved Count Grishnackh, she could do it all. She was a one woman music machine. She was a fucking creative genius!!!

"One day I'll show all those stupid cunts," she said.

Her platform boot pressed down even more heavily on the accelerator. She really had to blow off some steam tonight. Luckily there was a seminary school nearby. There was almost nothing she enjoyed more than seducing a seminarian. There was something about defiling a would-be man of God that just drove her crazy. The feeling of a holy man's cock in her mouth, hot and hard, the eager flesh contrasting with the tortured, ambivalent spirit within. When she drank a seminiarian's cum, she felt like she was draining his faith, draining his dignity, perhaps even draining his soul, siphoning off his connection to God in the form of salty droplets, thereby reducing him to the status of a mindless beast of lust, a hairless monkey with a big horny worm between its legs. It was perhaps their humiliation she craved above all, the shocked look in their eyes as their lust, now spent, sped down her gullet, and a fresh weight of guilt fell upon their shoulders.

She got wet thinking about it, and wriggled her pelvis, causing her cunt to rub against the tight PVC of her shorts. Vaginal juices mingled with Florida sweat.

She was so distracted by lust she almost missed her turn. The car squealed as she jammed on the breaks and skidded to a halt, smearing burned rubber behind her. She reversed the vehicle, cut across the left lane, and headed down a heavily-wooded road towards the seminary.

Insects and forest things swarmed unseen in the darkness, making all sorts of seething noises, as though they were involved in some nocturnal orgy. The sounds made her even hornier.

Before long she saw the seminary building loom from the shadows ahead, its greater bulk silhouetted against the night, its smaller patches lit by feeble outside lamps. The building was antique and majestic, demonstrating the seemingly infinite wealth of the

Catholic Church. Leper Licker pulled into the building's parking lot, got out, and hurried towards the towering brick mansion. The windows were mostly black, indicating the seminarians were mostly in bed. She thought of them lying beneath their sheets, praying for God to take away their pesky erections. Perhaps some were furtively masturbating over images of buxom mother Mary. Perhaps others were already dreaming lusty dreams, painting their blankets with nocturnal emissions. Oh how she wished she could be there amongst them, absorbing their lust like a tissue in a frat house, siphoning their faith and self-respect in the form of their seed.

She bit her lower lip in a gesture of lust and continued on her way toward the building. Mosquitoes swarmed around her. She smashed one into the pale flesh of her arm, leaving a satisfying blood smear behind. Another she smacked into the skin of her ass, leaving it squashed there. Perhaps her chosen seminarian could lick the tiny corpse from her dimpled cheek?

She drew close to the building, then paused, sniffing the air.

Cigarette smoke.

One of the seminarians must be smoking outside. That was a vice permitted by the Lord, considered much cleaner than eating a cunt. Leper Licker followed the scent until she spied a seminarian leaning against the side of the building, facing obliquely away from her. She crept toward him, stifling her footfalls against the lush grass. She'd catch him off guard, she decided. If only he was naked, she could leap from the shadows right onto his cock. What a surprise that would be!

Instead she crept up behind him, until she was just a few feet away. She could make out the side of his face. He was pale and blond, just the way she liked them. She bet he had blue eyes too. She always preferred blue eyes; to her, looking into brown eyes was like looking into a pair of shitty assholes.

"Hey there sexy," she hissed in the darkness, her voice matching the sibilance of nearby cicadas.

The seminarian jumped, wheeled around, and stumbled away from her, dropping his cigarette. His eyes flared wide in shock. They were definitely blue.

"Don't be afraid," said Leper Licker, stalking toward him. "God has sent me here to reward you. To give you a taste of heavenly delight..."

She licked her lips and drew closer to the seminarian, gripping her camel toe with one hand and massaging her breasts with the other.

"Get back, foul beast," said the wannabe priest as he continued backing away.

"I am no beast, but a child of God, just like you," said Leper Licker, though she knew her appearance must be shocking to him. She was still wearing her corpsepaint from the stage, smeared and distressed by her sweat. Her costume amounted to little more than a series of PVC straps cunningly arranged to hide her nipples and cunt while leaving most of her pale body bare. The flesh around the tight straps was angry, bulging between the constricting sections of the garment. Only her veil provided any modesty, concealing her blonde hair, providing a visual link to the nun she had once been.

"God sent me," she said again. "To reward you for your faith. He wants me to suck your dick."

The seminarian peered at her, still obviously in shock, as though he thought he might be dealing with a ghost. Then a look of understanding appeared in his eyes, and he stood up straighter, regaining his lost self-possession.

"I know you," he said, laughing in a show of relief.

"You're from that band that's touring around here! For a second I thought you were a demon or something."

"I'm no succubus," said Leper Licker, still drawing closer. "But I suck like one..."

The seminarian cocked his head. A look of wry amusement spread across his face, as though he thought something was funny. Then he composed himself, and peered at her with a more serious expression. Insulting compassion seeped into his eyes.

"I see you're as lost as they say you are," he said. "But it's never too late. You can always repent, and the Lord will forgive you. Why don't you forget this foolishness, and join me in prayer?"

"Very well," said Leper Licker, trying her best to look contrite. "Let's pray together. I feel *so* lost..." She whimpered, crowning the performance with crocodile tears.

The seminarian nodded to her solemnly, then knelt, bowed his head, closed his eyes, and sandwiched his hands in an attitude of prayer. Leper Licker knelt beside him.

"Let us pray," he said. "What is your name, Sister?"

"They call me Leper Licker," she said - just before she stuck her tongue in his ear and grabbed his cock.

"Ah, fuck!" he shouted, pushing her away and jumping to his feet. "Enough!"

She rose and stepped toward him, leering, like an animal waiting to pounce.

"Give me your seed, little priestling!" she hissed.

"You need to stop this," he said. "You're disgracing yourself. Why don't you calm down, and come inside for a cup of hot chocolate? Maybe you can talk to Father Ambrosio, he's –"

"Fuck Ambrosio! I want you, priestling. I want you in my mouth!"

"That is not going to happen," he said, stiffening his

back.

"Why? Don't you want a taste of pleasure before you sell yourself to God?"

"I've already had sex, if that's what you're talking about," he said. "Quite a bit of it, actually. I know what I'll be missing, and I don't really care."

"Bullshit!" she snapped. "You're telling me you don't want a piece of this?!"

Leper Licker gestured to her body, finding it literally inconceivable that anyone wouldn't want to fuck her. She was gorgeous, a goddess of beauty and raw, oozing sex. Even if she did have herpes and quite a bit of acne. And that scar from her harelip operation.

"I don't want you," said the seminarian, his voice sounding colder than before. "Even if I wasn't preparing for the priesthood, you still wouldn't be my type. You're too...hefty."

Leper Licker gulped and glanced down at her ample frame.

"Are you calling me fat?" she screamed. "I'm big boned. I'm robust. I'm not fat!"

The seminarian said nothing, just peered at her with a wry expression, as if to say "Honey, yes you are."

Leper Licker bared her teeth, then laughed at him. "Oh, now I get it. Now I know why you're here. You're a faggot! That's why you joined the church. You probably want to bugger little boys! Come here, and I'll cure you with my cunt. God has sent me —"

"Get away!" he said as she advanced.

Leper licker pulled out a switchblade and popped it open. The Floridian moon glinted on the killing steel.

"Fuck!" he screamed, turning to run.

Leper Licker tried to intercept him, but she stumbled in her massive platform boots and fell on her chest, almost stabbing herself accidentally with the knife as she went down.

"Shit!" she spat, while the seminarian sped away, screaming for help at the top of his lungs. Leper Licker scrambled to her feet as lights flickered on in the seminary windows, illuminating the lawn. Figures peered down at her from the portals above.

"Help!" shouted the seminarian. "Call the police!"

Fuck, thought Leper Licker. *Not the pigs!*

She abandoned the fleeing priestling and ran towards the parking lot as more of the seminary windows began to fill with light. By the time she reached the Fiesta she was even more drenched with sweat than she had been earlier. She jumped behind the wheel and turned the popsicle stick in the ignition. The lights flashed on and the engine asthmatically wheezed. In a moment she was rocketing down the Florida backroads, muggy wind blasting in her face through the window, full of insects and swamp smell. Burzum blasted from the speakers, feeding her wrath.

"That fucking faggot priest!" she screamed, punching the steering wheel.

She was too angry to drive. She pulled over, stopped the car, and sat there, squeezing the wheel, wishing it was that bitch seminarian's neck. How dare he. How fucking dare he! She'd been about to rock his pathetic little world, and he'd thrown it back in her face. He'd even made the outrageous suggestion that she was overweight! She was only a size 14 because she was big boned. Everyone knew that. She was a healthy Aryan female with massive child-bearing hips. Those smaller sizes were for gypsy smack whores and scrawny little jewesses with anorexia.

"Fucking cunt!"

She headbutted the wheel, blasting the horn. She turned to the seat beside her and slashed it open with the switchblade, imagining it was the smug face of the bastard who just got away. When the stuffing fell out from the upholstery, she saw it as his shit-filled guts. A few minutes later the seat was in ruins. She paused, panting heavily, dripping with sweat, corpsepaint running down her neck into her cleavage.

"He was a faggot," she told herself. "Probably liked little boys. If he was a real man, he would have been all over me, wannabe priest or not."

The thought calmed her, and her rage began to dissipate. She was still wound up tight though. She needed relief.

She glanced at the deserted road while slipping a pair of fingers into her weeping slit. Her herpes was active at the moment; she could feel the small raised sores surrounding her lips. They mingled with the rash she got from shaving her twat and wearing tight PVC all the time. The whole area was red, rashy, burning, just like her lust.

She wetted her fingers in her gash, then started teasing her clit. Semi-coherent images flashed through her mind as she tried to select her phantom lover for the evening. She rejected the handsome face of the seminarian with a tremor of loathing. She thought about her prince, Count Grishnackh, rotting away in that Norwegian prison. What would he do if he was with her right now?

She imagined him in her, but it wasn't enough. She needed something more potent to get her off tonight, to expel the weight of her towering frustration. As she worked her fingers feverishly, an image swam up from the depths of her mind - the face of Adolf Hitler.

It was not a random face. Hitler had been her dream lover since early adolescence. He'd been her dream daddy too, so much more potent than her weak biological sire. As a child she had always instinctively adored him, the way some children adore Santa

Claus or Jesus. The obsession followed her into adolescence, and led to her involvement with certain national socialist youth organizations. Together with her fellow Aryan warriors, she fought heroically to protect the white race from communists, Jews, and other sub-humanoids. Unfortunately the government frowned on things like firebombing businesses and curb-stomping people, and she found herself in prison. It was only by pleading her way into the sanctuary of the church that she was able to escape from the horrors of incarceration, and big Karlotta's cruel embraces.

After, in the convent, she tried to forget about Hitler and embrace Jesus instead. But often, when she prayed, and stared at the crucifix on the wall, it was the Fuhrer's face she saw, not the face of Christ. Other times it was both their faces combined into a single mutant image. It happened like an acid trip. She'd be staring at the wounded visage of the Lord, long-haired and shaggy, crowned with thorns. Then the hair would retract into the scalp, becoming short and neat. The beard would fall out, leaving only a stylish toothbrush mustache. The sorrowful eyes would turn hard as Krupp steel. The thorny crown would transform into a wreath of Jewish teeth, capped with gold and ripped from bleeding gums.

It was after many visions like these that she realized the truth – Christ and Hitler were the same person. When she told this to her superiors, she was sent to Hollóhegy Convent in Hungary, where the church kept the nuns it was ashamed of. That's where she met Blood, HOG, and Whoreface – that's where she met Black Metal Jesus himself, right before the whole place burned to the ground. Her Sisters denied it, but she knew the truth – Black Metal Jesus was Hitler too. She'd felt it when he'd fucked her in the ass.

"Oh my fuhrer," she whispered to herself, remembering that painful but wonderful moment.

Awkwardly she turned herself around in the driver's seat, clambering up onto her knees and sticking out her ass towards the steering wheel. She pulled down her PVC shorts, baring her backside to the night creatures. Mosquitoes landed on her cheeks, sucking her blood, but she didn't care. She was too worked up. She removed the thick wooden cross from her neck and slathered it up with saliva, then slowly inserted it into her ass. At the same time her other hand accidentally bumped the center of the steering wheel, sounding the horn. She imagined it was the horn of judgment, summoning her immortal Fuhrer to the war of Armageddon. She pictured him as a knight on horseback, much like he appeared in a certain famous painting, except that his face was covered in corpsepaint and his armor was black and spiky.

"Oh yes," she whispered.

He leapt off his horse and strode toward her, his eyes full of holocaust fire. His armor flew off as if by magic, revealing a physique that would have put the members of Manowar to shame. He stroked an eight-inch cock with the girth of a policeman's flashlight. Soon it was sinking into her stink hole, plowing her colon without mercy.

She moaned softly, plunging the cross into her anus, working her fingers on her clit, her eyes closed to drink in the fantasy. She felt an orgasm rising, rising, rising —

The sound of crunching gravel and a growling engine interrupted her ascension to climax. Her eyes flickered open, beholding a policeman on a motorcycle idling beside her stolen vehicle. His eyes were wide with amazement. He'd probably never seen a black metal nun ass-fucking herself with a wooden cross before.

For a moment Leper Licker's heart began to hammer with dread. The last thing she wanted was to be arrested again, locked up like an animal, forced to provide endless cunnilingus to violent psychopaths called Karlotta, Sigrid, or Susan. What could she do?

She peered at the cop. His vaguely fascist appearance was pleasing, and his eyes as he ogled her ass were filled with something other than professional detachment. She was starting to see a way out of this predicament already.

"Hello, orifice-er," she said huskily as she peered out the window. "Is there a problem?"

Half an hour later she was driving back towards the festival grounds, with a gaping sphincter and a belly full of cop cum. She'd made him put his truncheons to good use – both of them. It wasn't quite as fun as sucking the faith from a seminarian's cock, but it was good nonetheless.

Leper Licker was quite pleased with herself. Now that her sexual frustration had been dealt with, she could think about her other plans. She had to start spreading the True Message of Black Metal Hitler Jesus. She couldn't let the others hold her back anymore. She couldn't let Sister Blood stifle her creative genius. It was time to make her mark on the world, just like she'd made her mark on this car's passenger seat. She glanced at the ruined upholstery, and laughed as she sped down the road. Gators growled in the distance, echoing her infinite hunger.

Chapter 11: Whoreface

"Where have you been?" asked Sister Blood, looking the little nun up and down, her jaded eyes drinking in the dark spots on her clothing. "Is that blood? Have you been stabbing people again? You know they execute killers here. They are not as advanced and cultured as we are back in Europe. As a people, they are savages. So who have you assaulted now?"

Shit, thought Whoreface. She knew her Sisters would never be understanding of the situation. Even if she explained it was God's Will, she still had a feeling they wouldn't buy it. They never had before...

(Whoreface flashback, lalala....)

"Who stabbed that monk? Whoreface?"

"It was God's will."

"Who the hell stabbed our keyboardist?"

"It was God's Will."

"No! Again!? Who killed the bartender!? Whoreface!"

"It was God's Will."

(end flashback lalala...)

Yeah, she had definitely overused that excuse. It only ever seemed to work when HOG said it.

A lightbulb flashed in her head.

HOG, she thought, *of course!*

"It's from HOG, if you have to know, Sister," said Whoreface. "I stabbed her earlier, trying to get her out of one of her trances. What's the big deal with the third degree, anyway? You act like I'm a crazed killer. Why don't you back the fuck off?"

Blood turned away without a word and hurried toward the makeshift chapel at the back of the bus. Whoreface followed wordlessly. In the chapel HOG was kneeling in front of the Black Metal Jesus statue, her emaciated shoulders weeping from fresh flagellation marks.

"HOG, is this true?" asked Sister Blood. "Did Whoreface stab you earlier?"

HOG looked up from her prayers in a daze. "Stab?" she repeated, her voice slow and soft, like that of a catatonic lunatic.

"Yeah, stab!" said Whoreface. "Earlier, when I tried to get you to come out of the bus, you were in one of those trances. So I stabbed you in the arm. See?" Whoreface pointed to the blood-caked wound on HOG's lower arm.

HOG looked at the injury as if seeing it for the first time.

"Is this true, Sister?" asked Sister Blood.

"Yes, it looks like it," said HOG. "Unless my stigmata is now manifesting itself somewhere other than my cunt."

"That is not stigmata, Sister," said Sister Blood in an exasperated voice. She turned back to Whoreface, fixing her with a commanding stare. "No more stabbing," she said. "I have enough fucking problems with Leper Licker. Speaking of which, she should have been back by now. Have you seen her? Nevermind! I'll ask the stupid keyboardist, Sister…whatever her name is. Stupid sessional players…"

Sister Blood departed the bus in a huff. With Blood gone, Whoreface felt the full force of HOG's intense gaze.

"That is not my blood soiling your habit," HOG croaked.

"What?" said Whoreface. "Um, Yeah it is."

"No," said HOG as she stood up, towering over the tiny nun. "It is the blood of a douche."

Whoreface gulped. How could HOG possibly know? And what would she do with this knowledge? For a moment the two nuns stared at each other, Whoreface trying to hide her trepidation, while HOG's face remained eerily blank of expression, as though she were carved of stone, like some implacable angel. Her eerie eyes seemed to pierce the drummer's soul. Then, all of a sudden, she smiled, and pointed a scrawny finger at the altar of Black Metal Jesus.

"You please our Black Dragon husband," said HOG." Jesus weeps tears of blood for this happiness, yes? I will say no more. Wake me in a few hours for Matins. I will not neglect the Divine Office simply because of this tour."

"Uh, sure, no problem," said Whoreface, as the skeletal Sister wandered back to her bunk.

Alone in the chapel, Whoreface inspected the altar, wondering what HOG had been pointing at. She froze as she beheld the crimson drops spilling from the eyes of the Lord's statue. Quickly they overflowed the altar and pooled on the floor, soaking the gray carpeting.

Whoreface gasped. If she'd had any doubts before, they were long gone by now. Sister Whoreface had heard the word of God, and was truly blessed. She knelt before the crying statue and prayed.

Chapter 12: Ted & Kyle

(...Meanwhile, somewhere in Florida...)

"See, told ya, back in two seconds. It didn't get too hot for ya, did it, man?"

Kyle paused, waiting for Ted to answer him. After a silent minute Kyle laughed and started the van back up. The stale air from the AC did little to quell the humidity of the Florida evening.

"I, uh, got the beer you like," said Kyle. "I read all your interviews, man, so I know which one. It was a little expensive, but fuck it! You only live once, yeah? Cool."

Kyle pulled out in front of a red truck, then ran a stop light. He couldn't wait to get home and party with Ted.

It was dark when Kyle pulled into his driveway and took a sharp right, throwing Ted's body against the door. The singer's head made a heavy *thunk!* as it collided with the window.

"Ouch, sorry buddy," said Kyle, but Ted didn't complain. In fact, he didn't even seem phased. The guy was obviously tough, unlike those pussies in bands like Noose or Syndrome of a Down. Nodding in approval of Ted's silent stoicism, Kyle parked on the lawn just outside his front door.

"Let's get you inside, man. I don't know about you, but I could really use a tweak."

Kyle jumped out, then ran around to the passenger side and yanked open the door.

"Shit!" he cried as Ted tumbled out onto the weed-covered lawn.

"I got you man, *uh*! Don't worry, Kyle's got you."

Kyle huffed as he hooked Ted under the armpits and hauled him into the house. He kicked the door shut and dragged Ted to the futon in the corner. Thankfully Ted slid easily across the white tiles.

"There! Good as new. Perfect." Kyle straightened Ted's baseball cap and smoothed out his shirt. "Maybe just...um, here, let me just..." Kyle positioned Ted's legs so they stretched out casually in front of him. He put both of Ted's arms down by his sides, but it didn't look right, so he picked up one of the arms and stretched it out along the back length of the futon. Now Ted looked totally cool.

"There, that's chill," said Kyle. He sat down next to the singer's stiffening body, fitting himself perfectly in the crook of Ted's arm.

"That's cool, right?" he said. "You don't mind sitting so close, do you? Sh*ittt,* of course you don't! Ha! Alright, let's get this party started!"

Kyle rummaged through the messy pile of porn magazines and unpaid bills on his coffee table until he found a blackened glass pipe and a blue BIC lighter.

"Damn, it's even still got some crud in it," said Kyle with a grin as he inspected the pipe. He took a baggie out of his pocket and packed more rocket fuel into the mix for good measure. He lit the pipe and sucked white vapor into his lungs. The meth had a paradoxical flavor, wet but somehow desiccating, with a faint aftertaste of mothballs. But the flavor didn't matter; Kyle was after the feeling.

He leaned back, absorbing the static sparks of excitement exploding in his skull. He grinned at Ted, then exhaled a chemical haze into the singer's face.

"Motherfucker, shit cunt, that feels go*ood!*"

Kyle took another hit. Then another. Then one more.

"Want to watch something, Ted?" asked Kyle as he

fired up his sixty inch TV.

The television was Kyle's pride and joy. It'd cost him a lot of disability checks. His cable package, which boasted over fifteen hundred channels, was an ongoing expense. Luckily he still had enough cash for meth, cigarettes, and beer. Sometimes he even had enough to buy food, pay the rent, or finance other low priority stuff.

"Hey, you like Pacino?" Kyle asked as he selected a fim, then slumped against the cushions. As he sat back, something slipped off the top of the couch and rested against his shoulders. A surge of excitement ran through Kyle's entire body as he realized it was Ted's arm pressing against him.

"Pacino is the shit," said Ted, speaking for the first time since he and Kyle had met.

Kyle glanced over at him, beaming with joy and wonder. He'd been worried Ted might be, like, totally dead or something, but this was proof that a rocka rolla like Ted was just too cool to kick the bucket. Sort of like Keith Richards. Or Dracula.

"Pass me some of that shit, huh?" said Ted, nodding ever so slightly towards the glass pipe, which lay atop the tits of a Penthouse cover girl.

"Uh, yeah, sure man," said Kyle. "What are friends for?"

Kyle grabbed the pipe and the lighter, then held them out for Ted to take.

"Are you some kind of retard?" said Ted. "I'm dead, man. You need to help me out a little bit. Just blow some smoke into my mouth. I'll take it from there."

Kyle nodded. Thoughts racing, nerve endings tingling from the electrified footsteps of a thousand psychic spiders charging through his body, he took another hit, then leaned over so his face was right in front of Ted's.

"Like this?" he said, his lips clenched tight as he held the smoke in his lungs.

"Sure," said Ted. "Just get a little closer. Come on, you can touch my lips, it's no big deal. Helping another guy get high doesn't make you gay or anything. I won't tell anyone. We're bros, right?"

Kyle nodded his head. Ted was right, of course. Taking Ted's face in his hands, he parted the lips just so, then made a seal over them with his own before exhaling the smoke into Ted's mouth. There was some resistance, and he had to breath out pretty hard to force the meth-laden air into Ted's lungs. It was sort of like how people on TV gave CPR, except way cooler, because this air was filled with magic crystal power.

"Shit, it's good, right?" said Kyle as he finally pulled away.

"Really fucking good," said Ted. "Thanks bro. How about another? Wait, maybe a beer first. Where's that beer you bought? Let's crack a few of those open."

"Right on," said Kyle "Whatever you want, Ted. One sec."

Kyle hesitated for a moment, not wanting to get up. He liked the comforting feeling of Ted's arm pressed against this back. But Ted wanted beer, so Kyle had no choice. Besides, it wasn't like Ted was going any-where.

Kyle jumped up and hurried to the kitchen. He looked in the fridge. It was empty except for a few left-over pizza slices and a jar of Nutella. He slammed the door and scanned the kitchen, but the beer was no-where to be seen. A whirlwind of panic blew through his hollow bones and the flickering spider webs holding them together.

Where the fuck was Ted's beer?!

"I'm so fucking stupid!" shouted Kyle.

He punched himself in the side of the head. He

was screwing everything up!! His idol, his everything, was sitting in the other room, watching his TV, smoking his drugs, so fucking cool, like a dream come true, he was really fucking here, Ted was really here, Ted motherfucking Découché, and all Ted wanted was a fucking beer, and Kyle couldn't even do that, what the fuck was wrong with him?!

Kyle wrenched open the cupboards and started tossing things out, desperately searching for that six pack of expensive beer Ted loved so much. Soon there were overflowing boxes of stale cereal all over the floor, mingled with dented cans and Pop-Tart wrappers - but still no sign of the beer.

"FUUUUCK!" shouted Kyle. "They've got to be here somewhere!"

Spilled dry noodles crunched under his knees as he checked the lower cabinets. There was nothing but an old bong, some spider webs, and the broken pieces of all the clocks and smoke detectors Kyle had dismantled the previous week in an attempt to find the listening devices his asshole neighbors had planted in his house. As Kyle stared in horror at empty shelves, an impatient voice called out from the living room.

"Hey, how about that beer, buddy?" said Ted. "You get lost in there or something? Come on bro, don't leave me hanging!"

Kyle struggled to stop himself hyperventilating. This was all going terribly wrong. What if he couldn't find the beer?! There was only one answer. He'd have to kill Ted, then himself. It was the only way to save himself from the bitter shame of disappointing his hero. Heart racing, Kyle opened the cutlery drawer and reached for a kitchen knife big enough to co-star in the next Halloween movie.

"Whoa there," he told himself, stopping before he touched the handle of the blade. "Let's not get carried away. We can always go get more beer. There are stores and shit!"

Kyle felt a weight lift off his shoulders, but he wasn't out of the woods yet. The threat of Ted's disapproval lurked like a masked maniac, waiting to strike him down with unbearable pain. Sheepishly he crept back to the living room and loitered in the doorway, struggling for an excuse. He couldn't let Ted know he'd lost the beer, or he'd lose the respect of the coolest singer on the planet. He needed a cover story. His mind raced, while Ted's voice whispered from the living room.

"I'm gettin' awful thirsty, man. My throat's as dry as your mom's cooze."

"I know, bro," said Kyle. "And I'm sorry. But I can't get you the beer just yet. I've gotta duck out for a second. It's, like, an emergency and shit. It's my cousin, he's…been abducted by Satanists." Kyle peered down at his feet, terrified to look in Ted's face, lest he see a look of disbelief or disdain lurking there. "So, like, I just gotta go sort that out, then we can party, cool?"

Ted seemed less than enthused. "Fine," he said. "I guess I'll just sit here instead of going to that fucking killer afterparty filled with sluts and drugs."

"Two seconds, Ted, that's all," said Kyle. "Then, I promise, when I get back, it's going to be FUCKING EPIC!"

Kyle rushed out the door, praying Ted would still be there when he got back from buying beer at the all-night bodega. He sprinted to the car, climbed into the driver's seat, and slammed the door. He had to do this fast. His friendship with Ted was on the line! He reached into his pockets for the car keys, then froze as something shiny caught his eye amongst the trash on the van's floor. It was - THE BEER!

"Fucking stupid idiot!! I didn't even bring it in?

Thank fucking christ!"

Kyle grabbed the six pack and ran back inside.

"Ted! Ted!" he shouted. "I got your beer! Here man, let me open it for ya."

"About fucking time," Ted muttered, opening his mouth so Kyle could pour some expensive IPA down his gullet. Soon it was overflowing his mouth and dripping down his soul patch.

"That's better," said Ted. "My throat was dry as a housewife's cunt!"

Kyle laughed. Ted was so funny.

"Want more?" Kyle asked.

"Does a whore like to fuck?" said Ted.

"....um, yeah?"

"Then what the hell do you think?" said Ted. "Of course I want more! Load me up!"

Kyle drained the rest of the first beer, then cracked open a second, pouring half into Ted's mouth before swigging the rest. He tossed can after can onto the floor, until the six pack was empty, then relaxed on the couch beside Ted, enjoying the feeling of Ted's arm once again pressed against his back. They sat that way in silence for a while, until the Pacino movie ended and another came on.

"What the hell is this?" said Ted, punctuating his question with a belch. "Where the fuck is Al?"

"Oh bro, this movie is great," said Kyle. "Nic Cage is an angel and she's a woman. He falls in love with her, so he wants to give up being an angel so he can -"

"Enough!" said Ted, cutting him off. "I'm tired of screwing around. Kiss me."

Kyle turned slowly, peering into Ted's earnest face. "What?" he whispered. "Bro, seriously?"

"Yeah, what do you think?" said Ted. "You've been giving me hints all night. You're driving me crazy. Let's stop pretending this is something other than what it is."

"But…"

"It doesn't make you gay, Kyle" Ted said. "I thought you were my number one fan?"

"I am, I just didn't think…"

"What? That I'd be into guys?"

"Well, yeah," Kyle said, edging closer.

"I'm not. But I'm into you, Kyle. I think we've really got something here. A connection, I can feel it. Being famous is so isolating. People only want you to help make them famous too. But with us I know there's something there - something real."

Kyle looked away. He was lost for words, struggling to express his true feelings through a haze of beer and crystal. "Ted," he whispered. "Ted, I…I can't believe it." Kyle gulped, then glanced up, looking Ted right in the eye. "That's how I feel too!" he cried. "Even before we met, like, I just *knew* we were connected somehow. Everyone else said I was insane, delusional, or just too high, but I fucking *knew* you'd feel it too!"

Beaming with joy, Kyle leaned over to give Ted a kiss.

"Not there," Ted said.

"Right, man, of course," said Kyle, understanding exactly what Ted wanted.

He slid off the futon and got down on his knees between Ted's legs. Trembling with excitement, he opened Ted's cargo shorts, then drew back as he caught a whiff of something foul rising up from inside. At some point Ted must have soiled himself. Probably from partying too hard or something like that. But that was okay. All big rockstars party so hard they shit their pants. Kyle had heard all about it on that Ozzy Osbourne documentary.

Kyle placed a hand over his mouth and fought back his vomit reflex. Once he had the urge to puke under control, he glanced up at his hero.

"Hey Ted," he said. "Sometime, man, I think we need to get you into the bath."

"Sure, whatever," said Ted. "But for now, suck! There is no better way to end a night than with drugs and a blow job. Better make it good."

"Believe me, I will," said Kyle. "You fucking rock, Ted."

Kyle held his breath against the stench, then pulled Ted's flaccid cock into his mouth. He cupped Ted's balls with one hand and used the other to hold the limp worm between his lips.

"Oh Kyle," Ted moaned. "Fuck yeah...suck it bitch."

"I am your bitch, Ted," mumbled Kyle as he sucked and tugged. He felt his own heat and hardness begin to grow between his thighs, making it painfully obvious what he wanted to happen next.

"Mm-mm...Mm-mm!" murmured Ted as he finally exploded in Kyle's mouth.

"My turn," Kyle said.

"Sure, bro," said Ted. "What are friends for?"

Ted smiled, obviously happy to oblige, and Kyle guided him down until he was lying supine on the futon, one leg dangling off the side.

"I've been told I'm a real cocksucker," Ted bragged.

"I bet you are," said Kyle as he fumbled with his jeans.

He couldn't get himself out of his pants fast enough. He'd dreamt of this for two years, ever since he'd heard Jizz Biscuit's first album, *Two Bucks, Yo.* He yanked at Ted's jaw, trying to get it open a little wider, but it wouldn't budge.

"What's wrong? said Kyle. "I thought you wanted..."

"I do," said Ted. "It's just that my jaw's a bit stiff. Help a homie out, yeah?"

"Of course," said Kyle. "I just need something, like a tool or whatever..."

"Take your time," said Ted in a seductive voice. "I'll be right here waiting for you."

Almost tripping over his loose jeans, Kyle jumped up and hurried through the house, searching for anything which might help him pry Ted's mouth open a little wider. At last he found a hammer lying near the shattered remains of the back door. He'd locked himself out last week, and had been forced to use the hammer to get the door open. He still had to fix the stupid thing sometime, but right now he was way too preoccupied. He scooped up the tool and ran back to the living room.

"I found this!" he shouted, showing Ted the hammer.

"Great," said Ted. "Open me up and give me that delicious cum. I want to thank you for being my number one fan."

Kyle licked his lips excitedly, then wedged the flat end of the hammer between Ted's teeth and started levering the singer's mouth open, until he'd created a yawning chasm of pleasure.

"Damn, you sure are tight Ted!" joked Kyle as he tried to unwedge the claw of the hammer from one of Ted's teeth. The tooth cracked. Bits of it fell from Ted's mouth as the hammer finally came loose.

"Ted! I'm sorry!' said Kyle as he picked up the pieces of tooth and held them in his palm.

"Don't stress, bro," said Ted. "You can knock 'em all out if you want. It'll just make it that much easier for me to suck you. Mmmmm!" Ted licked his lips.

"No way!" said Kyle. "I wouldn't do that. But can I have this piece?"

"Sure! Enjoy! Now give me that cock, I'm hungry!"

Kyle tossed the tooth pieces into his mouth and swallowed them like a handful of benzos. It felt good to have a piece of Ted inside him.

"We're going to be one, Ted. You're inside me...and now I'll be inside you."

Kyle mounted Ted's head, squeezing it between his thighs and slipping his cock into the singer's yawning mouth.

"*Tedddddd*," Kyle moaned, rocking back and forth, plunging in and out, in and out, as deep as Ted could take him. A few minutes later Kyle lost control, and washed Ted's throat with bitter jizz.

"Fuck, that was amazing, Ted."

"It sure was."

Kyle flopped beside Ted on the futon. The two cuddled close.

"This is so cool," said Kyle.

"It sure is," said Ted.

"Oh, I know," said Kyle. "Want to take a snap for my webpage? Then we can remember this moment forever!"

"Wicked," Ted said.

Kyle fumbled in his pocket, pulling out a disposable camera he'd bought for taking photos at the festival. Positioning the camera at arm's length and pointing it toward them, he hugged Ted close so they'd both fit in the frame. The room was dark and hazy, the lighting terrible, but he figured the photos would turn out okay. He took several.

"Those will look sweet," he said.

"Doubt it," said Ted. "My face always looks fat."

"What? No it doesn't. No way."

Ted looked at him. "You don't think?"

"Ted, come on, no way! You're Ted motherfucking Découché, man! It's impossible for you *NOT to look* awesome."

"Fine, fine, fuck it. Go ahead and post it or whatever."

"Cool. I'll drop off the film tomorrow. Then, after I get them back, I'll scan the best ones and save them on my desktop. Then I'll log onto my webpage, go to my photos window, search for the photos, then upload them, and after like twenty minutes, bam! My website becomes *our* website. Isn't modern technology awesome?"

"I adore you, Kyle. You're the first person in a while to really see me, bro. I mean *really* see me. Sure, I'm a Grammy award-winning, rich, insanely good-looking musical prodigy, but you want to know something?

"Yeah?"

"It's all bullshit. I'm just a man. A lonely man...till now."

Kyle didn't say anything. Words wouldn't have been good enough anyway. He bent over and kissed Ted's gaping mouth.

"We're together now, Ted," he whispered. "You'll never be lonely again." Kyle fell silent for a moment, caressing Ted's cheek. "This might be a little soon," he whispered, "but...I love you, Ted."

Gazing into Kyle's eyes, his voice shuddering with emotion. "I love you too, bro." Ted said.

Chapter 13: Sister Blood

Sister Blood sat at the back of the tour bus and sighed. Black curtains decorated with crosses hid her from the world, giving her a chance at solitary reflection, even a chance to succumb to her exhaustion, if only for a moment.

Sometimes the burdens of leadership were great. Trying to keep her bandmates in line was like trying to herd horny cats. HOG's spiritual connection with the Black Dragon was a blessing, but it often made her very hard to work with. She always had her head in the spirit world. Whoreface was beyond difficult. Her violent temper was a blessing from Black Metal Jesus, and her random acts of violence always served to honor his name, but her brutality couldn't be allowed to jeopardize the music. Spreading the Word via song was their one true calling – and they couldn't do that if they were all in jail for one of Whoreface's murders.

Then there was Leper Licker. She used to be such an obedient Sister, but over the years she'd grown more and more arrogant. Now she was always challenging Sister Blood's position. Which was just ridiculous. Blood had the unwavering support of HOG and Whoreface. She even had the support of the keyboardist, not that it mattered. Sister Blood had *always* been the leader, even back at Hollóhegy, before they'd embraced their dark destiny. When Black Metal Jesus had come amongst them on that miraculous night, in that terrible storm, she was the first one he'd given communion. The first one he'd pierced with his lance of dark love. She was the leader, no doubt about it. She even played *lead* guitar. Leper Licker only played bass! Who ever heard of a bass player leading a band?! ...well a good band, at least. And yet, Leper Licker kept trying to steal away power, one piece at a time. Kept trying to pervert the band's lyrics with her sick Nazi sympathies. She had to be kept in line, or Temperance Holocaust would turn into a joke.

Sister Blood sighed again, and put the thoughts from her mind. Self-reflection was against the Holy Word; Black Metal Jesus had told her as much.

Don't, like, think about shit, he had told her in his resonant, holy voice. *Just, like, do shit instead.*

She followed his advice, retrieving her pad of paper and pencil from underneath the couch she was sitting on. It was time to get back to songwriting. She was halfway through composing her latest ode to the Dragon – *Anthem of Bile.* It would be a twenty-minute odyssey of darkness and doom, a prophecy of the end times, when Black Metal Jesus would manifest on earth, bigger than the Buddha and Muhammad combined, pouring out his hatred for wretched humanity. His bile would flow like magma from the cunt of Vesuvius, scouring the earth, burning the posers to ashes or transforming their bodies into statues frozen in timeless attitudes of agony and sorrow. Just thinking about that day of judgment made Sister Blood's heart sing. She thought of all those impure souls being ripped from their bodies and devoured by the Dragon – the souls of satanic black metallers, those worshippers of filth. The souls of nu metal imbeciles, those butchers of riffs and perverters of Sabbath's Black creed. The souls of anyone who denied the black blood of the Dragon!

Soon she felt high on her holy exultation. Furiously she wrote of bodies burning up in dark celestial bile. She wrote of her enemies, Flagermus, being turned into charbroiled skeletons by the fiery breath of her lord.

Your life is dead fool
Satanic whore shall kiss the brown ring no more

Flesh on the wind like ashes from a fag
You are the one who will die in your ass

She grinned. The lyrics were good, and her command of the tricky English language was getting better by the day. Much better than when she'd first started out, penning songs like *Centuries from the Pasts Hails the Dark Jehovah,* or *Shitting Poser I Will Make You To Be Dead.* She put her pen back to the paper – then froze as a loud CRACK! echoed through the bus.

Rising to investigate, Blood found HOG whipping her naked back with a cat-o-nine tails. Blood was already oozing from fresh lacerations on her pale skin.

"Do you have to mortify yourself now, Sister?" said Blood. "I'm trying to write a new song..."

HOG didn't answer; her eyes were filled with the dark love of Black Metal Jesus. She was off in a shadowy dimension, beyond the realms of life, beyond the realms of death.

Blood sighed and went back to her curtained-off alcove. She picked up the pen and paper, trying to concentrate even as the rhythmic whipping sound echoed through the air every few seconds. As she sat there, she became aware of all the other irritating noises in the Florida night. The sound of Whoreface snoring. Cicadas buzzing. Sirens blaring on the highways and backroads all around the festival grounds.

Then there were the sounds from the festival parking lot, where the tour buses were parked. With the final set over, the bands were settling in for the night, but none of them were sleeping yet. Blaring music came from the buses, punctuated by notes of laughter, booming voices, demented cries, and the occasional scream of agony or pleasure – it was often very hard to tell which. No doubt the other bands were all taking drugs, drinking booze, and taking sexual advantage of groupies.

Blood shook her head. She was so disappointed in herself. She should be doing the same thing! For
wasn't that the Word of Black Metal Jesus? Wasn't that
the commandment He'd given her, back at Hollóhegy?
She remembered His resonant words:

Do drugs. Drink booze. And, like, have lots of sex.

Sometimes Blood got so caught up in preaching
the Word of her Lord she forgot about following His
commandments herself. She threw her notepad aside,
and went in search of some groupies.

Blood found her way to the entrance of the festival,
which was now closed and guarded by security. But
the boundary was not impermeable. Attractive young
women were waved through the gates in the company
of sleazy and disheveled-looking roadies, who would
escort them to various afterparties taking place in the
buses and trailers of the bands. Many of the roadies
would no doubt receive blowjobs or other sexual favours from the groupies as payment for bringing them
face-to-crotch with their icons. Whenever famous musicians like Ben Balrog kissed a hot fangirl, they probably tasted the cum of roadies beneath a veneer of
hastily-swilled mouthwash.

Blood laughed, finding the whole thing amusing.
She didn't need roadies to find her someone to fuck.
Temperance Holocaust didn't even *have* roadies. They
couldn't afford them, and the ones who worked for the
Dark Ones of Darkness Tour refused to have anything
to do with them after a certain incident in which one
of their number had presented to the ER with a perforated bowel and a pair of Whoreface's drumsticks
stuck in his colon. Which meant the Sisters had to find
their own groupies, and lug all their own gear. Luckily Whoreface was very strong, despite her small stat-
ure, and Leper Licker was stout enough to carry all the
amps on her back.

Perhaps one day we will find some roadies who are believers of the Word, thought Sister Blood. *They will work for free, and fear no violence. They will be true soldiers of the Dragon.*

She strode to the fence and peered at the fans milling around outside. Most of them were young goth or metal girls, scantily-clad and covered in make-up. Blood had no interest in them. They were posers for one, and in any case Blood had no real interest in cunt. She kept on scanning the crowd.

Bingo, she thought.

Her eyes had alighted on two young men. They both wore poorly-printed *Dawning of the Death Gash* T-shirts, and their black denim jackets were covered in Temperance Holocaust patches, showing various versions of the band's logo, which had been redesigned five times in the last two years in a concerted effort to visually capture the true essence of Black Metal Jesus. Their faces were slathered in corpsepaint, and large metal crosses hung from their necks. One of them had dried blood all over his lower face. Blood remembered him vaguely as the one who'd taken cuntunion from her during the performance earlier that day. The memory was a foggy one; when she performed on stage she did so in an altered state of consciousness, an ecstatic union with her husband the Dragon.

Blood grinned to herself as she peered at the fans. It was still somewhat hard to believe they actually existed. There were true believers in Europe, of course, where the Sisters had been based for the last few years, but she'd hardly been expecting to find any here in America.

This is a sign, she thought. *A sign we're doing our job well. Spreading the Word in all its glory!*

As the young men saw her they rushed to the fence, followed by a small redheaded woman.

"Sister Blood!" one of them cried. "It's me! I'm still wearing your holy gore!" He pointed to his face, where the blood had taken on the color of rust. "Let us come and pray with you!"

She nodded to the fan, then walked over to a bloated security guard. The back of his neck, pallid and bald, looked like a pack of vacuum-sealed bratwursts.

"Those ones," she said, pointing at the two young men. "I want them in here."

The security guard looked at her wearily, then nodded and gestured to his fellow rent-a-cops.

"Those guys," he said. "Let 'em in."

Moments later the true believers were behind the fence with Blood, accompanied by the redheaded girl, who wasn't wearing corpsepaint, and whose skinny torso was covered by a sleeveless *Hog Head* T-Shirt.

"Have you accepted Black Metal Jesus as your master and defiler?" asked Blood, peering at all three of them imperiously.

"Yes!" shouted the two young men.

"Um...yeah!" said the girl, looking somewhat uncertain.

Blood stared at her. Did she have the makings of a True Believer, or was she merely a poser? Only time would tell.

"Sister Blood, this is such a fucking honour," said one of the young men. "We've been listening to your stuff right from the beginning, ever since your *Drunk on Christ's Cum* demo tape got circulated back in 96! It's so amazing – "

"Silence!" said Blood. "I do not need a lesson on my own discography. You will speak when spoken too."

"Yes, Sister Blood!"

"So, what are your names?"

"Patrick," said the boy with the bloody mouth.

"Benny," said the strapping young lad beside him.

"Katie," said the redheaded girl.

Blood frowned. "Those are insipid American names. You need true Black Metal names. You –" she pointed to Patrick – "you shall be known as Golgotha Skull-Fuck." She pointed to Benny. "You shall be The Lamb of Hatred." She pointed to Katie. "You shall be Angel Face Murder Cunt."

The three fans beamed with pride.

"Oh thank you, Sister Blood!" said the newly-christened Golgotha Skull-fuck.

"Follow me," she said.

Sister Blood led them back to the tour bus, past Whoreface's snoring body, past HOG, who had finished flagellating herself and was now sleeping soundly on her bed of nails. The fans glanced at the sleeping Sisters in awe, then joined Blood in her private, curtained chamber.

Blood opened a crate of whiskey bottles. She passed one bottle to the fans, then tore the cap off another and started drinking, letting the cheap American liquor defile her mouth. A pulsating warmth followed the stinging taste down her gullet and into her stomach, where it started rippling outwards in waves of sick recklessness.

"Time to follow His commandments," she said.

"Yeah – drink booze, take drugs, and fuck!" said Golgotha, quoting from the manifesto Sister Blood had released a few years ago on the teachings of Black Metal Jesus.

"Do you have any crack?" she said, peering at them intently. "I hear it is very popular here in America. I have never tried it."

"No, no crack," said the Lamb of Hatred. "But I've got some speed."

He took out a gram bag of white powder and dumped it onto the back of Black Sabbath's *Master of*

Reality LP, which sat on the small table next to Sister Blood's bunk.

"A glorious bounty," said Sister Blood as the Lamb took out his driver's license and began to chop the powder into generous lines. The photo on the driver's license showed a clean-cut young man, *sans* corpse-paint. Once he was done chopping the lines, he rolled up a one-dollar bill and handed it to Blood.

"Here you go, Your Holiness," he said.

"I'm not the Pope," said Sister Blood. "Though I ought to be."

Placing the rolled-up bill into her nose, she bent over the album and hoovered up the fattest white line. It surged into her body like spiritual rocket fuel, propelling her soul to a higher level of awareness, closer to her glorious husband. She felt her heart hammering fast, driving frenzied blood through her extremities. Her sexual need grew even more acute, fed by the amphetamine burn. She thrust the rolled-up bill towards the others.

"Hurry," she said. "Partake of the holy sacrament!"

As they snorted up lines she threw off her dress and began fingering herself, thinking of her Lord, Black Metal Jesus. She hoped He would return to earth again soon, not just to usher in the apocalypse, but to fill her once more with His hot, holy seed. She'd never felt so much pleasure from the touch of a man. But of course He was not a man, but a god...

"My Lord," she whispered, working the wetness from her cunt and down her upper thighs.

She noticed the two young men staring at her with faces of worshipful desire. The young woman looked excited too, mischievous, her pupils like black suns eclipsing her irises. Sister Blood turned to the Lamb of Hate. He was the tallest; perhaps he would be the most ample in the loins.

"Take off your vestments," she commanded.

The Lamb of Hate began to get naked, while Sister Blood caressed herself and quoted from the Bible.

"For she doted upon their paramours, whose flesh *is as* the flesh of asses, and whose issue *is like* the issue of horses..."

She watched the Lamb's erect phallus spring into view. She cocked her head, inspecting it. She was not wholly disappointed.

"It's not as big as my Lord's holy scepter, but it will do," she said. "Plunge it into my bleeding wound."

She knelt on all fours on her bunk, raising her wet cunt, from which a trickle of menstrual blood still flowed along with the vaginal exudate. She ignored the look of jealousy on the face of Golgotha Skullfuck, whose jaw was still marked with the rust-coloured remains of her menses.

"Open my red channel," she said. "Like holy Moses..."

The Lamb plunged into her. She moaned in pleasure from the sudden, joyful shock of it. She saw her Lord in her mind's eye, egging her own, speaking His commandments in that strange and resonant voice.

Just, like, do whatever makes you feel good, you know? Fuck everything else...

She felt the pleasure build and build, taking her higher and higher, into the upper reaches of the Sefirot, where the scales of the Dragon roll without end, lustrous and black in the terrible void. She moaned, and peered at the other True Believers, who stood there watching, eyes and pupils wide, sweat beads gleaming on their pallid skin.

"What are you waiting for?" she said. "This is supposed to be a holy orgy. The black dragon commands it. *No holes shall be spared!*"

Golgotha and Angel Face turned to one another, their faces awkward at first, then excited, then smiling with mutual lust. They peeled back just enough dirty denim to start fucking on the floor next to Blood's bunk. Blood watched them for a short while, enjoying the look on the girl's face as Golgotha's rod pierced her from behind, a fleshy surrogate for the penetrating power of the heavenly Dragon.

Blood closed her eyes, flashing back to that night at Hollóhegy when her husband had first entered her. She saw the lashing storm...the lightning...the beautiful cadaverous face with long locks and beard, with its bleeding wreath of barbs...she saw the flames, heard the dying screams of those who had not been chosen erupting like a musical flourish to crown her own blossoming ecstasy...

She felt a similar ecstasy building in her now, fed by waves of pleasure that rippled through her body with each plunging penetration. Each wave grew stronger than the last, the pleasure lasting longer, until they were almost overlapping, almost exploding –

"Hail Satan!"

The words boomed through the air, and Sister Blood's arousal died down like a flame doused in water, until it was barely a flicker.

"What the shitting fuck!" she roared, pulling herself off the Lamb's bloody prick and leaping to her feet as more cries rang through the air.

"Ave Satanas!"

"Hail Lucifer!"

"Shemhamforash!"

The sounds were coming from the bus next door – the bus that belonged to Flagermus.

"Those damn Satan Suckers," said Sister Blood. "How dare they ruin our holy orgy with their heretical chanting! We need to teach them a lesson!"

She stormed from the bus, naked except for her

veil. The True Believers followed in various states of undress. They gathered outside, staring at the neighboring tour bus, from which came the echoing voices of Satanists praising their goat-headed whore.

"I'll tell them to shut the fuck up," said the Lamb of Hate, who wore his denim jacket and t-shirt but no pants, so that his bloody erection throbbed naked in the hot summer night.

He stomped towards the door.

"Wait," hissed Blood. "They will not listen to the Holy Word. There's no point talking to them. We should take this opportunity, while they're distracted, to defile their blasphemous temple."

"You...you mean vandalize their tour bus?" said Angel Face.

"Exactly!" said Sister Blood. "Their Satanic vehicle must be smote with the power of the Dark Lord Jesus."

Angel Face peered back at the bus, which was branded with the logo *McPherson's Bus Rentals 1800 555 689*.

"Um...are you sure that vehicle is Satanic? It looks like a rental..."

"Of course it's Satanic!" snapped Blood. "It's inhabited by the whores of the Beast. It must suffer holy wrath. Go forth, True Believers, and take righteous revenge!"

She pointed theatrically at the bus. The three True Believers took a step forward, then paused.

"What should we do?" asked Golgotha, seeking Sister Blood's approval, like some sort of indecisive puppy.

She sighed. Sometimes being a leader meant you had to function as a surrogate brain for the sheep. And yet, it was better than having rebels in the flock, like Leper Licker. She fixed Golgotha with an imperious stare.

"What would black metal Jesus do?" she said.

The True Believers nodded, then strode towards the bus. Angel Face Murder Cunt took out a large black marker and started graffiting the vehicle with things like "The Devil is retarded" and "Satan is a gay porno star." She drew many crosses, which was pleasing to Sister Blood. Meanwhile the Lamb of Hate took out a butterfly knife and started puncturing the bus' tyres, causing the vehicle to slowly slump down by degrees.

While the others worked, Golgotha stood there, as if unsure what to do. At last he took his cock in hand and started pissing on the door. Urine splashed through the gaps, filling the bus with the incipient stink of piss, though Blood doubted the occupants would be able to smell anything over the pre-existing stench of Satanic incense and weed smoke drifting from within.

Golgotha finished pissing, but seemed unsatisfied with his vandalism. He scratched his head for a moment, then squatted down like an ape and began to defecate on the ground near the doors of the bus.

"Eww, gross!" said Angel Face, backing away from the growing stench.

The Lamb drew back as well, holding his nose.

"Dude...!" he said, in a voice of mingled admiration and disgust.

Golgotha stepped away from his turd, his eyes burning with holy conviction. Sister Blood felt a thrill run through her as her inner holiness responded to his.

"Good, Golgotha," she said. "Truly you are a vessel for the Lord's wrath. Now smear Satan's vessel with holy filth! Mark their door, as the people of Moses marked their doors in wicked Egypt! As the Lord marked the wall of Belshazzar's palace!"

Golgotha paused, contemplating his naked hand and the pile of shit on the ground. He glanced around for something to use as a makeshift glove. The parking lot was covered with ubiquitous Florida flotsam – hamburger wrappers, fried chicken buckets, used condoms, empty shotgun cartridges, alligator bones, rollerblades, and soiled pairs of neon leopard print short-shorts. Ignoring all of these items, Golgotha picked up a discarded Noose t-shirt, which showed all twelve members of the band wearing their signature masks and boiler suits. Perhaps it had blown away from a merch stand; more likely a fan had come to their senses and discarded the worthless trash.

"Good," said Sister Blood. "How appropriate. Use filth to spread filth!"

Gingerly using the crusty Noose T-Shirt like a catcher's mitt, Golgotha picked up a handful of feces and threw it at the door of the bus. It splattered outwards, like bird shit falling from on high. Was it just Sister Blood's imagination, or had the excrement taken on the likeness of a splattery cross?

She smiled. "Good work, True Believers," she said. "The whores of the goat have been chastised. We may now return to our holy orgy."

They went back inside the bus. Sister Blood wasted no time falling on all fours so the Lamb could enter her once more. She felt the pleasure building again as he fucked her with amphetamine roughness. The cries of Satanic worship coming from the neighboring tour bus didn't bother her this time. Instead, they filled her with mischievous laughter as she thought of the holy retribution she and her minions had wrought on their enemies.

Just another battle in the war that is the Eternal Conflict! she thought, as the waves of pleasure rose, bringing her closer and closer to climax. It sounded like Angel Face was close too, moaning as Golgotha impaled her on the floor.

"Yes," said Blood. "Let us all cum together..."

She felt the orgasm approaching fast, carried on waves that grew stronger and stronger, more and more intense and long-lasting, until the pauses between them were so brief they were *almost* overlapping, *almost* crashing together in a sensory apocalypse of uttermost pleasure. She was close, so close. She was going to –

> *Deutschland, Deutschland über alles,*
> *Über alles in der Welt!*
> *Deutschland, Deutschland über alles,*
> *Über alles in der Welt!*

Sister Blood bared her teeth in anger as the flames of her oncoming climax were once again doused. She leapt off The Lamb's cock and stormed from her curtained bedchamber, staring daggers at the singer.

"I told you not to chant that Germanic crap in this bus!" she roared.

Leper Licker stopped singing, peering back at her smugly.

"I'll sing whatever I want!" she snapped, then went back to reciting the anthem.

> *Deutschland, Deutschland über alles,*
> *Über alles in der Welt!*

Blood scowled at her. Leper Licker was acting even more uppity than usual. Her ego was out of control. She stank of lubricant, anal secretions, and cheap aftershave. She'd obviously been out somewhere, getting her asshole stretched out by some simian Florida native. And now she was singing this deplorable song, which glorified not God, but a dead and wretched empire.

"I told you not to sing that shit, Sister," snapped Blood.

"Fine," said Leper Licker. "I'll play some music, instead."

She took a CD from her purse and slipped it into the boombox. Burzum's *Filosofem* began to boom from the speakers.

"Oh no you don't," said Sister Blood. "This isn't true black metal. It's blasphemy. It's the screeching of a murdering Nazi bitch obsessed with faggoty hobbit novels. Turn that shit off!"

Leper Licker ignored her and started dancing ineptly, shaking her oversized ass.

"What the fuuuck?" groaned Whoreface, waking from deep slumber and rising from the couch nearby.

HOG remained still on her bed of nails, though she was obviously awake. Judging from the pained look in her eyes, she was more distressed by the unholy music than the metal spikes digging into her back. Meanwhile the three True Believers stood behind Blood, half-naked, watching the altercation with wide amphetamine eyes.

"I said fucking turn it off!" snapped Blood.

She rushed for the boombox. Leper Licker intercepted her, grasping her wrists. Leper Licker was much bigger, with thick bones and a fat, muscular build. But Blood had wiry strength. Even more importantly, she was a dirty fighter. She kneed her wayward Sister in the cunt and slammed her forehead into Leper Licker's nose.

"Ow! Goo Vitch! Ou oke my owse!" said Leper Licker as she stumbled back, bleeding from the nostrils.

Blood rushed over to the boombox. Her first instinct was to smash it, but she thought better of it, and simply hit the eject button. The cursed Burzum CD emerged like a circular turd from a black plastic anus. Sister Blood grabbed it and hurled it like a discus across the bus interior. It slammed into a wall and smashed into dozens of pieces.

"Die unholy thing!" shouted Blood.

"You cunt!" said Leper Licker, who seemed much more upset about her injured face than the broken CD. "You broke my nose, *again*!"

This was indeed the third time Blood had shattered her Sister's nose in a fight since the band had been formed.

"It is not I who have broken your nose, Sister," said Blood, "it is our husband, the Dragon, acting through me, to smite you down for your blasphemy!"

"Bullshit!" said Leper Licker. "I'm sick of getting pushed around by you. How's about I smite you back!"

She pulled the switchblade from her PVC shorts. It shone in the spooky light of the nearest crimson light bulb.

Sister Blood grimaced and glared at her Sister. She picked up a club with barbed wire wrapped around the end; it was but one of the many brutal weapons casually lying around the inside of the bus. Thus armed, the two Sisters started circling each other.

"I'm going to beat those Nazi sympathies out of you, Sister," said Blood.

"I'm going to cut off your slutty clitoris!" said Leper Licker.

Whoreface stepped between them, careful not to get too close. She pulled out her hunting knife.

"Whoa there," she said. "There's no need for violence. Now calm the fuck down, or I'll stab you both!"

HOG let out a strange, ethereal wail. She stood up, took a straight razor from her boot, and started slicing into her left arm.

"Sisters, don't fight," she said. "I will sacrifice myself for you, as He gave himself for the world. I will mutilate my flesh, so that you may be unharmed..."

The cut was deep; rich blood welled and started pouring down her forearm.

"HOG, stop that!" said Whoreface. "You'll end up in

hospital again!"

"She's right, Sister," said Blood. "You must save your holy mutilations for the stage!"

HOG didn't listen; she kept on carving. Blood dripped down upon her bed of nails.

Sister Blood glared at Leper Licker.

"This is all your fault," she said. "You're the reason HOG feels she has to sacrifice herself. You and your stinking blasphemy!"

"My fault?!" snapped Leper Licker. "You're the one who's torturing her with your tyranny!"

HOG screamed in agony. Sister Blood raised her club, ready to smite down Leper Licker. Leper Licker glared back at her, raising her blade in defiance. Whoreface brandished the hunting knife, as if ready to cut them both. For a moment they all stood frozen, poised on the threshold of holy brutality. Then a heavy rapping sounded on the door, and a loathsome Danish voice boomed through the air, stopping the Sisters in their tracks.

"Hey, you crazy Christian sluts!" roared Jokum Panzer. "What the fuck have you done to our bus? Get out here so we can talk to you!"

Sister Blood glanced at the door, then back at Leper Licker. Suddenly their internal squabbling seemed meaningless and petty in the face of this threat from their arch-enemies in the Eternal Conflict.

"Let's go talk to these ass clowns," said Whoreface.

They nodded to each other and moved toward the door. The True Believers followed, looking relieved that the fight between the Sisters was over.

Sister Blood pushed her way to the front, opened the door, and stepped into the sticky night, still wearing only her soiled headdress. The others followed after and fanned out beside her. Jokum Panzer and the other members of Flagermus stood opposite them, in front of the vandalized, shit-smeared bus. With them were some wasted-looking groupies and a pair of chubby roadies with thick dark bags under their eyes. Jokum glared at Blood, and gestured to the bus behind him.

"What is the meaning of this?" he cried. "You know this bus does not belong to us. It is hired by the tour! You have slashed all the tires. This is a lot of money to replace. Ben Balrog is going to be very angry with you!"

"Ben Balrog is not my master," said Sister Blood. "Only Jesus is my master! And as for your bus, I don't know what you are talking about. My Sisters and our followers have been in our bus all evening, enjoying holy prayer. We never touched your vile bus." She peered at the shit-smeared door and turned up her nose. "Why have you crapped all over your vehicle? You Satanists are disgusting."

Jokum bared his teeth in anger. "We did not shit on our bus," he said. "You did!"

"Nonsense," said Sister Blood. "We are sacred brides of the Dragon. We do not shit on buses. Besides, it's obvious who the culprits are. They even left their calling card. Look!"

She pointed to the shit-smeared Noose t-shirt lying on the ground nearby.

Jokum peered at the t-shirt. "Don't be ridiculous," he said. "Why would Noose do this?"

"Why would they have twelve members in a metal band that only needs four?" said Sister Blood. "Why would they wear halloween masks and overalls? Because they are simpletons and lunatics!"

Jokum paused for a moment in consideration, then shook his head. "Nonsense," he said. "You're trying to frame them."

"Outrageous lies!" said Leper Licker.

"Yeah," said Whoreface. "Stop talking shit, or I'll stick you!" She brandished her knife.

Sister Blood raised her club. Sister HOG raised the knife she'd used to cut herself. Leper Licker leered, waving her switchblade in the air. The Lamb of Hate took out the butterfly knife he'd used to puncture the bus' tires. Even without pants he looked intimidating, due to the knife and his blood-smeared erection. Golgotha Skullfuck, likewise pants-less and priapic from the speed in his veins, pulled a pair of knuckle dusters from his denim jacket pocket and slipped them onto his fingers. Angel Face Murder Cunt retrieved a can of mace from her purse.

The Flagermus clan responded in kind. Jokum Panzer withdrew a pair of black nunchucks from the waistband of his jeans. The two disheveled roadies produced matching blades with wicked curves and butt spikes that glinted in the leering flourescent lights of the car park. The rest of the band pulled out deadly weapons as well – except for the chubby guy with the fishnet top, who searched through his pockets but was only able to produce a comb. The stoned groupies cried fearfully and ran off, while the remainder of the group stepped forward, bracing themselves menacingly.

Temperance Holocaust took a step forwards in turn, so that the two groups were now almost in striking distance. The air crackled with the electric threat of violence. For the second time in under five minutes, Sister Blood found herself on the verge of a potentially deadly confrontation. The situation balanced on a knife edge, ready to tip into bloodshed –

"DOUCHE!"

Sister Blood turned to see a dreadlocked man in cargo shorts hurrying towards them, shouting.

"Douche! Douche!"

"Who are you calling a douche, asshole?" said Jo-kum Panzer, turning to face him while swinging his nunchucks. "Are you in league with these Christian sluts?"

The dreadlocked man paused, peering warily at both groups and their assorted weapons. His eyes lingered on Blood's naked body and the Lamb's gory erection. Then he stole his gaze away and peered back at Panzer. "I'm not calling you a douche, man," he said. "I'm trying to find Ted Douche..I mean, uh, Ted *Découché*. You know? He's gone missing. Has anyone seen him?"

Members of both groups mumbled and shrugged.

"Who the fuck is Ted Douche?" whispered Sister Blood, turning to the others.

"No idea," said Whoreface with a shrug, though Blood could tell she was lying.

"He's the singer from that shitty nu metal band," said Leper Licker. "Cum Cookie, or whatever it's called. He tries to combine metal singing with rap."

"Metal and rap?!" said Sister Blood, feeling her gorge rise. "Blasphemy!" She spat on the ground, and turned back to the man with the dreadlocks. "We don't know where this Douche of yours is," she said. "Perhaps he is off somewhere having sex with a woman who has low self-esteem?"

"Maybe," said the dreadlocked man. "But I don't think so. Something feels wrong. No one's seen him for ages. He's taken off in the past, but this feels different. Will you guys help us look? I'm worried he might be in trouble. Like, maybe he's OD'd somewhere..." He looked at them imploringly.

"Very well," said Jokum Panzer. "We shall help. If only to get away from these brides of the bearded whore." He sneered at the Sisters as he, his band-mates, and their roadies departed into the dark, calling out the name of the missing singer.

"Douche! Douche! *DOUCHE!*"

As the yells drifted off into the parking lot, Sister Blood turned to the others.

"My fellow black metal Christians," she said. "This is a sign."

"A sign of what?" said Leper Licker.

"A sign of our true purpose! We should not be bickering with each other. Our true enemies are those who pervert the purity of metal. Satanic fools and nu metal morons! We may have our differences, but we must stand united against the forces of all that is unholy and lame. Sister Leper Licker, I'm sorry I broke your nose, even though you did deserve it."

Leper Licker glared at her, then shrugged, neither accepting the apology nor challenging it. Either way, some of the tension seemed to drain from the atmosphere.

Sister Blood turned to the three True Believers.

"You have acquitted yourselves well..." She peered at them, feeling a flash of inspiration. "How would you like to stay on as roadies?"

The eyes of the two young men flashed with excitement. Angel Face looked more hesitant.

"What...what does that involve?"

"It is a thankless task that involves driving vehicles, lugging aroud heavy equipment, finding drug dealers, acquiring sex slaves, intimidating enemies, and basically obeying all of our commands without question no matter how maniacal, egotistical, or depraved. You would not be paid. Like those who have sworn a vow of poverty and obedience, you would be slaves of Black Metal Jesus. Wretched, penniless, inglorious slaves. What say you?"

"Yes!" shouted the two young men.

"I...I guess so," said Angel Face. "I mean, if we get

to stay with the tour..."

Sister Blood smiled. "Good," she said. "Welcome to the fold. And now, let us indulge in holy debauchery, in His name. All hail!"

She took The Lamb of Hate by his bloody cock, leading him and the others back into the bus – and into a maelstrom of flesh.

+++

A few hours later, Sister Blood lay on her bunk, naked and smeared with various fluids. Her bandmates and roadies lay unconscious all around her, similarly filthy and nude. The air stank of cunt, semen, vomit and blood. Empty liquor bottles were strewn about, their necks smeared with the juices of various bodily orifices. A dead raccoon, half dismembered, was on the floor nearby, having been involved in the orgy at HOG's instigation; the effluvium of death always aroused her unearthly senses.

Blood smiled to herself, but the smile was a weary one. The group was still together, but for how long? It was now becoming clear that Leper Licker would continue to rebel against Blood's leadership. Like Lucifer, she was full of pride, and would never relent until she was triumphant – or cast into perdition. And then there was The Eternal Conflict with those devilish Danes from Flagermus. Tonight it had almost come to bloodshed. How long until the two bands must meet in mortal battle, the Brides of Christ against the whores of Satan? And then there was this business with this Douche fellow. Whoreface was involved somehow, Sister Blood could tell. But how? Had she claimed another victim, another human sacrifice in honor of the heavenly Dragon? How long until the authorities locked

92

her away like the dangerous animal she was?

Sister Blood got up and went to the altar of Black Metal Jesus, which consisted of a statue of the Lord, purchased from a Catholic icon store, but adorned with corpsepaint, so that the figure bore a truer likeness to He who had visited the Sisters at Hollóhegy.

Blood knelt before the altar, dipping her knees in pools of semen and blood.

"Husband," she said. "Please help us spread your holy word of sex, drugs, and mayhem. And if we must all die horribly, or be sent to jail... then please let it happen in the most metal way possible. Amen."

Happy with her prayer, Sister Blood took another slug of whiskey, and passed out on her bunk.

Chapter 14: Hand of Glory

The caravan of tour buses pulled away from the festival grounds in the early morning. They wouldn't reach their next stop till late afternoon. The Hand of Glory had been up since Lauds for prayer (which, for those lazy sinners who choose to sleep rather than worship, is approximately 5am).

HOG had never been one to choose the easy path. She'd known from an early age her life would be difficult, and she'd chosen to embrace it rather than shirk her responsibilities like so many weak-minded lemmings. She was chosen. God had told her so.

At the age of seven, HOG informed her parents the voice of the almighty had commanded her to become a nun. At first her mother and father worried it was Satan's foul influence infecting their daughter's head with madness. But HOG knew better. She didn't give up. It took several more years, but she finally convinced them to give her to the Church at age twelve. But once inside, HOG found that life as an ordinary nun was still too worldly, too lavish for her tastes. She needed more deprivation, more isolation, to truly experience oneness with the Lord. *He* commanded it.

There was resistance to walling her up in the anchorite's cell, a small stone room only 12' x 15', which boasted only one tiny window just big enough to allow the entry of light, food, and other bare essentials of survival. The cell had not been inhabited by a living person for centuries, and instead had served as a storehouse for bottles of potent crab apple whiskey, which the Sisters crafted themselves and tried to sell to pilgrims in an attempt to supplement the Sisterhood's meager budget. Brewed according to an ancient recipe, it was known across Europe as being the foulest liquor, drunk only by the dying or the insane.

HOG still remembered the day they walled her up in that cell, and the fierce spiritual debates which had raged between some of the senior nuns about whether the decision was holy – or demented.

"This cell hasn't been lived in since the middle ages," said Sister Agnes, one of the oldest inmates of the convent. "It's unsanitary."

"Agreed," said Sister Bianca. "Besides, if we lock her in there, where are we supposed to put all the booze?"

"The girl is clearly mad," said the Mother Superior. "Do you want to wake up with her standing over your bed in the dead of night? Or will you sleep better knowing she's bricked up down here? If this is what she wishes, and her parents are fine with it, then don't argue, Sister. How about, instead of standing there bitching, you retrieve some of the brothers from across the river to help us, huh? We'll have her sealed up by nightfall."

HOG ignored their silly debate. As long as they followed His will, she didn't care about their interpretation of events. She began to spin her emaciated body round and round in a circle, extending her arms, singing about the sweet caress of Jesus, which she often felt all over her adolescent body. Sometimes she even felt him inside her.

"I feel him," she cried. "I feel him in me!!"

Sister Agnes sighed and glanced at the Mother superior. "You think it's really madness, or just hormones?" she asked.

"Who knows?" said the Mother Superior. "But it sure isn't God."

They walled her up that evening. And it was there HOG stayed, living on water and stale bread, seeing His face in the patterns of mildew on the walls, hearing His words in the cries of the wind as it blew

through the cracks. Inside the cell, the visions were almost constant. By the time the Sisters came and broke
down the wall of the cell HOG had already written
three full albums in His name.

Now here she was rolling along the Floridian coast
in a shameful bus filled with lazy, hung-over Sisters
who seemed more interested in quarreling with Danish fiends than bringing The Word to the sinners of the
States.

As she pondered past and present, HOG took a
sip from the bottle of crab apple whiskey she kept as a
memento of her time with the Sisters of Hollóhegy. The
bottle had lasted many years, even in the company of
dipsomaniacs like Sister Blood and Whoreface, who
refused to drink it on account of its extremely disgusting and bitter flavor. HOG enjoyed the painful bite as it
splashed down her gullet and undoubtedly ate holes in
her stomach lining. It helped her think.

After drinking three ounces - usually enough to
send a grown man into a Saint Vitus Dance - HOG began to experience a series of revelations.

With horror and contrition she saw the truth; she,
the Hand of Glory, had been blinded by pride. All this
time she'd arrogantly believed that these measly offerings of her own flesh and blood would be enough
for Him, but what her Black Dragon wanted was more
than that. He did not only want her to bleed, but for the
earth to bleed in His name as well. He wanted the misanthropic gospels of true Black Metal to spread over
land and sea, to be shoved down the heretical throat
of civilization like the oversized schlong of a coked-up
porn star. That is why He had seen fit to bring the Sisters to America in the first place, to this Godless land
of drive-thrus and strip malls.

There was only one thing to do. It disgusted her,
but HOG couldn't see any other way. The idea of toil-

ing for decades in the shadows, trying to get the sheep to follow one by one, sounded worse than Hell itself. No, there was only a single, guaranteed path towards salvation: Temperance Holocaust needed to get famous. Mega-famous, like Marilyn Manson, Bill Cosby, or McDonalds.

But how would that be possible? How could the band get famous without selling out? How could they convert the masses to the truth of Black Metal? People had short attention spans and horrible taste. They wanted cheap convenience, an insta-God they could take pics with and brag about on that horrible internet machine. *Everyone look at me! I was there!!! I saw God's miracles! Here's the photographic evidence. Read my fascinating blog...look at me…pay attention to me…please…?*

So desperate they were to be adored by other nobodies. It was pathetic!

Consumed with disgust, HOG took another slug of whiskey, savoring the heavy taste of wormwood. The answer was there, she was sure of it - she just had to open her heart, and He would show her. And so she sat by the window on the rollicking bus, her senses reeling in holy inebriation, trying to commune with her lord - but nothing happened.

'Fuck,' she hissed. 'I'm not drunk enough…'

She went to take another slug of the crab apple whiskey, but the bus jolted and she spilled some of the potent drink on her hand. It burned like paint stripper - and filled her with a holy revelation. As she watched the liquid dribble down her skin, turning it pink, a single word flashed into her mind - *Baptism.*

Of course! she thought. *But how does one baptize the masses?*

HOG drank more, pondering this quandary, but the answer eluded her. She was just about to give up and collapse into a drunken stupor, when she looked up and found herself staring directly into the eyes of her Black Metal Lord. His darkness blinded her. His presence gave her vertigo. She squinted, struggling to speak without losing her breakfast of booze and fresh air.

"My husband!" she cried. "Please, I am weary. Just tell me, how do I carry out this mass baptism? How do I -" HOG paused to swallow down a rising tide of puke. A small amount escaped and dribbled from her nostril. Her tongue flicked out quickly to lap it up. She waited for her Lord's answer, but all he did was look out the window and point with a pallid hand.

HOG looked to where he was pointing and saw a billboard flashing by.

All You Need is One! proclaimed the sign in screaming red letters. *The Devil's Den, Next Exit!*

Beneath the text was a woman dressed as a Devil with a black sex toy poised between her thighs.

HOG looked back to where Jesus had stood not a moment before, but he was already gone. No matter; she understood his message loud and clear.

"I received your word!" she cried. "Praise unto thee, Lord Husband! All Hail!"

Just one was all she needed, one great sinner to be washed in the blood of the Savior for the world to witness. Then surely all the soiled sodomizers of Satan would follow. Yes!

"Sisters!" she cried. "Sisters, awaken! Our Black Metal Lord has gifted me with a divine plan!"

But her Sisters were hungover and oversexed. They failed to rise for another four hours, during which HOG scribbled down her vision. She would find the worst, most depraved, most disgusting sinner in America. Then the chosen Sisters of Temperance Holocaust would baptize him, thereby snatching a powerful leader from the claws of the Devil and using his repentance to display the RAW POWER of Jesus! The weaklings would fall to their knees begging to be saved - and only then would HOG be able to rest.

+++

"We're not priests," said Blood. "The Pope will never let us baptize people."

"Of course he will!" shouted HOG. "You know we have his support in all things. Do you not remember our last trip to Rome, when his Holiness felt compelled to bless our divine mission with his Holy Seed? He does not do that for just anyone. He is old, you know it must be a strain for him. And yet I recall him doing just that, right on your face. Do you not remember his salty sacrifice?"

"I like the idea," said Leper Licker. "It'll get us more exposure."

"But who is this so-called 'Great Sinner?'" said Whoreface. "I mean, there are so many of them. How do we choose just one?"

As Whoreface spoke she rubbed her wrist. Stabbing so many people had given her carpal tunnel. It was one of the reasons HOG was always telling her to lay off the ultra-violence.

"That is a simple matter," said HOG. "We choose the most evil. Solved."

For a moment there was silence. HOG sat serenely, with total faith in His divine plan. The others seemed more dubious.

Blood began to speak, then paused to vomit into a grocery bag. Afterwards she wiped the corners of her mouth on her tattered veil. Smeared vomit mingled with cum stains, blood stains, and various other stains

HOG could not identify.

Blood began again. "The exposure would be great," she said, unleashing a foul breath as she spoke. "It would bring more people to our music..." Blood paused again, cradling her head. "Is there any fucking Aspirin on this damn bus?" she cried. Receiving no answer, she returned her attention to her vomit bag. With a horrid sound she hocked a wad of pink mucus into the bag, then tossed the whole soiled mess out the window of the speeding tour bus, into the path of an oncoming winnebago.

"You mean it would bring more people to *His Word*," said HOG, narrowing her eyes. 'Isn't that what you meant to say, Sister? Not to simply bring people to the music, but to *Him.* That is our purpose, yes?"

"Of course I was talking about His Word!" said Blood, rising from her chair as if ready for a fight. "That's what the music *is* - the essence of our Lord. Are you questioning my devotion, Sister?"

HOG turned away. "I must pray on this," she said. "My Lord Husband will reveal this Beast to me, then we shall convert him before the eyes of the masses."

"You mean *our* Lord Husband, don't you?" said Blood. "He is wed to all of us equally, not just you."

HOG turned back and glared at Blood. In moments like these she wanted to stab the lead guitarist. Instead she fled to the chapel, which was still blessed by the remnants of the previous evening's holy debauchery.

"Out, out!" she shouted to the naked roadies strewn across the floor.

The roadies fled, leaving HOG alone. She knelt on a used hypodermic, relishing the pain as she prayed to her Lord.

+++

100

Three hours later the bus jerked to a stop. HOG rose, pieces of broken glass embedded in her flesh. She passed her Sisters without daring to meet their eyes.

"I take it our Lord did not appear to you?" said Leper Licker, smirking.

"Shut up," said Whoreface. "Don't be a bitch to her. You know she gets upset when the visions don't come."

Inside the convenience store, HOG wandered up and down the aisles. Why would Jesus show her which road to take, but not how to find it? She was lost in the dark, surrounded by sin, like a hamster trapped in an A-list actor's colon.

"Can I help you lady, I mean Sister?" asked an unwashed, long-haired fellow standing behind the counter.

"Do you have any moldy bread?" HOG asked.

"Uh, no? Sorry. But sometimes the hot dogs are pretty old..."

HOG sighed. This day just kept getting worse. She settled for a dented can of lima beans, knowing that any attempt to open the can with her rusted pocket knife would surely lead to numerous cuts, a great amount of frustration, and perhaps even Tetanus. Such would be her penance for failing to commune with her Lord.

Holding the accursed can, HOG approached the counter.

"Your accent is cool, by the way," said the clerk as he scanned the can. "Where are you from?"

HOG ignored his question, fixating on a pewter talisman hanging on a black cord around his neck. It showed a dove hanging upside down, encircled by a viper. "What is that?" she asked, pointing a crooked finger toward the weird symbol.

"Oh, this?" The clerk looked down, fingering the talisman. "It's from the Ordi Templi Rubrum. Wicked, right?"

"Is this... a Christian organization?" asked HOG.

The clerk laughed. "No way," he said. "We won't be controlled by the false Church of Lies! We aren't afraid to embrace the darkness of the unholy legions. We are the *true* faith, the *true* believers! We meet every Thursday at 8pm for a black mass, and then we hang afterwards. It's super fun!"

HOG recoiled, unable to vocalize her disgust.

ANOTHER ONE, she thought. *Another slave of Beezlebub.* They were everywhere. HOG looked around, wondering where her Sisters were. Perhaps this was the sinner they were searching for, the Great Beast whose Black Metal baptism would set fire to the world? She turned her eyes back to him, as vile heresy continued to gush from his lips like blood from a menstruating cunt.

"Every week we have a black mass," he said. "Except for...except for *this week...*" The Satanic clerk's voice trailed off, and a look of sadness crept over his features. Were those tears in his heretical eyes?

"I'm sorry," he said. "It's just that our high priestess, the Great Red Dragon herself, Octavia Isis, passed away suddenly the other day. Hell has a new ruler, I suppose." He sniffed. "But still, it's a real bummer. She was an awesome chick."

HOG's revulsion at this abject display of human weakness was overshadowed by the intrigue she felt regarding this imbecile's words.

High Priestess...Great Red Dragon...Ruler of Hell....Dead...

HOG was so happy she decided to smile, which was not something she did very often. In fact, she'd gone without smiling for so long she could hardly remember how to do it. But it couldn't be too hard, could it? All one needed to do was pull the lips back from the teeth, like so...

The clerk leapt back as HOG showed her teeth in a cadaverous leer. Muscles in her cheeks, turned rigid from lack of use, began to flare with pain, causing her face to twitch. The clerk backed away even farther, until he bumped into the vast selection of cigarette packets hugging the wall behind him.

HOG was unperturbed by his reaction, and continued to smile despite the pain it caused. Her Black Metal Messiah had shown her the way once again. Truly she was The Hand of Glory, *His* Hand of Glory, given the power to discover all ways through the darkness.

"Tell me, gas station slave," she demanded, "where is this high priestess of yours, this Octavia Isis?"

"Huh? She's dead."

"I know this, fool!" shouted HOG. She threw aside the can of lima beans, then lunged across the counter and grabbed the clerk by his talisman. "Her remains! Her funeral! Where and when will this unholy service be held?!"

"Um, um, um, tomorrow at the Happy Acres Cemetery!" stammered the terrified clerk, his words blurring like speeding cars down a rainy highway.

HOG released him, yanking his talisman off as she did.

"Ouch! What'd ya do that for, lady?"

"This will not save you," said HOG, stomping on the pewter talisman. "Jesus, the true Black Dragon, will fuck that beastly bitch of yours. And when it is over she will submit, and thank Him! With his holy cum her soul will be saved. For there is no greater power than the dark power of Black Metal Jesus! All hail!"

"Huh?" said the clerk, looking bewildered.

But HOG was already out the door and rushing to

the bus, abandoning her dented can of beans.

"Sisters!" she cried as she climbed into the bus. "I have found the red dragon we must slay!" she turned to the driver. "Indentured bus slave, you must -"

"My name is *Ron*," said the driver testily, his face buried in a newspaper.

HOG's eyes widened as she saw the page he was perusing. She ripped the paper from his meaty fingers.

"Hey!" he said. "I was reading that!"

"Look at this!" shouted HOG, slamming the newspaper down on a nearby table. "I just met one of this succubus' followers!"

HOG's Sisters gathered round to look at the paper, while Ron grumbled something about "crazy rock n roll bitches." There, on the bottom of page thirty-two, was a photo of a scantily-clad woman of about forty holding up a sword. Underneath ran the caption: *Local witch, political activist, and high priestess of the Ordi Templi Rubrum, Octavia Isis (real name Kimberly Sweet) dies after getting hit by a drunk driver.*

"So?" Whoreface said.

"So this is our sinner!" shouted HOG. "We shall baptize her."

Sister Blood took the paper and read the article out loud. It turned out that not only was Octavia Isis a senior leader of the Ordi Templi Rubrum, but she also volunteered at the puppy shelter and ran a local group for recovering alcoholics.

Blood chuckled. "The irony, huh? A former alcoholic getting run down by a drunk driver. Ha! And what a wholesome devil's whore she was. It even says she wrote a book - *Serving Satan: The Ultimate Guide to Worship and Devotion of the Dark Angel.* Pugh! Disgusting! And it says this temple of hers has chapters all across the country, servicing thousands of wretched, cocksucking posers!" Blood paused for a moment, fuming with hatred at the dead blasphemer and her vile congregation. A resolute expression hardened her hungover features. "HOG is right," she said. "This Satanic harlot is the perfect candidate for a black metal baptism. Her conversion will show her legions of followers the true power of the LORD! Are we agreed?"

For a brief moment there was silence, in which the unified will of the Sisters seemed to crackle in the air like static electricity awaiting the breaking of a storm. The atmosphere made HOG feel high. Finally, after so much division, she and her Sisters were of one mind, one purpose. The words that followed were barely necessary.

"In the name of the Lord," they screamed. "All hail!"

Chapter 15: Soiled Purity: Flagermus

What follows is an excerpt from an interview between Jon Vertigo, editor of *Soiled Purity Extreme Metal Fanzine,* **and Jokum Panzer, lead singer of the Danish Satanic black metal band Flagermus.**

JV: So, you guys have described yourselves as "anti-cosmic Satanists." Can you explain for our audience what exactly that means?

JP: It means we worship SATAN, the primordial chaotic force of creation. We despise the false cosmos created by God, the demiurge, the pretender. It is our mission to tear down his fake reality and escape from the prison he has created for our souls! Human society, human laws, human beliefs, they are all a part of that false reality. We have to tear them all down, rip them all apart like wet toilet paper, so that the true ancient darkness can emerge, and we can become one with it!

JV: Okay, thanks for that explanation. I can't help but notice that your beliefs sound a lot like Christian Gnosticism, except that you've swapped God and the Devil around...

JP: The Christian Gnostics were fools who didn't see the truth. God is the deceiver, the demiurge. Satan is the liberator, the true primal force. Like Tiamat, he is the black Dragon of Chaos, he is –

JV: Wasn't Tiamat female? Also, she's never specifically referred to as a dragon in the *Enuma Elish.*

JP: (stares for a moment) You know some obscure facts, Mr Vertigo.

JV: I studied comparative religions at college.

JP: I see. Well, your studies are meaningless, because they are based on stupid books! *We* have communicated with Satan, the Red Dragon of Chaos, through powerful rituals. I have communicated with him myself. I have felt his serpentine presence enter into me, penetrating my very soul. He has filled me with the Venom of Truth. He has shown me the dark light of knowledge!

JV: Right, I see. Jokum, has anyone pointed out that your references to Satan sound very...homoerotic?

JP: I don't know of this. What is this word, "homoerotic?" Sometimes my English vocabulary is not that totally potent.

JV: Well, basically, what people are saying is that based on your lyrics, it sounds like maybe you think of Satan as your lover?

JP: (scoffs) Don't be silly, little man. Of course lesser-minded people will say things like this. They conceive of everything in terms of the flesh. They are like stupid animals, thinking everything is about sex! When I sing about Satan entering me and filling me with his darkness, it's about a spiritual experience, not this disgusting gay sex stuff to which you are referring.

JV: So you are against gay sex?

JP: Yes, I think you could say that.

JV: But didn't you say you were against all human laws and beliefs? And against Christianity? And surely homophobia is a product of human belief systems, especially Judeo-Christian ones? So shouldn't you be trying to destroy homophobia? Shouldn't you in fact be encouraging gay sex?

JP: I see you are a man who likes to argue. Maybe at school you are leader of the debate team, yes? Well, you can't use my own words against me. When I say I am against all human beliefs, I am also against human logic.

JV: So you mean your beliefs don't have to be consistent?

JP: Yes, that is right.

JV: Okay. Well, I've got a letter here from someone who has a question for you. Let me read it. It says "Jokum Panzer, in your song 'The Serpent's Rod,' you sing about how your heart burns with love for Satan. Isn't this totally gay?"

JP: (frowns) I thought we were done with this whole gay topic! I have already explained that there is nothing gay about loving Satan and wanting to have him inside of you, filling you with his darkness.

JV: Of course. Sorry, I'll move things along.

JP: You had better, or this interview is over.

JV: Okay. Can I ask you another question from a letter?

JP: Sure, as long as it is not about being gay.

JV: No, it's about something else. The question is: "Jokum Panzer, all your songs are about loving Satan. If someone were to take the word 'Satan,' and replace it with 'Jesus,' you would sound almost exactly like a Christian rock band. And everyone knows Christian rock bands are the faggiest thing on earth. Doesn't this make Flagermus sort of faggy too?"

JP: (scowls, swears in Danish) I thought we were done with these questions about homosexuality? You are trying my patience, Mister Vertigo!

JV: Sorry, Jokum, but this question isn't about homosexuality. When this person says your band is "faggy," they're not saying you like to have sex with men. They're using the word "faggy" in a looser derogatory sense, to refer to something stupid. Basically, what I think they're saying is that religious music is inherently lame, whether it be Christian or Satanic.

JP: Well, you can tell them I think they are lame. They are stupid assholes and wimps who suck oversized cocks.

JV: Okay, I'll tell them that. Now, perhaps we can talk more about these beliefs of yours. You say you are against the whole universe, against human society, against all law and order. What does this actually mean? Do you think people should commit crimes? Should they commit rape and murder? Is that the sort of thing you are into?

JP: (pauses) We in Flagermus make music, so we are not into rape and murder specifically. But I think if other people are...if that is how the spirit of Satan moves them, to be a rapist or a serial killer, then yes, they should follow that calling. It will help to destroy this false society.

JV: What if someone raped you?

JP: Excuse me?

JV: I said, "what if someone raped you?" Would you think that was okay, if Satan told them to do it? Would you call the police, or not worry about it?

JP: That's a ridiculous question. No one would ever rape me, I would kill them. If anyone ever messed with me, I would annihilate them!

JV: Have you ever killed anyone before?

JP: I have never felt like it, so no. But if I wanted to or needed to I would not hesitate.

JV: Okay. Let's talk more about your religion. You're part of an official church, is that right? The Church of the Dark Light?

JP: That's right.

JV: And it was founded by Emil Pedersen, from the band Mutilation.

JP: That's right.

JV: And Emil Pedersen killed himself shortly after founding the church. He was clinically depressed. Do you think his belief in anti-cosmic Satanism contributed to his depression? Do you think his belief system is a product of his mental illness? Are you maybe following in the footsteps of a very sad and unfortunate individual, who was in dire need of psychiatric help?

JP: Emil is with the Red Dragon now, nestled in his coils. He was not sick. He saw this shitty world for what it is, a worthless illusion!

JV: So you advocate suicide?

JP: Suicide is the best way to escape from this prison of lies!

JV: So why don't you kill yourself?

JP: Flagermus has too much work to do. We have to spread Satan's message through music. We must tell people to cause chaos and violence. Break all the laws. Smash all the traditions of humanity. Destroy this false reality! Soon there will come a time when all this comes undone. The twilight of humanity. This false edifice will be destroyed and Satan will reign supreme. His enemies will be annihilated. He will recreate the cosmos in a different light - in the Dark Light!

Chapter 16: Baptism

The cab pulled up outside the cemetery just before the ceremony was set to commence. Despite numerous threats from the Sisters, Ron the bus driver had refused to deviate from his pre-planned route, forcing Temperance Holocaust to call a taxi. Presently the Sisters sat in the back of the cab, all bunched up together, staring out the window at a horde of black-clad heretics. Hundreds of people had turned out to pay their respects to Octavia Isis, Satanic Priestess and renowned animal lover.

"This entire flock is hers?" said Whoreface. "How will we ever get to the body?"

"What do you mean?" said HOG. "It's right there." She gestured towards a large black coffin in the center of the crowd. "Besides, we are wives of the Great Black Dragon. Who would dare stand against us?"

"Uh..."

"And if they do rise, we will strike the fools down! Now, no more talking." HOG opened the cab door and tumbled out onto the warm cemetery grass. Her Sisters watched her run across the green towards the gathering, leaping over headstones and plots as she went.

"We should probably go after her," Blood said. "If anyone interferes, maybe just stab them, but don't kill them. A stabbing can be considered an accident, but murder not so much."

"That's not entirely true," said Whoreface, who had tried the "accidental stabbing" defense many times, only to be met with the outright disdain of law enforcement agencies all over Europe.

The three remaining nuns exited the cab without paying. After their conversation about stabbing, the cab driver didn't reprimand them, but drove on quickly, thankful to have the soiled foreigners out of his vehicle. They smelled like sex, vomit, and Frankincense, a disturbing combination which made him want to pray and womanize simultaneously. Crossing himself, he cut off another car and sped onto the highway, anxious to get away lest the strange women should return to flag him down for a ride back to the circus or wherever it was they had come from.

+++

At first the mourners were simply too shocked to try and stop the molestation of the corpse. The high priest of the Ordo Templi Rubrum, Castor Stone, stood stunned and motionless as the spectacle of strange violation took place before him. He had never seen anything like it, and he'd been a black magickian for more than two decades. The Hand of Glory had come out of nowhere, interrupting him as he'd begun to read from the Order's most holy text, *The Grimorium Ruben*, which, according to Temple belief, had been dictated to the Order's founder, A. A. Zorpa, by Satan himself, back in 1963, while Zorpa had been deep in the throes of a five-week binge of rent boys and heroin. Charging through the congregation, HOG mounted the corpse and began grinding her hips whilst howling out prayers to her black metal lord.

Confused whispers and glances passed between members of the crowd, many of whom were unsure if this was the criminal act of a deranged lunatic or some sort of esoteric death ritual planned by the temple. Castor Stone, on the other hand, was certain that this was *not* a part of the official ceremony.

Feebly, Stone tried to collect himself in the face of this madness, and restore some sort of order to the fu-

112

neral of his beloved Satanic whore.

"Miss?" he called. "Miss, what are you…stop that… stop it!"

Other members of the congregation were more forceful. A hefty woman in a corset lurched forward, intending to remove HOG from the casket.

"Do not touch the prophet HOG, you sinister cunt!" Whoreface shouted, placing the point of her blade against the woman's throat. The Satanist felt the cold steel against her flesh and stopped in her tracks. Confusion and terror spread through the crowd, but no one seemed willing to take decisive action. The Satanists weren't as militant as republicans or Evangelicals. They didn't believe in guns, and practiced non-violent protests in the form of interpretive dance. They also mistrusted the government and constantly annoyed the police and local council, so they couldn't count on The Man to come to their aid. What could they do, other than scream?

"Who are you people?!" A tattooed woman cried.

"Calm down little sinners," said Sister Blood as she strode into their ranks. "We are the Sisters of Temperance Holocaust. Perhaps you have heard of us?" Blood waited for some sign of recognition, but the crowd just looked even more confused, and so she continued her speech. "We have come to save your souls by saving the most sinful among you - your priestess, Octavia Isis. In life she was a hollow-headed goat-sucker. In death, this Satanic she-whore shall be devoured by the jaws of the Lord and vomited back into an eternity of His divine lust. In death, her soul shall be anointed by our Lord's holy cock, washed in His sweet white seed. Thus shall her spirit be saved. Amen!"

Mostly still clueless as to what Blood was talking about, the mourners turned their attention back to

HOG, who had pulled out a flask of whiskey and doused the dead woman. Leaning down, HOG licked some of the acrid liquor from the dead woman's face. She squeezed the priestess' breasts, then started caressing her own meager bosom. Her moans and pelvic gyrations atop the corpse caused outrage amongst the mourners, not to mention a certain measure of perverse jealousy amongst the male members of the congregation, many of whom had lusted after Octavia, but had failed to ever consummate their longing in the bedroom.

"Fuck this!" shouted one of the men. "Get the hell off of Octavia, you crazy Christian bitch!" He grabbed HOG, trying to wrench her away from the body. HOG made the sign of the cross, trying to ward him away as though he were a vampire, but he continued pulling at her arms. Unusually strong for her size, HOG remained immovable, her legs clamped around Octavia's hips in a vice-like grip. The casket rocked as the struggle raged. All the motion and pushing had the unintended side effect of heightening the friction between HOG and the corpse, against which she continued to grind her hips in a frenzy of mystico-sexual mania. Her cries of pleasure increased. A tide of horny gibberish poured from her mouth as she spoke in the Tongue of Lust her husband had taught her.

"Your devil whore is *o'* so lucky to be baptized by the holy seeress," said Leper Licker, seizing HOG's assailant. "You should be kissing her cunt."

Leper Licker held a knife to the man's throat with one hand and fondled his cock with the other. Cringing in terror, the man stepped back from the coffin, weeping as Leper Licker squeezed and caressed him.

"Octavia, *noooo!*" Castor Stone cried, falling to his knees in horror as he realized the meaning of the ritual taking place before him. "She can't be a Christian!

You can't do this to her!" He ripped at his hair in a fit of helpless rage, while HOG tore open Octavia's bodice, sprinkled cocaine onto dead woman's chest, and began to hoover it up with both nostrils, while continuing to grind her hips and moan as though she were close to a mind-blowing orgasm.

At the same time Shawn Harcross arrived on the scene. A local newspaper reporter for the North Florida Sentinel, he'd been tasked with writing a piece on the quirky spectacle of a Satanic funeral ritual. All too aware from his college days about just how dismally boring Satanists actually were, he'd approached the task with a distinct lack of enthusiasm, hence why he had arrived so late. Now, as he saw HOG riding the corpse of Octavia Isis, he knew something way more exciting was happening than some lame Satanic ceremony for an alcoholic animal lover. This was real news!

Harcross whipped out his camera and started snapping photos like a paparazzi at a Hollywood fist fight. He got some choice shots of HOG gyrating atop the corpse, her soiled hairshirt hiked to her hips as she ground her cunt into the corpse's pelvic triangle.

"This is great," said Harcross, more to himself than anyone else. He turned to the only nun who wasn't having sex with a corpse or holding a knife on someone. "Can I get a statement?"

"Of course," said Sister Blood. "We shall talk. But first, you should keep taking photos. The great moment is at hand!"

Harcross turned back to the spectacle of HOG and started snapping more photos. He acted not a moment too soon, for just a moment later HOG arched her back and let out a wild orgasmic shriek.

As her Sister climaxed atop the sinner's body, Blood was allowed a glimpse through the Veil. She grinned as she saw His Holy Spirit surging through

HOG's loins like lightning through the belly of a cloud. A moment later HOG collapsed into a gasping heap, a single hand raised toward the heavens.

"It is done!" she shrieked, slamming down the rest of the whiskey. "Help me out, Sister, for I am weak from my exertions!"

HOG reached out for Whoreface, who grabbed her by the arm and dragged her from the casket. The empty whiskey bottle tumbled to the ground. The corpse lay in disarray, its clothing ripped open, smeared with liquor dusted with cocaine.

"What just happened?" asked Harcross, turning back to Sister Blood. "Are you real nuns? Surely you can make a statement now?"

"YES!" shouted Blood. 'Do not be so impatient, chronicler of doom! All shall be presently revealed. We are Temperance Holocaust, the true Servants of the Black Dragon, chosen to inflict His Word on the weak minded posers of this earth! We are the brides of Black Metal Jesus, He who screams forth the gospels of Suck, Fuck, and Drug. He who in his fathomless, holy lust has saved this whore pretender, this so-called Octavia Isis, from the flaming hemorrhoids of Hell! Now her soul fornicates with the true Jesus. She cries out his primal gospel of penetrated bliss beyond the Veil for all to hear. You maggots of Lucifer, take note! We will be at the North Florida Fairgrounds for three days. Just three!" Blood held up three fingers while scanning the traumatized eyes of the crowd. "All those who wish to be saved are welcome! Those who wish not to be - may you know a thousand deaths, infidels!"

"And do not forget," said Leper Licker, attempting to soak up some of the limelight. "It is only through -"

"That is enough, Sister," said Blood, cutting her off. "I have said all that needs to be said. Do not overegg the pudding, yes? Besides, we must leave this place before the authorities arrive. Come."

Leper Licker glared at Sister Blood. Trapped between the two of them, Harcross felt his pulse begin to quicken from fear. He was no stranger to intimidating people, having interviewed Tory McCracken, the Chicken Nugget Killer, while the latter was on death row. And yet, these women scared him all the same.

"I said come," snapped Sister Blood. "*Now.*"

As Leper Licker reluctantly acquiesced, Blood turned to Harcrosss.

"What is your name, chronicler of doom?" she asked.

"Shawn," he said, trying to keep a tremor of dread from his voice.

"Shawn, our cab has left us stranded," said Blood. "You will give us a ride back to our tour bus."

"Uh, sure," said Harcross. "But first, can I get a group photo?"

"Of course," said Sister Blood. "We must spread the word about this glorious baptism."

The four Sisters stood close together, Whoreface supporting the lank body of HOG, who slumped like Christ on the cross, wearing a stupefied look that was one part post coital bliss, one part religious mania, and one part sheer drunkenness. As Harcross knelt down to get a good angle, Leper Licker peered at him eagerly.

"You fuck?" she asked.

Shawn gulped and tried to avoid eye contact. "I'm engaged," he said.

Leper Licker shrugged. "That is fine. I don't mind."

+++

117

The members of the Ordo Templi Rubrum gazed upon the ruined remains of Octavia Isis. Her makeup was smeared. A crude cross, drawn in blood, was drying on her forehead. Her torn gown reeked of booze, and a wet stain on the crotch bore a mute - but moist - testament to Sister HOG's humping.

"She was sober for three years," sobbed one of the mourners, distressed to see the body of the abstinent priestess stinking of liquor. "Oh, Octavia!"

"But I don't know," said Castor Stone in a contemplative tone. "She seems at peace, doesn't she?" Stone looked down at his former lover's face. Was it just his imagination, or was that a faint, blissful smile on her lips? Dead and soiled by a black metal nun, she seemed more beautiful than ever. A nimbus of light seemed to cling to her. What did it all mean? Either Castor was microdosing too much LSD, or he was experiencing a mystical revelation.

"What do we do, Castor?" asked one of the temple members.

Castor glanced at his confused followers, then back at Octavia, whose radiance only seemed to intensify with each passing moment. The answer was obvious.

"We shall go to the black metal church of Temperance Holocaust!" he shouted, ripping the talisman from around his neck, feeling a sudden disdain for the icon of Satan. "All this time I was wrong," he said. "Lost! I did not know the way. But now I see! Octavia has been saved! She has been embraced by this great Black Dragon. He accepts her as the alcoholic lesbian she always wanted to be, but was too ashamed to embrace! The filth has been scraped from our eyes, for we have witnessed the truth! Who will come with me to embrace the eternal darkness of Jesus Christ?!"

The mourners grew silent, looking at each other,

all of them thinking the same thing. Their high priestess was dead. Their high priest wanted to get baptized
by some horny nuns at a heavy metal festival in Talla-
hassee. There would probably be drugs, fist fights, and
rampant fornication. So why not tag along? After all -
What had Satan done for them lately?

Chapter 17: Ben Balrog

Ben Balrog raised the spoon to his lips and took a sip of French Onion soup. He closed his eyes, savoring the flavor. When the world went to shit – when the chips were down, when Ben got a cold, or some jumped-up skank kicked him out of bed – French Onion soup was always there to make him feel better. French Onion soup and a chicken sandwich from Wendy's. Those two items together would always take his blues away.

He slurped the soup by the light of a solitary candle. The flame wavered, casting shadows across the inside of his private trailer. Ben glanced at himself in the mirror opposite. He looked like a true lord of darkness, with black hair streaming to his shoulders and pale skin that hardly saw the light of the sun. His bare chest was waxed as smooth as a baby's ass. He never wore a shirt, so he could show off his sculpted pecs and chiseled abs. Lately people were saying he looked fat. What a load of bullshit. Looking in the mirror, all Ben saw was buff perfection. So what if his belt buckle, in the shape of a sinister bat, was digging into his gut? That didn't mean anything. Everyone had a little bit of fat around the belly. And so what if his leather pants were feeling much tighter than usual? Leather shrinks, everyone knows that. He smiled at his reflection, and took another sip.

The candle fluttered again, moved by a draft, flaring as oxygen fed it, lighting up the contents of the room. Ben was surrounded by trappings of his success – framed t-shirts, album covers, movie posters, relics of his miraculous career. It had all started in the late seventies when Ben fronted a punk outfit, The Misfires. Their music was never that popular, but their logo was very eye-catching, consisting of stark, distorted lettering along with the image of a ghostly face Ben had traced from an old Italian fumetti. The combination was instantly iconic.

So while hardly anyone actually bought the Misfires' albums, millions of kids bought t-shirts with the Misfires logo just because it looked so cool. T-shirts were just the beginning. Soon there were Misfires lunchboxes, lighters, baseball caps, stickers, badges, iron-on patches, skateboard decks – the merchandise was never ending. At first Ben got screwed out of his rightful cut by the record label, but after a series of lawsuits he started getting paid. By the mid-1990s he was making millions of dollars a year from merchandising royalties alone. It allowed him to finance his many passion projects. He released his own line of erotic horror comics, Demonerotika, including his flagship title *Demon Gash Inferno*, about a demonic chick with a dick for a clit who specialized in sodomizing angels.

He made a number of feature films, paying homage to the great European B-Movies of the sixties and seventies with titles like *Horror House of Whores* and *Death Killer in the House of Death*. His movies featured lots of fake blood, porn stars with silicone tits, and soundtracks by Ben Balrog. Of course, his passion projects didn't stop there. He had his own record label, through which he released his own lavishly-produced but poorly-selling solo projects. He had his own fashion label. He even had his own touring company, which had led to his greatest passion project of all, the Dark Ones of Darkness Tour, which allowed him to select the greatest fucking metal bands on earth and take them all around the United States for the peasants to witness.

And yet, being Ben Balrog wasn't all sunshine and roses, which was why he was eating French Onion Soup. The tour was in trouble. That loud-mouthed asshole Ted Douche had run off somewhere, leaving his band without a singer, which meant they couldn't play. And since Jizz Biscuit were one of the biggest bands on the tour, a lot of fans were angry. Thousands of people were demanding refunds, and the bad publicity was pouring in like acid rain.

"Fucking Ted Douche," hissed Ben Balrog. He knew he never should have trusted a grown man who dressed like a twelve year old boy.

Ben drained the last of his French Onion. In a sudden fit of rage he threw the empty bowl like a frisbee toward the door of his trailer. At the same time the door opened, revealing Ben's tour manager, Ray Withers. Ray's eyes went wide with shock as he saw the bowl spinning towards him. He had no time to duck. Luckily he didn't have too. The bowl passed over his head, ruffling his hair, then smashing against the side of a tour bus across the way.

"Jesus, Ben, what the fuck?" said Ray. "You almost took my head off!"

Ben Balrog did not apologize.

"What is it, Ray?" he said. "You bring that extra chicken sandwich I asked for?"

Ray shook his head. "The sandwich isn't here yet. I'm here about something else, something you gotta see." He hurried into the trailer, carrying a stack of newspapers under his arm. "Here, take a look," he said, dumping the papers on Ben's desk.

Ben peered down at the mixture of newspapers, some local, some national, all with the same photo on the cover, showing a semi-naked nun with bandaged arms straddling a corpse while a crowd of horrified mourners looked on. There were all sorts of headlines, some more creative than others —

Deranged Nun Interferes With Dead Body
Heavy Metal Hedonist Fondles Cadaver

Sick Sister's Sapphic Frenzy with Suicide Satanist
Defrocked Deviant Defiles Dead Diabolist
There were a bunch of shorter, even catchier ones,
like "Bad Habits," "Nun so vile," and the very predict-
able "Twisted Sister."

It took Ben a moment to recognize the woman in
the photo. "Holy shit, that's the batshit crazy bitch singer from Temperance Holocaust – HOG!"

"It sure is," said Ray. "And check this, it's all over
the news."

Ray picked up a remote, turned on the TV, and
flicked to the 24-hour news channel. Beside the talking
head of a plastic-looking newsreader hovered a small
reproduction of the already infamous photo, along with
a caption reading "Has Heavy Metal Music Gone Too
Far? The Vatican denies all knowledge of death metal nuns."

"Fuck me," said Ben Balrog, staring at the screen.

"So, what do you want me to do, boss?" said Ray.
"Should I kick them off the tour?"

Ben stared at him as though he were growing a
large, veiny cock from the side of his head. "Are you
fucking kidding me? This is exactly what we need!
Bring those chicks to me now, I need to have a word
with them."

+++

Balrog had never met the Sisters of Temperance
Holocaust before. There were dozens of bands on
the Dark Ones Of Darkness tour, and they were perhaps the most obscure. He'd only picked them for the
lineup because the idea of black metal nuns was like
a teenage wet dream come to life. He'd heard about
their crazy antics – menstruating on stage, self-mutila-

123

tion, huffing bags of roadkill – it was extreme, but not all that different compared to what some of the other bands got up to. But disrupting a funeral and molesting the corpse of a Satanic priestess? That was next-level demented, and it had garnered them nation-wide media coverage.

Balrog stared at the Sisters, who now stood before him in his trailer. They weren't as hot as he'd thought they'd be. The one called Whoreface was short and wiry. There was something scary about her, a sense of barely-controlled aggression, as though she were a coiled spring about to SNAP, or a stick of dynamite about to explode. He looked away from her instinctively.

Sister Blood and Sister HOG weren't so hot either. Both of them were skinny as junkies. HOG was especially emaciated, almost like someone from a concentration camp. Her eerie eyes seemed to stare right through his flesh and into his soul. It gave him the willies. Blood just peered at him imperiously, like a dominatrix or a dictator, ready to give him some orders. The only one of them he fancied was Leper Licker. She had big tits and a big ass, just how he liked it. She looked like a chick from a Simon Bisley comic come to life. He didn't even care about the cellulite on her exposed thighs. She was just so *ample*. It was as if she was overflowing with curves. Shame about the harelip scar, the acne, and the large cold sore on her face, but still, Balrog wouldn't mind slipping her the sausage, bending her over his desk and –

"Mister Bullfrog?" said Sister Blood in the cold and emotionless tones of a European cinematic villainess. "You summoned us?"

"My name's Balrog," he said.

Sister Blood did not apologize. She took a long drag of her unfiltered cigarette, exhaling with a bored expression. "Yes?" she said. "And?"

"Don't you know who I am?" said Balrog. "I'm the tour organizer."

"Oh," said Blood. "So you are the one who put us together with bands like Noose and Jizz Biscuit, who are making heavy metal sound shittier than disco." She stared at him with a look of disdain and took another drag. "What do you want? We are supposed to be performing a mass right now. If HOG doesn't flagellate herself before noon she gets very upset. And I need to take communion of holy methamphetamine. So if you are going to kick us off your gay tour, you had better do it fast before I go into withdrawals and puke all over your office."

Ben Balrog stared at her, feeling a surge of anger – which just as quickly gave way to laughter. "Oh my God, you chicks are hilarious!" he said. "I love these personas you've created."

"What's he talking about?" whispered Whoreface as she played with her butterfly knife.

"No idea," said Sister Blood.

Balrog laughed again. "Amazing. Just amazing. You girls are showbiz geniuses. Molesting that corpse, that was the best publicity stunt I've ever seen. And it's only a misdemeanor, so you won't even –"

"It was not a publicity stunt," said HOG. "I rode that Satanic whore to free her soul from the cold caress of Satan's thorny cock! Now she's in Heaven, receiving the love of our Lord."

"Right," said Balrog, winking at her. "Totally. I get it. You girls are the real deal. That's perfect, that's just what we need to take people's minds off this Ted Douche fiasco –"

"Who's Ted Douche?" said Whoreface.

Balrog peered at her. "The singer from Jizz Biscuit," he said. "The one who disappeared? Anyway, we're getting our asses kicked because Jizz Biscuit can't play, so we need something to distract people. This is perfect. I want to move you girls to the main stage. You can take Jizz Biscuit's slot from now on. Also, I'd like you to increase the, uh, the *theatrical* aspects of your show. You know, make it really extreme —"

"We are not whores," said HOG. "We don't serve you, Balrog! We serve the Holy Black Dragon of Heaven."

"That's right, Sister," said Blood. "Besides, we like playing our sets on East Stage Three. The space is very small, so less posers are able to fit into the audience. If only we could have an even smaller area, then only the Chosen of the Lord would be able to witness our performances. Perhaps it would be best if we played in a small basement with only enough room for ten or twenty people at a time?"

Balrog peered at the Sisters, wondering *Are they fucking serious?* He couldn't be sure if this was an act or something real, but either way he decided to play ball.

"I understand what you mean Sisters, I really do," he said. "But think about it this way – the bigger the audience, the more, um, souls you get to save – "

"What makes you think we are trying to save souls?" said Blood. "We are here to spread the Word of Black Metal Jesus. Sex, drugs, violence – the world must be destroyed."

"Right," said Balrog. "And you can spread that word best if you have a bigger stage, and a bigger audience. Don't you think so?"

The Sisters glanced at each other, as if trying to decide.

"He's right," said Leper Licker. "The bigger the audience, the better. It'll help us spread the Word!"

"But the Word of Black Metal Jesus is only for the chosen few!" said Sister Blood. "For didn't the Black Dragon himself say unto us 'all the posers must die?'"

"He did," said Leper Licker. "But think about it, Sister – it's only by exposing ourselves to the largest possible audience that we can touch the hearts of the true believers, the ones who are destined to find Black Metal Jesus! Otherwise they'll never hear His Gospel. Remember – 'neither do men light a candle, and put it under a bushel – '"

"Do not quote from the second testament, Sister," said Blood. "It is outdated. Better to quote from the third testament of the Black Metal Messiah!" she paused. "And yet, you have a point. Maybe we should play on this main stage, even if a horde of stinking posers surrounds us like flies around a corpse...we can smite them with the Word of the Lord, and speak to the chosen ones amongst them, who alone are worthy of our message...Whoreface, what say you?"

The small nun shrugged. "I don't give a fuck."

"What about you, HOG?" said Blood.

"This is not a decision for us to make," said HOG. "As in all things, we must follow His will..."

"I think His will is pretty clear," said Leper Licker. "Otherwise why would Balrog be offering us the main stage? The Dragon is working through *him*. I bet it was the Dragon who made Ted Douche disappear, and created this whole situation."

"Totally," said Whoreface. "It was definitely the Lord who got rid of that Ted guy, rather than an actual person."

For a moment Blood and the others peered at her with furrowed brows.

"Anyway," said Leper Licker, "it seems our path is clear. Doesn't it?"

Sister Blood paused, as if in contemplation, then

turned back to Balrog.

"Very well, onion breath," she said, "We shall claim your main stage in the name of Black Metal Jesus!"

Balrog smiled. "That's good to hear. We should celebrate."

"Do you have any holy cocaine?"

Balrog nodded, reached into a drawer, and pulled out a mirror already covered with pre-cut lines. He rolled up a fifty dollar bill and offered it to the Sisters. Leper Licker stepped forward to take it, but Blood cut her off, snatching the bill from Balrog's hand. Balrog sensed the friction in the air between them; it was thicker than one of his own French onion farts. He'd seen enough ego battles in bands to know that those two were heading for a violent clash of personalities, and only one would be standing by the end of it. He hoped it was the one with the big ass. He winked at Leper Licker, who winked back, shooting him a look so voraciously slutty, so tinged with malevolent insanity, that it almost made him gasp and fall back into his chair.

This bitch is crazy, he thought. *But I still want to bone her.*

Blood leaned down and snorted a line, just as Ray Withers barged into the trailer.

"Boss," he said, sounding almost breathless. "There's loads of press outside. There's some cops too. They want to talk to the Sisters!"

Chapter 18: Talking To The Cops

Officer Reiner stared at the black metal nuns. Despite the Sisters all looking drugged-out, disheveled, and unwashed, they were also disturbingly sensual on some level he couldn't quite explain. It was easy for him to zero in on the one who'd starred in that infamous photo. She stood out from the others by virtue of her emaciated frame and hauntingly penetrating eyes. The black of her habit was faded. What once had been white was now a dingy yellow speckled with brown, which Reiner assumed could only be blood, judging by the scars and bandaged lacerations covering the Sister's exposed arms and legs.

Reiner shifted slightly in his chair, trying to hide his unease. He'd never seen women like this before. Here in Florida, women tended to wear sundresses or bathing suits, the fabric often strained and stretched from having to contain a wealth of overgrown curves. Also, Floridian females tended to be golden brown, and often reeked of greasy sunscreen. The color of their skin, combined with their ample size and glistening coating, made them look like oily roast chickens fattened by steroids in a battery farm. Their stickiness made the ever-present sand of the Floridian beaches cling to them like glitter at a dance party. On more than one occasion, Reiner had discovered sand in the moist pink folds of a date, a place where no sand had any business being. Presently he found himself wondering what might lie between this skeletal creature's slit. He bet it would be warm and wet, like usual. It would be her hips, sharp and jutting, which would make the ride different. Captivated, he stared into the bloodshot eyes of The Hand of Glory, and she stared right back, unflinching.

"What is it you wish to speak about?" said the one

called Sister Blood. "We have praying and drugs to do."

Reiner cleared his throat and reached into a manilla folder on the table, withdrawing an 8 x 10 black and white photo of HOG in all of her glory, riding the corpse of one Kimberly Sweet, AKA Octavia Isis.

"Is this you, uh..ma'am? Sister?" he asked.

The Sisters leaned in to study the photo. Sister Blood remained blank-faced. The chubby one smirked. The tiny one exhaled as if a huge weight had been lifted from her shoulders. Sister HOG spat on the floor at Reiner's feet.

"That's not very polite, Sister," said Reiner, trying to hide his shock. He'd dealt with behavior like this from gangbangers, but never from nuns. Then again, he'd never met a heavy metal nun before.

"Are you here to punish me for this greatness?" said HOG. "The way Pilate punished the Lord? Very well. What will it be? Burning at the stake? Stoning? No matter what you do to me, I will not yield to your blasphemous bureaucracy. I will spread the WORD until my dying breath!"

"What?" said Reiner. "You've got the wrong idea, Sister. We don't stone people to death here. Or burn 'em. Well, not unless you count the electric chair. Sometimes those fuckers fry a little." Reiner chuckled. When the nuns didn't crack a smile, he cleared his throat and continued. "But uh, anyway, I don't know how they do it where you're from, but here, abuse of a corpse is illegal, and it carries a fine of fifteen thousand dollars and up to five years in prison."

"Abuse?" shouted HOG. "PUGH! I was saving that poor woman's soul! I will not be insulted by your heresy. Either hang me from the nearest tree for all to see, or this farce is finished. We have more disgusting souls than ever to collect for Him."

"Whoa now," said Reiner, "no one is hanging anyone."

"A flogging then?" said HOG.

Before Reiner could respond, the Hand of Glory ripped off the tattered remains of her habit - which
looked almost as old as she was - and bared her svelte
ass. "Mind the hair shirt," she said. "It was worn by
the Blessed Jutta of Sponheim. It is irreplaceable, and
most holy!"

As HOG grabbed her ankles to brace for a spanking, Reiner glanced at the other three Sisters. None
of them seemed phased by this display. Reiner himself had dealt with some weird shit in his time - quite
literally, as in the case of the the Brown Ninja, AKA
the 7-Eleven Shitter, a mysterious defecator who ter-
rorized a local convenience store for months by rushing inside in the early hours of the morning and taking
a dump in the middle of the floor. Cameras had been
unable to identify him on account of his full ninja costume - brown in color. Reiner had tracked him down
with good old-fashioned police work. The guy turned
out to be a native Florida man with a grudge against
the convenience store, whose bad hot dogs had given
him a bout of violent food poisoning. "I just wanted to
give 'em a taste of their own medicine," he had said as
Reiner led him away in handcuffs.

So yeah, Reiner had dealt with some weird shit
- but this crazy nun took the cake. For a moment he
froze, not sure how to handle the situation. The woman
was clearly mad. Maybe he should call an ambulance
and have her put on a 72-hour hold for psychiatric observation?

"Just get on with it, pig!" shouted HOG, still holding
her ankles so that her bony ass stuck out towards him,
both cheeks covered in faded whip marks. "The world
will know I graciously accepted this punishment in ex-

change for saving their wretched souls. I will wear the scars on my flesh as I wear all others - with pride!"

Reiner's blood began to quicken. The four nuns were all staring at him, silently urging him to spank HOG's ass.

Maybe I should? He thought. *Maybe it'll do her some good. And there's no one around to see, other than these four crazy women...*

Heart pounding now, Reiner extended his hand so that it hovered just behind HOG's narrow backside. He could feel the heat coming off of her, as though she were aroused by the promise of punishment. A feeling of sick, giddy excitement flushed through Reiner's body. His cock twitched in his trousers.

"Alright," he said. "If this is what you want..."

Reiner drew back his hand, ready to deliver the slap -

"Reiner, what the hell is going on?" asked Officer Waters, Reiner's partner, who had suddenly burst into the room.

Reiner drew back his arm. "I was, ah, I was just trying to cover her up. She went crazy and tore off her dress. Why, what do you think I was doing, trying to give her a spanking?" Reiner laughed and smiled nervously.

Officer Waters peered back at him, looking completely unconvinced. He grabbed Reiner by the arm and dragged him outside.

"Reiner, what the fuck?" he whispered. "You know the department can't handle another sexual misconduct case. Trying to spank a suspect's ass? A *nun's* ass, for fuck's sake? This sort of thing is why you got kicked out of Miami Metro!"

Reiner didn't know what to say. Cheeks turning red, he lowered his gaze to the floor.

"It's okay," said Waters. "We'll just do a quid pro

quo, that's all. Get the charges against them dropped in exchange for them signing a statement about being happy with their treatment by the police. Come on, let's get the ball rolling..."

+++

Reiner opened the back door of the police cruiser. Having jointly signed a statement which cleared them of all charges and exonerated Officer Reiner of any and all inappropriate behavior, the Sisters of Temperance Holocaust were being dropped back at the festival grounds.

"All right," said Officer Waters. "I think we're good here. Sisters, no more baptizing the dead, ya hear? Not unless asked by the family directly."

HOG stared back at him. Her habit was shredded, leaving only her antique hairshirt, which was so skimpy - and so ancient - that it barely covered her modesty. Not that she seemed to care. "We saved the woman's soul from Satan's throbbing member and delivered her into the arms of Jesus," she said. "If such a sinner can be saved, then so can two heretical pigs like you. What say you? Do you wish to be washed in the blood of the cunt? Swallow your pride, humble yourself, and pass beneath the yoke of Christ!"

"All hail!" The other Sisters shouted in unison, causing both officers to flinch.

"Come on Reiner, we're done here," said Waters, hurrying back into the car. Reiner could tell he was spooked. Religious fanaticism had always scared officer Waters more than drug dealers and murderers ever could. Like he always said - Zealots were capable of anything.

Reiner followed after him, taking a final longing

133

glance at the band of holy women. His gaze lingered on HOG's scrawny legs. A part of him wanted to stay, and find out exactly what a baptism from these Sisters would entail.

"Reiner, come on man," said Waters.

Giving his head a short, sharp shake, Reiner dragged himself free from the grip of carnal temptation.

"Have a good day, Sisters," he said as he returned to the cruiser.

"You'll burn in Hell!" shouted Whoreface as she climbed into the band's tour bus.

The rest of them followed without so much as a polite wave, or *have a nice day, thank you officer.* Reiner's smile withered a little around the edges, while that primal lust continued to tug at his brain. How he suddenly wished to reach out and caress one of these elusive angels. Even the fat one with the cold sore on her face. Yeah, he'd even take her.

As the cruiser pulled away, Reiner looked back to see The Hand of Glory staring out of the bus window toward him, her middle finger extended and pressed against the glass. The gesture had the look of a blessing, and before he knew what was happening, Reiner found himself slumping back in his seat, overcome by a heavenly wave of euphoria. He bit his knuckle to prevent a sob of sheer bliss from escaping his mouth. All at once he had realized on a conscious level what his soul - and his penis - had already sensed: HOG was truly holy. He had just met a heavenly creature made flesh, and she had blessed him. *Him.* And to think he had almost sent her to jail!

There was only one option. He would have to atone. He would have to return to the Sisters, and surrender to baptism at their hands. Maybe he could swing by after his shift? Unless his girlfriend was home. Then it would have to wait for the next day. Either way, he would be sure to take lots of lube. He had a feeling this baptism was going to live up to all his wildest fantasies.

Chapter 19: The Rise of Black Metal Christianity

The following is an excerpt from the article "Temperance Holocaust and the Rise of Black Metal Christianity," written by Rubert Harrison, first published September 11 2001 in *Sargeant Pepper's Lonely Music Magazine.*

On June 3rd, 1999, an extreme metal band called Temperance Holocaust entered the United States to take part in the annual Dark Ones of Darkness Tour. To say the band was obscure at this stage in their career would be an understatement. According to their record label, Blood ov the Lamb records, Temperance Holocaust's first studio album, Dawning of the Death Gash, had sold less than fifty copies worldwide, and only a dozen of those sales had taken place in the United States. The band's only other source of exposure was the small number of controversial live shows they had performed in Norway, and the three demo tapes they had released between 1996 and 1998 - "Drunk on Christ's Cum," "Cuntuntion," and "The Ten Cuntmandments" - which had been traded by small cliques of extreme metal fans worldwide. They had never been played on radio, and it is doubtful if more than five thousand people had even heard their name, let alone their music.

That all changed on June 13th, 1999, when the members of the band barged their way into the funeral of Octavia Isis, a Satanic priestess affiliated with the now-defunct Ordo Templi Rubrum. What happened next is now common knowledge. Sister

HOG, a former anchorite, who is often credited as being the most spiritual member of the band, as well as the most psychotic, climbed into the casket and proceeded to engage in an act of frenzied necrophilia. A local journalist, Shawn Harcross, was able to take photos of the incident. The now iconic image shows Sister HOG writhing atop the body of the dead woman, ribs jutting from her bony frame, mouth open in a mixture of sexual ecstasy and spiritual rapture.

The image flooded the media and captivated minds all over the country. There was something about a half-naked black metal nun molesting the corpse of a Satanic priestess that fascinated the American people. Within a matter of hours, the band's fame had exploded. Their name was on millions of lips. Young people were especially excited. All over the nation, teenagers went out in search of Temperance Holocaust CDs and t-shirts. The ten thousand existing copies of Dawning of the Death Gash sold out almost overnight, prompting Blood ov the Lamb Records to immediately commission the manufacture of a hundred thousand more. All remaining tickets for the Dark Ones of Darkness Tour likewise sold out within a matter of hours. Temperance Holocaust fever had gripped America, and a brand new subculture was about to be born: Black Metal Christianity.

All around the country, young people started identifying with the new movement. Young women and girls began wearing habits and painting their faces with ghoulish black and white corpsepaint. Young men donned the corpsepaint as well, while dressing as priests or cardinals.

But Black Metal Christianity wasn't just a fashion statement. Members of the movement followed *in the footsteps of their icons, absorbing the bleak, destructive messages Temperance Holocaust had presented in their lyrics and in interviews with extreme metal fanzines. Soon parents' groups and conservative Christian organizations were up in arms. Black Metal Christians didn't just pray to God – they also carried out a host of illegal activities. Drug use, assault, and even murder were soon associated with the movement, whose members spent just as much time getting drunk and having unprotected sex as they did fasting and flagellating themselves.*

Members of mainstream Christian organizations were quick to denounce the movement as blasphemous, unholy, and dangerous. Reverend Nicholas Bolack of the New Christian Temple dubbed Temperance Holocaust "she-wolves in sheeps' clothing, here to serve the will of the Prince of Darkness." Father Frederick Fiddler of the Jesus Christ Congregation said Black Metal Christians were "the spawn of Beelzebub, whose heathen buttholes will burn in Hell for all eternity." Peter Guest, a Lutheran Pastor, called Temperance Holocaust and their fans "very sick people, who need professioanal psychological help."

The public furore over the band was only fed by the Catholic Church, who refused to make any official statements about the group, despite persistent rumours that the Pope himself was a fan, and had given Temperance Holocaust a private audience at the Vatican in 1994.

In a phenomenon considered by many to be deeply ironic and perverse, Temperance Holocaust were also denounced by numerous Satanic organizations, including The Temple of Lucifer, whose high priest, Hannibal Darkfate (AKA Bri-

an Stevens), made the following statement: "We at the Temple of Lucifer wholeheartedly denounce the members of Temperance Holocaust and all their fans. They are dangerous, antisocial maniacs. Their use of violence is totally against our Satanic Commandments. Temperance Holocaust embody the true face of Christianity, which has always been a religion of cruelty, intolerance, and madness. Hail Satan."

The violent behaviour of Temperance Holocaust's fans drew both police attention and national media coverage. In Phoenix, a young Temperance Holocaust fan, Dwight Carmichael, was sentenced to six months imprisonment for assaulting a fan of the nu metal band Noose, whom Carmichael claimed were "blasphemous, retarded, and totally gay." In Houston, two young women in leather habits were arrested whilst trying to set fire to the local chapter house of the Temple of Lucifer. They said they were trying to "do the Lord's work." In San Francisco, fans of the black metal nuns were fined over ten thousand dollars for hosting a drug-fuelled orgy in the courtyard of the Cathedral of Saint Mary of the Assumption.

And yet, despite the reckless criminal behaviour of their fans, the Sisters of Temperance Holocaust would outdo them all, slipping into a spiral of self-destructive behaviour so extreme it would see one of them dead, another in intensive care, and two of them carted off to jail...

Chapter 20: Flagermus

"Hail Satan!"

Jokum Panzer held his mildly-lacerated pinkie finger above the chalice, allowing his blood to drip down. He was shirtless in front of the altar at the back of the tour bus. His dark hair cascaded over his pale shoulders. His torso was covered with monochrome tattoos, the most prominent of which was a large figure of Baphomet in the center of his chest. The goat-headed figure had an enormous penis.

"Hail Lucifer!" he said again, squeezing his pinkie so that another small drop of blood came out. There wasn't much blood in the chalice. He supposed he should really cut deeper, but he didn't want to injure himself too badly. He thought of that crazy Sister HOG from Temperance Holocaust, mutilating herself on stage until her arms were ragged ruins. Something like jealousy flared in his heart, but he tucked it away.

She is just a crazy whore, he decided.

"Hail Satan," he said again as another drop of blood trickled down. At this rate it was going to take ages to get enough blood into the chalice...

The sound of someone clearing their throat distracted Jokum from his ritual. He turned to see his three bandmates standing nearby, waiting to get his attention.

"What is it?" snapped Jokum. "Can't you see I am worshiping Satan?"

"I know what you are doing," said Church Burner, whose real name was Christen Christensen. "But the ritual is taking too long. There are things that need to be done." He held out a small piece of paper.

"What is that?" asked Jokum.

"A shopping list."

"For the black mass?"

"No, for groceries. We have run out of some essential supplies. Malthe needs his fair trade organic muesli."

Jokum glared at Malthe, AKA Nun Raper, the band's lead guitarist. "Can't you just eat the cereal provided?" he said. "There is endless cereal for free!"

"It is all just disgusting American cereal," said Malthe with a look of abhorrence. "There is too much glucose in it. They don't even use real sugar, just that horrible high fructose corn syrup. If I eat that stuff I will get diabetes! Besides, I need my muesli, otherwise I will get constipated. You know I hate to play when I am constipated!"

"It is true," said Christen. "His playing is better when he has gone to the bathroom. Besides, cereal is not the only thing we need. We also have run out of imported beer. All we have is this horrible American Budweiser and Coors Light."

"It is like the watered down piss of a syphilitic whore," said Oscar the drummer, stagename Mother Mary's Assfucker. "We need proper European beer."

"Yes," said Christen. "And I need some vitamins. And also, we have run out of lubricant —"

"Fine, Fine!" snapped Jokum. "So we need to go to the shops. But why do I have to go?"

"Because it is your turn!"

"I thought it was Malthe's turn."

"It would have been Malthe's turn, but he cleaned that shit off the bus instead. So now it is your turn."

Jokum sighed. "Fine," he said. "Just let me finish this invocation of the Dark Lord."

"You can invoke the Dark Lord when I have my cereal!" said Malthe.

"And when I have my beer!" said Oscar.

Jokum grumbled to himself, then nodded to the others. He put some antiseptic wash on his lacerated pinkie finger, then wrapped a band-aid around it. The band-aid had pictures of Hello Kitty all over it. He would have preferred a Satanic band-aid, but Hello Kitty was all he'd been able to find at the last drug store they'd visited.

He put on his black t-shirt and black leather jacket, took the shopping list from Christen's hand, and stepped outside. He wrinkled his nose as he saw the tour bus of those Christian whores from Temperance Holocaust, parked right next to his own. He scowled as he remembered the humiliating vandalism those sluts of the bearded whore had inflicted. He thought about spitting on one of their windows – but something held him back.

Jokum closed his eyes and offered a prayer to the Dark Lord, asking Lucifer to annihilate the Bible-licking bitches. He imagined the skin of this false reality ripping open, allowing Satanic black tentacles to emerge from the fathomless void like entrails from a gaping abdominal wound. He saw the tentacles grasping the bus, twisting it, crushing it, tearing it open. The whores of Christ toppled out onto the asphalt, crying and screaming, calling on their impotent God. But He did not answer. Instead Satan's black phalloi snaked down towards them, grasping them, violating them, impaling them, devouring them with lamprey mouths which sucked the moisture from their bodies and the blood from their veins, until they were nothing but desiccated husks dispersing on the wind like ashes from a campfire.

Grinning at the scenes of cruel destruction, Jokum opened his eyes – and saw that nothing had happened. Which was not a surprise. Satan just wasn't that overt. No doubt the Dark Lord would have a more subtle and insidious form of destruction to work against the sluts of Jehovah. Grinning with malevolent smugness, Jokum continued on his way. He had a mission to carry out.

First he had to find out where to get the items he required. Not just any shop would stock Malthe's organic muesli or Oscar's imported Belgian Beer. He asked around for a while until he found out about a place called Whole Foods. It was thirty miles away, but he had no choice. He borrowed one of the vans belonging to the Dark Ones of Darkness tour. As he drove out of the parking lot he grumbled to himself. They should really have roadies to go on missions like this, but Flagermus didn't have their own roadies, only the ones who worked for Ben Balrog, and those guys flat out refused to do stuff like this unless they were bribed with amphetamines and sexual favours from groupies. Only the really high profile bands – like Noose and Jizz Biscuit – had their own personal road crew.

+++

Jokum pulled out of the parking lot and drove towards the distant supermarket. He got stuck behind a slow-moving winnebago doing twenty miles under the speed limit. He was tempted to honk his horn, but something held him back. He prayed to the Dark Lord to devour the driver of the winnebago. He imagined a black mouth opening up in the black top to consume the recreational vehicle. In real life, once again, nothing happened. The Dark Lord truly worked in mysterious ways.

Finally, two and a half hours later, Jokum arrived at his destination - Whole Foods. He smoked a cigarette in the parking lot before hurrying inside. He had no desire to make this tedious mission take any longer than absolutely necessary.

Once inside he grabbed a trolley and loaded it up with everything he needed – five boxes of organic cereal, a case of Belgian beer, and five tubes of banana-flavored lubricant. He rushed towards the express checkout aisle, only to be cut off by an elderly lady who arrived just a split second before him. Her shopping cart was practically overflowing with groceries. Tins of cat food and cookies were stacked up in teetering piles, threatening to spill out onto the floor.

The sign above the express aisle said 15 ITEMS OR LESS. Jokum estimated the old lady had more than fifty. He was about to say something to her, but he held back, silently waiting. After all, why should he be the one to challenge the old bag? Surely she would not be allowed to violate the rules like this. Surely the checkout attendant would tell her to go use another aisle.

The old woman pushed her trolley towards the attendant, a young woman with dreadlocks, who stood chewing gum distractedly beside the register.

"Hello dear," said the old lady in a soft, croaking voice, which seemed to rise up from the depths of withered lungs like dust from the floor of an ancient tomb.

The attendant glanced at the old woman's full trolley with a look of bored indifference.

"Start putting your items on the conveyor belt please ma'am," she said.

Jokum's eyes went wide with horror. This checkout whore was failing to perform her duty! Why wasn't she telling the old woman she was in violation of the fifteen items or less policy? Now he was going to be stuck waiting here for ages!

He peered intently at the attendant, clearing his throat to draw attention to himself, but she totally ignored him, popping another stick of pink gum in her mouth and chewing it insolently.

Jokum fumed. He glanced at the other aisles to see if he could switch, but none of them had item limits, and all of them were busy. The supermarket was packed. If he left his spot now, he might end up in an even longer line.

He sighed and waited as the old lady began to place her items on the conveyor belt with painful slowness. Her skin was withered like crinkled tracing paper. Her fingers were twisted, the knuckles bulbous and red, as if she suffered from some kind of arthritis.

One by one she took the cans of cat food in her shaking grip and placed them on the belt. Each time an item was placed on the belt, the attendant would pick it up, scan it, and bag it with comparatively blinding speed, leaving the belt empty while the old lady retrieved the next item.

The slowness was agonizing...

[What feels like fifteen minutes later...]

... The attendant continued to just stand there, chewing gum, casually waiting, while Jokum grew more and more annoyed. This was intolerable! At this rate he'd be here all afternoon. He had to do something.

He thought about offering a prayer to the Dark Lord to destroy the old lady with a heart attack, but that would probably slow things down even more. No, a prayer to Satan would not work in this circumstance. This time he would have to take action. He would have to take matters into his own hands.

He stepped closer to the old woman, his heart pounding with frustration and rage as he loomed over her spindly frame. He cracked his knuckles.

"Miss?" he said. "Miss, allow me to help you."

He reached into her trolley and started unloading yet more cans of cat food. The old lady squinted at him, as though she were half-blind. She peered at his long hair and dark eyeliner.

"Oh, thank you young lady," she said. "You're so kind."

Jokum grimaced with annoyance. He noticed the checkout attendant peering at him with a smirk on her face.

Lord Lucifer, please kill both of these people, he thought as he tossed stacks of frozen TV dinners onto the belt.

As soon as the trolley was empty, he began loading up the bagged goods into the trolley once again so the old lady could take them to the parking lot.

"That will be one thirty-five ninety," the Whole Food slave said.

The old woman nodded, took out her purse, and started fumbling with the clasp. By the time Jokum was finished loading her bags into the trolley, she was still fumbling with the clasp. His muscles trembled with tension. Would this ever end?

The old woman finally got the clasp undone and started searching through the seemingly endless items in her oversized purse.

"One thirty-five ninety," repeated the attendant, still chewing gum.

The old lady pulled out a large stack of coupons painstakingly cut from a local paper and the backs of various shopping receipts, many of which were yellow and brittle with age. The attendant rolled her eyes and began to sort through them.

"This one expired two years ago," she said. "This one is for a different store. This one expired two years ago. This one expired six months ago. This one is for Home Depot. This one expired last month..."

The old lady grumbled about supermarkets releasing coupons with a use-by date. They expire too quickly, she said. The whole thing was deceptive and unfair.

The attendant rolled her eyes again. "Do you want me to throw them out, ma'am?"

"No," insisted the old lady, who snatched them back and returned them to her purse.

"That's one thirty-five ninety," repeated the attendant once again.

The old lady pulled out a stack of bills, counted them, counted them again, then handed them to the attendant, who counted them much faster.

"You're five dollars and ninety cents short, ma'am," she said.

Flustered, the old lady went back into her purse and started rummaging for coins. She spilled a handful of dimes on the floor.

"Oh dear," she said. "I'll never be able to get those, not with my knees."

Jokum's fingers twitched with longing to strangle the old woman. He stepped toward her –

...And descended to his knees, collecting the coins and handing them to her.

"Thank you," she said. "What a kind young woman you are."

Jokum said nothing. The attendant smirked at him again, then counted the coins.

"You're still short five dollars," she said. "This is only ninety cents."

"Oh dear," said the old woman. "That's all I have. I thought I'd have more than enough, because of the coupons, you see..."

"You'll have to put something back," said the attendant. "Choose five dollars worth of items to put back."

The old woman made her way to the trolley and started slowly sorting through her items, looking for something to return. Jokum's head filled with the white-hot pain of a migraine. He glanced at the other aisles and saw they were all moving much faster than this one. People who'd started waiting at the same time as him were now leaving the store. Even the longest line would have been faster than this!

"Here," he said, handing the old woman five dollars. "Take this."

"Are you sure, my dear?"

"Yes, I'm sure, just take it."

"Oh, that's terribly kind of you. Such a sweet young thing."

The old woman handed the note to the checkout attendant, who took it, filed it away in the register, and handed the old woman a long receipt. There were coupons on the back. The old woman folded the receipt carefully, placed it in her purse, and began to push her trolley away. She turned back to Jokum as she left.

"Thank you so much dearie," she said. "There are so few kind young people around these days, so few with manners. You're a lovely young woman. I bet you'll find yourself a wonderful man." She smiled, showing a largely toothless mouth, then turned and went on her way.

Jokum held his head, feeling the headache waxing. He loaded up his items and quickly paid. Less than a minute later he was out in the parking lot. He threw his bags in the van and jogged around to the driver's seat. He was about to get in, when he saw the old woman struggling to load her groceries into the back of her sedan. Some terrible instinct gripped him, a dark urge he could not control. He strode over to her.

"Miss, can I help you with those?"

[Three hours later...]

Jokum sat drinking sweet tea in Miriam's kitchen. Miriam - that was the old woman's name. He'd helped her put her shopping in the boot of her car. He'd driven to her house to help her take it inside. Once there, he'd helped get her cat Flossy out of a tree in the backyard. He'd also helped her change two lightbulbs, plus clean the gutters around her one-storey home. He'd wiped a few windows too.

"I can't believe I thought you were a lady," said Miriam, sitting across from him. "I'm so embarrassed. It's because of your long beautiful hair."

"Don't worry about it," said Jokum, sipping his tea. He'd removed his leather jacket and was now wearing a sweater Miriam had given him. She'd knitted it herself, before her rheumatoid arthritis had gotten too severe. It was lemon yellow with a distorted figure of a purple cat. Miriam said the cat was supposed to be black; it was clear she was color blind, as well as short-sighted. The sweater was originally knitted for her son, Jacob, but he had died in the Gulf War. Jokum had given her his condolences.

"I suppose a lot of young male musicians have long hair these days," said Miriam. "It's been the fashion ever since the hippie days. I never much cared for any of that though. I still love my Elvis." She gestured to the walls, where framed pictures of the King, smiling massively, loomed on all sides. "What did you say your band was called? Flavour Moose? It sounds very interesting. And you're a singer! You must have a beautiful voice. Maybe you can sing a song for me? Oh, please do! Sing me 'Blue Moon,' it's my favorite."

Jokum sat in silence for a moment. He hated sappy songs like that. But for the upteenth time that day, some dark compulsion moved him. The same dark compulsion that had dogged his heels ever since he'd encountered Miriam at the supermarket. He opened his mouth, and began to sing. He didn't use the goblin-like screeching he used while on stage with Flagermus, but a different voice, a clean voice, sweet as honey and soft as velvet.

Blue moon
You saw me standing alone
Without a dream in my heart
Without a love of my own...

Miriam sat entranced by his smooth voice with its heavy Danish accent. When the song was over, she said "My that was wonderful! They must have a lot of good singers in France or wherever it is you come from. Would you like some more tea, Mister Prancer?"

"No Miss, I'm afraid I must go. I have to get these supplies back to my band. They will be wondering where I am."

"Oh. Okay." Miriam's voice and face momentarily filled with the sorrow of loneliness. She took a breath and composed herself, offering him a smile. "Thank you for all your kind help, Mister Prancer," she said. "Next time I'm at the record store I'll be sure to look out for an album by Flavor Mouse. I'm sure your music is wonderful."

Jokum nodded and smiled. He picked up his leather jacket and headed to the front door.

"Thank you Miriam, for the tea," he said. "It was a pleasure to meet you."

"The pleasure was mine, young man. Say 'hello' to your bandmates for me."

She waved from the porch, while her black cat

purred around her varicose legs. Jokum waved back to her, then got into his van, fired up the engine, and drove away.

+++

"What the fuck took you so long?" said Malthe. "I need my muesli. If I don't have fiber I can't shit. You know that!"

The lead guitarist snatched a cereal box and stalked away. Oscar picked up an overpriced imported beer and cracked it open, taking a swig.

"Fuck man, this is not even cold!" he said, spitting it out.

"What the fuck is this?" said Christen, pulling the pale yellow sweater from the boot of the car. He glanced at Jokum. "Dude, why do you have such a gay sweater? Were you shopping at the faggot store while you were out? Ha-ha!" Christen looked at his band-mates, who both started laughing uncontrollably. Jokum fumed, glaring at them.

"You idiots know nothing. I did not buy that sweater! I...I took it. I took it from the house of a woman I raped and murdered in the name of Satan! Look on the news tonight, and you will see. This is a trophy of the sacrifice I have made in the name of the Dragon, a memento of murder. The next time I fuck some teenage slut, I will wear this to re-live the excitement of my crime all over again."

He stared at the others with intense, unblinking eyes. Christen and Oscar gulped, glancing at each other uneasily.

"Wow, man," said Oscar. "That's really intense. Like, really fucking cool, I mean..."

"Yeah," said Christen. "Way to go, man, serving the

151

Dark Lord..."

"Hail Satan!" barked Jokum.

"Hail Satan!" they repeated.

Together the three of them carried the shopping back to the bus. On the way they passed Sister HOG. She peered at Jokum as if piercing his soul.

"You are a kind man at heart," she said. "Jesus hates you."

Chapter 21: Sister Blood

Sister Blood scowled as she saw the horde of mongoloids waiting for her backstage. There were dozens of them, a mixture of fans and reporters. The fans were screaming excitedly, holding CDs and T-shirts to be signed. The media monkeys were snapping photographs, trying to blind her with their camera flashes. Only a wire fence prevented them from stampeding forward like a herd of mad cows.

"How did these maggots get back here?" she growled.

"Must have been Balrog," said Whoreface. "He's such a publicity whore."

"Why does he want *more* publicity? This stupid tour is already sold out!"

Sister Blood strode towards the fans and journalists, grimacing. She had to walk past them in order to escape the backstage area and get back to the tour bus. Soon she was just inches away from the fans, who poked their fingers through the gaps in the fence and screamed with demented admiration, worshipping her as though she were a golden calf.

"Disgusting idolaters!"

She gripped her cunt with one hand and flipped them off with the other. The fans just went wilder, while the paparazzi snapped even more photos, perhaps hoping to capture yet another iconic image.

Sister Blood shook her head in annoyance and strode past them as fast as she could, followed by her three Sisters and the three roadies, who now doubled as security guards. Sister HOG remained aloof from the crowd, her face marked with a look of holy agony as she martyred herself to the irritating attentions of the masses.

In a disgusting display of blasphemous commercialism, Leper Licker began to sign CDs and touch the outstretched fingers of the fans, collecting their sickening germs. Whoreface slapped the face of a groupie who was pressed against the chainlink. The young girl turned the other cheek, hoping to receive another blow, but Whoreface just sneered in disdain.

Soon the ordeal was over, and the Sisters were out in the parking lot, heading for their bus, which was now parked at the rear of the main stage, next to the bus being used by Noose. As she strode towards what passed for her home, Blood glared at the tinted windows of Noose's vehicle. The nu metal morons were probably inside right now, dressed in clown masks and coveralls, injecting heroin into their eyeballs. Their heroin use was the only thing Sister Blood respected about them.

One minute later, Sister Blood collapsed onto her bed at the rear of the bus. She felt so terribly tired, and not just because the cocaine was wearing off. Ever since Sister HOG had saved the soul of that Satanic whore just two weeks previous, things had gone downhill.

Thanks to their media exposure, Temperance Holocaust had been moved to the main stage, while hordes of idiots all over the nation were now worshipping them like idols. Their performances were thronged by screaming philistines misinterpreting their messages. Blood could tell most of these so-called "converts" were just band wagon whores following a fad. They consumed Temperance Holocaust's music the same way they consumed McDonald's, Pizza Hut, and all those despicable movies about talking animals and magical princesses – it was just another facet of their sickening culture of vacuous hunger. They did not really *hear* the music. They did not really *hear* the message of Black Metal Jesus. They just wanted a new identity, something to wrap around their emptiness, like a facade around a building whose rooms have been gutted by fire. Blood wanted to spread the Word of the Dragon, but not like this. For verily, had not Black Metal Jesus himself said unto her, when He had visited her in the flesh, to shun the posers and vilify the herd?

"Most people suck," He had said. "They're just, like, parasites. They'll never understand cool music. That's why everything popular always sucks, because most people are shit. Only a small number of people are cool enough to like cool stuff. The rest are just posers, and all posers must die, you know?"

How right He was, she thought. How could she have lost sight of His Holy Word? How could she have been seduced by Balrog's entreaties, by Leper Licker's crass manipulations? Appealing to the masses wasn't the best way to find True Believers – it was the best way to ruin the band! She could almost *feel* all those vacuous souls out there, all those empty-headed fans, trying to feed off her like vampires, trying to taint her dark art with their grubby little fingers and stupid little brains. It was almost enough to make her puke. She groaned as she lay on the mattress.

"Are you okay, Sister Blood?" asked Golgotha Skullfucker, who stood above her bed like the loyal servant he was.

Blood smiled up at him in a rare display of affection. He was a proper True Believer, a proper devotee of the Black Metal Messiah. He hadn't found his way to the band through the wide easy road of mass media hysteria. He'd discovered them the right way, by being a part of the black metal underground, by listening to bootlegged demo tapes he'd received through the post from his penpal in Rotterdam. People like Golgotha, *those* were the fans Temperance Holocaust needed, not those screaming lemmings backstage. Oh how

Sister Blood wished they could go back to East Stage 3, where the audience was small and the sets were performed so early in the day.

"Sister?" said Golgotha. "I said are you okay? Would you like the holy whiskey? Maybe I can eat your cunt? Or I could bring some people back here, for a holy orgy —"

"No," said Blood. "None of those things interest me tonight. Bring me...bring me the holy heroin!"

Chapter 22: Ted and Kyle

[Kyle's house, somewhere in central Florida]

"Everyone thinks I'm crazy," said Kyle. "My friends, the cops, the judge, even my mom. My own fucking mom, how wack is that? And I'm like mom, *seriously*?! She won't even let me have a key to the house after this thing that happened with her cat. But that cat was fucking asking for it! He seriously said, 'lick my -'" Kyle paused, deciding to cut the anecdote short. "You know what? It's not even important. What's important is that you *get it*, Ted. I read that interview you did about your childhood. Your mom never believed in you either, and look at you now, you're a fucking star."

"That's right," said Ted. The singer was sitting on the couch beside Kyle, shades down, arms crossed, looking chill as fuck.

The two of them had enjoyed three straight weeks of passionate romance. Kyle knew neither one of them had ever experienced anything like it. It wasn't just the amazing sex, but the sense of freedom they enjoyed in one another's company. Together they were truly able to be themselves. Ted had been living a lie, screwing whores and singing about bitches. Kyle had been confused about his sexuality, but now it had all become clear. Ted and Kyle were made for each other.

"I put those pics up on my webpage yesterday," said Kyle. "You look hella awesome in them."

"I bet," said Ted. "I love that webpage. Only you really understand what I'm trying to do with the music. Sometimes you just gotta break it down and change shit up, you know? Like with the beats, I want them like *ba-da-ba ba-da-ba,* thick and compressed. Not like that cookie cutter *da-da-ba-brrrrr* messy shit every other fucking band is doing these days."

"Yeah, I feel you," said Kyle, stumbling over pizza boxes, beer cans, and debris to get to his Windows 98 across the room. "Let's see if we got any hits."

Kyle sat down and turned on the screen, then leaned back, waiting for the heavy gray box to load. He took a deep breath - then almost puked. There was an awful smell in the air. It reminded him of that time he and his friend Reggie McManus had found a rotting raccoon in that old shack by the freight yard, all bloated and pregnant with flies. Maybe some rats had died in the walls? Or under the couch? Or...

He turned to Ted. It couldn't be, could it? Nah. Ted was fine. A rockstar like him would never decompose.

"It's starting to stink in here," said Kyle, lighting up a cigarette to chase away the smell. "We should clean sometime."

"I feel you, bro," Ted said, without offering to help. Ted Découché did not clean, and Kyle respected that.

"Holy shit, Ted!" said Kyle, sitting bolt upright in his chair as the computer screen finally flashed to life, showing his webpage. "We got like 804 hits! That's like 800 more than normal! Shit is goin' viral. Look at this! These comments are off the hook. Oh! Fuck! Now it's up to 823 hits! In, like, just a few seconds! Fuck! Ted! Ted! Check it out, bro!"

Ted, always the cool cat, remained seated on the couch while Kyle scrolled through the comments people had made about the photos he'd uploaded of Ted and himself. One choice pic showed the two bros chillin' together on the sofa. Another showed Kyle wearing Ted's backward baseball cap. Then Ted wearing Kyle's boxer shorts. Then both wearing sick shades.

"Some of these assholes don't think it's you, Ted." Kyle glared at the screen. With caps lock engaged, he

began to type furiously until every comment, every insult, every incredulous asshole, had been well and truly dealt with.

IT'S THE REAL DEAL, DOUCHEBAG.
TED IS WITH ME!
IT'S US AGAINST ASSHOLES LIKE YOU! WE AIN'T
NO POSER BITCHES!
TED DÉCOUCHÉ DOES NOT FRONT!!

When the war had been won, Kyle let out a sigh
and turned to the love of his life. "Don't worry Ted, I got
your back bro. There's bound to be a little backlash.
Shit like this doesn't happen every day."

"Like what?"

Kyle lit another cigarette, took a drag, and breathed
out a thick plume of Marlboro perfume. He couldn't
tell if Ted was being obtuse, or teasing him. "Like *this*,
bro," he said. "Like us. I mean, I always kinda knew
we should be together in one way or another. That's
why I started this fan page in the first place, www.
découchéismyhomie.com. It was because, like, your
soul totally *spoke* to my soul. When you wrote about
doing it all for the shtupping, so you could get that biscuit, it was, like, a metaphor for my whole universe,
you know?"

"That's why I wrote that music," said Ted. "I knew
you were out there somewhere, Kyle. I knew that if I
wrote those words, and released them in the form of a
top 40 single with a ballin' video, my soulmate would
hear them and be drawn to me. It was, like, a message
in a bottle. Except way cooler than that fucking Sting
song." Ted paused for a moment, signaling that he was
about to get even more real. "Kyle, I fucking love you
man."

"Same, Ted. Same. It's fate, that's all. None of
these assholes will get it, but fuck 'em, right?"

Kyle turned back to his Windows 98 and started a

new blog post titled *Ted Is OUT of the closet.* When he felt satisfied he hit publish and watched the hits come rolling in.

"Fuck yeah, this is going to be *THE* number one site for all things Jizz Biscuit and Ted Découché for life!" Kyle laughed. "Stupid fuckers thought you were missing or dead or something. Now everyone's freaking out that you're alive. How fucked is that? But don't worry, Ted, I told them no interviews until you're ready."

"Thanks bro, you're way cool. Better than my useless manager, or any of those posers in the band. From now on, Jizz Biscuit is just us."

"Really?" Kyle's chin quivered. He had to swallow back a tear. He couldn't believe this was happening. He and Ted really were soulmates. Before they'd met, he'd tried writing to Ted for years to explain their mystical connection, but had never heard back. And now here they were, sharing everything together. It was paradise on earth.

The only problem was that damn smell.

Leper Licker awoke to the sound of someone tapping on the door of the bus. She rose and hurried over, stumbling as she shook off her sleepiness.

"What is it?" she said as she opened the door.

Outside was a weedy-looking man with long hair and a goatee. He glanced around nervously, as though he were trespassing. Perhaps he was some deranged stalker, she thought, here to take her prisoner and keep her in a basement while subjecting her to endless rounds of sodomy.

"Hi," he said. "I'm Everett Steele, from *Bizzang Magazine.* I've been trying to get an interview with you guys for a couple of weeks, but no-one is returning my calls, so I thought I'd try the direct approach. Is there any chance I can get an interview? Temperance Holocaust is huge right now. I can promise you'd be the cover story."

Leper Licker's eyes lit up with excitement. Here was her chance to get some of the attention she so truly deserved, without Blood and the others getting in the way and hogging all the limelight!

She glanced at the back of the bus, where her Sisters were sleeping, still knocked out by liberal injections of heroin. Leper Licker had done just as much as the rest of them, but as usual she'd been able to shake off the attendant lethargy much faster. Whoreface said it was because she was so fat, but that was ridiculous. It was obviously her superior Aryan biology which allowed her to metabolize the smack so effectively.

Having scanned the sleeping bodies to make sure they weren't stirring, she peered back down at the journalist.

"Sure," she said. "I can give you an interview."

"You're Sister Leper Licker, right?" he said. "The

bass player? I'd definitely like to speak to you, but I
was also hoping to speak to Sister Blood, and especially Sister HOG, that would be really great."

Leper Licker scowled at him. "They're asleep. And
anyway, they won't talk to you. They hate journalists.
So you can either talk to me, or you can talk to no-one.
I'm the true creative force behind Temperance Holocaust anyway."

She folded her arms across her ample aryan bosom.

"Sure, okay," said Everett Steele. "I'd love to interview you. Should we go inside, or..."

He tried to peer inside the bus, but Leper Licker stepped down towards him, blocking his view and
causing him to back away from her womanly curves.
"No, people are sleeping in here. We can talk there, instead." She pointed to a port-a-potty nearby.

"In there?" he said, sounding reluctant. "Okay..."

They entered the cramped space of the cubicle.
Leper Licker closed the door after them, leaving only a
crack for the lights of the parking lot to peek through.
Everett glanced around.

"Jesus, is that blood?" he said, peering at the
stains on the walls.

"Blood or shit, who cares?" said Leper Licker.

He knelt down and picked up a baseball cap
streaked with dry blood. The logo of a band called
Five Finger Prostate Massage was embroidered on
the top. On the inside of the cap someone had written
"Découché" in black felt tip marker.

"Do you think this could belong to Ted D–"

Leper Licker snatched the cap, threw it in the toilet, closed the lid, and pressed the flush button. She
peered at him aggressively as water surged from the
cistern.

"Are we here to study toilet artifacts, or talk about

me?" she snapped.

"Sorry. Of course, your time is precious. Okay, let's start the interview. Do you mind if I record you?"

"No, that's fine. That way you won't mess up my words."

Everett took out a dictaphone, pressed record, and placed it between them on the lid of the toilet.

"Okay," he said. "I'd like to start by asking about what happened at the funeral —"

"I'm not going to talk about that. We already talked to the press, and the police. Sister HOG was saving that Satanic whore's soul, and that's all there is to say."

"Okay, thanks. I guess we won't talk about the funeral any more. Let's talk about the music then. Your album *Dawning of the Death Gash* is very exciting. People say it has the raw primitivism of Hellhammer mixed with the eerie darkness of Bathory's *Under the Sign of the Black Mark*. Were those bands a big influence on you? What would you say are your biggest inspirations?"

"For me, my biggest inspirations are Burzum, and of course the music of Wagner, the greatest composer of all time. As for those other bands, I don't really care about them. I've never even heard of them."

"Right...and when it comes to writing songs for Temperance Holocaust, what's the process there? I've heard Sister Blood and HOG write all the lyrics, and the guitar and keyboard arrangements, while Sister Whoreface is in charge of the drums."

Leper Licker scowled. "It's more of a group effort than that. We all get involved. There are a lot of things I've added to the songs, even though I haven't received any official credit. I don't need any credit because I don't have a big ego. But yes, when it comes to composition I have a lot of influence. I'm the only member of the band who's traditionally trained in mu-

sic. Blood, HOG, Whoreface, they only started playing music four years ago, after we left Hollóhegy. But
I've been playing all sorts of instruments and singing
ever since I was a little girl. I was a musical prodigy
at age eleven. I even got sent to a special school. But
the teachers were envious of me, and gave me bad
grades out of jealousy. So I left. But I still know how to
play all those instruments – the piano, the violin, lead
and bass guitar, the oboe...I can make electronic music too."

"It sounds like you're really talented. Are there any
compositions you've written completely yourself?"

Leper Licker paused, then nodded. "Yes!" she said,
lying. "I've written many songs that will soon become
a part of our playlist. In fact, I'll be singing one of them
for the first time during our next performance."

"You'll be singing? Instead of HOG?"

"Yes, for that song, I'll be singing," said Leper Licker, digging herself into the lie even deeper. "I wrote the
song, so I'll be singing it, and playing lead guitar."

"That sounds exciting. Hopefully I can hear a recording. Now, this philosophy you follow, this Black
Metal Christianity, can you tell me a bit about it?"

"Sure," said Leper Licker. "My Sisters and I were
visited by Black Metal Jesus in the flesh. He gave us
His gospel, told us we had to help Him destroy human
civilization. He said all sorts of things, but reading between the lines, it was clear He was talking about how
western society has become decadent, corrupted by
the degenerate morals of certain undesirable peoples,
so it has to be purged..."

"Right...and this Black Metal Jesus, that was the
second coming of Christ?"

"No, Christ has come back before, many times, in
many different guises..." She paused, wondering if she
should tell him that Hitler had been an incarnation of

Christ. She decided he wasn't ready to receive such a powerful truth - at least not directly. "...for example, he was reincarnated in Austria during the previous century, and in other shapes as well..."

Leper Licker kept talking, growing more and more confident and increasingly verbose as she explained to him all sorts of things about the true nature of Jesus, authentic black metal, and the future direction the band would take, which would involve a lot more of her own compositions, and a lot more songs with her playing lead guitar. Eventually Everett picked up the dictaphone and switched it off.

"Okay, I think I've got everything I need for the interview. Thank you so much Sister, you've been great."

He reached out his hand. She took it, shook it, then pressed it against her cunt. His eyes went wide with shock.

"Our business isn't over just yet, Mr. Steele. These cubicles *always* make me horny."

It was true. There was something about the barely-suppressed stench of human waste that always got Leper Licker wet. She pushed the journalist onto the toilet seat, then straddled him, holding him down with her healthy feminine bulk. She was grateful for the poor lighting. Her herpes was active again; she didn't want him to see her suppurating sores.

Chapter 24: Whoreface

Voiceover Man: The Debbie Lyons show is filmed before a live studio audience!

Debbie Lyons: Obscene Nuns! Yes, you heard me. *Nuns* are turning on the youth of America, not to the wholesome Christian values of yesteryear, but to something dark and sinister instead. They are not preaching *love thy neighbor.* Chastity, charity, humility? Forget about it! The Sisters of the heavy metal band Temperance Holocaust preach what they call "The Gospel of Black Metal Jesus," a messiah that they claim has appeared to them, defiled them, and now inspires every aspect of their music, from their lyrics right down to the soiled and mutilated habits they wear. Here with us today is the drummer known only as Sister Whoreface, to give us an inside view into this strange phenomenon. Parental discretion is *strongly* advised.

(Upbeat music swells, then fades to the sound of the audience cheering and clapping)

By the time Debbie's opening monologue finished, Whoreface was already bored. The pear-shaped host did little to inspire her. And yet she must endure this trial, for it was she who'd been chosen as a sacrifice to the Media Moloch of America. As the audience clapped like a pack of deranged circus seals, her mind flashed back to a few weeks previous, when she and her Sisters had met with the band's new manager, Zed Rifkin...

"Who the fuck is this guy again?" Whoreface asked.

"He's a media whore," said Sister Blood. "Ben Balrog found him for us. Like a human syringe, he will help us inject the holy blood of Christ into the veins of retarded America."

"I'm your new manager," said Zed, apparently unsatisfied with Blood's introduction. "And yes, I'm going to help spread your message. I can get you in all the best magazines, on all the talk shows - speaking of which, I've already got you a headlining slot on Debbie Lyons!"

The Sisters stared at him blankly.

"It's a talk show," he said.

The blank stares continued.

"Anyway," said Zed, "It's all set up. They want just one of you - some sort of insurance thing - and I think Whoreface would be perfect."

"Me?" said Whoreface. "Fucking why?"

'Yeah," said Leper Licker. "Why her? I would be happy to go. It think I-"

"Whoreface is more photogenic," said Zed bluntly. "Don't forget, the camera adds ten pounds."

For a moment Leper Licker looked like she was going to leap across the table and attack Zed Rifkin like a savage beast. Then she saw the outline of the revolver in his pocket. Someone had obviously forewarned him about the type of musicians he'd be dealing with.

"Nothin' personal, Sister," he said. "Whoreface is just the right gal for the job."

"No I'm not!" said Whoreface. "I don't want to be on some stupid TV programme. Why can't Blood go? She's the best talker!"

"I've had enough of dealing with the media," said Blood. "I'd rather get AIDS than talk to another reporter."

"Well, what about HOG then?" said Whoreface. "She can go! Can't you, HOG?"

By way of an answer, HOG launched into a long allegorical speech about rotting doves and black holes in space, which had the unintended effect of illustrating exactly why she *shouldn't* be sent to deal with the media.

"Ugh," said Whoreface, growing resigned to her fate. "Fine, I'll do it. But what is it, anyway? A *talk* show? Sounds super lame..."

"Actually it's not that bad," said Zed. "Basically what happens is people go on there and argue. Maybe a guy reveals he's been unfaithful. Or a girl will tell her boyfriend she used to be a man. Then the parties involved try to beat each other up, but a fat security guard gets in between 'em."

"There's violence?!" said Whoreface. "Why didn't you say so earlier?"

"You can't stab anyone on TV," Zed said, beating her to the punch. "You'll be on camera. Fuck this up, they'll crucify your skinny ass on live television. Just push the upcoming tour dates. Think you can handle that?"

Whoreface paused in contemplation. She supposed there could be an upside to this Debbie Lyons thing. It might do her good to win the love of the American people, just in case she ever had to stand trial for any of the holy acts of violence she'd committed since arriving in the country. Rumors were already flying that Ted Douche was living with a lover somewhere in central Florida. If the guy really was alive, she figured it was only a matter of time before he fingered her for attempted murder. And he wasn't even the only person she'd stabbed in the state of Florida! If the American authorities found out, they'd lock her away and melt the key with acid - *unless* she was a bona fide celebrity, rather than just a drummer. Celebrities in America could get away with murder. Just look at O.J. Simpson. Yes, the more she thought about it, the more she figured going on TV might just make her immune to going to prison.

"I'll do it!" she said.

"Great," said Zed. "But you can't take any weapons."

"Fine," said Whoreface with a shrug, knowing that if push came to shove, she could always bite someone's throat out, just like that time back in Odense...

And that was how she had ended up on stage at the Debbie Lyons show, slouched in an uncomfortable chair before a beige and buttoned-down suburbanite crowd. Whoreface assessed their bulging eyes and concerned frowns. She found the females especially disgusting. They were fat and wore ugly sweaters. The men all seemed to have curly, awkwardly-cut hair. Their buttoned-down denim shirts were tucked into pants the shade of baby shit.

Whoreface scowled in disgust. These people sought to judge *her*? Ha, such frightened sheep. Look at them, all cowering together in tight rows, their stomachs bloated with TV Dinners and mediocrity, their heads fat with backwards Christian ideology that did more to glorify Satan than invoke the true dogma of The Holy Dragon. How blind and weak they all were!

The divide between them and the followers of the Black Metal Messiah was obvious. The true believers had been placed right at the front of the audience. Whoreface could glare down into their charcoal-smudged eyes and see that they held no fear. Judging from their scarred, stained, emaciated bodies, she could tell they took of the vows sex, violence, and true black metal seriously. They had devoted themselves with blood, cum, and pain!

Whoreface nodded approvingly at the disciples, just as the applause ended and Debbie raised the microphone back to her lips.

Debbie Lyons: Sister Whoreface, first off - what kind of name is that? And the black lipstick, the spikes, why? What are you trying to prove?

Sister Whoreface: The name is a pet name given to me by loving parents **(members of the audience gasp).** I have nothing to prove. Not to you, Debbie Lyons, or these assholes in the audience. The fans have made their choice. They desire the true Word of the Lord, and the Sisters of Temperance Holocaust give that to them. It is no mystery.

Debbie: And your, uh, dress, is that meant to be part of the message as well? Why can't you dress like nice nuns? If you're truly all about preaching the word of Jesus Christ, wouldn't more people listen if they weren't so shocked by your appearance?

Whoreface: This outward appearance you focus on is nothing! I am who I am. I am shocked by *your* appearance, *Debbie Lyons!* Your uniform of conformity disgusts me! I would be out here naked if your people would allow me! I am real, it is *you* **(she points to the crowd)** that are the fakes and phonies! You are frightened of the free thought the Black Metal Messiah offers to your children! We are gathering the youth of this country, and every country we visit. No church or doctrine will censor us! Your children are ours! We come not to bring peace, but a sword!

(The crowd is a mix of outraged horror from the suburbanites and smirking grins from the True Believers)

Debbie: Well, that is one serious claim. I don't know... audience, does this sound very Christian to you?

170

(A woman with permed brown hair and a faded T-shirt showing a cartoon Tinkerbell stands up and grabs Debbie's microphone)

Woman: Just who do you think you are? You speak nothing but hate and blasphemy! You are not a servant of God! **(the woman crosses herself)**
Beige Suburbanites: Amen! Amen!
True Believers: Bless you, Sister Whoreface!

(Both sections of the crowd begin to shout back and forth. Debbie Lyons yanks back the microphone)

Debbie: (shouting) Oh-*kay*! Okay, everybody! Calm down!

(On stage, Whoreface grins, thinking it is just too easy to upset the collective)

Debbie: I hear your shows can get very violent. In fact, you yourself were briefly incarcerated for manslaughter. What do you say to the parents who are scared for their children attending your concerts?
Whoreface: If people embrace the Black Dragon they should expect to be kissed with a fist. When they come to mass and take cuntunion, *there will be blood*. There will be violence - so saith *HIM*. Kicked, stabbed, punched, or raped, the followers of the Radical Gospels know there is a war going on and we need to fight! Some people just have to get stabbed.
Debbie: But it's just a rock show! Yet you are encouraging violence! Girls across the country are leaving their jobs and boyfriends to take part in this Black

Metal Messiah charade that you and your Sisters have cultivated! You are ruining lives!!

(conservative members of the crowd shout in agreement!)

Whoreface: Debbie, this is bullshit. Ruining lives, *pugh*! People *want* to be there. They love the blood, the excitement! Those left standing at the end prove they are worthy to follow Black Metal Jesus. And those who aren't, they deserve to fall!! I say let the cunts come - fight, fuck, and fill your veins with junk!

(The fans of Temperance Holocaust shriek with delight!)

Debbie: Who are you? You're a fan I take it? What is your name?

(Debbie hands the mic to a teenage girl dressed in a vinyl nun costume)

Teenage Girl: No, Debbie, I'm not a fan, I'm a true believer in the Word of Black Metal Jesus as preached by the Sisters of Temperance Holocaust!
Debbie: Uh-huh...have you taken vows?
Teenage Girl: I have taken cuntunion, yes. And it was bloody delicious! **(the fan wiggles her tongue at the rest of the audience. Members of the crowd shriek and cry out, covering their faces with their hands. *The horror!*)**
Debbie: And you're willing to give up everything for the modern incarnation of Black Metal Jesus and these...*these*...nuns?

172

Teenage Girl: Of course! Look, no one is forcing you to listen to their music or go to the shows. Sure, sometimes it gets violent but everyone knows the risk! If you don't want to get punched, don't go into the pit! It's that fucking simple! They are the messengers and HE is GOD!

(A woman in the crowd starts shouting from two rows back)

Upset Woman: Debbie! Debbie, this is just madness! **(Debbie rushes to give the mic to the upset woman)** You can't believe that. You're only a young girl! Oral sex, lesbianism, and violence!! This is just a ridiculous cry for help! It's nonsense!! There's no way -
(The teenage fan shouts over the top of the upset woman)
Teenage Girl: You don't know me! You need to sit your fat ass down! You'll never get -
Upset woman: I go to church every Sunday! I teach Bible School, and let me tell you -
Teenage Girl: OH! OH! You teach *Bible* School?! You don't know shit, cunt! I will fucking kill you! Do you hear me?! I will look right in your shit-stained face and I WILL END YOU!!
Upset Woman: Don't threaten me! Sit down! You just sit down!!
Teenage Girl: You sit down! Down, down, bitch! Down!

Debbie: Ladies, ladies! There is no place for threats on this show. (The two women sit down. The crowd claps)

Debbie: Sister Whoreface, what do you think about

all that?

Whoreface: You should never accept what the schools or the false doctrines try to spoon feed you. The Black Metal Messiah wants only those with strong minds who do not gobble down just any crumb that is tossed to them called truth.

Debbie: Your band often encourages not only violence against other people but also violence against one's own self. There are deeply disturbing videos of your singer slashing her arms and spraying the audience with her blood. Does this "Black Metal Jesus" also embrace suicide?

Whoreface: Yes. **(she folds her arms and falls silent, feeling like she really nailed that question)**

Man in Khakis: You are going to BURN IN HELL, you whore of SATAN!! How dare you!

Whoreface: Pfff….Hell….if the soul is strong it will live on in the eternal bed of Christ, rocking his cock long after the body rots and the fires of Hell burn low. There is no fear of that. You sir, you are the one going to Hell. And I will gladly send you there…

Man in Khakis: Did you just threaten me?! You crazy bitch!

Debbie: Did you just threaten that man by saying you were going to kill him?

Whoreface: It was not a threat but a promise, Debbie. My English is not so great, but I feel my point was clear. He wants to see Hell so badly, I will send him there **(Whoreface's lips twitch, thinking about the petite pocket knife she has smuggled inside her cunt. She will be seeing this man in the parking lot later, she decides…he can count on it).**

(The crowd descends into an uproar, screaming and shouting)

174

Debbie: Now there will be none of that! We do not threaten people on this show, Sister Whoreface. I already said I would not stand for it! **(members of the audience clap)** We need to take a break. When we come back, the parents of a *four-TEEN* year old girl who says their daughter wants to be a nun and play the drums instead of going to college and getting married. Stay tuned!

(crowd claps and cheers. The screen cuts to black)

Chapter 25: Ted and Kyle

Word has spread that Ted Découché is homosexual and has taken a lover of whom little is know. The music world is on fire with speculation and gossip. Even Découché's manager, Barry Overman, can't get information on Ted's whereabouts. However, Ted and Kyle have bigger things than fame and avoiding the national spotlight to worry about. Ted is in a state of rapid decomposition and is melting into Kyle's futon. Kyle is seeking to remedy the situation via the only means he can think of - by preparing a romantic shower...

"Sorry Ted, but fuck, you're heavy man."

Grunting from exertion, Kyle dragged Ted off the futon and onto a skateboard.

"You're alright babe, I got ya."

Kyle positioned Ted so he could pull him by the arms across the floor to the bathroom down the hall. Unfortunately the path was littered with household debris.

"Ugh! Fucking bottle. Where the hell did that bag come from? This is why you're so heavy, Ted! Did you eat that entire bag of chips after I told you to save some for me? Dude, I know you're rich and everything, but I'm on a budget."

"Wash me, fucker." Ted ordered.

Kyle stared back at his lover, his face darkening. The first two weeks had been bliss, but now it seemed like some of the romance was starting to wear off. Ted never wanted to go out anymore, not even for car rides on Sunday mornings. He never wanted to make love anymore either, just eat junk food and smoke meth. In the past that would have been just fine with Kyle, but experiencing true love with Ted had opened his heart to the true richness of existence. He wanted more - he *needed* more than just an endless crystal meth marathon. Plus, Ted's bossiness was starting to bug him.

The nu metal icon had become increasingly demanding of late, even more so than usual. If Kyle wanted to be bossed around, he could call his mom, his parole officer, or his court-ordered psychiatrist. He didn't need this kind of shit from his number one bro. Of course he had tried talking to Ted about all this stuff, but it had only ended in a fight. Ted just couldn't take criticism. Everything had to be his way - or no way at all.

And then there was the smell. Kyle had tried to deny it at first, even to himself, but Ted was really starting to stink. Also, really weird *things* had started happening to Ted's body. He'd put on a lot of weight, often in weird areas. His testicles, for example, had swollen to three times their original size. At first Kyle had thought it was just all the junk food Ted was devouring, but that just didn't add up. Since when did junk food make your balls get fat? And it couldn't be an excess of semen, either, because Kyle dutifully went down on Ted three times a day.

Sometimes, when the two of them cuddled, parts of Ted would deflate, and he would let out the most horrible farts Kyle had ever smelled. The farts didn't always come out of his asshole, either. Sometimes they came out of his mouth, or those holes in his abdomen. His skin wasn't looking too good either. Some parts were black, some parts yellow, as if Ted were trying to escape his wigga status by turning multi-racial through sheer force of will. But if that was the case, what about the purple parts? Kyle had never seen a purple person before. He was pretty sure they didn't exist.

All of these changes with Ted were deeply upsetting. It'd gotten to the point where he couldn't even stand to share a bed with the guy, and had started placing Ted in the freezer overnight. It was one of those big freezers, large enough for a person to climb in, or store a few hundred frozen pizzas in. Ted's stints in the cold had gone some way to arresting the weird changes happening to his body, but they only seemed to make him more frigid in the bedroom. It was almost as if his heart was hardening, freezing along with the bristles of his soul patch...

Shaking off the sudden urge to cry over all these dark developments, Kyle continued dragging Ted down the hall, kicking trash out of the way as he went.

"Okay, here we are," said Kyle as he wheeled Ted into the walk-in shower. Once inside, Kyle slumped down and panted. "Damn, this shit is exhausting. Maybe we should try a wheelchair next time?"

Kyle thought about his grandmother's retirement village and the rows of wheelchairs he'd seen sitting around there every time he'd gone to visit her to pickup some of the benzos she kept in her medicine cabinet. Maybe next time he could nab one?

With a sigh, Kyle got back to work, grunting as he positioned Ted in the shower. He peeled Ted's soiled clothes off and tossed them aside. It was hard work; some of the clothes were stuck to the skin. As he ripped off Ted's cargo shorts, the singer let out a sickening fart.

Kyle stood and stumbled back, feeling almost faint from the overwhelming stench.

"Dude, seriously!" he said.

Ted chuckled. "It wasn't me, bro, I swear," he said. "Whoever smelt it dealt it."

Kyle glared down at him, but couldn't make eye contact as Ted was hiding behind his shades. Always hiding behind those fucking shades.

Steeling himself, Kyle got back to work again. He managed to get the rest of Ted's clothes off, but when it came time to turn the water on and start the actual shower, Ted wasn't playing ball. He kept slumping over, like someone playing possum.

"Ted, fuck! Just sit up for a second!" Kyle said, struggling to hold Ted in a sitting position against the wall beneath the showerhead. He kicked the skateboard away to make more room, almost tripping over in the process.

"AH! Fuck!" he shouted. "Ted, why you gotta make this so difficult?"

"Stop bitching and scrub my crack," said Ted. "I got something wiggling back there, I know it. Little rice babies I bet. Yum, yum, yum! You said you got them all last time, but I know you didn't..."

"Ah, what? For real?"

Kyle's lip curled. He hated bugs, but bugs seemed to love Ted. Ever since the singer had moved in, the house had been full of maggots and flies. Kyle had tried everything - fly strips, bug bombs, industrial amounts of fly spray - but it never seemed to be enough. The bastard insects had infested Ted somehow, buried themselves in his crevices. Maybe that was why Ted was being such a dick?

I won't let these insects take him away from me, thought Kyle. *I won't let them ruin our love!*

Giving Ted a final good push to keep him upright, Kyle turned on the showerhead. Hot water splashed down over Ted, carrying strange goo from his pores and openings down towards the plughole.

"One sec, bro," said Kyle. "I'll be right back."

Kyle left the stall for a moment, and came back with a toilet brush.

"That?" said Ted. "You're gonna use *that?* That's for cleaning up shi, bro. Do you think I'm shit, Kyle?"

Kyle had had about enough of Ted's constant complaining, but decided to keep playing it cool. After all, it was the fault of these damn creepy crawlies, not Ted.

These bugs were messing with Ted's head!

"Of course I don't think you're shit, bro," said Kyle. "But we need something better than a rag and I ain't got nothing else. Do you want me to clean your cracks out or not? Because if you're going to bitch about it..."

Ted sighed, but it sounded more like another fart, this time delivered from his mouth. "Just do it then," he said. "I don't wanna be in here all fuckin' day. This water is making my skin all pruny. Look!"

Ted held out his arm to show Kyle his wrinkled hand. The flesh was receding from the nail bed, making the nails look long, like a drag queen's.

"Then just let me do this!" snapped Kyle. "Just stop bitching for two seconds. I'm doing everything and you're doing nothing!"

"That's because I'm Ted fucking Découché, and if you can't DEAL with that fact, then maybe I should just leave. I can get any whore to scrub maggots out of my ass."

Kyle felt his heart seize in his chest. He couldn't believe what Ted was saying! Sure, they were having some problems, but this was true love. You can't just give up on true love!

"Come on Ted!" he said. "Come on bro! I was just fucking with you. It's all cool. I don't mind giving you a shower."

Ted gave him a knowing look. "Uh-huh. In that case, let's get cleaning."

"Fuck, yeah! Okay, here we go."

Kyle gulped and turned Ted over. Ted slumped sideways and slid down so that his face was pressed against the corner of the floor, his ass exposed. Dark purple splotches covered his lower back and thighs. Kyle dumped half a bottle of liquid soap onto the sagging skin, then pressed the bristles of the toilet brush between the misshapen cheeks of Ted's ass. He gagged as small white larvae began to wiggle from the crack.

"Why are you doing this to ussssss?" They squealed, as rushing water picked them up and carried them off towards the drainpipe.

"Fuck you, you little shits," said Kyle. "You tried to fuck up our shit!"

"Nooooo, Kyleeeee, we're sorrrrryyyyyyy…" wailed the maggots as they vanished down into the black abyss.

Kyle couldn't help but feel a twinge of guilt. Sure, those little fuckers had tried to turn Ted against him, but they were only babies, and Kyle was slaughtering them. What sort of monster was he becoming for the sake of love?

"What's going on back there?" said Ted. "Are you getting the fuckers that are eating my ass? You know I only want you eating my ass, Kyle."

"Just a sec, Ted...uh…oh fuck, there's more!"

Kyle looked down in horror at the host of white worms teeming from Ted's asscrack. As Kyle tried to brush them aside, they clung to the bristles for dear life.

"We're too young to die, Kyle!" they moaned "No, Marty!" they shrieked as one of their brothers was swept down the drain.

"Smash the fuckers! Kill 'em!" Ted ordered.

Kyle gritted his teeth, trying to keep his shit together in the chaos of the moment. The water was pounding down on his back, echoing like thunder in the confines of the cubicle. Maggots were crawling all over, some of them screaming abuse, others begging to be spared. Ted was barking orders - *finish the job, kill those rice babies!*

Just as Kyle was starting to think that this was all too much to handle, he heard a loud banging at the front door.

"Mr. Lewis? Mr. Lewis! It's Carol, your social worker! We had an appointment. Mr. Lewis! I know you're here, I see your van on the lawn."

"Fuck that cunt," said Ted. "Scrub my ass!"

"NO, *Kyleeee!*" screamed the maggots.

"Uh…uh...uh..."

Kyle froze, unsure whether to keep washing Ted, apologize to the fly babies, or rush off to answer the door.

"Mr. Lewis!" shouted the social worker as she continued battering the door.

Kyle decided right there - this woman had to be dealt with first.

"Ted, I'll be right back," he said.

"Don't answer that door Kyle! You better not fucking leave me here, you -"

Kyle threw the brush aside and ran out of the room, slamming the bathroom door behind him. In the hall he paused, catching his breath, trying to push down the panic. Damn, dating a famous rock star was tough.

"Mr Lewis!"

Kyle looked up and saw the social worker's head pressed against a window, trying to peer through the gauzy curtains.

"Fuck!" hissed Kyle under his breath. Speaking louder, he said "Coming, Miz Carol!"

He rushed to the front door and opened it, just as the social worker returned from snooping around the side of the house.

"Sorry, Miz Carol," he said. "I was, um..."

"Taking a shower?" she said, peering at his sopping wet hair and shorts.

"Yeah, that's right, just taking a shower. Sorry. Do you need to come in?"

"That would be preferable." She smiled, but the

smile didn't reach her eyes, which seemed to be filled with a cold, laser-like scrutiny.

Kyle ushered her into the living room.

"Oh! What is that?" cried Carol, shrinking back towards the door as she saw the soiled futon against the far wall, soaked in Ted's mysterious body juices. She took out her notepad and began scribbling notes. "I thought we talked last time about how important hygiene is, Mr. Lewis."

"I know, I know," said Kyle. "I've just been super busy. My website is really taking off and I haven't had much time for anything else. Want to sit?" Kyle offered her his computer chair.

"No, thank you," said Carol, holding her nose against the stench of Ted. "I can't stay. What I am going to do though, is call a cleaning service for you. This is not an environment for wellness, Mr. Lewis. You really need to take better care of yourself. You don't want to have to go back to the hospital, do you?"

"What? No! But I don't want strangers coming in here touching my stuff either. I'll clean the place up, I swear! I was just telling my friend how we needed to clean..."

Kyle paused, trying to remember when he and Ted had talked about cleaning the house. Had it been last night? Last week? It was all a blur. Crazy love will do that. So will meth.

"Okay Mr. Lewis," she said. "I'll be back in one week. If this place isn't in better condition, I'll have no choice but to write up a formal report. Are we clear?"

She hardly waited for Kyle to nod before hurrying out the door. Kyle trailed after her, waving to her as she rushed to her car. As she pulled out of the driveway, he slammed the door and kicked it with the back of his heel.

"Fuck!" he hissed.

Ted was *not* going to be happy about this development. So far, Kyle had been able to maintain the secrecy of their love nest by using the pseudonym Wicked Dude online, and by keeping his face obscured by rad shades. But if these assholes from the state kept coming around, it would only be a matter of time before the secret spilled out. And once people discovered the current whereabouts of the famous Ted Découché, the place would be swarmed by press, paparazzi, and demented super fans in a matter of hours! Kyle knew there was nothing Ted dreaded more than being sucked back into the stinking butthole of pop star success. To save Ted - to save their relationship - Kyle realized he had only one choice: he had to get both him and Ted the fuck out of town!

Chapter 26: Sister Blood

Blood stared at the sheets of lyrics and music spread out on the table in front of her. There was nothing blasphemous or heretical about them. The words were congruent with the gospel of the Dragon, while the music was a worthy example of brutal black metal.

"So what do you think? Can I play it tonight?" asked Leper Licker, her voice both hopeful and cajoling.

Sister Blood sighed. Leper Licker had been harassing her for days, seeking permission to perform her solo song during one of their sets. She was like a child pestering their parents to be taken to some infernal shithole like Disneyland or Movieworld, constantly wheedling, begging, manipulating, then throwing bitchy tantrums when all else failed. Trying to resist her entreaties was exhausting, and Sister Blood was feeling almost too tired to care. Perhaps she'd been doing too much holy heroin? Or perhaps the vampiric force of newfound fame was siphoning her strength. In either case she was tempted to let Leper Licker have her way. There was only one thing that made her hesitate, and that was Leper Licker's history of blasphemous beliefs.

In the past, Leper Licker had voiced the belief that Hitler was the reincarnation of Jesus Christ. It was this demented claim, among other things, which had caused the church to banish her to Hollóhegy Convent. Whilst at Hollóhegy, Leper Licker had recanted her heresy. Then, when Black Metal Jesus arrived at the convent, giving the Sisters his Holy Word and bathing their bodies in his Holy Seed, Leper Licker had been just as receptive as Blood and the others.

Sister Leper Licker had become a true devoted wife of the Black Dragon, helping to spread his gospel.

And yet, she still showed traces of her old heretical beliefs. She still seemed obsessed with Nazi Germany, often wearing the iron cross, singing *Deutschland Uber Alles*, and making sinister references to Nazi ideology, using terms like "The Aryan Race," "ubermensch," and "World Jewry." All this made Sister Blood wonder if Leper Licker was still a Nazi underneath, just waiting for the chance to unveil the swastika tattooed on her soul.

"This song of yours," said Blood suspiciously. "It doesn't have any hidden content, does it? No nasty surprises? You're not going to say anything...political, are you?"

She almost said *You're not going to mention Hitler, are you?* But she didn't want to trigger her Sister's heretical psychosis.

"What do you mean?" said Leper Licker. "Of course not! All the lyrics are on the sheet. It's all right there in front of you."

Blood scrutinized her, then sighed and rolled her eyes. "Fine," she said. "I suppose you can perform the song in the middle of the set. Whoreface, what do you think?"

"Sure, whatever," said the drummer, who sat gazing out the window, her face covered in crimson light from a crimson lightbulb, making her look as if she were covered in neon blood. She seemed far away. Had she even heard the question?

"That settles it then!" said Leper Licker. "Three of us agree, that's a majority."

"We should still ask HOG," said Sister Blood. "HOG, what do you think?"

"I have inspected the lyrics," said HOG as she knelt shirtless nearby, lashing herself with a knout. Slivers of broken glass and sharp metal nails dug into her emaciated back, shedding blood that flowed to her bony behind and into the crack of her scrawny ass. "Leper Licker's words are pure in content, even if the black fire of the Dragon does not truly inhabit them."

"What's that supposed to mean?" snapped Leper Licker.

HOG said nothing, just closed her eyes and kept on whipping herself, spraying a mist of blood all over the tour bus interior.

Sister Blood peered at her. The former anchorite seemed even more aloof than usual, as though she were on the verge of completely detaching from the material world. She was also mortifying her flesh more than ever before, and hardly seemed to eat any food. Was it their newfound fame which had led to this acceleration of her self-destructive behavior? It seemed to be affecting them all. Leper Licker had become even more obsessed with increasing her role in the band. Whoreface had become even more violent, starting fights on an almost daily basis. And Sister Blood herself...well, she'd been using a lot of the Holy Narcotics, and indulging in a lot of Holy Orgies.

I suppose everyone deals with the sickening specter of fame somewhat differently, she thought. *Perhaps the Dragon is testing us...*

Having waited in vain for HOG to make a reply, Leper Licker shrugged.

"Fine then, just go on whipping yourself," she said. "It doesn't matter anyway, because the matter is settled – I'm playing my song."

Someone knocked on the tour bus door.

"Sisters?" It was Golgotha, their faithful servant. "It's time for you to go on. Actually, you're ten minutes late. Balrog is starting to complain..."

Blood sighed. "Come on Sisters," she said. "Let's give these filthy heathens the Word of the Lord!"

They nodded to each other and made their way

from the bus to the main stage, dressed in the special new costumes Balrog had provided for them. Other than their trademark corpsepaint and habits, they all had fancy new adornments to accompany their rise in status from demo-tape obscurity to cultural sensation. Whoreface had steel-toed boots embossed with crosses, along with a chainmail tank top and matching chainmail short-shorts. Leper Licker had a long black robe which covered her beefy frame almost completely, adorned with iron crosses forged from purest silver. Sister Blood had the most expensive garment of all – a black dress sewn with countless holy relics. The body parts of long-dead saints – finger bones, jawbones, calcified hearts in jars, strings of teeth, strips of mummified flesh - covered her costume, making her look like a walking charnel house, a human reliquary. She thought it looked metal as fuck.

Only HOG had refused a new costume, preferring to wear only her antique hairshirt, though she had made the addition of a barbed wire g-string underneath, which she wore to increase her level of constant discomfort and pain.

With Blood in the lead, the Sisters mounted the stage and stood behind the curtain. Above them stood a massive neon crucifix glowing blood red. It was part of the lavish stage production Ben Balrog had organized. On either side of the stage, two men dressed as black metal Jesus were suspended in mock crucifixion. The sight of them made Blood's pulse quicken with anger. The imagery was all wrong! Not only were these minstrels mocking the suffering of Christ, they were misrepresenting the nature of Black Metal Jesus. For Black Metal Jesus was not like the suffering, self-sacrificing Jesus who had appeared on earth two thousand years ago. He was the wrathful, violent Jesus. He would not go meekly to be crucified; he would burn his foes with eyes of black fire and tear them apart with his bare hands. This whole display – it was heresy!

"What the fuck are they doing there?" snapped Sister Blood, gesturing to the crucified men.

"They're part of the show," said a roadie who was dashing around, making last second preparations. "Ben Balrog said to set them up."

"Take them down!" said Sister Blood. "They're an insult to the Dragon!"

"No can do, Sister," said the roadie. "Your set's about to start!"

He scurried away like a miserable rat. Sister Blood scowled. That fucking Balrog was a minion of Satan, trying to corrupt them with crass commercialism! She scowled even harder as she heard the crowd beyond the curtain shouting –

Temperance! Holocaust! Temperance! Holocaust! Temperance –

Blood shook her head. Those heathens should be shouting the name of the Lord, not the name of his messengers!

"It's all wrong," she hissed to herself. "All fucking wrong!"

She felt the rage and frustration bubbling up inside her. Only Holy narcotics could help her now. She took a small blue pill from her pocket. It was embossed with the symbol of an anvil. She had no idea what was in it, but she was sure it was sufficiently intoxicating to meet the standards of her Lord. For verily, had he not said unto her, on that blessed night at Hollóhegy, that she should "get fucked up as much as possible, and don't give a shit about anything?"

Slipping the pill under her tongue, she picked up her guitar and took her position on the stage. The others followed suit, Whoreface sitting behind the drums, Leper Licker picking up her bass, HOG standing in

189

front of the microphone. The wretched keyboardist took up her place in the shadows. Blood could never remember her name.

The curtains parted, exposing the Sisters to the crowd. There were thousands of people in the audience, all screaming and chanting like lunatic lemmings. Their collective stench almost made Sister Blood gag; she was grateful all the holy cocaine had diminished her sense of smell. It was a shame she still had 20/20 vision, because not only did the audience stink, but they were ugly as well.

Her soul surged with revulsion as she gazed down upon them. They were not True Believers, they were whores. Whores who did what they were told. They weren't here because the holy sounds of black metal had called to their souls with a siren song of dark brutality – they were here because a media sensation had captured their sheep-like minds. The corpsepaint they wore was not an expression of devotion, but a token of make believe, like a mask worn by a child at Halloween. These were empty people, following the media frenzy to the place of greatest noise. As they stared up at her, screaming with rapture and total adoration, Sister Blood felt only disgust. People like this would have licked the gilded anus of the Golden Calf itself, just because everyone else was doing it. People like this would have stood on the hill at Golgotha, jeering at the lord in his misery, because that's what Caesar would have told them to do. People like this would have voted for Hitler.

As the crowd continued to scream and chant, the smoke machines activated, oozing out tendrils of thick white vapor which quickly turned red in the light of the great neon crucifix, turning the stage into a phantasmagoric nightmare of holy blood.

Sister Blood rolled the decomposing pill under her

tongue, feeling a surge of holy amphetamine power. There was speed in the tablet, that much was certain. Speed, and Christ knew what else. She nodded to her Sisters, and began to play.

The sound of her chainsaw guitar screamed through the air, empowered by the tall banks of amplifiers into a sonic death shriek of mutilated decibels. Leper Licker followed suit, strumming her bass to add to the onslaught of holy noise. Whoreface hammered her drums as if she were trying to beat them to death. In a voice that seemed far too guttural and deep for an emaciated nun, HOG began screaming out the lyrics to "Braineating Lazarus."

The song told the story of how Lazarus had really been the first-ever zombie, whose thirst for brains had taken him all across the eastern Roman provinces. Everywhere he went he left slaughter and death in his wake. Some of his victims rose up, eager to devour the pink squiggly meat lying in the skulls of the living. The whole thing was a true story, which had for some reason been left out of the Bible. Black Metal Jesus had told them all about it, back at Hollóhegy, when he'd given them His gospel.

"And Lazarus, you know, he was like, the first zombie and shit. And Moses? That motherfucker was a sorcerer, like Aleister Crowley. Fact."

Fuelled by holy rapture and holy amphetamines, Sister Blood managed to lose herself in the music, ignoring the morons in the crowd, even though some of them were blasphemously sporting Noose or even Flagermus t-shirts. The Holy Sisters blazed through a couple more songs – "Dismembering the Concubine," "Defiling the Philistines," and "Satan's Rectum is Always Bleeding." Then it came time to play their most iconic track – "Cuntunion." HOG sang the lyrics –

The red blood of Christ

Flows from my Cunt
Transubstantiation
Suck on my clit and be saved from damnation

Like many of their songs, the track and its accompanying ritual had been born at Hollóhegy, when Blood's Holy husband, Jesus Christ himself, had insisted on eating her cunt even though she was menstruating.

"Don't worry babe," he said. "Eating your bloody cunt is truer than any communion wine, any of those little wafer things. The holy blood of women should be savored, worshiped. Your gash is a true chalice of life. Fact."

And so, by licking her gore with His holy tongue, He had shown her the truth – that her very own cunt was a mystical font of His divine force. Since then she had performed the ritual many times.

"Cuntunion! Cuntunion! Cuntunion!" shouted the audience as the song entered its dark and meandering middle section, when Blood would often let someone from the audience sup on her menstrual blood.

Unfortunately tonight she wasn't menstruating; her period had stopped the day before. Normally, that would mean no more Cuntunion for a while, but Ben Balrog had convinced her to carry out the ritual tonight anyway.

"It's an iconic part of the show," he said. "You have to give the crowd what they want."

"But I'm not bleeding," she said.

"So what? If we can put an asshole on the moon, we can make blood trickle from your pussy..."

And so he provided her with an apparatus of tubes and bladders designed to make fake blood pour from her vagina and into the mouth of a kneeling supplicant. Blood had been disturbed by the idea of using fake blood, so she'd swapped the bag of coloured corn syrup with some real gore squeezed from a dead raccoon she'd found in the parking lot. Surely raccoon blood would be more likely to transubstantiate than corn syrup, right? Still, she almost felt like a heretic. Was she betraying the Lord by altering the ritual? A part of her wanted to just keep playing, and refuse to go through with the charade, but the audience kept screaming –

"Cuntunion! Cuntunion! *CUNT*-union!"

Fuck it, thought Blood. *I'll go ahead with the ritual. If the supplicants are true believers, then the raccoon's blood in the bladders will transform into the blood of the Dragon. If they are blasphemers, they will drink the filth of vermin!*

Sister Blood hiked up her dress, revealing her cunt. The audience howled with excitement. Members of the crowd began to scramble up onto the stage to partake in Cuntunion. Golgotha and the Lamb of Hate stood nearby, ready to bludgeon anyone who got too rough with her or overstayed their welcome.

The first crawling supplicant wore a Noose t-shirt. His chin was defiled by the presence of a soul patch. Sister Blood's skin crawled with disgust as she thought about his tongue on her cunt.

"Do not lick me, foul beast!" she said, grasping him by the forehead and forcing him down so his tongue was out of reach. "Open your mouth and drink the sacred blood!"

The wretch nodded and opened his mouth, while the audience screamed "Cuntunion! Cuntunion! Cuntunion!"

Sister Blood positioned her gash above his face, squeezing the bladder filled with raccoon blood. It oozed from the end of the tube hidden among her pubes. The blood of carrion gushed into the Noose fan's mouth. He gagged, recoiling in horror and disgust at the taste.

I guess that didn't transubstantiate! thought Sister Blood.

Meanwhile the audience kept chanting - "Cuntunion! Cuntunion! Cuntunion!"

Three more supplicants came and drank, all of them retching as they tasted the gore. None of them were true believers, that much was obvious.

With the blood bladder empty, Sister Blood let her skirts fall to cover her cunt, then sang the rest of the song. When the track was over, Leper Licker stepped forward assertively.

"It's my turn," she said. "It's time for my song!"

Chapter 27: Leper Licker

Leper Licker's heart hammered with excitement as she took her place center stage. This was it – this was her chance! Finally she'd get to show everyone the truth. That *she* was the most talented member of the band. That *she* was a musical genius of Wagnerian proportions. That *she* was the true prophetess of Black Metal Hitler Jesus!

She was going to tell the truth about the Lord, just as she'd done all those years ago. The world hadn't been ready for it then. They'd called her horrible names and locked her away in that damn convent deep in the *Highlands of Dunántúl*. But now the time was right, she was sure of it. The audience would see the light. Her Sisters would see the light. Everyone would see the light!

The scripted song she had shown them was nothing but a fake, a decoy to get them to agree to give her some time in the spotlight. Her actual song was filled with truths her Sisters were too afraid to acknowledge. And yet, she was sure that when she began to sing and play guitar – when they heard her immaculate voice and sublime riffs soaring through the air – they would be seized with heavenly rapture. They would see her true genius, and fall to their knees before her. Afterwards they'd make her the head of the band, and Blood and HOG would crawl at her feet, possibly even licking her toes.

"Right," she said, pointing to the keyboardist. "Start the drum machine!"

The keyboardist went to flip a switch. Whoreface went red with anger.

"What the fuck?" she said. "What do you mean 'drum machine?' We don't use a drum machine. I'm the fastest fucking drummer in the world!"

"I'm using a drum machine for this song," said Leper Licker. "I programmed it myself. I told you about this already!"

Whoreface looked incredulous. "What the fuck is she talking about?" she asked, glancing at HOG and Sister Blood. "I don't remember hearing anything about any drum machine!"

"She's been talking about it for days," said Blood. "Weren't you paying any attention?"

"Obviously not," said Whoreface. "Otherwise I would have said no! I'm the fucking drummer in this band. I'm not getting replaced with a machine!"

"Too fucking late," said Leper Licker. "The machine's been programmed. You, keyboard person – turn the fucking thing on!"

"Don't you fucking dare!" shouted Whoreface.

The keyboardist paused, obviously terrified of both Whoreface and Leper Licker, and unsure which of them was the scariest. She was just a session musician, not a proper member of the band. What was her name again? Leper Licker could never remember. Whatever the bitch's name was, she clearly needed some encouragement.

"Hit that fucking switch or I'll turn you into mince meat!" snapped Leper Licker, pulling an antique German bayonet from her belt.

The keyboardist's eyes went wide. She flipped the switch and the drum machine started pounding, drowning out the sound of Whoreface's furious swearing. Leper Licker grinned. It was time for her to make her mark on the world!

She threw off her black cloak, revealing her nearly naked body. Black duct tape swastikas covered her nipples; black duct tape sig runes adorned her belly, hiding most of her stretch marks, as well as her appendix scar. Her only other items of clothing, besides

her headdress, were a black leather miniskirt, fishnet stockings, and huge black platform shoes adorned
with iron crosses. She picked up her lead guitar –
which she had never played before – and gave it a
single violent strum, filling the air with a rusty sonic
scream. Then she opened her mouth and sang with all
her might.

In 1889
Jesus returned
To save his chosen people
In 1889
Jesus returned
To save the German people
His name was Adolf Hitler
Defender of the volk!
Hitleeeeeeeeeeeeeeeeeeeeeeeeeeeeeeeeeeeeeeeeeerrrr –
She sang the name of her Fuhrer, her God, drag-
ging out the final syllable as long as she could, but
before she could even finish intoning the holy name,
someone hit her over the head.

Chapter 28: Sister Blood

Sister Blood's guitar crashed into the back of Leper Licker's skull, knocking her down onto her knees. The name of her false god died in her throat.

"I told you back at Hollóhegy," said Blood, "If you ever started spewing that Nazi shit again, I'd break your fucking face!"

Sister Blood swung the instrument again and again, bashing Leper Licker around the ribs and hips. Her muffin top wobbled. The nun screamed in pain, stumbling forward on her knees, trying to cover herself with her arms. At the same time the air exploded with a deafening screech of ungodly feedback noise. Blood glanced around to see Whoreface stabbing the drum machine with her sticks, as though she were trying to stake Dracula through the heart.

As the sticks tore deep into the circuitry, the feedback died, as did the fake drums, plunging the stage into relative silence. There was only the ringing of tinnitus in Blood's ears, along with the howling of the crowd. Like the filthy Romans at the circus, they were shouting for blood.

Blood turned back towards Leper Licker, ready to give her another whack with her guitar, but the Nazi Nun had taken advantage of Blood's moment of distraction, and was already on her feet, wielding her own guitar like a weapon.

"You fucking cunt," said Leper Licker. "You ruined my moment!"

She flew at Blood, swinging the guitar like a club. Blood parried with her own guitar, and the two instruments, still both plugged into their amplifiers, smashed together with a terrible explosion of noise. Again and again the instruments clashed between them, like dueling blades between a pair of medieval knights.

"Nazi cunt!" growled Sister Blood.

"Junkie slut!" roared Leper Licker.

The guitars connected again with a sonic scream. Leper Licker's instrument snapped at the neck, leaving her unarmed. Blood felt a surge of triumphant aggression, but before she could take another swing at her disarmed opponent, Leper Licker let out a terrible roar and stampeded toward her like a homicidal cow, barrelling into her and knocking her flat on her ass.

Sister Blood's guitar went flying as Leper Licker crashed on top of her. Blood tried to struggle, but it was no use – Leper Licker was twice as heavy as she was, fattened up by countless extra helpings of bratwurst, strudel, and Häagen-Dazs. She pushed Blood down and hit her in the face, tearing open her cheek with a heavy silver ring. Blood growled, grabbed one of Leper Licker's tits, and squeezed it as hard as she could. Leper Licker screamed and scrambled backwards, fleeing from the pain.

Blood rolled onto her hands and knees, and began to rise, but she wasn't fast enough. Leper Licker leapt back on top of her, wrapping a guitar cord around her neck and pulling it tight. Blood gasped, alive to the horrible sensation of not being able to breathe. Instinctively she clawed at the cord as it sank into the skin of her neck, trying to pry it loose, but it was far too tight. In desperation she ripped a piece of bone off her chest – the shattered femur of Saint Grobian – and thrust it back towards Leper Licker, stabbing her as hard as she could. Leper Licker screamed in pain, but didn't let go. Blood's vision began to go dim. It wasn't just her airways being strangled – it was the supply of blood to her brain. The noose was so tight it was choking her carotid arteries.

"Skinny cunt," said Leper Licker. "I'll rip your fucking head off!"

Blood heard the audience screaming as she began to lose consciousness. She faded in and out, from light to blackness, from blackness to light. In her mind's eye she saw the face of Black Metal Jesus, smeared with blood from her cunt, smiling and wiggling his tongue.

I'm coming to you, my husband, she thought. *It is time.*

Then something flew through the air and smashed into Leper Licker, knocking her backwards. The noose came loose and fell from Sister Blood's neck, finally allowing her to breathe. She sucked in air as color flooded back into the grayed-out world. Turning around, she saw Whoreface on top of Leper Licker, whaling on her with a pair of drumsticks.

"I'll give you a fucking drum machine you cunt!" Whoreface screamed.

Sister Blood picked up her guitar, brandishing it like a club, and stepped towards the two fighting nuns.

"Get off her, Whoreface," said Blood. "It's time to finish this!"

Whoreface climbed off Leper Licker, whose face was a bloody mess after its dramatic encounter with the drumsticks. Sister Blood stepped towards the Nazi Nun, raising her guiter, ready to smash her foe. Then a steel-toed boot slammed into her cunt.

Blood stumbled backwards, dropping her guitar as pain radiated outward from her bludgeoned pubis. She could almost feel the cross-shaped imprint left by Whoreface's boot.

"What the fuck was that for?!" she growled, peering at the drummer.

"Because fuck both of you," said Whoreface. "You and her!"

Blood's mind filled with burning rage. She launched herself at the drummer, tackling her to the ground. They rolled across the stage, punching, kicking, biting each other. Then a murderous scream shot through the air and Leper Licker leapt atop both of them, turning the battle into a three-way brawl.

Sister HOG tore off her hair shirt and began punching herself in the stomach and face, as though she were joining in the brawl by attacking herself. The whole time the crowd's screaming had steadily increased, and was now at a lunatic pitch. Finally the curtains were drawn, and a bunch of burly security guards came charging in, dragging the Sisters away from each other.

Whoreface flailed, elbowing one of the rent-a-cops in the nuts. He went down wheezing, while two more took his place, each grabbing one of the drummer's wiry arms. HOG was restrained, but managed to keep doing violence to herself by biting her lip. Blood and Leper Licker were dragged in opposite directions, but their eyes remained fixed on each other.

"You're out of the band, you Nazi sow!" shouted Sister Blood.

"You can't kick me out of the band," said Leper Licker. "I fucking quit!"

Chapter 29: Ted & Kyle Forever

Ted Découché - Found! shrieked the headlines.

Kyle could feel the sweat beading on his forehead, and it wasn't just due to the jungle heat of southern Florida. Him and Ted had been on the road for weeks, zigging over to Clearwater before zagging back to Kissimmee. They were ghosts. They were gangstas. Windows down, fucking free, with nothing before them but true love and endless possibility. Things had been going great until they'd hit Melbourne, a few hours south of Orlando. Then it all went to shit faster than you could say *pussycat! Kill! Kill!*

Kyle had parked at a gas station to acquire some essential supplies - tin foil, lighters, Red Bull, and lollipops. On the way in, he passed three teenage girls leaving the store. They couldn't have been older than seventeen or eighteen. Kyle glanced at them, but they didn't seem to notice him, like always.

Kyle stepped into the store, an endless stream of thoughts buzzing in his skull, unrelenting. Where would he and Ted go? What would they do once they got there? Would the world ever leave him and Ted alone? Kyle's phone had been ringing and chiming nonstop for the past two days. Messages from that bitch social worker, from his mother, from a couple of so-called friends he knew from his time at the halfway house, all of them just kept fucking calling. In the messages they all said the same sort of thing, but with subtle variations, as if they were all reading from a script, but adding a bit of improv, just to throw him off the scent.

"Hey honey, it's me, your mother, call me back..."

"Bro, what up? Been a few, hit me back..."

"You holding? Give me a ring bitch..."

"Mr. Lewis. *Kyle*... this is your social worker, Carol. Call me back as soon as you get this. Have a nice day."

They'd thought they could fool him, but Kyle had noticed the suspicious pattern right away. They all wanted *him* to call *them* back! But why? So they could set him up, that's why. Kyle knew they were all reporting straight back to the judge, trying to fuck up his bail and take Ted away from him. *He fucking knew it!*

Kyle paid for his items and left. In the parking lot it took him a fraction of a second to take in the scene.

"What the hell?" he shouted. "Get the fuck away from there!"

He ran at the van, trying to shoo away the three girls crowding the passenger side. Thankfully he'd rolled up the window and locked the door, but Ted was still visible inside. He might have been partly obscured by his baseball cap, a haze of cigarette smoke, and the dirtiness of the van's windows, but the three girls had obviously recognized him, probably because of his wicked sick trademark shades.

One of the girls, who had poorly-dyed blue hair and chains hanging from her black jeans, was snapping a photo, while her friend with badly bleached hair was rapping on the window.

"Ted?" she cried. "Hey Ted! We love you!"

The third was pulling a pen from her coffin-shaped purse and holding it up, her eyes wild with excitement. "Can we get an autograph?" she asked. "And a pic?!"

"Hey, put the camera away!" Kyle shouted as he reached the van. He'd expected the girls to flee from his presence, but they stubbornly hung around, like tenacious flies obsessed with a singular pile of shit.

"Is that really Ted Découché?" asked the blue-haired one. Kyle thought she looked more like a junkie smurf than a true Jizz Biscuit fan. He couldn't believe he used to bang bitches like that. Who'd he been trying to kid? It should have always been Ted.

"Yeah, it's fucking Ted Découché!" Kyle snapped. "But he's taking his nap and doesn't like to be woken up. He's shy. So, uh...move along."

The girls pouted at being denied. The one with too much metal shit in her face began to raise her camera again, snapping a series of photos.

"Nah! Get the hell out of here!" shouted Kyle, standing between the girl and the van in an attempt to block the photos.

But the girl just pointed her camera around him and kept snapping pics of Ted - Ted with his shades on, his hat pulled down, and a blanket over his legs (Ted always seemed to be cold these days. Maybe it was all those nights spent in the freezer?).

"Come on!" shouted the bleached blonde. "Let us see him! Who are you anyway, his manager?"

"Yeah! Who the fuck are you?" echoed the blue-haired one. "Get a life!"

Ignoring Kyle, the girls pressed even closer to the van, banging on the window.

"Ted!" they cried. "Ted! *Ted!*"

Kyle dashed to the driver's side and jumped in, shoving the key in the ignition. The van struggled to start, wheezing like a sick animal. Kyle gritted his teeth as the girls hammered on the door. Finally the engine turned over. The sound system, already cranked to the loudest setting, boomed automatically to life. Jizz Biscuit's top single *Butt Stuff* rattled the windows as Kyle threw the van into reverse, hit the road, and pumped the gas.

In the rearview mirror, Kyle watched the Jizz B. groupies growing smaller and smaller.

A few miles later, Kyle was standing by the roadside, ripping his hair out.

"Photos! Fucking photos!" he turned to Ted, who was still sitting in the car, chill as fuck. But Kyle just couldn't be that calm, not now that their cover had been blown. "Bro, what are we going to do? You know if they find us they'll separate us. You'll go back to being a rockstar with all the groupies and coke you could ask for! You'll totally forget about me!"

"Calm the fuck down, babe. Here, smoke this, it'll help." Ted reached out the window and handed Kyle his glass pipe. "I'll even light it for ya, big guy. Come on, suck it down. You deserve it."

Kyle took a deep hit of meth. Suddenly the stress maggots of fear were replaced with marching ants on a mission. "We need to find a place and chill," he said, pacing on the roadside. "A place where no one can find us. Like, off the grid and shit. Fuck, I still can't believe they recognized you. I mean, you had on shades *and* a hat. I told you it was a fucking shit disguise! We should have gone with my mom's cancer wig and bathrobe..."

"You're fucking losing it, Kyle!" Ted reached out the window and slapped Kyle hard across the face.

"Damn! Ted, why'd ya hit me, bro?"

"Because shit happens," said Ted. "And no one is gonna give a damn what some skanks with blurry pics have to say. Have you seen the quality of those disposable cameras? They're shit! I'm sure everyone is laughing in their faces right now. Let's face it, Kyle, I'm not going anywhere. Now take another hit and pass that shit back."

Kyle took another hit and exhaled. His body was amped, but his mind felt calm. The power of the crystal, combined with Ted's unrelenting cool, had pulled him back from the brink of hysteria. But his calm would only last until dawn two days later, when he entered another gas station and saw the front page of the *Fort Lauderdale Leader.*

"Look! Look at this!" he shouted, thrusting the

newspaper onto Ted's lap.

"Uh-huh...just what am I looking at here? '*Police Pursue Man on Jet Ski.*' Ha!" Ted shook his head. "Fucking Florida, man! I love this state."

"No, Ted. Below that." Kyle pointed to a blurry photo of Ted napping in the van, beneath the headline *Ted Découché - Found!* A smaller, more conservative caption read *Jizzcognito: Découché on the run?*

"I knew those hos were going to sell those pics!" said Kyle in despair. "Damn it! We need to get as far south as possible, some shithole backwater island where no one can read!"

"We sure do, bro," said Ted, staring at the paper in his lap. His customary cool had evaporated into a semblance of stark, silent dread. His eyes were distant, remote, but Kyle could tell exactly what he was thinking, sort of like Professor X or some shit. He figured it was the mystical power of true love - with a bit of help from the crystal.

I can't go back, thought Ted.

Fame was a thirsty beast, a double-edged sword, a bitch in a nice dress. Whatever you wanted to call it, it wasn't good. One day everyone loved you, the next they were ripping you off and calling you a wigger. Ted had thought he could conquer fame and use it for a good cause - like banging fugly chicks - but that was before he'd met Kyle.

Kyle was really fucking cool. Washing him, cleaning him, giving him all the sex and meth he could ask for, without ever requesting anything in return. Never once did the guy ask for money - and he was fucking broke! All Kyle did was protect him like a lover should. And that meant more to Ted than all the tattooed cunts and backward baseball caps ever could.

"Kyle," he said. "I -"

"I know, bro," said Kyle. "Believe me, I know. And I

feel it too."

For a moment they stared lovingly into each other's eyes. Then a lightbulb flashed in Kyle's brain. He snapped his fingers and laughed. "Bro, I've got it! The Bermuda Triangle! Boats and planes disappear all the time in that shit."

Ted was skeptical. He'd heard aliens lived there. Sounded like a pain in the ass; he hated people that couldn't speak English.

"Nah, we need to disappear in the swamps," said Ted.

"Think so?"

"Fuck yeah, think about it -

1: It's closer

2: We can actually locate it on a map

3: It's got gators and giant snakes and shit, plenty of stuff to keep unwanted people out."

Kyle nodded, *yeah made sense...*

"No one will want to waste their time battling fucking man-eaters and shit trying to find me," continued Ted. "I mean, maybe they will, but they'll get fucking killed in the process! Ha-ha!" Ted cackled. An iridescent blowfly flew from his gaping mouth.

Kyle swatted it away, and grinned. He was starting to like this idea. "We could build a fort!' he said. "It could have a moat, and we could fill it with crocs! It'll be so fucking cool."

Ted nodded. "Damn right, babe. I always wanted a treehouse."

Kyle fumbled for the blackened pipe and took a few victory hits. Between him and Ted there was nothing they couldn't do, no problem they couldn't solve.

Stuffing the pipe back in the glove compartment, Kyle keyed the ignition. The old van roared to life as though it were brand spanking new.

"Ready?" he said, turning to Ted. "I bet if we leave

we can be in the Everglades by early afternoon."

Ted just nodded, shades down, head tilted back, looking cool as can be.

Pulling out of the parking lot, Kyle felt like a million bucks. Ted wasn't going to leave him and go back to his superstar baller lifestyle. They were true soul mates, together till the end. Pretty soon they'd have a real house, and wouldn't have to keep sleeping in his van next to the beach. He pictured lying awake at night with Ted in their custom-made fortress deep in the everglades. Maybe they'd have a skylight over their bed? Then they could look at the stars while listening to the insects sing.

"I love you, Ted," said Kyle.

"Love you too, babe," said Ted.

The two of them shared a loving fist bump.

"You want another hit of this?" said Kyle, retrieving the pipe from the glove compartment. It was still warm. "Hopefully we've got enough till I can find us a line down in the swamps. I'm sure some redneck is cooking."

"That's cool," said Ted. "You have it. I'm high on you anyway. You're better than any fucking drug." Ted smiled, rubbing Kyle's leg.

Kyle couldn't help but blush. Ted was the fucking best. As Kyle pumped the gas and hit the pipe, he felt like he was living the dream. But two hours later, shit was about to get real.

+++

The sun burned high overhead. Kyle turned off the main highway onto a side road. The less traffic the better. He could feel eyes searching for him and Ted. Every stop sign, every passing car, pushed them one step closer to discovery, and the death of all their dreams. Kyle knew he'd do anything to make sure that didn't happen.

The van rolled toward a stop sign at an isolated crossroads.

"Fucking stupid," said Kyle. "Why the fuck is there a stop sign out here? There ain't shit to stop for."

Slowing but not stopping, Kyle rolled the van through the intersection. No sooner had he done so than a police cruiser appeared like a bat out of hell from behind a copse of needle pines, lights and sirens blazing.

Kyle dropped his hash pipe, hot ash spilling in his lap.

"FUCK!" he shouted as the sirens pierced his brain like sonic ice picks. "Ted, wake up! It's the pigs! Ah, man! FUCK!" Brushing embers from his crotch with his free hand, Kyle pressed the pedal to the floor. The van rocketed off down the dusty side road with the cruiser in pursuit.

Ted woke up with a start. "Kyle, what the hell?!"

"They found us, Ted. I don't know how, but they fucking found us. They were waiting there like fucking ninjas! Just hold on. I'm going to try and lose 'em!"

Kyle took a deep breath, trying to focus all his attention on the road. It wasn't easy. The meth he'd smoked for breakfast had sharpened his senses, but the weed he'd smoked for lunch was making him hazy. He gritted his teeth. Ahead of them the road coiled and twisted like a serpent, flanked by ominous swampland.

"Faster, Kyle!" Ted shouted.

The van protested with a constant groan as Kyle took it up to 85mph. He knew he should have traded it in for that Oldsmobile last year.

"Come on... come *on*..." said Kyle, willing the engine to hold itself together.

Kyle felt the panic rising in his breast as the cruiser drew closer to the van's dented bumper. Rivulets of sweat crawled down his face. This couldn't be how it all ended, it just *couldn't.* He and Ted had only just met. They had a plan, a future together. What about their house in the swamp? Their desire for a simple life away from the spotlight? They'd even talked about collaborating on an acoustic album.

"It can't end like this," said Kyle, echoing his own thoughts. "I won't let it!"

Kyle kept one eye on the road in front of him, the other on the rearview mirror as the high-speed chase continued. The cops maintained a conservative distance. Within a half hour there were two more cruisers and a chopper overhead.

"Fuck, fuck fuck!" Kyle cried. Then he saw it - a service road coming up on the left. It seemed to offer their only hope of escape. "I'm taking it, Ted. Hold on."

Kyle made a hard left. Ted's bloated body flopped against the door, his head banging on the window.

"Whoa...whoa!! Ted!!"

The van swerved onto the sandy service road at just over 85 mph. The tires slipped in the sand, sending the van hurtling into a swampy channel running alongside the lane. As the van sped towards the water, Kyle closed his eyes and reached for Ted. "I fucking love you Ted!" he cried.

"Together, babe!" Ted said, gripping Kyle's hand.

Kyle felt a strange moment of calm as the van flew through the air. Time seemed to slow down, even to stand still, leaving Kyle poised on the edge of oblivion. But he wasn't afraid. If this was how it had to go down, then he was okay with that. Fuck the police. They'd never take him and Ted alive!

+++

Kyle came to with a groan of pain. His head was throbbing. Warm, sticky blood was all over his face, clogging his eyes.

"What the...? Ted, I don't think we're dead..."

"Hold tight in there, son," came a voice from nearby. "We're going to get you out."

"Who the fuck are you?" asked Kyle, trying to wipe the blood from his eyes.

"Florida highway patrol. You sit tight and -"

"Fuck you pig!" Kyle screamed.

Frantically blinking the rest of the blood from his eyes, Kyle glanced around. Through the shattered windshield he saw the van had come to rest in the swamp, surrounded by about five feet of water. But what about Ted? The rock god was nowhere to be seen. In horror, Kyle's eyes fixed on a large, Ted-sized hole in the windshield just in front of the passenger seat. Ted must have been thrown from the vehicle into the swamp.

He'd always been too cool to wear a seatbelt.

"Ted, no!" screamed Kyle as he tore his own seatbelt off and climbed out the window.

"Stay in the car!" shouted the highway patrolman. "There are -"

"Fuck off, pig!" shouted Kyle as the swamp water surged up to his nipples.

Trying to ignore the uncomfortable feeling of something slithering past his ankle, as well as the incessant oinking of the pigs, Kyle splashed away from the van, searching for his soulmate. He quickly spotted Ted's body up ahead, drifting slowly towards open wetlands.

"Hold on," Kyle shouted. "I'm coming!"

Kyle slogged forward, trying to catch up with Ted. At first it had looked as if Ted was just floating around, but as he drew closer, Kyle saw the truth. Ted, cool as ever, had a plan. They were going to swim out of there!

The cops would never be able to follow. They'd lose the pigs in the swamps. Ted was a fucking genuis!

"Ted, wait up!" said Kyle, excitedly paddling towards him. He froze as Ted's body suddenly jerked below the water.

"What the? Ted?"

Kyle drew closer, peering at the spot where Ted had been. Bubbles popped on the surface of the water. Agitated currents roiled around Kyle's lower body. In horror he realized he and Ted weren't alone in the swamp.

All at once the cries of the pigs, previously blocked out by Kyle's crystal meth zen meditation, came rocketing straight into his consciousness.

"Son, stop, don't move!" shouted a highway patrolman. "There's a -"

A gator. A big, ugly, prehistoric monster, chewing on Ted's ass. Kyle saw it just below the water.

"No, Ted! Let him go! Oh, no! *Teddddd!*"

Kyle shrieked and leapt on the swamp beast, punching it in the face. Ted's body surged back up to the surface as the monster released him, and turned its attention to Kyle. Shots rang out from the shore, peppering the water all around them as the pigs took aim at the gator. Once again time seemed to slow down, almost stand still. Was the gator hit? Was Kyle hit? Even worse, was Ted hit? Kyle glanced down at Ted's body, but it was the gator that filled his vision instead, launching up from the water and clamping its jaws around his midsection. It dragged him down, then rolled beneath the water, spinning his limbs like the rotors on a windmill. Swamp water clogged his nostrils. Reptile teeth shredded his belly. Animal terror scrambled his thoughts into a frenzy of horrid sensations. In a final moment of clarity, he saw Ted floating above him, face peering down into the water. His shades were still on.

Chill as fuck, thought Kyle, before the darkness claimed him.

+++

The police stood on the shore, waiting for backup. There was no way in fuck they were going down in that water. They tried a few times to shoot the damn thing, but missed its thrashing head.

Yup, they concluded, *that boy was dead.*

+++

The following is an excerpt from the article "Temperance Holocaust and the Rise of Black Metal Christianity," written by Rubert Harrison, first published September 11 2001 in *Sargeant Pepper's Lonely Music Magazine.*

Less than 24 hours after the recovery of Ted Découché's half-eaten corpse, the story hit the AP, and a vast wave of prayers and tributes began pouring in from all around the world. People formed prayer circles. Candlelit vigils were held in major cities, with mourners pledging to be more tolerant of sexual orientation and alternative lifestyles.

The coroner would later declare that Ted had been dead for several weeks prior to the alligator attack, and had also been the victim of repeated postmortum sexual acts. Mourners and fans were shocked. Some commentators condemned the entire event as nothing more than a sordid sex crime. Others took a more sympathetic approach. Kyle Lewis replaced Jeffrey Dahmer as America's most beloved gay necrophiliac. A national campaign called Cold Comfort was created to bring awareness of postmortem homosexual relationships to the public eye. Ted and Kyle were named as posthumous spokespeople for the Rainbow Hugs Foundation, an international organization seeking to encourage tolerance towards practitioners of alternative sexual lifestyles, both living and dead.

Soon after the confirmation of Découché's death, the remaining members of Jizz Biscuit announced the dissolution of the band, stating "there's no point going on without Ted." The demise of the band allowed the remaining members, still on tour with The Dark Ones of Darkness Festival, to quickly form a new band with Sister Leper Licker, who had just been exiled from Temperance Holocaust as a result of the dramatic incidents reported above. The new band, called White Vengeance, immediately attracted hordes of fans thrilled to see what such a supergroup might accomplish. Their wishes were destined to be crushed on July 10, 1999, when mayhem and death of biblical proportions descended on the Dark Ones of Darkness tour, claiming the lives - and arguably the sanity - of many musicians involved.

Chapter 30: Sister Blood

The black ceramic bong flew through the air and smashed against the interior wall of the tour bus. It was only the latest in a series of objects Blood had destroyed in her wrath. She paced, clenching her fists, grinding her teeth like a rabid animal.

"That Nazi fucking whore," she growled. "I can't believe she betrayed us like this! She's turned her back on everything we stand for. She's betrayed our husband, the Dragon! No fate is too cruel for her. We must have revenge. That fat skank must be punished for her sins! Don't you agree, Sisters?"

She turned to HOG and Whoreface, who'd been standing by silently this whole time, watching her rant and destroy their possessions.

They remained silent.

"I said don't you agree, Sisters?" said Blood, peering at them.

HOG peered back, her eyes filled with eerie intensity, as though she were inspecting Blood's soul. "Let she who is not a poser break the first face," she said, paraphrasing one of the thirteen new commandments the Dragon had given them.

Blood stared at her in shock. Had HOG just called her a poser? She couldn't believe it. There was no word more disgusting, no insult more vile, no sin more grotesque in the eyes of Black Metal Jesus than the foul state of poserdom. She felt her heart thunder with rage. Her corpse-painted face twitched with uncontrollable anger.

"You fucking bitch!" she screamed.

She slapped HOG across the face. HOG received the blow without flinching, then turned the other cheek. Blood slapped it. HOG received the second blow just as placidly as she'd received the first, then

turned her back, hiked up her hairshirt, and bared her
ass, presenting two more cheeks to be slapped. Her
pallid rump was already covered with welts and whip-
marks, some of them from HOG's daily sessions of
self-flagellation, others from the Sisters' nightly orgies,
which HOG could only be persuaded to join if she was
thrashed both before and after.

Blood stared at HOG's ass in rage. Those sca-
brous and lacerated butt cheeks seemed to be mocking her. She kicked HOG in the ass, sending the former anchorite crashing down onto her own bed of
nails. HOG landed on her chest with a grunt, then lay
like a stoic martyr on the rusty points of iron, unspeak-
ing, unmoving. Blood turned away from her in anger,
and peered at Whoreface.

"Sister!" she said. "Surely you are with me. Together we can punish that fat Nazi sow. She's the one
who's the real poser!"

Whoreface scoffed and sneered. "Whatever, man,"
she said. "As far as I can see, you and Leper Licker are just about the same. You're both egomaniacs.
You're the ones who agreed with that Bullfrog guy to
take the main stage and have all these gimmicks and
shit." She paused, gesturing to her chainmail tank
top and short-shorts. "You're the ones who wanted to
have, like, an audience and shit. You're the ones who
wanted to sell albums. All I ever wanted to do was
get high and start fights, just like Jesus told us to do.
HOG's right – you *are* a fucking poser."

She turned and headed towards the exit from the
bus.

"Sister!" shouted Blood. "Don't you dare turn your
back on me!"

Whoreface gave her the middle finger without
turning around, grabbed a bottle of half-drunk whiskey from a pile of soiled clothing, then jogged out the

door and into the parking lot, leaving Blood alone with HOG's prostrate body and the three faithful roadies.

Blood glanced at the true believers. Was that disappointment in their eyes?

A sense of shame welled up in her. Beneath the corpsepaint her cheeks were burning.

"Get out," she said. "Get out! I must pray."

The true believers fled before Blood could attack them or throw something at them. She went and knelt before the altar of black metal Jesus that stood in the corner, splattered with blood and covered with offerings of roach butts and roadkill. She inhaled its stinking miasma, and closed her eyes.

To Blood's surprise she found she was almost crying. Her Sisters' rebukes had cut her to the core. Was there truth in what they'd said? Was she really a poser, an egomaniac? A part of her wanted to brush aside those accusations and stubbornly cling to a sense of self-righteousness. But another part – the part that was closest to her God – caused Blood to reject those self-justifying lies, and peer deep into her soul. What she found there was sin.

She looked back on the terrible train of events that had led them to this moment in time, and realised it had mostly been her fault. She was the one, back in 97, who'd pushed them to record *Dawning of the Deathgash* and release it on CD for commercial distribution, rather than just trade poorly-mastered demo tapes with the black metal underground. She was the one who'd pushed them to leave Trollskjede Farmhouse in Norway in order to participate in Ben Balrog's Dark Ones of Darkness tour, even though she knew very well the tour's lineup was clogged with shitty posers, satanic fucksticks, and nu metal abominations. She was the one who'd decided to give that interview to *Soiled Purity* Extreme Metal Fanzine, rather than maintain a deathlike silence with the media monkeys. Then, more recently, it was she who'd sided with Leper Licker and accepted Balrog's offer to perform on one of the main stages. She'd even encouraged Whore-face to go on that stupid American talkshow! And why? Why had she done all these things? Every step of the way she'd told herself she was doing it for Black Met-al Jesus, to spread His glorious Word. But had He not commanded her to shun the limelight, to rebuke all posers, and to remain forever true to the underground roots of black metal darkness? Hadn't He said unto her, verily, "people are just retarded worms, they're too stupid to appreciate good music. Real black metal bands should tell people *not* to listen to their albums."

Blood had betrayed his teachings, and look where it had gotten her. The band was falling apart. Leper Licker had crawled up her own asshole and was lost in Narcissistic neo-Nazi insanity. HOG was starving herself to death. Whoreface was surely on the verge of committing mass murder. They were all being taint-ed by the sticky filth of fame, which the media, like a diseased monkey, was constantly hurling at them like so many handfuls of simian faeces. Fame was defil-ing them, defiling the band itself. Posers were wear-ing their merchandise. Their albums were being pur-chased by Hot Topic refugees with eyebrow rings and PVC fat pants. People who liked nu metal were attend-ing their shows! And it was all because of Blood's own hubris, her secret, perverted desire for success. She'd told herself she'd been doing it all for the Dragon, but now she knew that was a lie. It had been her ego. Whoreface had been right – she really *was* like Leper Licker.

The thought was enough to make her puke all over the altar. Though maybe the bad chilli she'd had for breakfast and the six fentanyl tablets she'd recently

stuck up her ass had also played a part in her nausea.
Nevertheless she still felt sickened by her behaviour.
She had betrayed her Lord in her own secret heart.
What sin could be worse? The puke-covered image of
Christ seemed to be rebuking her.

"Forgive me husband, for I have sinned," she said.
"I must do penance!"

Blood lit a Marlboro, inhaled deeply, then hiked up
her dress and pressed the burning tip of the cigarette
to the flesh of her inner thigh. The searing pain shot
through her nerves, making her jolt, but she held the
flame close nonetheless, until she smelled the scent
of her own roasting skin mingle with the rich tobac-
co aroma. The jolt of pain made her heart beat faster, filled her with a strange sense of power, a sense
of explosive release. And yet, that sense of release
was dulled. So was the pain. Those pills she'd stuck
in her ass were really starting to kick in. She dropped
her cigarette into the puke, then staggered to her feet.
She took a step, then fell backwards onto the couch.
Her heart rate grew slow. Her breathing grew slow. Her
mind became a haze in which all guilt was lost. The
pain of her burn retreated into nothingness. Her consciousness followed, down into oblivion.

+++

Sister Blood found herself on stage, guitar in hand.
HOG and Whoreface were there. Even Leper Licker
was present. The nameless keyboardist stood in the
background, her forgotten face replaced with a swirl of
black shadows.

Blood looked into the audience, and cried out in
disgust. The whole crowd was made up of posers and
mindless consumers. Most were obese and unspeak-

219

ably ugly. They were all eating hamburgers and drinking thickshakes. They were all dressed in virtually identical clothing, all wearing the same label, the same icon, as though they had been branded with the Mark of the Beast.

"...that no man may buy or sell, save he that had the mark, or the name of the beast, or the number of his name," whispered Blood as she stared in horror at the crowd.

Her horror increased as she saw the nature of the mark they all bore – it was the Temperance Holocaust logo. They had branded themselves with it like a horde of willing cattle. They wore it on their t-shirts, their baseball caps, even tattooed on their flesh. The women had Temperance Holocaust purses, the men had Temperance Holocaust chains around their necks. Some even had Temperance Holocaust dolls, miniature effigies of Blood and the others, like Barbies given a black metal makeover. Even their thickshake cups and hamburger wrappers were marked with the Temperance Holocaust logo, as though the essence of the band had somehow been transformed into saturated fat, salt, and sugar for the masses to consume. As the members of the horde finished off their meals, they all let out a singular burp that shook the earth like a blast from Gabriel's horn. Then they started chanting.

"Temperance Holocaust! Temperance Holocaust! Temperance Holocaust!"

They were calling for the band to play. But Blood didn't *want* to play for these wretches. Just the thought of it made her feel degraded. She turned to flee, then realised in horror that she couldn't. She was trapped, like a puppet on a string – literally. Her wrists and ankles had been brutally slashed open. Long red strings extended from the wounds and into the sky above the stage, where the monstrous form of Ben Balrog loomed, holding her strings in one of his gigantic hands. The others were his puppets as well. He jiggled their strings, forcing them to posture and strut before the crowd. The posers in the audience screamed with mindless approval. They drew closer to the stage, staring with black hole eyes, as though they could devour by seeing. Their mouths hung open hungrily, as though they wanted to eat Sister Blood and the others, gobble them up like pre-packaged Happy Meals. Blood screamed in absolute terror as she realized she was about to be consumed. They would eat her up, digest her, shit her out, then move on to the next mindless craze. This was all she was now, all any of them were – fast food entertainment.

The consumers crawled onto the stage like zombies in a Romero movie, eager to devour. Blood knew her time was almost over. This was her fate, now that she'd sinned against her Lord and embraced the path of fame. The obese mutants crawled towards her legs...

Then froze as lightning crashed above. From a black sky where black clouds clung to the even blacker face of night came the terrible apparition of Black Metal Jesus, as big as Godzilla but far more attractive. First came His fingers, piercing the clouds, just as they had pierced Sister Blood's cunt back at Hollóhegy. Gripping the sky like a curtain He tore it open and stepped into the world, glowering hatefully, His huge, corpse-painted face creased with furrows of unfathomable anger. Black metal riffs and ceaseless drumbeats exploded from the heavenly abyss behind Him, where nought but darkness reigned.

He slashed Ben Balrog's throat with a huge broken bottle of cheap Hungarian wine. Balrog fell back, his putrid blood evaporating, his whole body fading on the wind like smoke from a thurible, as though he had never been more than an overblown image without any substance. The strings binding the Sisters disintegrated too. Blood was free!

She got down on her knees and prayed, while her husband unleashed His wrath upon the posers below. First He extended His punctured hands and held them high above the masses. Instead of blood, crimson insects swarmed from the wounds and down into the audience, devouring their flesh like airborne piranhas. They screamed as many of their number were reduced to walking skeletons covered in His wrathful ichor.

Black Metal Jesus was not content with just one brand of smiting. He opened His mouth and unleashed His hatred in the form of a torrent of pitch-black vomit that dissolved many members of the crowd into a sludge of bones and disintegrating organs. And yet even this was not enough. He unzipped His fly, flopped out His cock, and delivered a stream of deific urine all over the heads of the audience. The acid piss stripped off their skins and left them rolling around, screaming, their raw nerves bared to the world.

"Hallelujah!" said Blood.

Her divine husband reached down, picked her up, and carried her high above the remains of the wretches below, most of them already dead, the rest of them melting, skinless, or screaming as the ichor insects devoured their flesh and progressed to the bones. Blood smiled up at her husband. She couldn't wait for His loving touch, though she wasn't quite sure how they were supposed to make love now that he was the size of a Japanese movie monster. Perhaps she'd be martyred to his massive prick over and over again. Would that be her heaven?

He raised her to His corpse-painted face. The black pigment was deepest black, like starless night, but the white was whitest white, like the stars themselves. The radiance blinded her, covered her, and filled her with warmth. The sense of wellbeing was incredible. She hadn't felt anything like it since Hollóh-egy. In a way this was even more profound, a sense of all-pervasive bliss, better than the best heroin hit. She closed her eyes to bask in the feeling –

Then awoke in the tour bus with a start. Her heart was pounding. Someone had torn off her dress and attached plastic pads to either side of her chest. Wires ran from the pads to a defibrillator with blinking lights, which sat in the hands of a uniformed paramedic. Another paramedic loomed over her, staring intently.

"She's back," he said.

Blood sat up, gasping. Behind the paramedics stood HOG, Whoreface, and the True Believers – Golgotha Skullfuck, the Lamb of Hate, and Angelface Murdercunt. They stared at her as though she were Lazarus rising from the dead.

"What the fuck is going on?" she said.

"You overdosed on opiates, ma'am," said one of the paramedics. "You went into respiratory arrest, and your heart began to beat irregularly. We had to defibrillate. We also gave you something to counteract the narcotic in your system. It should kick in any second now. Basically, it's going to reverse the effects of any opioids in your body. You might feel some discomfort –"

Blood cried out as waves of pain flooded her body, not just from the cigarette burns on her thigh, but from all the other injuries she'd sustained in her battle with Leper Licker on stage, which were no longer masked by an opioid haze.

"Like I said, ma'am, it might hurt a bit. I'm sorry but –"

"Do not apologise, resurrectionist!" shouted Sister Blood. "This pain is a welcome gift. I deserve to suffer for my sins. Through this agony I shall be absolved!"

223

She turned to HOG and Whoreface. "My Sisters, you were right. I was infected with the sin of pride and poserdom. Do you forgive me?"

HOG stared at her with soul-searching eyes. "Of course, Sister. I see you are back on the true path once more."

Blood smiled as she felt the former anchorite's forgiveness wash over her like a glorious ketamine high. "Thank you Sister," she said, then turned to Whoreface. "And you? Do you absolve me as well, Sister?"

Whoreface shrugged. "Sure, why not," she said.

Blood smiled even wider. She leapt off the couch and ran to her Sisters, embracing them both. They hugged her back.

"Come on slaves," said Blood, gesturing to the roadies. "Even you may join this hug!"

Golgotha and the others moved in, wrapping their arms around the Sisters and each other, until Blood was at the centre of a warm collective embrace.

Meanwhile the paramedics packed up their equipment, then stood staring at Blood and the others with looks of puzzled amusement.

"Hey, aren't you those nuns who had sex with that corpse?" said one of them.

"Begone, Ambulance slave!" said Sister Blood. "Your services are no longer required here!"

The paramedics glanced at each other in jaded disbelief, then back at Sister Blood. "You should seriously consider coming to the hospital, ma'am. You almost died. Clinically speaking, you really were dead for a short period of time."

"Pah!" said Blood. "I was not dead, I was communicating with my husband. And there's no way I'm going to this hospital with you. I will not set foot in your vile church of health, where insurance is worshipped like the Golden Calf!"

"Does that mean you don't have insurance, ma'am? Because if that's the case, you're gonna be on the hook for a lot of –"

"Do not bother our Sister with this blather!" shouted HOG in a voice that seemed too loud and terrifying for her emaciated frame. "She has just had a holy experience. Besides, we are insured by the tour. If filthy lucre is what you are after, go speak with one of Ben Balrog's pencil pushers!"

"Yeah," said Whoreface. "Get the fuck out of here now, or someone's gonna have to restart *your* hearts!"

The paramedics looked at each other again, then hurried toward the door. One of them glanced at Blood as he went. "You're welcome, miss," he said sarcastically.

"Come on Steve," said the other one. "Let's go take our break at that strip club over by Eaglemont Road."

"Sure, why not," said Steve. He shot a final look at Blood as he prepared to exit the bus. "You should lay off the narcotics, Sister."

"Don't be ridiculous," said Blood. "It was the power of Holy Fentanyl that gave me a vision from the Dragon himself!"

Steve rolled his eyes and vanished out the door. Sister Blood turned to the others, who had ended their group hug and were now standing in a circle around her.

"Sisters, I'm sorry," said Blood. "It was my perverted, ambivalent lust for success that led us down the excremental path to musical stardom. I almost led us straight into the anus of Satan himself! But now I've seen the error of my ways. I see now that we should never have departed from the black metal underground. But fear not, for I know how things can be fixed. Our husband showed it to me..."

She told them about the divine vision she had

seen. HOG's eyes filled with wonder as she heard the tale. Even Whoreface looked impressed.

"Okay," said the drummer. "So what does it mean? Is the Dragon gonna come and kill all these posers by peeing all over them?"

"It's not a literal prophecy, Sister," said HOG. "It's a coded message, like the Book of Revelations, or that episode of *Married with Children* that told me I had to cut off my little toes with an electric carving knife. We just have to interpret it for ourselves."

They stood there in silence for a while, then one by one started smiling.

"Are you thinking what I'm thinking, Sisters?" said Blood.

"I'm pretty sure we are," said Whoreface.

"We all know what must be done," said HOG. "We must make your vision come true. We must unleash divine wrath upon these shit-eating heathens! But how?"

They sat down and began to plan. A whole hour passed as they scrawled notes on pieces of paper, then rolled them up and set them on fire, totally dissatisfied with all of their ideas. They took a break to fornicate and smoke some holy crack. It was then that the answer came to Sister Blood, as she sat wreathed in crack smoke and covered in bodily fluids. She scrawled down a shopping list for the materials they would need, and handed it to Golgotha.

He looked at it with wide open eyes.

"Are you sure this isn't a bit too...extreme?" he said.

Blood merely laughed. Her Sisters joined in, filling the bus with the sound of their echoing amusement.

Chapter 31: Leper Licker

A crack pipe shattered beneath one of Leper Licker's boots as she stomped across the carpark. She didn't know where she was going, just that she had to keep moving or the murderous energy inside her would force her to scream or rip out her hair.

Leper Licker's whole body jiggled with rage as she walked. Her teeth were clenched, her skin was hot, her heart pounded so fast she thought it might explode. How dare they betray her – how dare they ruin her moment of glory! Her solo song had been intended to teach the world the truth about Jesus, and propel her to absolute fame – but Blood and the others had ruined it.

She pictured killing them all in numerous violent, agonizing ways. She'd Start with the most satisfying - stomping on Sister Blood's head until the skull cracked and the brains flew out like candy from a waterlogged pinata. Leper imagined holding a blowtorch against HOG's face until the skin turned black and her strange eyes melted like marshmallows on a grill. She thought about shoving Whoreface's drumsticks so far up the drummer's own ass that they punctured her bowel, subjecting her to a horrible septic death as her shit seeped out into her bloodstream.

"Those sluts," she growled. "Those blind, self-righteous bitches. I'll kill them!"

She stomped onwards. A wave of emotion rose up from her guts, threatening to overwhelm her. She choked back tears. She couldn't believe she was out of the band. Temperance Holocaust had been her whole life for years. She felt like a seaman adrift on the waves, far from the comfort of shore.

"Never fear, fräulein."

The voice was familiar – abrasive, German, Hitleresque. She turned and saw the Führer himself beside her, astride a pale unicorn. Impaled on the unicorn's horn were the heads of all the famous dead Jews who had ever lived – Albert Einstein, Sigmund Freud, Karl Marx, all of the Marx brothers – in fact, there were so many prominent Jews, and therefore so many heads, that the horn seemed to spear off into the stratosphere, all the way to the sun, though it didn't seem to weigh down the unicorn's head, which was raised up proudly, smeared with gore.

Hitler looked much like he did in Leper Licker's masturbation fantasies, with oiled pectorals and six-pack abs, the body of a male stripper manscaped to perfection. Only his head looked the same as it had in life – small and rounded, with flat dark hair, beady eyes, and his signature toothbrush mustache. He was dressed only in leather jodhpurs and motorcycle boots. As he smiled at her he tugged at his nipple rings in a gesture of sadomasochistic lust.

"Oh my God," said Leper Licker, staring up at him in awe. "My God, my Führer!"

Ecstasy filled her as she bathed in his radiance. Truly this was a divine visitation. It definitely wasn't just a result of the four tabs of LSD she'd taken before the set.

"Don't worry about those bitches, fräulein," said God-Hitler. "They are just jealous of you. That's why they attacked you. They knew as soon as you showed your true talents in public no one would care about them anymore. That's why they stopped you from singing. Sheer fucking jealousy." He tweaked his pierced nipples until holy blood flowed out, sparkling like the paint on a vintage cherry red Cadillac.

"You're right!" said Leper Licker. "They've always been jealous of me. That's why they kept calling me names, like 'behemoth,' or 'chubby,' or 'fat ass.' They are simply envious of my robust Aryan physique! And that's why they never let me play lead or sing. They said it was because I couldn't play, that my voice was off-key – but that was a lie. They were afraid I'd out-shine them, make them look like the talentless losers they are!"

"That's right, mein little saurkraut. You don't need them. They were holding you back. Now you're free to be the shining star you were always meant to be."

Leper Licker beamed. "You're right. Thanks Hitler!"

She wrapped her arms around his leather-clad leg and held it close to her bosom. When she opened her eyes, she was clutching the hard iron girth of a streetlamp.

"He's gone," she said, gazing up toward heaven. "I guess he must be very busy, giving children AIDS, and making sure antisemitism stays strong all over the world."

She genuflected, then walked on, feeling her anger dissipate and be replaced by the cold fire of endless ambition. Now that the others were no longer holding her back, it was her time to shine, just as the Führer had said. All she needed was a band. A group of mu-sicians who would play her songs, follow her orders without question, and not try to stand between her and the God-like fame she so richly deserved. But where would she find such people?

A sheet of wet newspaper flew through the air and stuck to her thigh. She wrinkled her nose, displeased by its slimy texture. She plucked it off her leg, ready to throw it away – then paused as she read the headline:

Gator Bait: Pop Star's Homosexual Elopement Ends in Bizarre Tragedy!

Beneath the headline were two photographs - a head shot of Ted Douche with his trademark backwards baseball cap and dark sunglasses, and a blurry photo of a bloated alligator. Leper Licker's eyes widened as she scanned the accompanying text.

...said he was "swallowed up like a large fried chicken." The alligator in question has been shot dead, and is currently on its way to the coroner's office, where the remains of Découché will be extracted for an autopsy. Many commentators have blamed this regrettable incident on the atmosphere of homophobia still present in some parts of the music industry, particularly in the heavy metal and rap subcultures, the latter of which is especially notorious for its homophobic messages. Gay Rights activist Taylor Jerome said that "if Ted had been allowed to express (his) sexuality openly, well then he might not have come to such a tragic end." Ted Découché was the frontman of famous "nu metal" band Jizz Biscuit, which is now in mourning, and without a singer...

Leper Licker grinned to herself. She looked up from the sodden piece of newspaper and found herself staring straight at the Jizz Biscuit tour bus.

"It's providence," she said. "Sheer fucking providence. Thank you my divine Führer!"

She tossed the newspaper aside, then stomped her way to the tour bus and banged on the door. A moment later the door folded open with a hydraulic *CLUMP.* The smell of weed smoke, stale vomit, and sweaty male perineums seeped out into the parking lot air.

The disgraced nun looked up. Before her stood one of the members of Jizz Biscuit. She had no idea what his name was or what instrument he played. He was short and pudgy, with bleached dreadlocks and a soul patch. He looked at her with a dazed expression.

His eyes were so bloodshot everything outside of the iris was crimson. Had he been crying, or was he just really stoned?

"Hey," he said, inspecting the PVC habit she wore. "You're that chick from the nun band, right? Cripple Kisser?"

"My name is Sister Leper Licker," she said. "And I'm here to share something huge with you!"

Bleached Dreadlocks stared down at her. "Something huge, huh?" he said. "You here to share your ass?"

"Out of the way, fool," she bellowed. "I'll talk to your bandmates instead!"

She moved to push past him, but the doorway was too small for her robust Aryan physique. The two of them got stuck in the entrance together, wriggling and muttering, trying to get loose. Finally Leper Licker squeezed her way past and stomped into the center of the bus. In the struggle she had lost one of the duct tape swastikas covering her nipples; it was now stuck to the front of Dreadlocks' t-shirt. Sister Leper Licker didn't care - that was her good nipple. She didn't mind showing it off.

She peered at the rest of the band with a brazen, imperious expression.

There were three more of them, all sitting on a couch. She had no idea what their names were or what instruments they played. One had cornrows despite being white as a sheet. Another was bald with a soul patch and an eyebrow ring. The fourth had spiked hair with bleached tips and a black goatee. They all dressed like twelve-year old boys in t-shirts, board shorts, and sneakers. On the table in front of them sat a smoking bong, a pile of cocaine, and various bottles of whiskey and rum. A naked young woman lay passed out beside them on her belly. Someone had drawn a silly face on one of her ass cheeks, with horns and a Hitler mustache.

"My Lord," whispered Leper Licker, "it's yet another sign!"

"What did you say?" asked Cornrows in a low, slow voice.

"I said the Lord has brought me here," said Leper Licker. "This is providence!"

The bandmates glanced at each other.

"Providence?" said Baldy. "What's she talking about?"

"It's that place in Rhode Island, man," said Bleached Tips. "Remember, where you got crabs from that chick at the Dairy Queen."

"Oh yeah," said Baldy.

"I speak not of dairy whores and sinful cities," said Leper Licker. "I speak of the will of the Lord! For he is the reason why your singer is dead. He is the reason why you are now in mourning!"

"We're not mourning Ted," said Cornrows. "We're, like, celebrating his life and shit."

"Yeah," said Dreadlocks, moving past Leper Licker and sitting himself down on the couch. "Ted was an awesome guy. And he wasn't no faggot either, no matter what the papers are saying."

"Yeah," said Bleached Tips. "Ted hated queers more than anyone. Remember that time in San Francisco – "

"Silence!" cried Leper Licker. "I care not if your singer was a sodomite. I'm not here to talk about him. I'm here to talk about *me* – and *us*. I'm here because we all have a common need, something that unites us."

"Is she talking about crack?" said Bleached Tips. "Because I don't want to share any of the crack."

"Nah, man," said Cornrows. "She's talking about sex. She wants to bone us."

"I'm talking about none of those things!" Leper Licker roared. "I'm talking about destiny. Providence. The hand of fate. The crossroads of fortune!"

The nun strutted back and forth, gesticulating wildly, just like the Führer during one of his speeches. The band mates watched her, entranced. Their eyes seemed to be glued to her exposed left breast, which bounced every time she waved her arms or pointed her finger. She was glad the duct tape hadn't come off her other breast; the nipple on that one had been bitten off by Cannibal Klara, back when Leper Licker had been in prison for grand theft auto and various other criminal acts. Beneath the duct tape was nothing but an ugly lump of scar tissue that would never give milk, even if she decided to stop having abortions and produce some Aryan babies.

"...and so," she said, winding up her epic speech, "the path before us is clear. I am no longer a member of Temperance Holocaust. You have lost your singer. The answer is obvious. We must unite – and form a supergroup!" She raised her arms in a grand gesture, panting, staring at them intensely with wild eyes.

"Hold on," said Baldy. "You want us to form a band with... *you*?"

"Yes!" said Leper Licker, on the verge of exasperation. How stoned were these guys?

"But aren't you, like, just a bass player?" said Bleached Tips. "Ted was a singer..."

"I'm a singer too," said Leper Licker. "And I can play lead. I'm a musical genius. I was classically trained!" she paused, taking a breath. "So, what do you say? Shall we combine our forces, and create the greatest metal band of all time?"

The remaining members of Jizz Biscuit glanced at her, then at each other, then back at her. Bleached Tips ogled her body. A sleazy smile spread across his face.

"Sure," he said. "We'll start a band with you. On one condition – you have to give us all a blowjob, right here and now."

His sleazy smile turned into an even sleazier grin. His comrades giggled and laughed.

"Yeah," said Cornrows. "You have to blow us all at once, while we stand in a circle. You have to do that, what's it called, that Japanese thing..."

"Hari kiri?" said Dreadlocks. "Pokemon?"

"No, dumbass," said Cornrows. "Bukkake. She has to do bukkake." He turned his gaze back to her. "So, whatta you say?"

Leper Licker peered at them for a moment, then shrugged. "Sure," she said. "You've got a deal."

The remaining members of Jizz Biscuit stared at her incredulously, as though they couldn't quite believe what she was saying. Dreadlocks giggled to himself, sounding almost nervous. Leper Licker got down on her knees in front of the couch.

"Come on!" she snapped. "Let's get on with it."

The men looked a bit intimidated now – intimidated, but also horny. Their stoned eyes roved across her ample curves, her ruby lips, avoiding the cold sores that flanked her mouth. All four of them stood up, dropped their shorts, and started to masturbate. Slowly their pricks got bigger – but not by much. Leper Licker had never seen such short, thin penises before. Back in Schwarzenau prison she'd known a woman whose clit was bigger than any of their cocks. As they stood around her, caressing their tiny bratwursts, she sensed a strange reluctance in them.

"Come on," she said. "Bring those sausages over here. I want a taste..."

Leper Licker licked her lips – and her cold sores. She was no stranger to providing oral sex for groups of people. Back in the showers at Schwarzenau she had almost worn out her tongue licking the cunts of the older, more violent inmates. And before that, on the streets of Vienna, she'd been one of the only female members of her Neo-Nazi youth gang, *Junge Werwölfe*. The boys had been all over her. Her mouth was always their favored orifice – especially after they found out about her hep C, herpes, and syphilis. She'd often gone down on her knees to suck them all off at once. It was something she enjoyed. She loved to be the locus of attention, the focus of everyone's lust. Even now, despite how unattractive these men were – how small their penises were, how much they smelled like unwashed chode, cheese crackers and bong water – even now she still found her cunt moistening as their pricks pointed towards her from all four cardinal directions, as though she were the center of some universe of lust.

She took the first one in her mouth, then the second, then the third, then the fourth in quick succession, getting their dicks all wet with her saliva. While one was in her mouth she jerked another two off, while the forth stood waiting in frustration. She never let them wait long. Like a plate spinner toiling to keep all their pieces of china twirling on their sticks, she moved from one prick to another, making sure they all stayed at the peak of arousal. One of them got carried away and started violently fucking her face, but luckily he wasn't long enough to reach her tonsils, otherwise she might have vomited all over him.

Sixty seconds after she'd started, Cornrows let out a groan and shot a rope of semen straight into Leper Licker's eye. She blinked, spreading the stinging white all over the surface of her eyeball. As though they were all connected to each other via some sort of douche bro hivemind, the others all groaned as well, and began to explode in quick succession, one on her cheek, another on the back of her head, and the fourth into her mouth. His foul-tasting cum, tainted by the chemical byproducts of cigarettes, liquor, and crack cocaine, was almost enough to make her puke. She spat it all over the floor of the bus, then tried to wipe the other load of semen from her eye. The bandmates backed away from her, laughing.

"Okay, slut," said Bleached Tips. "Time for you to go."

Leper Licker looked up at him – or at least she tried to. Her vision was still blurry from the seminal onslaught on her eyeball.

"What are you talking about?" she said. "We're supposed to be forming a band!"

The remaining members of Jizz Biscuit peered at her, then at each other, then burst out laughing.

"Don't be ridiculous," said Cornrows. "As if we'd form a band with some fat, crazy ho. We just said all that for the nookie."

They laughed again. Leper Licker reached into her right boot and pulled out a bayonet. Before they knew what was happening, she grabbed hold of Cornrows' cock and placed the dagger's slender tip into his urethra.

"Don't move," she said, "Or I'll skewer your piss hole."

Cornrows froze, peering down at her in absolute terror. A tiny rivulet of blood dripped from the tip of his penetrated prick.

"Hey," he said. "Wait, please – "

"Don't move," said Leper Licker, "or I'll fuck your dick with this knife. Now, why don't we have a little talk about forming this band?"

"Of course," said Cornrows. "We can totally form the band. We were just joking! A deal's a deal, right, guys? You sucked our dicks, so now you're the lead singer."

"And songwriter!" snapped Leper Licker.

"Sure, and songwriter too!" said Cornrows. "Right guys?"

The other band members nodded their heads.

"Good," said Leper Licker. "Now repeat after me – Heil Hitler!"

The four men paused, eyes wide.

"What?" said Cornrows.

Leper Licker jammed the knife deeper into his urethra.

"Aaah!" he said. "Heil Hitler!"

"Say it!" screamed Leper Licker, glaring at the others. "Or I'll shish-kebob your cocks one by one. I mean it!"

"Heil Hitler!" they shouted.

Leper Licker peered at them. They were terrified. Their tiny penises were even smaller now, shrunken into their fatty pubic zones. She smiled smugly, secure in the knowledge that she had dominated them utterly. They might affect the behavior of street thugs, but they were spineless middle class bitch babies. She knew they'd be her slaves as long as she threatened their tiny little kranskys with violence.

"Good," she said, rising to her feet. "Now kneel before me, worms!"

They knelt, sniffing as tears rolled down their cheeks. Leper Licker felt a glorious rush of power flowing through her. This was the way it was meant to be. Her own band, ready to follow her orders without question. Forget the decadent democracy that had been Temperance Holocaust – this was a dictatorship. This was musical totalitarianism, her very own Reich! She stared down at them with the burning eyes of a tyrant.

"Say my name," she said.

The members of the band formerly known as Jizz Biscuit glanced at each other in terror, then peered up at her sheepishly.

"What's, um, what's your name again?" said Dreadlocks.

"I told you, worm, my name is – " Leper Licker paused. Somehow her name no longer felt appropriate. It was a name she'd taken as a member of Temperance Holocaust, but those days were over. The title no longer suited her; she'd outgrown it. Now she needed something that truly expressed who she was. Her power, her beauty, her beliefs. She pondered the issue for a moment, until a lightbulb sparked in her head. She grinned like a hungry piranha in a pool full of chum.

"Call me Sister Blitzkrieg!"

Chapter 32: Hand of Glory

The altar before which HOG knelt had become more holy and obscene as the tour progressed. One evening, just after they'd crossed the Texas state line, HOG had communed intimately with her husband. Through a haze of holy opium she'd heard the whispered word - *stigmata*. Obeying the command, she'd dug an ice pick deep into the sole of her foot, then smeared the scarlet offering in a wild blaze around the altar's crucifix.

Hog felt it was an incredibly sacred relic. Black twinkle lights had been added to it. A brass bowl offered a cornucopia of cigarette butts and roaches, among other things. The ash from the dish was used daily to adorn the Black Dragon with His holy corpsepaint. It was quite fitting for a warrior king such as He.

HOG dipped her fingertip into the broken bottle that functioned as the altar's font. It contained not blessed water, but something far more holy - *Spirytus Rektyfikowany*, 95% proof. The stink of the potent liquor burned her nose, then stung like acid as she used it to purify the gashes she had made upon her chest. HOG closed her eyes to fully absorb His throbbing love as the pain of a thousand searing needles danced in her wounds. And yet it was nothing compared to the pain He had experienced as a mortal being of flesh and blood.

She would never forget the stories He had told her at Hollóhegy, tales of His incredible suffering. Of screaming followers clawing at His flesh, desperate to bathe in His cum and wear His t-shirts. Of enemies slandering Him, claiming His third and fourth gospels were not as good as His first two. Of critics blaspheming His name and calling Him a has-been. The nerve! Even His apostles had betrayed Him. Those who had once been His most intimate companions - those who had helped spread His misanthropic message of drugs, sex, and death - gradually lost faith and departed, leaving Him to carry the heavy burden of The Word by His lonesome. One apostle took a job at a Sunglass Hut. The other started teaching high school band class. The drummer joined a reggae band, and the fifth, truly lost in darkness, became a DJ. The horror!

Therefore, while HOG often despaired at her own situation on earth, she knew it could be much worse. For she had not truly suffered as He had. Though of course it was not for lack of trying. Between self-flagellation and the horrible headlining shows she'd been forced to perform night after night for the last month, she had made herself into a true black metal martyr.

She shuddered as she thought about it. Playing at night, on a big stage, amidst flashing pyrotechnics, before a massive audience, as though she were a common, heretical rock star - everything about it reeked of sin.

Each night, during those shows, HOG had looked out over an ever-growing pit of damned souls jumping and crawling like blowflies on a bloated corpse. They begged for The Word, but she could tell by the Noose t-shirts they draped themselves in, by their glow-in-the-dark eyebrow rings, by their black phat pants with rivets and shit hanging from them, that they were heretics of the lowest rung! None were worthy of The Dragon's Black Metal Gospels or His holy sodomy.

But of course that hadn't been the worst part. The worst had been when her Sisters had been clawed away from righteousness by the talons of ego and fame. In silent revulsion she had watched their hedonistic displays. Their on-stage battle had been fought not in *His* name, but their own. Signs of the end time had fallen upon them. HOG had been sure it was al-

240

most time...

But then the arch-heretic Leper Licker had been expelled from the fold, and Blood had been reborn onto the true path. A glorious future lay before them, a black metal apocalypse of their own making, which would chastise the world and show the True Way of the Dragon for all to see. And yet, would it be enough? Would the tumult to come satisfy HOG's spiritual craving? Was it her lot to follow the same path as the others, or must she carve out her own? To answer all these questions, she couldn't simply follow Blood's spiritual vision. She needed to experience her own.

With a throat perennially cracked from shrieking His hateful love, HOG gulped the rest of the liquor from the font. The jagged vessel cut her tongue and lips. The *Spirytus Rektyfikowany* stung her wounds like manifest sin, and her whole gullet throbbed with holy fire.

HOG began her holy ejaculation. "LORD! Jesus fucking Christ! Son of His most unforgiving Father. Give me no mercy for I am a sinner. *Your* sinner... as you told me you like." HOG rocked back and forth on crystals of shattered glass, used condoms, and trash. She clawed at the scabs on her arms, feeling the power of prayer intensified through her beloved suffering.

It hurt so good.

"Your word has been made flesh with the use of my body, my Lord Husband. I am your faithful whorewife. Come and make me all Thine before I am to die! Make me your saint, my Black Dragon Lord!"

HOG wailed, feeling the acid she had slipped beneath her tongue earlier begin to unfurl within her skull. The holy, dry death winds that brought Him blew his message through the holes and cracks in the lobes and bones within her bent and mutilated frame.

"My most loyal of whores, my Hand of Glory," He

said. "The wealth of souls you deliver to me is most satisfactory. Even if most are posers and wimps."

HOG stopped rocking and looked up to see her Lord hovering cross-legged above the filth of the altar, exhaling cigarette smoke, his unwashed hair hanging heavily around his pockmarked face, making his smeared corpsepaint all the more ugly. HOG felt herself grow moist between the legs as she took in His greatness.

"My Lord," came her raspy voice, "My Sisters, they -"

The Black Metal Messiah put up his hand to stop her. "I know, I know, all them bitches be crazy, right? Yeah, I see."

HOG nodded her head solemnly. "I thought about killing them often in the preceding weeks. Especially Blood and Leper Licker. But now Leper Licker is cast out like Cain, and Blood is back on the path. I no longer think about poisoning her heroin, or torching the bus while she sleeps. And yet, even if she were still a foul sinner deserving of death, there would be no justice in ending her life. For truly death is a blessing for the faithful, not a punishment for the wicked. It is *I* who wish to linger for eternity in your bed of bloody sheets and rusted thorns. I want your metal spikes to pierce me, to be covered in your holy paint of death. Mark me with your blood, and bless me with your cum, My Lord." HOG lowered herself to kiss the dirty floor. "Tell me, have I not suffered enough, having to endure this....this *fame*?" Even as the word rolled off her tongue she cringed. Thinking of her holy work appearing on *music charts* and being written about in *magazines* filled her with rage along with a violent urge to vomit. "Their mocking whispers surround me day and night, Husband," she continued. "A most dark evil thing they threaten me with, a... a *Grammy*..." HOG choked out the last word in a tone of utter horror.

Her black metal god seemed to take this very seriously. His brow furrowed. "I see... I see... that is too bad. Just horrible..." He lifted his round black glasses, revealing the dark, twisting cosmos that sat in lieu of his eyes. HOG looked deep into the eternity of Heaven from which she had slithered, and to which she so longed to be returned. A deep cold abyss of dead stars and deafening silence. She saw her body floating there in the blackness, rapidly decaying until it was one with the dust of nothing. How she longed for such peace.

"Spreading the Word," The Black Dragon began, "is no easy task. You have done well and have suffered well too. You have completed all that I asked. You have perverted the Satanic church with gospels of unprotected sex, drug addiction, and true black metal, among other things. Soon you will destroy the Dark Ones of Darkness Festival with mayhem and madness. Do you therefore deserve an eternal reward? Hmmm...a wise bastard once said that to live is for the weak, but to die is for the true believers. Yeah, suicide! Go for it! Martyr yourself for me, slut!"

HOG threw herself forward, kissing his filthy hippie feet.

"Thank you, most foul Husband! My Black Dragon! YES! I shall burn for you as my love burns so deeply in my loins! Give me strength!"

HOG ripped her hair shirt from her bony body and splayed herself on the floor amongst the cum-filled condoms, chip wrappers, and broken bottles.

"Anoint me!" she screamed.

Black Metal Jesus didn't need to be asked twice. He defiled that crazy nun on the chapel floor.

[an unknown time later...]

HOG woke up, her cunt throbbing with His holy seed, her soul begging for release. Staring up at the ceiling, she knew it would soon be time.

There is a time for everything,

and a season for every activity under the heavens...

A time to cry, a time to die.

A time to smoke, a time to shoot.

A time to mutilate, a time to titillate.

A time to spurn, a time to burn.

A time to abort, a time to snort.

A time to kill, a time to thrill.

A time to hate, a time to masturbate.

A time for warring, a time for whoring.

A time for wickedness, a time for sickness.

A time for genocide, a time for suicide.

Yes, for everything there is a time...burn....burn... burn...

HOG fingered a book of matches near her fingertips. She had used most of them on herself during her ecstasies with her Black Metal Lord, but a single one remained. It would light the way to her personal End Times. The Hand of Glory had never belonged here. She would light herself on fire, and cut her own throat. And if that didn't work, she'd simply throw herself into the pit, naked and bloody, ready to be pulled apart by the heathens below. Her flesh, eaten. Her blood, drank. Thus purifying the wretches of this place with her holy carcass.

It would come as no surprise to anyone, for she wasn't dying suddenly. No, she'd been dying since the day she was born. And what of the songs and work she left behind? What of her holy, saintly remains? They could do whatever the fuck they wanted with them. Wrap them in gauze and leather, or let them rot on display in a glass coffin. Or snort her bones and see God for themselves. It didn't matter. She was done with these posers and wimps. When Temperance Holocaust next played - when they unleashed Holy Hell on the sinners and posers in the audience - HOG would not be coming back.

Chapter 33: Ben Balrog

You know how people say a movie is "so bad it's good?" Well, this isn't one of those. This movie just plain sucks. The story is retarded. The dialogue is shit. I don't even know how Ben Balrog got people to act in this piece of trash. He must have kidnapped their children and held them at gunpoint like some kind of Mexican drug lord. The rest of the cast were probably crackheads he picked up off the street. The sort of people who'd lick a fat guy's crack for a sprinkle of rock. Most of the extras look like street whores. The rest look like over-the-hill porn stars from the 80s with giant fake tits that would explode like balloons if you pricked them with a sewing needle. Are these the type of gross sluts Ben Balrog is into? That guy's dick must be a fucking biohazard zone. I bet he's got more gonorrhea than the French Navy.

The worst thing about this movie isn't just that it's a worthless piece of crap straight from Satan's asshole. The worst thing is that this movie is fucking pretentious. It's trying to look like a 70s B-movie, like something by Jean Rollin or Jess Franco. Basically, it's trying to suck, but it's not even trying to suck in an original way, it's trying to suck in an outdated, pretentious, affected way, like Ben Balrog thinks he's making an ode to the great grindhouse films of yesteryear or some shit, but really all he's doing is taking the smelliest cinematic dump since Stephen King's Maximum Overdrive. *Don't watch this movie unless you're retarded and want to get even more retarded in an attempt to win the retarded olympics. I'd give it zero stars if I could, but the lowest I can give is one. Which I guess is for the soundtrack, which doesn't totally suck.*

Ben Balrog should stick to making music because as a director he makes Uwe Boll look like Stanley

Kubrick.

Ben Balrog growled and turned away from his laptop screen. This was just one of the many harsh reviews his latest film, *Death Killer in the House of Death,* had received. The movie had a rating of 10.7% on Rotting Vegetables, and a score of 2.3/10 on the Internet Film Archive.

Who gives a shit, thought Balrog.

It wasn't his fault people didn't get the point of the movie. Besides, most of them were probably just jealous. A guy like Ben Balrog attracted a lot of envy. He was rich, famous, multi-talented, and he got more ass than a toilet seat. Plus he was almost fifty and he still had a rocking body. He could *still* fit in the black leather pants he'd worn on his 1991 Prince of Darkness Tour. Though they were getting very tight. But that was only because they'd shrunk in the wash. Everyone knows leather shrinks.

Anyway, it was only natural he'd attract a lot of enemies because of his success. People who wanted to get to him somehow. If they weren't writing mean reviews of his films, they were making stupid fan fiction comic books that made him out to be a queer. What the fuck was wrong with people? They always tried to drag down great men, like those midgets in *Gulliver's Travels.*

A sound at the door interrupted his thoughts. He rose from his chair with the grace of a panther and immediately went into a fighting stance. A guy like him had to always be on guard, just in case a crazed stalker or some psycho rival from another band decided to go on the warpath. Luckily Balrog had been trained in martial arts by none other than Bruce Lee himself (not the one from *Enter the Dragon,* the one who taught karate at a strip mall in Phoenix, Arizona).

The sound came again. Someone was fiddling with

the handle. Why hadn't they knocked?

"Who's there?" he said. "If you're trying to get an autograph, you have to talk to my assistant..."

No answer came. Instead, whoever was out there kept fiddling with the handle more and more violently, like a poltergeist. Was it Balrog's imagination, or was the air getting colder? He felt a chill run down his spine. He knew all about poltergeists and other spiritual phenomena; he'd been studying the occult for decades.

He picked up the crucifix that lay next to the inverted pentagram on his desk, and held it up towards the door.

"Unquiet spirit, begone!"

The door handle stopped shaking, and suddenly all was silent, save for the distant sounds of revelry that followed every concert. Balrog took a breath, feeling relieved.

Then the door smashed open and a figure with a deathly-white face hurtled into the room.

Balrog gave a scream that wasn't girlish at all, then jumped back from his desk as the figure came tearing towards him. Another second passed before Balrog realised it was one of the nuns from Temperance Holocaust, the one with the huge ass. She sped towards him awkwardly on her clunky platform boots, her big tits bouncing as she came. She crashed into the front of his desk, panting and staring at him intensely. Her eyes were filled with maniacal fire. She had the gaze of a dictator, a serial killer, someone whose ego was fettered only by the limits of flesh. He recoiled from her Manson lamps instinctively, then composed himself and countered her stare with one of his own.

"What do you think you're doing, barging in here?" he said.

"I needed to talk to you," she said. "It's a matter of

dire importance!"

"Why didn't you knock?"

"Sister Blitzkrieg does not knock!"

"Sister Blitzkrieg? Who's that?"

"It's me! I'm Sister Blitzkrieg. I've changed my name."

"Why'd you do that?"

"Because I'm a new woman. I've been reborn, and Temperance Holocaust is no more!"

A surge of panic rose in Ben Balrog. Temperance Holocaust were the most controversial and exciting band on the tour. Ever since molesting that corpse they'd become the hottest new musical sensation in America. They were the reason all the shows were sold out. People couldn't get enough of their crazy antics. And they'd just topped it all by having a violent altercation on stage! The video of the brawl had already gone viral, generating millions of hits and increasing their fame even further, as well as the fame of the tour. People were more desperate than ever to see their show. Scalped tickets were selling for over four hundred dollars each, more than ten times their original price. Temperance Holocaust couldn't break up now, or the tour would be fucked!

"What are you talking about?" he asked. "What do you mean the band is 'no more?'"

Blitzkrieg shrugged, looking irritated. "Well, technically Temperance Holocaust still exists. HOG, Whoreface, and that bitch Sister Blood" – she paused and spat contemptuously on the floor – "are all still in the band. So is that stupid keyboardist, what's-her-name. But I've left them for good. And everyone knows *I* was the real creative force behind the music. I was the only one who was classically trained. I was a musical prodigy as a child, you know. I'm multi-talented, I can play dozens of instruments. So without me, they're screwed."

"Weren't you the bass player?" asked Balrog.

"I was," she said. "But only because they wanted to stifle my genius. In my new band, I'm going to be singing, writing all the songs, and playing lead guitar. Sometimes I might play the cello."

"Your new band?"

"I've formed a supergroup with the remaining members of Jizz Biscuit. We're calling ourselves 'White Vengeance.'"

"That's cool," said Balrog. "People always like stuff that's named after cocaine. What sort of metal are you going to play?"

"It's going to be a fusion of styles. We're going to be the greatest nu black metal band the world has ever seen!"

Balrog nodded, considering her words. Jizz Biscuit was famous because Ted Douche had just gone on a cross-country cock-sucking spree before being eaten by an alligator. Temperance Holocaust were famous for fucking a corpse and being all-round crazy. A supergroup made up of members from both bands might just have the makings of a cult phenomenon - even if their music just happened to be retarded. He smiled, hearing cash registers go CHA-CHING! in his mind.

"This sounds like it might be a really good idea," he said.

"Of course it will!" said Blitzkrieg. "Especially since we'll be the greatest band of all time. We just need a proper time slot to play in. I was thinking we should get Jizz Biscuit's old time slot, on the main stage."

"But I already gave that slot to Temperance Holocaust."

Blitzkrieg's face twitched with rage. Balrog almost physically recoiled from her. The woman was giving out a scary vibe. Balrog was glad for his martial arts expertise. If she went berserk, he'd be able to neutralize her with some of the special pressure point moves he'd learned back in Phoenix.

"Temperance Holocaust only got that slot because Jizz Biscuit couldn't play," said Blitzkrieg. "But now I'm the singer –"

"But you're not the singer of Jizz Biscuit," said Balrog. "You're the singer of a new band, White Vengeance. Right? So how can I give you Jizz Biscuit's old time slot? Ted Douche is still dead. Plus, I gave that slot to Temperance Holocaust, and they're super popular, so..."

His voice trailed off as Blitzkrieg's face twitched with rage once again. She looked as though she were about to leap across the desk like an angry doberman and bite his nipples off. Balrog knew he had to think fast. The gears in his brain began to spin. Luckily those gears were well-oiled, like the gears of a bullet train. In a matter of moments the lightbulb of sweet inspiration flashed in his mind, accompanied by the sound of even more cash registers clanging.

"I think I've got an idea," he said with a smile. "How about this – we split the time slot between both bands."

Blitzkrieg growled. "That's ridic –"

"Hold on," said Balrog, interrupting her. "I'm not finished. How about we split the time slot between both bands, but only for one show. We make it a competition. White Vengeance versus Temperance Holocaust, head-to-head. We'll get a panel of judges and some random people from the audience to decide who gave the best show. It'll be like a battle of the bands. Whoever wins gets to keep the time slot and the spot on the main stage. The loser gets banished to East Stage Three. How does that sound?"

Blitzkrieg grinned like a hungry hyena. "It's perfect!" she said. "We will crush them. Destroy them.

They will be *vernichten! Ausrotteten! Sie werden durch vernichtendes Feuer ausgelöscht! Sie werden...*"

She continued ranting in some strange lingo, pointing her finger and gesticulating wildly.

"Hey!" Balrog said. "Cut it out, will ya? This is America, speak damn American."

"Apologies, Mister Balrog," she said. "I just got so excited. This is the best idea anyone's ever had. You really are a genius!"

Balrog smiled. Now this was a chick who appreciated him properly. Maybe she'd like his movies? She might even give them positive reviews, help beef up that aggregate score on the Internet Film Archive...

Blitzkrieg began to slowly walk around the desk toward him. He could tell she was trying to strut in a sexy way, but her giant platform shoes and large backside made her ungainly, and she ended up clumping awkwardly, like old Boris Karloff playing Frankenstein's monster. And yet her clumsiness didn't bother him. He was too busy staring at her tits. Not for the first time he noticed that one of them was completely exposed, while the nipple on the other was obscured by a duct tape swastika. Some sort of fashion statement. Young people these days wore all sorts of crazy shit. He watched the crooked cross jiggle as she stepped even closer towards him, until her lips were just a few inches from his.

"So," she said. "Do you want to seal the deal? Defile my holy body in exchange for this once in a lifetime opportunity?"

Balrog drew back. "Whoa," he said. "You've got me all wrong, kid. I don't trade favours for sex. I'm not into sexually exploiting women."

She glowered up at him. "Are you saying I'm not good enough to be sexually exploited?"

"Huh? What?"

"Are you saying I'm not beautiful enough?" her voice was threatening. She stepped towards him, pressing her large breasts against his torso. Her left nipple stabbed him like an accusing finger tip.

"No, of course not," he said. "You're, um, you're definitely hot enough to be sexually exploited..."

"Then hurry up and exploit me!" she said. "I demand it. I demand you coerce me to have sex with you!"

"Um, okay," said Balrog, feeling more than a little uncomfortable. He was starting to get scared about what she might do if he didn't take sexual advantage of her.

He grasped her corpse-painted face and planted a kiss on her lips. Her mouth had a peculiar salty flavor that was very familiar. He'd tasted it before on the lips of many groupies who'd been brought to his trailer by members of his road crew. He figured all these girls must like that weird salty licorice from the Netherlands or something.

She kissed him violently, invading his mouth, then pulled away and began to awkwardly clamber up onto his desk, until she was sitting on her haunches with her ass towards him. Slowly she began to lower her PVC skirt, revealing more and more of her ample backside. It was definitely big. Balrog loved the way it jiggled, even when it was sitting still. She pulled her skirt lower still, until a round metallic object was revealed, glinting in the candlelight: the base of a butt plug embossed with a swastika.

This chick really likes swastikas, he thought. *I wonder if she's a Hindu?*

"Remove my plug, Balrog," she said, "And defile my ass with the holy sin of sodomy."

Balrog shrugged and pulled out the plug. Mucous trailed from the tapering tip; her asshole gaped like a lamprey's mouth, sans teeth.

"Hurry up and take advantage of me!" she cried.

Balrog set down the plug and fumbled with the button on his leather pants, which had become stuck underneath his overhanging six pack abdominals (it definitely *wasn't* stuck under a protruding lump of abdominal fat. He definitely did not have a muffin top. It was just that his abs were so developed, sometimes they looked like one. Okay?).

Finally he managed to undo the button. His leather pants sprang open. He pulled down his fly and grabbed his prick. He had to massage it a little; the tightness of the pants had made it go numb. Finally it sprang semi-erect, which was more than hard enough to enter such a gaping hole. He pushed it up her asshole with a single thrust.

"Oh yes!" cried Blitzkrieg. "That's it Balrog, you disgusting pig. Push my shit in. Fuck me like I'm George Michael!"

"Maybe cut out that sex talk?" said Balrog as he pumped her gingerly. "It's kind of a turn-off..."

"Fine," she said. "I'll talk about something else, like...like the concert! The battle of the bands. It has to be – UGH! – the best – UGH! – spectacle of all time. There should be – OW! YES, IMPALE MY CO-LON! I WANT YOU TO MAKE ME INCONTINENT! – there should be a sausage sizzle for the fans, with plenty of complimentary bratwursts. It should be like – TOO GENTLE! HARDER! I WANT THE NEXT SHIT I TAKE TO LOOK LIKE A BROWN PLASTER CAST OF YOUR COCK! – it should be like Oktoberfest, with weiss beer, and free lederhosen for everyone. And for the stage, I want – UGH! GOOD! I CAN FEEL THAT IN MY ILEUS! – I want a giant, ten foot swastika made out of scrap metal, with – DON'T SLACK OFF! I WON'T CUM UNLESS YOU MAKE ME BLEED! –

with glowing crimson lights all over it. And I want it to spin around like – UGH! – like a propeller, shooting out sparks from the side! Will you give it to me? Will you – UGH! – give it to me?!"

"Yes!" said Balrog as he spilled his seed into her colon. "Yes! You can have it *ALL*!"

Chapter 34: Ezekiel Leake

"...and when you purchase just one of these gorgeous turquoise belt buckles, you will receive two more, absolutely free..."

Zeke sat in the eerie blue glare of the television, smoking meth. He kept his eyes glued to the TV as he sucked on the pipe. He had to keep watching, otherwise he might miss the messages. There hadn't been any so far today, but he knew They'd be contacting him later in their special code. Probably after he'd smoked more meth. They usually contacted him after he'd smoked more meth. He wasn't sure why. Probably They had him under surveillance somehow, and could tell how much he was smoking.

"Ow, fuck!"

He took his finger off the lighter, which was getting painfully hot. Risking a glance away from the TV, he saw the pipe was empty and blackened. Blindly he fumbled on the coffee table for his bag of crystal so he could load up the pipe again. He had just placed his fingers on the little plastic baggie when a terrible impact shook his tin cabin. It sounded like the roof was about to cave in! Had They found him? Maybe it was the government. The government was the real threat. Those sick bastards in the government were trying to take over the whole goddamn country, and no one was doing shit about it.

The terrible rumbling sound came again. Zeke thought about hiding under the couch, but even he wasn't skinny enough to fit under there.

"Zeke! Zeke! I know you're in there. Open the fucking door!"

It was Marty's voice. Zeke rose, twitching. He hid the pipe and the crystal between two of the couch cushions, then walked, still twitching, to the door of the cabin, which like the walls was made of corrugated tin. He drew back the bolt and opened the door. Marty, his employer, was standing on the porch. Marty was a squat man in dirty boots and shorts, with tribal tattoos on his meaty calves. Behind him was a sprawling field of scrap metal. The skeletons of cars, washing machines, pieces of rebar, even the odd disintegrating school bus, filled the expanse as far as the eye could see.

"Jesus fucking Christ, Zeke," said Marty, looking him up and down. "You've gotta lay off the crystal. Your teeth look like balsa wood, and you're skinnier than Iggy Pop on Weight Watchers."

"Whatta you want?" said Zeke, wishing he was back in front of the TV, smoking his pipe and waiting for the messages. Shit, what if the messages were on the screen right now? He might miss them.

"What do you mean what do I want?" said Marty. "I want you to do some fucking work. Why else do you think I let you live in this shack rent-free?"

Zeke scratched the back of his neck. "Does that mean there's a job then?"

"It sure fucking does. Crazy bitch from a rock band called up ten minutes ago, says she wants a twenty-foot metal swastika with flashing lights rigged up by Saturday night."

"Saturday?" said Zeke. "Wasn't today Saturday?"

Marty sighed. "Jeezus Zeke, you don't even know what day it is. Saturday is tomorrow. Still, that doesn't give you much time to rig this thing up. You might have to go without sleep. Reckon you can manage that?"

Marty grinned. He obviously knew as well as Zeke did that Zeke almost never slept, he just stayed up all night smoking meth.

"Sure, Marty, no problem," said Zeke.

Marty fixed him with a gaze that was suddenly serious. "Now listen here, Zeke. This is a big job, and you're not gonna get much time to get it done. I need to know for sure – are you up to it? Because if you're not, I can always tell this crazy broad to forget about it. We don't want another incident –"

"Fuck that shit!" said Zeke. "Are you forgetting who you're talking to? I'm the two-time Mississippi welding champion!" He pointed at the two tarnished trophies sitting atop his television set. "I'll weld this fuckin' swastika before tomorrow morning, or my name isn't Zeke Leake."

Marty stared at him for a moment, then shrugged and handed him a folded piece of paper containing the specifications for the piece of metallic artwork Zeke had now been commissioned to create. He scanned the information and nodded.

"No problem," he said. "I'll get onto it pronto."

He slammed the door in Marty's face and went back to his couch, pulling the glass pipe and the lighter from between the cushions. He'd need the pipe if he was going to complete this job by tomorrow. Only the power of methamphetamine would give him the strength to weld such a monstrous object in such a short time. He smoked a few crystals, then went out into the junkyard, searching for the metal he would need.

Chapter 35: Sister Blitzkrieg

Sister Blitzkrieg strode onto the stage, her heart jackhammering from a mixture of excitement and cocaine. But mostly from excitement. This was it! Without those losers from Temperance Holocaust holding her back, she was free to show her true talents to the world. She was free to speak the truth about her God.

Grinning with satisfaction, she nearly tripped over a snaking power cable. Her huge platform boots were hard to walk in as usual. But she needed them to complete her image. As always she was dressed in corpsepaint and habit, with the new addition of a Gestapo-style leather trench coat with a swastika patch on one arm. Beneath the coat she was naked. She liked the feeling of her bare, sweaty skin against the oiled cowhide, and the thought of being nude under the coat gave her a sexy thrill.

The former members of Jizz Biscuit – now members of White Vengeance – followed behind her like a pack of loyal slaves. Their body language demonstrated their utter submission. Middle-class pussies like them could never stand up to a woman like her, who'd faced the horrors of Schwarzenau and Hollohegy. She'd broken their wills, turned them all into her bitches. Their faces were marked by cold sores contracted from Blitzkrieg's own lips. She had marked them in more ways than one. She smiled to herself as she thought of the herpes sores already blossoming on their crotches.

They were dressed as she had commanded them to dress, in the uniforms of the Hitler Youth. Their shorts were very short, leaving their chubby, tattooed legs mostly bare. As per her instructions, they had all shaved their heads. In hindsight that had perhaps been a mistake, since without their distinctive hairstyles she could no longer tell them apart. Their facial hair didn't help, and neither did their piercings: they all had soul patches and eyebrow rings, making them look utterly homogenous.

The four identical Untermenschen took up positions behind her, readying their instruments. Behind them was a gigantic metal swastika, which had earlier been brought in on a truck. Blitzkrieg looked up at it with a sense of awe. It was truly magnificent. The engineer had constructed it exactly according to her specifications. The swastika was made of jagged scrap metal, giving it a brutal, industrial look. The arms were covered with red neon lights and strapped with pyrotechnics that would soon be ignited. Twelve feet high and just as wide, the swastika stood attached to a tall metal frame. The whole thing looked almost like a scrap metal windmill, for the swastika itself was designed to spin around and around like the blades of an electrical fan. When the lights were on, the pyros were burning, and the swastika was spinning, the effect would surely be majestic.

Blitzkrieg took in the scene. Everything was perfect – the costumes, the props, the pyrotechnics. Only one thing made her anxious – the music. White Vengeance had barely had time to rehearse. They'd only been formed two days before! They only had one new song – *An Ode to Hitler,* which was really just the same song Blitzkrieg had tried to play the last time she'd been onstage when Blood had smashed her over the head with a guitar. Now she was recycling it as a White Vengeance original. But still, one song wasn't enough. She'd been forced to take some old Jizz Biscuit songs and change them to suit the band's new message and aesthetics, adding black metal aggression to the music and Nazi idealogy to the lyrics. She'd managed to salvage seven such songs for their set list –

1. Break Stuff (But only if it's owned by Jews)
2. I'm Broke (because of World Jewry)
3. 9 teen 30 nine
4. Hot Bratwurst
5. Full Goering
6. Stink Finger (in my Aryan ass)
7. Nobody loves Winston Churchill

So that was it. Eight songs to show her genius. Eight songs with which to crush Temperance Holocaust under her boot heel. Eight songs to show the truth about Hitler Jesus. Would it be enough? A shadow of doubt flitted across Sister Blitzkrieg's hammering heart.

Do not fret, mein sauerkraut said the voice of her Lord in her head. *You are ze chosen vun. You cannot fail. You vill bring about ze new vorld order!*

Chapter 36: Ben Balrog

"What's with all the swastikas?" asked Ray Withers. "Are they Nazis?"

"What?" said Ben Balrog. The two of them stood on the left wing of the stage, watching the band get ready. "Nah, no way. They're just being controversial. You know, like Alice Cooper or Marilyn Manson. Or how Slayer did that song 'Angel of Death,' which made it sound like they might have been Nazis, even though they weren't. It's all just showmanship, man."

Ray Withers peered at him with raised eyebrows. "Are you *sure* they're not Nazis?"

Ben Balrog shrugged. "I'm pretty sure. I mean, she's a nun, right? Who ever heard of a Nazi nun?"

The curtains drew open, revealing a massive crowd. News of the battle between Temperance Holocaust - the most controversial band in the world - and White Vengeance - a super group featuring the artist previously known as Leper Licker, as well as the former members of Jizz Biscuit, whose lead singer Ted Douche had just been eaten by an alligator in a strange homosexual suicide pact - had attracted a massive audience. The fans were packed in like proverbial sardines. Many of them were wearing Jizz Biscuit T-shirts, while others were sporting the corpsepaint and strange religious paraphernalia that marked the fanatical fans of Temperance Holocaust. Ben Balrog smiled to himself. These fanatical nuns had really put the Dark Ones of Darkness tour on the map!

Many people in the crowd started to cheer as the curtains opened, though the sound wasn't as loud as Balrog had expected. Looking out into the audience at a somewhat oblique angle, he saw that quite a few members of the crowd looked confused, distressed, even disgusted. They must have been freaked out by the Nazi imagery.

They'll chill out when they realize it's just a gim-mick, he thought.

"We are White Vengeance," said Sister Blitzkrieg in her thick Austrian accent. "The five apostles of our lord God Hitler!"

The music began to play, a strange and unwieldy combination of ravishing grimness and nu metal funk riffs. Leper Licker began to sing –

It's just one of those days
Where you don't want to wake up
Everything is fucked
Everybody sucks
Because the Jews
Control all the banks

As he listened to the lyrics and watched Sister Blitzkrieg awkwardly strut the stage in her Gestapo trench coat, a wave of realization began to flow over Ben Balrog.

"Oh shit," he said. "I think she might actually be a Nazi."

Ray Withers slapped a palm against his face and groaned.

262

Chapter 37: Temperance Holocaust

"This is fucking disgusting," said Whoreface.

"This is an abomination against the Lord," said HOG. "This black Nazi nu metal is an abortion straight from Satan's cancerious rectum."

Sister Blood stood with them on the right wing of the stage, watching the hideous performance. She was so angry she couldn't even comment. Given the amount of heroin she'd injected, the valium she'd inserted in her ass, and the ketamine she'd snorted, she should have been placid as a lamb, unmovable by anything. Instead she was raging. Her heart hammered, her teeth ground together so hard she thought they might snap. Her anger at Leper Licker was greater than the cocktail of narcotics swimming through her blood. What she was witnessing was absolute blasphemy. Black metal was being defiled. *THE LORD* was being defiled. Her ears were being defiled!

"I can't take this shit anymore," said Sister Blood. "I'm gonna end this bitch. I'll see you in a few decades when I get out of jail for murder!"

She drew a dagger from her belt and stepped towards the stage. HOG grabbed her and held her back; the former anchorite's scrawny limbs were filled with unusual strength, as though she were channeling the power of the Dragon.

"No, Sister!" said HOG. "No violence – not yet. We must have faith. We must pray, pray for the Lord to smite these philistines down!"

Blood stared at her, her teeth still chattering, her whole body literally itching with desire to slaughter Sister Blitzkrieg – though maybe the itching was mostly to do with the heroin. Either way it was hard for her to give up her wrath. But Sister HOG seemed to be speaking with the voice of the Lord.

"Very well, Sister," said Blood. "Let us pray!"

The three Sisters knelt down. Sister HOG led the prayer.

"LORD! O that Thou wouldst slay the wicked, treacherous, fallen slut, Leper Licker! O God, she speaks filth and blasphemy, claiming Hitler was made in the image of thee! I shall not forgive her my Lord, for she perverts your name for the sake of her own self."

As the Sisters prayed, a pair of roadies crept onto the stage and started up the engine attached to the huge metal swastika. The engine itself was quite large; it looked like it had once belonged to a piece of powerful farm equipment, like a tractor or a combine harvester. It let out a rusty growl and began to belch diesel fumes. Soon the swastika began to spin like a huge electrical fan. The neon red lights went on, covering the stage with the lucent likeness of blood. The spinning of the crooked cross ignited the pyrotechnics, which began to belch sparks of flame in all directions. The crowd howled as the light show began, while the three Sisters continued to pray.

"RISE UP, king of kings!" shrieked the Sisters in unison. "Rise up, Great Black Dragon, and strike the whore down! Down to the bowels of Hell where her soul is ripped from her bones. May she burn for eternity in agonizing torment and humiliation. All HAIL! Amen!!"

A spark, then a flicker of flame on the other side of the stage captured HOG's attention. She froze in her devotion as her Sisters continued to wail and chant their love for their Black Dragon husband. Smoke began to pour onto the stage, but it wasn't from the smoke machine. It was acrid, toxic - dangerous.

HOG squinted at the smog. The noise of the so-called music faded into the background as her senses focused on the spiritual world. She saw nothing but His face in the smoke cloud. Raging eyes of vengeance burned into hers. Black Metal Jesus was here - and he was pissed.

While HOG stared at the smoke, Sister Blood prayed. She had never prayed so hard in her life. Her focus was absolute as she poured all her hatred and malice into the words of the prayer.

The sound of tearing metal broke her concentration. She looked toward the sound and saw the giant spinning swastika wobbling as though it were about to tear loose from the hub.

Which is exactly what happened a split second later. The crooked cross crashed to the ground, flattening the White Vengeance rapper. Not sharp enough to bisect him, its edge simply crushed him, the way a blunt knife crushes a loaf of bread. Like a wonky wheel it rolled off his body and over the bass player, who vomited blood as his abdomen was flattened. The crooked cross paused atop the cadaver for a split second, leaning towards the center of the stage like a dreidel about to tumble over.

Blitzkrieg looked up at it, screaming. She had just enough time to turn and take a step away before it crashed down on her. The arm of the swastika pinned her to the ground, crushing her ass and the small of her back. She shrieked in agony, along with the drummer and guitarist, who were likewise trapped beneath the blasphemous arrangement of metal. The audience screamed as well, backing away from the stage in terror. Blitzkrieg tried to crawl out from under the wreckage, but the weight of the swastika was too great. Shattered neon lights stabbed into her back. Burning pyrotechnics roasted her legs and set her habit on fire, haloing her head in flames. At the same time the pyrotechnics scorched the insulation from various electrical cables snaking across the floor of the stage. Naked wires touched the Nazi cross, sending electrical death shooting through the metal. Sparks exploded like neon fireworks; tendrils of murderous energy arced through the air like the wrathful fingers of God.

Sister Blitzkrieg went into a seizure as the voltage flowed through her flaming body. As Blood watched the Nazi nun burn, her heart filled with joy, and she started to laugh.

"Hallelujah!" cried HOG. "The wicked have been punished!"

The three Sisters beamed at each other. Grabbing one another's hands, they began to jump for joy, dancing in a circle like children playing ring around the rosie.

"Hallelujah!" they cried. "Praise Black Metal Jesus! All hail! All hail!"

Roadies and security staff with fire extinguishers rushed into the wings, but wouldn't approach the bodies for fear of being electrocuted. Blitzkrieg and her boy toys continued to burn until they were nothing but blackened husks. The stench of burning human flesh, strangely appetizing, filled the air. People in the crowd screamed, but most did not flee. Instead they stood watching, transfixed by the scene. Many looked excited, their eyes wide with awe as the spectacle of mortality unfolded before them, grislier and more immediate than anything they'd seen on *Faces of Death* or Rotten.com.

Finally the fires went out and the sparks stopped flying, but the roadies and security staff were still too afraid to set foot on the stage. A strange hush filled the crowd, punctuated by the occasional hysterical shout of delayed horror.

The Sisters stopped dancing.

"Now is the time," said HOG. "For our final performance."

Blood nodded. "Time to unleash the biblical plagues."

"Time to fuck shit up like it's never been fucked up before!" said Whoreface.

They nodded to each other, then turned to the roadies.

"Gather the instruments!" they shouted.

The roadies rushed into action, gathering Whoreface's drum kit.

"Wait, what the fuck!?" said Ray Withers, approaching them in the company of Ben Balrog. "You can't go onstage. It's not safe! Some of those wires might still be live. And there are *bodies* out there, for Christ's sake! Don't you —"

Blood slapped him. "You will not take the Lord's name in vain!" she cried.

Balrog stepped forward as his minion drew back in terror.

"Look Sisters," he said, "This crazy shit has gone far enough. I'm all for controversial publicity stunts, but those people are dead! We have to stop the show. Besides, if you get electrocuted too, who knows how high my insurance premiums are going to be on the next Dark Ones of Darkness tour! I might have to start charging the bands for the right to come and play! How fucked up would that be?!"

"Back off, fatso!" said Whoreface. "We don't care about your stinking premiums!"

Balrog glared at the little nun, wondering *Who the fuck does this bitch think she is?* Balrog didn't know how they did things in Estonia or wherever the fuck she was from, but here in America, his word was *The Word.*

"I'm thinking maybe you ladies don't speak English very well so I'm going to say this one more time, slower, so you understand. The show is canc-"

Whoreface knocked the words right out of his mouth, along with a couple of teeth. Ben Balrog hit the floor with a heavy *thud!* He was out cold.

"What the fuck did you did that for?!" shouted Ray Withers, grabbing at his own hair in a gesture of total vexation. He didn't need a genius to tell him shit was spiraling out of control. Nazis, fires, belligerent nuns, dead bodies, and now Ben was on the deck. What could possibly go wrong next?

Whore face pointed at Balrog's limp body. "Tie him up," she said, sounding almost bored.

The three roadies stood in stunned silence for a moment, glancing between Whoreface, Ray Withers, and the supine figure of Balrog.

"But uh, Sister," said Angelface Murdercunt, "that's Ben fucking Balrog. The man is a punk rock legend. We can't just -"

"You can't just what?" Whoreface pushed her sharp little fist under Angelface's quivering chin. For a moment it seemed as if a second person would be knocked out cold. Then Golgotha Skullfuck cut in.

"It's nothing," he said. "We can totally do that, no problem. Right guys?"

"Sure," said Angelface, quivering. "No problem..."

Whoreface lowered her fist.

"I'll just go get some rope or something," said the Lamb of Hate.

"No, use the wires," said HOG. "And tie him there." She pointed at a selection of scaffolding which had been knocked over by the falling swastika. By some strange fluke - or a dark miracle - pieces of the scaffolding had come to rest in the precise shape of a crucifix.

"Whatever you want," said Angelface. The other roadies nodded, and together they dragged the unconscious body of Balrog towards the dented metal cross.

Glancing at each other as they toiled, all three of them silently agreed - they hadn't done anywhere near enough drugs for this shit.

"Grab those cords," said The Lamb of Hate as they began to drag Balrog's body onto the cross.

"Good thing he's a little fucker," said Skullfuck. All three of them chuckled.

"I still can't believe he went down so hard," said Angelface. "I mean, isn't he supposed to be a kung fu master or something?"

The three of them pondered this questions as they wound the cords around Balrog's wrists, ankles, and flabby belly, until he was suspended from the crucifix, facing the stunned audience, who had watched the whole thing unfold with a mixture of excitement, confusion, and fear.

"It's time for the plagues!" shouted Blood. "No slacking off, roadie slaves!"

The roadies nodded, then rushed off stage in search of the special materials they had acquired during the preceding two days.

Whoreface watched them leave, then turned towards the center of the stage, sensing more than ever that the time was at hand. The scene was set for the pinnacle of their career. They were about to make the ultimate show of faith, and the whole disgusting earth would bear witness. The Sacrifice would bleed. Plagues would be unleashed. Screaming canticles of ecstasy would shatter the heavens. The Black Metal Messiah would bear witness to all, and would never dare doubt their devotion to Him.

The three Sisters trod across the charred remains of White Vengeance and took their places on stage.

As she took her position in front, HOG looked down at the ruined face of their former Sister. Leper Licker's skull was half caved in, her demented brain weeping from the wound. Did HOG turn away? No! For she knew that in such visions of gore was the face of The Dragon and all that he stood for. An echoing voice commanded her -

DESTROY THE WICKED, HOG.

HOG pressed her bare foot down into the mess of Leper Licker's head. Splintered bone cut into the sole of her foot; warm, squishy neural tissue oozed between her toes like fresh dogshit. HOG shuddered in ecstacy, absorbing the pain and pleasure of stomping her former Sister's face in. Better late than never.

"ALL HAIL!" shouted Blood and Whoreface, pleased with her action.

HOG gave a cadaverous smile, feeling closer to sainthood than ever before. All that remained was to immolate herself, and her devotion would be clear to the church and the mighty Pope himself. Then she would forever be known as the first and most devoted martyr of Black Metal Jesus.

"Witness, filthy sinners! The End Times are upon us!"

HOG's voice crashed into the mic and blasted from the sound system. Feedback flared from some of the damaged speakers, making her tones sound even more eerie, even more terribly sublime. Arcs of electricity flashed and crackled from stripped and damaged wires; small fires flared and gouted from pieces of damaged equipment. Burnt Nazi carcasses smouldered where they lay. The stage looked like a death trap from Hell, but none of the crew would dare cut the power after what had happened to Ben Belrog. The Sisters were in control now, and their set was about to begin.

Blood's guitar cried its banshee song. Whoreface hammered out funereal drum beats. HOG split her lungs with blood and pain as she roared the opening lyrics to their earliest song - "Black Metal Jesus."

There was no keyboardist to muddy the composition; the nameless sessionist had fled long ago. And who the fuck needed a bass player? They were nothing but trouble anyway. So prideful were they, Blood thought, always wanting two more strings, trying to be something they would never be - lead guitar. With only three musicians, and with eerie feedback blasting from flaming equipment, Temperance Holocaust sounded more brutal and primitive than ever before. Here, at the height of their fame, they'd returned to their roots in the black metal underground.

The crowd jumped to life as the music began, forgetting the carnage they'd witnessed only moments ago. Were they stupid enough to believe it was all just a part of the show? Probably. At least that's what most of them would tell the cops later.

Two songs in, the first of the Plagues was unleashed on the audience.

"Blood and Pestilence!" bellowed HOG, as the roadie slaves wheeled three large barrels on stage.

The unsuspecting crowd screamed with excitement, while the Lamb of Hate pried the lid off the first barrel of assorted animal parts acquired from a slaughterhouse across town. Blowflies buzzed forth from the putrescent assortment, their white babies wiggling amongst the decay. The Lamb of Hate gagged as the stench assailed him.

Sensing the weakness of the roadie, HOG tossed her mic aside and reached into the cylinder of rot. She hauled out a severed pig leg and flung it forth into the crowd. Someone screamed. HOG reached back in and tossed out a sheep's head.

"Open the other barrels, you fools!" she screamed, while tossing more and more ripe animal segments into the audience. HOG couldn't tell if the people in the pit were crying in delight or in abject horror. Either way, her holy duty was being done. Let the chosen ones delight in the onslaught of filth, while the posers vomit and squeal in squeamish abhorrence.

Angelface kicked over a barrel of pig's blood. It gushed across the front of the stage, splashing the security guards who remained lined up in front of the pit. They fled, allowing the audience to surge even closer to the stage, just as the seal on the third barrel was broken. It was hard to tell if the people in the pit were advancing deliberately towards the scene of bloody mayhem on stage, or whether they were being driven forward by a stampede of curious onlookers rushing from behind. Either way, they were soon perfectly positioned to get covered in entrails and organs from the barrel of offal.

"Take that, you sinning heathens!" shouted HOG. She kicked the charred corpse of the White Vengeance rapper, sending a charbroiled hand flying into the pit. The addition of human body parts to the mosh seemed to act as a trigger for the true horror to begin.

"The time is now," said HOG. Her voice, eerily calm and weirdly fractured, like fingernails dragging through gravel, was barely audible over the shouts and screams rising up from below. Fights broke out. Girls had their clothes ripped off amidst the stinking gore. A scene from Sodom and Gomorrah unfolded in the mosh.

On stage the music slowed. Whoreface's drumming shifted from a furious onslaught to a tribal beat, while Blood slowed her strumming, unleashing a tortured trickle of tritones.

"Ugh, what is going on...?"

Balrog groaned as he awoke on the cross and tried to take in the scene. His head was killing him. How had he ever ended up here? He couldn't remember having been knocked out. It must have taken all three of the nun whores and their stupid-looking roadies to take him down. Had it been a fair fight, one-on-one, then he would have kicked ass, he was sure of it.

Balrog blinked his eyes. Through un-blurring vision he saw Whoreface heading over to him.

"Bitch," he cried, "Let me down N-*OWWW!*"

Balrog's commanding voice became a yelp of pain as Whoreface stabbed him through the foot. She wasn't about to waste any time. The Black Metal Messiah's commandment was clear: *The blood of the posers must flow!*

Grinning like a shark, Whoreface watched the garnet liquid leak from Balrog's boot as she yanked out the knife.

"Stigmata," she cried. "You are blessed!"

Whoreface laughed as she stabbed his other foot and twisted the blade.

"Hey, you stop that!" shouted Bill Withers, watching from the wing. "Enough is enough! This isn't a rock show, it's a damn slaughterhouse. You can't do this!"

Whoreface just laughed and kept twisting the blade while Balrog screamed.

"Why you…!"

Ray Withers gritted his teeth. He knew he had to do something. He couldn't stand by any longer while this crazed little foreigner stuck his boss full of holes. He had to intervene, even if it meant charging full bore into the sparking, flaming, electrified death zone of the center stage.

Steeling himself, Ray Withers swallowed his paralyzing fear. He was going to fucking do this! She was just a little nun. Slipping back into the habits of his linebacker days, Ray positioned himself for the charge, then ran full force at the little cunt, shoulder-first, catching her by surprise and knocking her away from

Balrog.

"Don't worry, man. I'll get you down," said Ray as he began to gingerly remove Whoreface's blade from Balrog's foot.

"Hurry up," said Balrog. "Ah, fuck!"

He screamed as Withers removed the weapon and began to cut through the ties binding him to the cross.

Whoreface stood watching with a twisted smile. How naïve these men were, she mused, thinking they could just walk away from all this. A Sacrifice was needed; the Black Metal Messiah had decreed it. One of these men was destined for the altar of blood. One, or even both - it didn't matter to her.

Freed from the cross, Balrog leaned on Withers, who helped drag his hobbling body towards the wing. They had almost escaped the stage when something jerked Withers backward, leaving Ben standing alone. Struggling to stay upright on his mutilated feet, Balrog turned to see Whoreface strangling Ray with an extension cord. The poor guy was down on the ground with the homicidal nun wrapped around him in a fearsome death grip. He thrashed, grasping at the ligature, fighting for a single breath of air.

Ben froze for a moment. He knew he should stay and help, especially since he had a blackbelt and was a lethal killing machine, *but*... he was bleeding from the feet, and his head hurt. He wasn't in any shape to battle a mad Scandinavian midget on a stage dotted with naked wires and dancing flames. Sadly, it was going to be him or Ray.

"Sorry Ray, you understand," muttered Balrog as he turned and limped backstage.

He decided to head straight to his trailer and lock himself in until the cops arrived. Even *he* wasn't punk rock enough for whatever the fuck these nuns thought they were doing. Maybe they thought it was a stage show, but it looked like the goddamn End of Days. Blood, animal parts, fires, burnt corpses, flies...and the cries of the audience...*the screams*...Ben Balrog knew those sounds would haunt him for the rest of his life.

Ray Withers fell limp in Whoreface's grip, unconscious but still breathing. She turned to the largest of the roadies.

"Toss him into the pit!" she cried.

The Lamb of Hate glanced at Ray's body, then at the grisly maniacs down in the pit. Something primeval had taken them over, stirred up by the music and the iron tang of blood. Throwing a human being to them would be like throwing a puppy to a shiver of sharks.

"What are you waiting for?" screamed Whoreface. "The heathens are hungry!"

The Lamb of Hate froze, battling a crisis of faith. He was prepared to do a lot of things for Black Metal Jesus - vandalism, assault, unprotected sex, rampant drug use - but cold-blooded murder? He wasn't sure he could handle that. Then he saw the spine-chilling look on the drummer's face, and did as he was told.

Fuck I hope I don't go to prison for this, he thought as he dragged the body toward the pit.

Ray Withers woke to find himself being propelled through the air. A moment of weightlessness surrendered to a sharp impact as his body collided with the ground. Then came the stomping of boots and the cruel caress of countless filthy hands.

"*Nooooo!*" screamed Ray as the frenzied audience ripped him apart.

"Angel dust for all!" shouted HOG. "Witness the end!"

HOG pulled a clear plastic bag from her robe, did a bump of the powder inside, then knelt face-to-face with a fervent fan gripping the side of the stage. Members of the audience were climbing on top of each other, forming a slithering pile of grisly, semi-naked bodies as they struggled to reach the stage towering over them.

"Hand of Glory!" screamed the fan. "All for you! I worship you!"

The man reached out for her. HOG opened her palm and gently blew a white blessing directly into his face.

"Dust to dust!" she cried. "Prepare to meet your Black Metal Messiah, worm. You are blessed!"

HOG made the sign of the cross before moving on to the next available fan, then the next, and the next, until her bag of PCP was empty. She staggered back from the edge of the stage, beholding the masses before her. Crazed fans were maiming and raping each other, while others kept moshing. Blood and liquor flowed by the bucket load. Explosions sounded in the distance; someone had lit the tour buses on fire, as well as other buildings dotting the fairgrounds. One fan climbed the scaffolding like a naked, blood-splattered Spider-man, then leapt into the audience from a height of thirty feet, ending his life in a final, grisly stage-dive.

HOG smiled serenely. This was all she could have hoped for, and more. She knew that when they wrote the story of Her it would end with this scene of beautiful devotion. Which was all well and good, for she could wait no longer. Her soul was shrieking for release from this flesh bag she'd lugged around for far too long.

"The fire of life will no longer burn within me," she cried. "Take me, Jesus!"

The Hand of Glory turned her back to the audience. For her the show was over, but her Sisters were still playing, as if possessed by the Holy Spirit. Blood's guitar screamed in a ceaseless Black Metal jam, while Whoreface hammered out nonsense only saints and angels could ever understand. Absorbed as they were in the music, HOG knew they would not interfere with what she had to do next.

She turned to the roadies. "Light my garments ablaze!" she demanded.

The holy slaves stared at her in horror.

"I said burn me, you fools!" she cried, as black clouds rolled across the moon, blocking out the light, beckoning her up into the dark embrace of her most holy husband.

"HOG, we...we *can't!*" said Angelface. "This has gotten out of hand. I didn't take this job to kill people!"

She turned away, hyperventilating, unable to take any more of this madness.

HOG snagged the roadie's wrist and pulled her close.

"This is not murder but a blessing, child," she hissed. "I will meet my blessed death with eyes wide open. Now *do it*, or I'll take you with me!"

She shook the frightened girl like an abusive mother reprimanding her child. Angelface wept hysterically, babbling "No, no, I can't!"

"Here!" said the Lamb of Hate, snatching his friend from the claws of the singer. "I'll do it." After all, he thought, what did he have left to lose? He'd already tied up a rock legend in a mock crucifixion, covered the audience with rotten animal remains, and hurled Ray Withers to a gruesome demise. What was one more felony?

He picked up a broken guitar neck and shoved it into a fire burning nearby. As it burst into flames he turned to HOG.

"Fucking die, crazy cunt!" he said, lighting the remains of her tattered hairshirt and habit. Already soaked in *Spirytus Rektyfikowany,* the black metal mystic lit up like a match.

"AHH!" cried HOG, her arms outstretched and her

face turned heavenward. "I feel you in me!" The fire engulfed her limp hair, licked her neck and kissed her face, causing her flesh to bubble and spit.

"JESUS FUCKING CHRIST!" shouted someone HOG couldn't see.

Heavy boots thundered onto the stage. Someone was here - police, paramedics, firemen, maybe all of the above. But such things no longer mattered to HOG. She fell to her knees, inhaling the holy heat and smoke of her Black Metal Messiah.

"Deliver me," she managed to groan before slipping off toward sweet eternity.

+++

Ben Balrog breathed a sigh of relief when the people banging on his trailer door turned out to be the cops he'd called and not the blood-soaked maniacs setting fire to the tour buses. He supposed it wasn't very punk rock to call the pigs, but then again, it also hadn't been very punk rock for those bitches to try and kill him. Him, the God of punk and all-round badass. Those murderous nuns needed to be stopped by any means necessary. Now all Ben wanted was a week in bed with a whore, some chicken soup, and a sandwich from Wendy's. He was getting too old for this shit.

Chapter 38: Epilogue

Miami Tribune, June 1999

Family, friends, and fans all gathered at The Miami-Dade County Fairgrounds on Thursday night to pay tribute to their beloved hero, friend, and inspiration, Theodore (Ted) Hamish Découché, along with his partner Kyle Patrick Lewis, both of whom died suddenly this Sunday at the tender ages of 34 and 28, respectively.

The music world was rocked this summer by the sudden departure of Découché from the Grammy award-winning band Jizz Biscuit. The singer's absence was noted by fans and the press alike, leaving everyone wondering - what happened to Ted Découché? It wasn't until a few weeks after his mysterious disappearance that photos began emerging of him in the company of Kyle Patrick Lewis of Homosassa Springs, FL. Based on the photos in question, and the contents of Lewis' blog, it is believed the two men were lovers. Though rumors of necrophilia are circulating among fans, nothing has been officially confirmed at this time.

According to statements made by Lewis in online forums - under the pseudonym "Wicked Dude" - the couple fell for each other right away, and planned on collaborating together in the future. But their plans were dashed on Sunday afternoon when Lewis' van, driven by Lewis, veered off the road into alligator-infested waters inside the Everglades National Park. It has since come to light that Lewis was speeding to evade police, but the initial reason for the chase is still unknown. Kriss Moony, a spokesperson for the Rainbow Hugs Foundation, claims the incident is just an-

other example of police prejudice towards the LGBTQ+ community. "If they had been Florida good ol' boys in a pick-up out gator hunting, the cops would have never stopped them. But because Ted was famous, and Kyle had a mental disability, they were perfect targets for the police department. The whole thing is heartbreaking. It's a hate crime pure and simple. We need to defund the police, NOW!"

Other members of Jizz Biscuit were not present at the memorial, having tragically died on stage just a few short days after Découché himself passed away.

Donations can be made in Ted & Kyle's name to the Rainbow Hugs foundation.

If you or someone you know has witnessed or been victim of a hate crime due to your status in the LGBTQ+ community, there are resources available to you. You are not alone. Call or text 0434-918-905 to talk to a caring volunteer at the Rainbow Hugs Foundation help line today.

LOUISIANA (AP)

A shocking scene unfolded at Airline Highway Park in Baton Rouge Saturday night when the traveling hard rock music festival, The Dark Ones of Darkness, turned from a carefree evening of music into a scene straight out of Revelations. It began and ended with the depraved nuns from the Neo-Christian black metal band, Temperance Holocaust. Sister Leper Licker, who had recently departed the band over creative differences, was left crushed to death beneath a swastika stage prop during the one and only performance of her newly-formed group White Vengeance. Despite the sudden and gruesome demise of all five members of the band, the Sisters of Temperance Holocaust took to the stage immediately following the incident. It is unclear at this time whether the festival organizers allowed this stunt, or if the band took it upon themselves to continue with the show as planned. Within an hour riots broke out amidst the audience, while live animals were said to have been sacrificed in the name of the "Black Metal Messiah," Jesus Christ. Ray Withers, senior tour manager and assistant to Ben Balrog, was dismembered in a gruesome attack which is still being investigated by police. The singer of Temperance Holocaust, known only as The Hand of Glory, was set ablaze on stage. She remains in critical condition at Baton Rouge General Hospital. Accused of murder, battery, and tampering with a corpse, both the drummer, Sister Whoreface, and the guitarist, Sister Blood Cunt Christ Fucker, have been arrested and await sentencing, along with several of the band's roadies.

When reached for comment, musician and organizer Ben Balrog was dismissive of rumors regarding a brutal assault on his person by Sister Whoreface. "It's a rock show, shit happens. Look, I knew there were probably cameras around filming, so when that nun took a swing at me, I couldn't necessarily swing back, ya know? That's how these small bands are - they're just looking for a reason to sue you and make a name for themselves in the process. Could I have defended myself? Yeah, that was my right as an American citizen. But I, uh...I don't believe in hitting women, and I don't have the time to deal with another bullshit lawsuit from some wannabe rock star, ya know? It's all about practicalities. Everyone knows I'm trained to kill. My hands are officially registered as lethal weapons in twelve different states. Fuck, see this paperclip? I could easily jab it in your neck and end your life like that (snaps fingers). But the art of Jeet Kune Do teaches one discipline and respect for human life above all else. So no matter what the rumors are, or what the video shows, that's not the whole story."

When asked if the Dark Ones of Darkness festival would continue to tour, despite the numerous deaths and pending lawsuits, Balrog was confident that the carnage experienced Saturday night would not affect future tour dates. "Yeah, we're rolling right along as planned. Thankfully I know some good people from some fucking great bands like Bassinet of Decay and Backgash, who have offered to fill the slots previously taken up by Jizz Biscuit, White Vengeance and Temperance Holocaust. And my own band will be playing a double set to close. See? Problem solved. Fuck those crazy nuns. I mean, I'm not mad about the rampant drug use, orgies, violence, or the fact they're women, ya know? It's about respect for how things are done. You can't just come onto a scene, start murdering people, and think you're going to get anywhere but fucking deported."

The Dark Ones of Darkness music festival plans to play The Four States Fair Entertainment Center & Fairgrounds in Texarkana, Arkansas this coming Friday, Saturday, and Sunday. Tickets are available.

282

After nearly a month in critical care, the singer of chart-topping black metal band Temperance Holocaust has been awakened from a coma. The Hand of Glory (real name Agnes Paprika) was placed in a medically-induced coma while recovering from self-inflicted third-degree burns after a stunt gone wrong last month at a fairground in Louisiana. One source, who wishes to remain anonymous but is said to work inside the hospital, and to have witnessed the singer's injuries first hand, is quoted as saying "It is truly a miracle. If you'd have told me a person could have survived something like that, I wouldn't have believed it unless I saw it for myself. She's a lucky woman, and will be in need of a damn good plastic surgeon, that's for sure."

The remaining members of the band, Sister Blood Cunt Christ Fucker (real name Helga Chelovekonenavistnichestvo) and Sister Whoreface (real name Svetlana Dragoste), were deported and banned from playing further shows in the United States as part of a plea agreement rather than face charges. When reached for comment, Sister Blood characterized The Hand of Glory's recovery as a true miracle from Christ. Upon release from the hospital, the singer is scheduled to be canonized by the Pope to become the first-ever living saint in the history of the church.

Temperance Holocaust will be entering the studio this winter with plans to record a second album.

Black Metal Jesus

Jesus had to admit the convent looked metal as fuck. It sat alone atop the peak surrounded by nothing but utter desolation. There were no trees on the range, just rocks with peculiar red stains, as if they'd been left over from some ancient, barbaric execution festival in which thousands of people had been stoned to death - the Woodstock of stoning.

As for the convent itself, it managed to look dark and evil despite being covered in crosses and other sickening marks of the Christian faith. The bricks were a dirty red, like dried blood, and there were black marks and smudges all over the building as if people had tried to burn it down several times without success. Everything was rimed with frost - the bricks, the stones, the solitary tree stump outside the convent. Even Jesus' hair and beard were frosty, and he'd only been outside the van for a couple of minutes.

He glanced back at the van with a sense of betrayal. The engine block was smoking. To put it mildly, the vehicle was fucked. He walked over and kicked it. Unsatisfied with this minor act of violence, he punched the van, which had "Virgin Raping Wagon" stenciled on the side in barely-readable black metal lettering. The rings on his fingers tore through the paintwork and a bolt of pain travelled up his arm.

"Ah, fucking, fucking cunt, cunt mobile!"

He kicked the side of the vehicle again, then hugged himself. It was freezing out here. Even his trusty leather jacket couldn't keep him warm, and it had plenty of insulation in the form of dozens of patches for bands like Mayhem, Hellhammer, Darkthrone, and Sigh.

"I'll freeze to fucking death out here," he said to no one but himself. Once again he cursed his craven bandmates for abandoning him before the border crossing.

"Sorry man, but we just don't want to cross the border with all those drugs in your guitar case," Sven, the
pussy fucking bass player, had said.

The others had agreed, and they'd forced him to
drop them off before the Hungarian border. Now here
he was, alone, lost, and contemplating an act of desperation that made him sick to his black metal stomach - the act of seeking shelter at a den of Christianity.
He hated Christianity, just like all true black metallers
should. He never let anyone call him by his Christian name, and always went by his black metal moni-
ker - Jesus Heretic. Could a man with such a name really bring himself to beg for assistance at a place of
worship, even if it looked like the coolest metal album
cover ever?

"Fuck it!" he said.

He would take advantage of their weak Christian
virtue of charity. He would take what he needed and
be on his way. Perhaps he'd even fulfil a personal fantasy, and defile a nun.

The thought made him smile as he slammed open
the van door and retrieved his most precious posses-
sion - the case containing his Gibson Les Paul and
(approximately) five thousand dollars worth of LSD,
speed, cocaine, and PCP.

With guitar case in hand, he strode to the gate
which led to the convent grounds. It was covered in a
thick patina of rust. Next to the gate, on a stone arch,
was a rusted plaque bearing the following inscription in
Roman script:

Hollohegy Home of Wayward Nuns

*...and ye shall overthrow their altars, and break
their pillars, and burn their groves with fire; and ye*

shall hew down the graven images of their gods, and destroy the names of them out of that place.

Deuteronomy 12.3

"Fuckin" weird,' said Jesus.

He pushed at the gate, but it only moved a little. He kicked it, and it opened all the way with a scream of rusty hinges that echoed amidst the crags of the convent.

The sudden explosion of sound made him feel exposed. He paused on the threshold. The earth on the other side of the fence was just as rocky and desolate as the earth outside, and he wondered why they bothered having a fence at all, unless it was for the purpose of giving unwanted guests tetanus should they try to scale the high bars, which were topped with spikes and garlanded with rusted barbed wire.

He strode on to the building and its grim towers. Gargoyles and grotesques perched on the gutters and ledges. Looking closer, Jesus saw some of the gargoyles had been sculpted to look like drunken or naughty nuns frozen in the act of vomiting, pissing, or menstruating. The grotesques were in the more classic style of leering devils.

Jesus wished he had a decent camera. One photoshoot here and he'd have enough material for a dozen album covers. But covers for what? There was no one left in the band but him. What was he supposed to do, jump on the synth and crank out a one-man album like that arsewipe Count Grisnack?

Movement from a window above shook him from his thoughts. He caught a glimpse of a young woman's face framed by the crisp white of a nun's headscarf. She caught his eyes for a moment, then was gone from the window, like a mouse scurrying under a table.

The large front doors stood in a recess between two projecting turrets. For a few paces as he walked

287

towards them there was no sound but the crunching of his black boots on the gravel. Then he heard it -
frantic praying, accompanied by the rhythmic lashing
of a whip against flesh. It seemed to be coming from
the base of the turret to his right, muffled and distorted as if the owner of the voice were inhumed within
the bricks. Other voices drifted from the bowels of the
convent - screaming, shouting, off-key singing. Jesus
wished he had some recording equipment on hand.
Those voices would make some sick samples for song
intros.

At last he arrived at the imposing front doors of
red-painted timber banded with studded iron. As he
reached for the door knocker, a shudder of excitement
passed through him, and somehow he knew, deep inside, that whatever he would find beyond these doors
would change both his life - and the face of the black
metal scene - forever.

+++

The Mother Superior peered out the window at the
man on the doorstep. The sound of him hammering
the door with the brass knocker echoed through the
halls. He'd been knocking for several minutes.

'Hey!' he cried. 'What gives? It's cold out here,
man. I'm fucking freezing my dick off! Can't you help
me out? I thought you were supposed to be Christians!
Come on and open the door!' He continued to bang on
the wood.

'What should we do, Mother Superior?' asked Sister Dorcas. 'He won't go away. Maybe we should shoo
him with a broom? I fear if he doesn't leave, he might
endanger the spiritual recovery of some of the more
troubled Sisters. For example, what if - '

288

Mother Superior silenced Sister Dorcas with a raised hand. She knew very well the spiritual danger the young man on the doorstep represented. His very appearance screamed the word "antichrist," from his swarthy skin to his hideous t-shirt with its image of a woman impaled on a wooded pike through her exposed vagina. Every time she looked at him she felt like crossing herself and saying a prayer. Even his long hair and beard - which gave him a superficial resemblance to the Saviour - could not prevent him from looking unholy. And yet, Mother Superior knew she could not turn him away to die of exposure on the merciless plain. Her faith forbade it. And perhaps there was some greater force at work here too.

'We shall not turn him away,' said the Mother Superior. "Instead, we shall welcome him among us. And we shall assign the most wretched of our ranks to wait upon him and serve his needs. Our three most wayward sisters.'

'You don't mean -"

'I do. Those girls have been skirting the brink of damnation since they arrived here. This shall be their final test. Either they shall meet this antichrist and succumb - or they shall pass through the fire of his presence and be redeemed. Sister Dorcas, go fetch Sisters Helga, Svetlana, and Hildegard!'

+++

Apocalypse is coming, it's time to prepare,
Brace for the chaos, the end is near,
Jesus is watching, with eyes full of blood,
But sinners and heathens, surely won't rise.
Lust may tempt, and I feast on his flesh
Death to sinners, as they're gnashed by his teeth

But for those who follow, Jesus will provide
Eternal life, in the holy heaven
I, bathing in his seed
Brace for the brimstone, the fire and smoke,
As the beast rises and the ground shakes
It is He
The holy husband stands by my side,
In His glory
In His filth
All Hail!

Sister Helga sat back and looked over her poem.

It was brilliant.

It was brutal.

It was holy.

Thinking of her Saviour, her husband, Jesus Christ the warrior king washed in the blood of sinners, ignited a fire within her pelvis. She looked at the plastic clock on the table with *Made In The USSR* printed across the face; she had time before evening prayers.

"Ah..." escaped Sister Helga's lips. She kept her eyes locked on the dead stare of the faded wooden icon nailed to the wall before her. She struggled to part her robes. Layers of black and white, this cotton prison she had been forced to cover herself with, would not stop her displaying her deepest devotion to her holy spouse.

"Ugh," she said, getting her wrist tangled in her belt. Her rosary fell to the floor. The beads shattered and rolled under the bed. "Damn," she said, knowing Mother Superior was going to give her shit for wrinkling her tunic and destroying yet another set of beads.

Finally, there it was, exposed for Him to see. Sister Helga relaxed on her wooden chair and let her legs fall open. It had been too long...

"Sister Helga? Sister, are you in there?"

At the sound of the voice Sister Helga sighed in frustration. Her burning loins instantly cooled as the pig face of Sister Dorcas peeked around the door. That little porkchop wasn't fooling anyone, Sister Helga thought. She was as guilty of gluttony as Helga was of lust. But at least Helga's lust was pure. It was for Him and not for a berry pie with cream.

"Oh!" cried Dorcas. "Sister Helga, you need to cover up this instant! Mother Superior requires your presence in the main hall."

"What is it now?"

Sister Dorcas tried to look away but couldn't help sneak a glance at Sister Helga's exposed cunt. The coil of red hairs resembled a nest of burning snakes. They say redheads are more likely to sin because of their fiery nature. Seeing that cunt, Sister Dorcas believed it to be true.

"Now, Sister," Dorcas said.

"Yes, fine." Sister Helga stood and followed Sister Dorcas, adjusting her robes as she went. Her tunic was soiled and her fingers smelled of her body's most holy incense, pungent and thick.

+++

The Mother Superior guided Jesus along corridors where the smell of fresh timber contrasted sharply with the damp scent of old stone.

"Have a little accident with some candles, Sister?" he asked.

The Mother Superior looked around as if just noticing the construction. "A few of our sisters got a little overzealous at Candlemas. It is nothing. In a place like this, the wood goes up like a matchstick. Let's just hope it doesn't happen again." She stopped and glared at the cigarette dangling from his mouth. "No smoking," she said.

Jesus sucked in as much of the methamphetamine-laced stick as he could, then snubbed it out on the stone wall. Him and the old nun locked eyes for a moment before she gestured for him to continue following. As they walked Jesus felt the eerie sensation of someone watching him but shook it off. God was dead and this was his tomb, what did he have to worry about?

The pair entered a large hall in the centre of the convent. Pale light streamed through a glass-domed ceiling. Wind squealed through a crack in the wall like a rabbit on a hook.

A moment later three nuns stumbled in. Mother Superior had them line up before Jesus. "Sisters, this stranger has had car troubles and is in need of food and drink. You will aid him on this cold evening and see that his van is repaired tomorrow morning, and nothing more. Is that understood?" No answer. "Sister Helga? Sister Svetlana? Sister Hildegard?" Mother Superior's voice was stern as she looked down her nose at each of the young nuns slumped before her. "Is this understood? You will not mess up again, girls. This is your last chance, and you have God to thank for it."

"Yes, Mother Superior," Sister Helga said.

Jesus admired the crude cross tattooed on Sister Helga's cheek. And was that the faint stench of cunt wafting off her? He wondered how long it had been since a cock had slipped between those frowning lips of hers.

Mother Superior turned to the other two sisters, neither of which had spoken. "Sister Svetlana?" she said. "Answer me!"

Sister Svetlana was small and looked like a delinquent schoolgirl with a switchblade friend. Still, Jesus bet she had to be eighteen at least. And if not, then hell, when had that ever stopped him before?

"Whatever," said Svetlana. She glared at Jesus, clearly unimpressed by his scarred leather and unkempt beard.

Jesus wasn't concerned. He knew it was what lay beneath the leather and hair that the ladies liked. At that moment he could feel blood running under his skin like cars hurtling down a wet freeway. He couldn't shake the idea of peeling the clothes from his body and getting a rub down from these nuns. Well, maybe not from the third one, who Mother Superior was presently yelling at.

"Sister Hildegard! One last time, before you are locked in the dungeon! Will you serve our guest?!"

Sister Hildegard was big, about six feet and built like a brick shithouse. Her head seemed to melt directly into her shoulders, her thick neck a mere nub. A smile not even a mother could love added further disfigurement to her pockmarked face.

"Yes, I will service our guest," she finally said. When Mother Superior turned her back, Sister Hildegard waggled her tongue at Jesus, then flipped the middle finger at him.

The signals seemed mixed, but he was pretty sure she was flirting with him. He was a big guy, but the idea of having this heinous creature on his dick made him break out in a cold sweat. She was the foulest thing he'd ever come across. And yet, maybe, if he were drunk, really drunk... It wasn't like he hadn't fucked plenty of skanky metal sluts in the past. And at least she was probably a virgin, which meant no STDs.

+++

293

She heard the sound of the stranger coming near. Footsteps both familiar and foreign entered the main chamber. Through the narrow slit in which her bowl of gruel was passed each day the Hand Of Glory observed the scene between the man and her Sisters.

Mother Superior had instructed three of her Sisters to attend to this man's needs. Why not cast him out? Hand of Glory squinted, and took note of his ragged long hair, the threadbare clothing, and the wide hazy eyes. Then, as if struck with divine inspiration, it all became clear. Of course. He had finally heard her call!

Hand Of Glory had been locked in the anchorhold since she was twelve. She was now older, exactly how much she couldn't say. She bled the holy Stigmata from her cunt once a month, which made her old enough to be His eternal bride. The days passed with only a stray beam of light coming through the rectangular opening in the brick that allowed food, books, and soap to be passed to her.

Hand of Glory had her first vision at three years old. It took her until she was eleven to convince her parents to send her to a convent. The first one they placed her in was too cushy. There was heating, beds, and joyous nuns who roller skated through town on Sundays and played the ukulele for school children.

After a month, Hand of Glory had enough of those posers and wimps who called themselves the "wives of Christ." She began wearing a hair shirt made from her own hair and flagellating herself at least once a day for an hour, if not more. That was how she discovered He had chosen her. She had her first orgasm during a particularly intense session in which the lashing went on for five hours. After that, the Sisters of Happy Doves sent her here, to Hollohegy, where the Mother Superior finally relented and allowed Hand of Glory to fulfil her deepest desire and become an anchoress. The sisters walled her up in this 12 x 15 foot cell, and that had been that. She had dwelled in religious ecstasy ever since.

Presently she turned from the slit and rushed to the back of her narrow cell. She went over the illuminations she had painted on the wall in a mixture of her own blood and gold paint. She traced the crudely-drawn images with the tip of her finger. As she did so, she sensed a presence lingering just beyond the edge of her vision.

"I've seen you before," she said to the angel no one else could see. "No, it is not Him... He has come?"

The Hand of Glory dropped to her knees in disbelief. Her Holy husband had disguised himself in the black rags of an earthly heretic. He had finally revealed Himself to her in the flesh.

"My Holy Love, it is you...!"

The Hand of Glory fell forward in tears and kissed the hard floor with her forehead. She smashed it a second and then a third time in ecstasy. She raised her fists to the air, feeling triumphant.

"He has RISEN!"

She attempted to sing, but her ragged throat turned the words into a fierce shriek instead.

+++

"...And this is the dinner hall," Sister Helga said. She was bored. All this guy did was follow them in silence. When he thought no one was looking he'd scratch his balls or pick his nose and wipe it on the wall.

Sister Hildegard leaned against the long wooden table with her pelvis thrust toward him. "Have you ever thought about shaving that beard into a mous-

tache?" she asked. "Maybe a classic toothbrush mous-
tache?"

"Uh…" Jesus was kinda freaking out. He want-
ed to rip his skin off and bathe in these chicks' juices.
Instead he said "I could eat. Mind if I smoke?"

"Only if I can have one," Sister Svetlana said.
She slid beside him. The top of her head was barely
level with his shoulder.

"Sister," said Dorcas, who had been charged
with chaperoning the group. "What do you think you're
doing? You know there is no smoking, not after what
happened last time. Do I need to get Mother Superi-
or?"

"Fuck you, Dorcas," Sister Svetlana said.

"That is it, Sister. I am tired of your constant
verbal abuse. I'm going to tell Mother Superior!" Sister
Dorcas tried to leave, but Sisters Helga and Hildegard
grabbed her and wrestled her onto the table.

Jesus stood back and watched. "Shit…" He
couldn't believe this was happening. These were the
most hostile nuns he'd ever seen.

Sisters Helga and Hildegard held the piggy nun
down and yanked up her robes so her thighs were exposed. The sight made Jesus hungry for more than
just food.

"You are going to tell Mother Superior on me
again? I don't think that is a good idea. Remember
what I said last time?" Sister Svetlana reached under her robes and retrieved a carving knife she'd stolen from the kitchen. The steel glinted in the weak
light from the buzzing bulbs overhead. It was a glaring
threat that even a simpleton like Sister Dorcas could
understand. "I..I…" she stumbled over her words.

"I think what she needs is a good fuck," Sister Hildegard said.

Sister Helga nodded. All eyes were on the stiff

blade in Svetlana's hand. She traced the tip of the blade up the frightened nun's leg, leaving a run in her stocking and a red scratch on her thigh.

"It's been a long time, hasn't it, Sister?" Svetlana asked. "It's been a long time for my friend too."

Sister Dorcas choked on her terror. Her face turned pink.

"Oh, is this your first time?" said Svetlana. "Too bad, because it's going to hurt." She drew back the blade, preparing to plunge it inside Sister Dorcas.

"Whoa!" said Jesus as he grabbed her arm at the elbow.

Svetlana twisted loose from his grip and glared at him. "Do you want some too, you asshole?" she jabbed the knife in the air between them.

Jesus disarmed the tiny nun and shoved her to the ground.

"Enough!" he said. "Fucking someone with a knife is metal and all, but…I'm just saying, there are better ways to get deflowered."

Svetlana spat on his boot and climbed to her feet.

Helga and Hildegard laughed and let Dorcas go. She scrambled to her feet, her face sparkling with sweat.

"What is going on?"

They turned to see Mother Superior standing in the doorway taking in the scene.

Jesus looked at the nuns, who looked back at him.

"Nada, Sister," he said. "Nothing's going on."

Mother Superior glared at the cigarette between his fingers. "I said no smoking. Put that out. And girls, it's time for dinner. Help me in the kitchen, will you?"

Jesus stamped out his cigarette and slumped onto the bench. Damn, he was tired, and these nuns were fucking crazy. He couldn't decide if he should fuck them or slap them. He half expected to wake up in the morning with a dagger between his legs. "Shit," he said. He ran his fingers through his greasy hair. It had been four days since his last shower.

+++

"Wine?" Sister Helga asked as she carried in a tray with glasses. She set it down and poured wine into each cup. "Food will come soon. But it is gruel. You might as well drink. The wine is good. We make it ourselves from crabapples in the orchard. It is most holy."

"Uh-huh," Jesus said. He watched her leave. From somewhere in the convent he heard the banging and shrieking of a lost soul. He wondered if they kept crazies here or something, like a charity hospital. He examined the wine. It looked like brown water, and was the worst thing he'd ever tasted. "Damn, fuck, shit," he said.

He wondered if this night could get any worse. Then a thought occurred to him; he certainly knew how to make it better. He reached into his jacket and pulled out a half-used sheet of LSD. To the uninitiated observer it looked like a scrap of white perforated paper with a pattern of tiny black skulls on it. They were Black Death trips from Hanover. Jesus used them to commune with the Old Gods when he went camping. He wondered what a taste of acid would do to religious nuts like these chicks.

Jesus listened for a moment for footsteps. When all was clear he ripped several trips from the sheet and dropped them into the wine glasses. The flimsy paper quickly dissolved into the caustic wine.

Jesus sat back and smiled to himself. He might enjoy this night after all.

298

Ten minutes later the Sisters merched in one after another. They set the table while Jesus relaxed with a stupid grin on his face.

"What are you looking at?" Sister Hildegard said.

"Sister," Mother Superior said. "Lower your voice."

"I will when this asshole stops looking at me. Why are you looking at me?"

"Sister!" Mother Superior said. "Go take Hand of Glory her meal. Don't forget her wine this time. I will know if you drink it all."

"Fucker," Sister Hildegard said before breaking eye contact.

Jesus laughed. "These are some god-fearing women you have here, Mother Superior."

"Yes, well, we work with what we have. The powers that be have seen fit to place me in charge of this facility, so here I am. If I don't help these wretched souls, who will?" Mother Superior motioned with her hands for them all to say grace. Her prayers were interrupted by a tortured howl that carried an undertone of carnal bliss.

"My GOD!" it cried.

Jesus jumped in his seat. "What the hell was that?"

The nuns ignored him and began eating.

"Didn't any of you hear that?" he asked.

The nuns giggled, but said nothing.

"That," Mother Superior finally said, "is our anchoress."

"Come again?" Jesus said. He took a spoonful of gruel, then spat it back out and pushed the bowl away. He guessed he would have to fill up on wine. From the looks of it, that was what the others were doing.

"Our anchoress," repeated the Mother Superior. "Sister Agnes, or the Hand of Glory, as she has named herself. From time to time she receives ecstatic visions from our Lord. She is very excitable. But do not worry, she is walled up. You won't be seeing her."

"Walled up, really?"

"Do not think us monsters. It was at her request. She's been in her cell for, oh, about six years now."

"Seven," Sister Dorcas said.

"Right, seven." Mother Superior finished off her drink. Jesus watched the others refill their glasses. In about twenty minutes he bet they'd all start having some ecstatic visions of their own. He himself was already feeling the effects when Sister Hildegard came back into the room with a frown that made her resemble a flea-bitten bulldog. She growled at him and began to slop up her food with stale bread.

"What happened to your face?" he asked her.

"What do you mean? This is how I look." A line of gruel had dribbled down her chin. She didn't appear to notice or care.

+++

"He has risen. Can't you see him? Fire, the… the… flames, how they dance! You shall all burn and We will be reunited in carnal bliss! Let me out! Do you hear me?!?! Tear down the wall! I will bleed for youuuuuuuuuuuuu! HA-ha!"

The crazed ranting had been going on for the past several minutes, making conversation all but impossible. The nuns treated it with practised indifference, but Jesus couldn't ignore it anymore.

"Is that that anchoress chick again?" said Jesus.

"Indeed it is," said Mother Superior. "She is unusually agitated tonight. Though it is not uncommon for her to pray fervently until the early hours of the morn-

300

ing..."

"Attend me or you shall suffer the caress of burning genital lice for all of eternity!" screamed the Anchoress.

"Shouldn't you, like, go and see what she needs?"

Hildegard and Svetlana scoffed.

"No, our guest is right," said Mother Superior. "We should attend to our Sister's distress. Sister Hildegard, go and look in on her."

"But I already took her the wine!" said Sister Hildegard, sounding more like a petulant child than a woman of God.

"So take her more," said Mother Superior. "Perhaps it will calm her excited nerves."

Sister Hildegard groaned like an angry she-boar and rose from the table.

Soon she was stomping down the corridors towards the screaming anchoress. As she walked she imagined herself feeding the Mother Superior into a woodchipper, covering her with scorpions, and rolling her down a hill in a barrel lined with barbed wire.

How dare that old bag boss me around. One day I'll teach her a lesson!

She paused for a moment as she drew close to the anchoress' cell. There was a peculiar lightness in her step, coupled with sickness in her gut. Was her untreated syphilis playing up, or was something else going on? She looked down at her hand and saw the veins crawl under the skin like blue worms.

"Strange. I haven't seen anything like that since I did acid with Gunther, Hans, and the rest of the New Hitler Youth back in Berlin. Maybe I'm going crazy, like the poor old Hand of Glory..." She laughed to herself. Somehow the thought of going insane wasn't very frightening, more like the thought of diving into a swimming pool at a house party. Still laughing, she approached the slit in the wall which offered the only access to the anchoress' cell.

"What is it, Sister Agnes?" she snapped. "You're annoying the whole convent. And you interrupted my dinner. You know I need to keep meat on my bones, or I'll lose my sexy curves!"

"Silence, you vainglorious sow!" shouted the Hand of Glory, her intense eyes peering through the slit. "I have grave news more important than your whorish hips. News I must share with you and the rest of my Sisters in person. Sister Hildegard, I command you in the name of our husband - unleash me from this cell!"

"But…but you never want to leave," said Hildegard. "You love it in there!"

"For everything there is a season. A time for peace. A time for war. A time for being walled up in a disused storage closet. For me that time is over! I come to share the truth with you. I come to share a holy vision. Now hurry up and release me, or I shall squeeze myself through this hole by cracking every bone in my body. My husband shall give me the strength!"

The Hand of Glory screamed, and the sound of a cracking bone echoed in her cell. Hildegard laughed. The thought of her mad sister shattering her entire skeleton, then trying to push herself through a slit in a wall like a dead mouse through a letterbox, was comedy gold. And yet, if Hildegard let it happen, she'd almost certainly be punished by that miserable Mother Superior.

"Enough!" she said. "I'll get you out, just wait a moment. And stop trying to break your damn bones!"

"Be quick about it!" said the Hand of Glory.

Hildegard looked about for something to smash the wall down with. The brick was old, the mortar crumbling. Feeling a surge of confidence and power she clenched her fist and punched the wall with full force.

"Ow," she said. "Fuck!"

Her hand was red and throbbing. It hurt, but not as much as it should have hurt. The wall was untouched.

"You fucker!" she shouted, kicking the wall. Grit crumbled out from the decrepit mortar and fell from the ceiling. Was it just Hildegard's imagination, or had the bricks given way, ever so slightly?

"That's right, my Sister," said the Hand of Glory. "He has given you the strength to set me free. Smite this wall like Samson smiting the temple of the Philistines!"

With a mighty roar, Hildegard launched herself shoulder-first toward the bricks.

+++

Jesus heard a distant crashing sound but ignored it. The important thing was that the mad nun had stopped screaming. Even better, the killjoy Mother Superior had fallen asleep in her chair, leaving him alone with the three younger nuns, two of whom were pretty fuckable. They stared at him as if in a trance, and he could tell by their expressions the LSD was starting to affect them. It was starting to affect him too. So was that horrible wine. He felt loose, buzzing, invincible - and horny as fuck. It was time to get these nuns into an orgy or die trying. But how did one go about seducing a nun?

Fuck it, he thought. *I'll just do what I always do, and use the power of rock and roll.*

Jesus opened up his bag, rummaged through it, and pulled out a copy of *Soiled Purity* magazine, the world's most obscure - and therefore the world's most authentic - underground extreme metal zine.

He held up the cover and pointed to it.

"Check it out," he said. "That's me and my band, Virgin Raper, when we were doing our Rape the Netherlands tour back in '91. Pretty fucking cool, huh? I bet you Sisters don't get too many black metal legends coming through here, huh?"

Sister Dorcas recoiled from the image as if from a snake and crossed herself.

Sister Svetlana squinted at it. "Are you sure that's you?" she said. "I can't see shit."

The cover, like those of all great zines, was poorly-photocopied. It was also crinkled and stained with blood, wine, coffee, and several other fluids, making the image somewhat hard to make out. Even so, Jesus knew his image was unmistakable.

"Of course it's me!" he said. "Look at that tattoo. It's the same as this one!"

He turned around and pulled down his trousers to show the inverted cross tattooed on his left buttock. "See? This ass is recognizable anywhere!"

Sister Dorcas crossed herself again and stared in frozen horror at his hairy backside.

Sister Svetlana erupted from her chair with her switchblade in her hand. "What is this blasphemous shit? I'll cut it off your arse!"

Jesus' eyes widened. Suddenly he no longer felt so invincible. Had he overestimated his ability to seduce a group of wayward nuns? He was about to pull up his jeans and make a run for it when a wild shout echoed through the room.

"Sister!" shouted the Hand of Glory. "Get away from him. Come over here. You too, Sister Helga. And even you, Sister Dorcas. Though you are not worthy, you too shall know the truth!"

The three sisters rose and walked over to Hand of Glory, a woman so pale and emaciated she resem-

bled an inmate from a concentration camp. She wore
a hairshirt and her exposed legs and arms were criss-
crossed with welts and marks of self-mutilation.

Jesus smiled as he saw her. She reminded him of
a chick he used to bang in Amsterdam.

With her was Sister Hildegard, her massive form
covered in dust, as if she'd just smashed her way
through a wall like some kind of human demolition machine. Jesus was lost for words and stood with his arse
out as the nuns began to whisper to each other.

+++

"The truth is simple," said the Hand of Glory. "He is
the saviour. Just look at him! Surely you can recognize
your own divine husband?"

Sister Dorcas squealed and clutched her hair.

"Divine?" said Sister Svetlana. "He's got an inverted crucifix on his arse! Doesn't that mean he worships
Satan?"

"Do not be so literal and naive," said the Hand of
Glory. "Did you think the Son of Man would return in
his previous, passive guise? The first time he came
it was to save humanity. Now he comes to judge humanity! To cast the unworthy down into the lake of fire!
He is a vengeful Jesus, come not to bring peace but
a sword. He is Jesus inverted. He shall be the cruci-
fier, not the crucified! He is the one who shall ram in
the nails. He has travelled through the realms of death,
only to rise again, upside-down! Where once he was
peaceful, now he is violent. Where once he was a
lamb, now he is a wolf. Where once he was white and
pure, now he is black and filthy. Now he is The Un-
clean, he is Black Metal Jesus!" The Hand of Glory
glanced at Helga. "What say you, Sister? I know you

too have experienced holy visions. Surely you can see what I see. Surely you can recognize our husband!"

Sister Helga was silent, too busy staring in awe at the man with his arse hanging out of his jeans. For many minutes she had already been aware of the presence of the divine, but had been unable to put her finger on it. And yet, there had been many signs - blood dripping from the ceiling, the icons on the walls winking and fornicating with each other, faces appearing in the wood grain patterns on the table, and a chorus of wailing souls in purgatory flowing with the cold mountain wind through the window. All of these signs had been there, all of these and more, yet Helga had not known what to make of them - until now. For now, she could see Black Metal Jesus in all his glory.

She could see the heavenly fire in his eyes, the nimbus of divine darkness wreathing his body, the blood which flowed not like blood but like strange smoke from the phantasmal wounds on his palms and feet. If she squinted hard enough she could even see the crown coiled around his head, made not of thorns this time but of rusted barbed wire dripping with glorious gore. The icons in the alcoves knelt for him. The saints in the stained glass windows hailed him with wanton displays of their wounded bodies - Bartholomew with his shredded skin and naked redness, Lucy with her empty sockets, Cecilia with her neck wound gaping like a hungry cunt. And if she squinted even harder, Helga could see the hosts of angels behind him, terrible Black Metal angels, wheels of burning black flame, winged skulls dripping blood, and four-faced cherubim with the features of vultures, zombies, and wolves all hideously fused into a heavenly visage of nightmare. And beyond them, seen as if through a wound in reality, loomed the towering divine host of black metal saints bedecked in black robes and corpse paint, playing Fenders and Les Pauls on black clouds dripping blood into the yawning abyss below.

Sister Helga let out a wild hallelujah as she saw that yes, it really was Him, the Son of Man returned in a new incarnation! "It's Him, it's really Him!" she wept and fell to her knees along with the Hand of Glory.

"If you say so," said Sister Svetlana. She joined the others on the ground. When Dorcas failed to take a knee herself, all three of them dragged her down.

"All hail," they cried. "All hail!"

+++

Whoa, thought Jesus. *Even nuns are sluts for rock and roll gods!*

He strode towards them with a giddy feeling in his guts. He could hardly believe his ultimate dream of defiling nuns in a blasphemous orgy was about to come true! Surely this would be the most metal night of his life, and the depraved acts to follow would form the basis for many killer tracks.

It was all worth it, to get to this point, he thought. All his trials and tribulations had been leading to this reward. Getting dumped by his band. Getting dumped by his whore ex-girlfriend for that asshole drummer in Flagermus (a fucking drummer!). Getting dumped by his record label for being "too egomaniacal" (Ptah! As if black metal lead guitarists weren't meant to be that way!).

It's all been leading to this, he realised. *This is it, this is the night!*

He stopped in front of the five nuns. Their eyes all seemed to shine different colours, like Halloween lights. Despite their habits, they looked like succubuses hungry for his man-meat. He dropped his jeans and showed them his rod.

"You," he said, pointing his prick towards Svetlana. "You've got a nice little whore face. You suck it first."

"He has blessed you, Sister Whoreface," said the Hand of Glory. "He has given you a new name. Now accept His baptism!"

The crazy anchoress grabbed the newly-Christened Whoreface by the habit and shoved her onto Jesus' cock. He felt himself slide past her lips and deep into her throat. She bobbed her head, taking him in and out of her oesophagus like a seasoned sex kitten. *Whoa,* thought Jesus. *There's no way this nun is a virgin!*

He closed his eyes and surrendered to the pleasure of her mouth. Then a sharp pain in his side made him open his eyes again. When he looked down he saw Whoreface's switchblade slicing a shallow wound across his abdomen. Her eyes locked with his as she took him in deep and slashed his flesh at the same time.

"Fuck!" he said, but made no move to stop her; it was way too hot.

"The stigmata," cried the Hand of Glory. "The Holy Blood!"

The anchoress licked the wound. Sister Helga shoved her face into it as well. Ecstatic, smeared with blood, the two sisters began to kiss, then fought with Svetlana for a taste of Jesus' prick. Soon all four of them - Helga, Svetlana, the Hand of Glory, even big Hildegard - were sucking on his shaft and balls, trading his length between them like a bunch of homeless diabetic hookers desperately sharing a lollipop to fight off hypoglycemia.

When Jesus first watched his member pass between big Hildegard's lips he winced in fear, worried she might bite it off. Instead, her mouth was wide and

deep, and her gag reflex was like a keyboard in a true
black metal band - barely there at all.

Watching those blood-smeared nuns fight over his
prick with their mouths was the hottest thing Jesus
had ever seen. He felt like he'd died and gone to black
metal heaven. Even the sound of the Mother Superior
snoring couldn't dampen the festivities (*Damn, that old
battleaxe could sleep through anything*). The only one
not getting into it was Sister Dorcas. The poor chick
was obviously having a bad trip. Her eyes were wide
with horror and she kept crossing herself. When the
others tried to shove her mouth onto Jesus' cock she
cringed away from it and cried.

"Oh ye of little faith!" screamed Hand of Glory.

"Service your husband, you ungrateful skank!"
shouted Whoreface.

"Heretic," shouted Helga. "Apostate! Suck his heavenly rod or go to hell!"

Sister Dorcas screamed like a person whose soul
was breaking in two. With a wild look in her eye she
wrapped her lips around the tip of Jesus' prick. She
may have looked like Miss Piggy in a nun's habit, but
the sight of her sucking on his manhood was possibly
the hottest thing Jesus had ever seen, because it was
obvious from her sloppy technique she'd never given
head before. She may have eaten a lot of sausages in
her day, but she'd never taken a prick into her mouth.
Out of all these wayward nuns, she was obviously the
only virgin. Her cheeks were burning as red as a cartoon devil's ass.

"Oh God," said Jesus, driven to the brink. "Oh
yeah, oh fuck yeah!"

He exploded all over Sister Dorcas' lips. She
screamed in shock, while the other sisters fought to
get splattered with subsequent jets of semen.

"The Holy seed," cried the Hand of Glory. "The

True Baptism!"

"Give it to me, husband!" cried Sister Helga. "Dorcas isn't worthy!"

With wild lust and devotion the sisters licked his seed from wherever it fell. From their habits, from the floor, even from each other's faces. Dorcas trembled as Helga and the Hand of Glory licked her semen-smeared mouth clean as a rose.

Holy shit, thought Jesus. *Being stuck in a convent really turns women sex-crazy!*

+++

The Sisters continued to lick and caress Jesus as he lounged spreadeagled on the dining table. He finished the wine and threw the bottle against the far wall. The Sisters watched it explode like fairy dust. Glitter wafted through the air, adding to the surreal feel of the scene, while Jesus continued to rant about his trials and tribulations as a black metal messiah.

"....Fucking Sven, he thinks he knows what's what. He's the damn bass player. Does he really think anyone gives a shit what he thinks? Whatever, let the fuckers try to kick me out, man. I've got my own shit to do anyway. They'll be playing weddings by the end of the year. Fucking wimps. I *am* Virgin Raper."

"What does he speak of?" Sister Whoreface mumbled.

"The betrayers," Hand of Glory said. "He is disgusted by humanity."

"Oh." Whoreface returned to the task of carving her initials on Jesus' abdomen. He flinched beneath her knife but seemed to enjoy the shallow cuts nonetheless. As Whoreface cut him, Sister Hildegard tongued an open sore on his inner arm.

"You like that?" he said.

"I do," she said.

He looked at her with a mixture of disgust and pleasure. "How about we call you Leper Licker? It suits you. That's seriously black fucking metal."

Her eyes lit up, "It would be an honour, Husband," said Sister Hildegard, now Sister Leper Licker. She went back to cleaning Jesus' ragged wound with vigour. "Even your infection is most delicious," she said. She gazed into the wound, which seemed to spiral into eternity. She bet if they cut Jesus open the whole of the cosmos would explode from his insides and the world would end. Armageddon, an event which had always filled her with longing. Could today be such a day?

"What of I?" Sister Helga asked as she rode atop Jesus, menstrual blood pouring from her gash. "What will be my most holy black metal name?"

"Ha, that's easy. You..." he pointed at her and thought a second longer. "You will be called Blood Cunt Christ Fucker, ha-ha! How do you like that?"

"Oh, I like it very much, Husband. Very much!" Sister Blood moaned. The sound of her new name, given to her by the black metal messiah himself, turned her insides hot. A gush of fluids, both his and hers, made her thighs slick.

While the nuns carried on in holy bliss, Sister Dorcas remained frozen against the far wall. Her eyes were wide as she watched foul demons possess her sisters' bodies in a black mass of the likes she'd never even imagined. Satan himself had named them his whores, and they liked it! Even Dorcas herself had been tricked into tasting his unholy rod. She prayed silently that she would have the courage to save them. But she felt paralyzed by Satan's claws. He rolled his lazy head and winked at her. Sister Dorcas cringed and hid her face away. It was so hard to think over all the moans and groans of carnal pleasure. Not to mention the tingling warmth between her own legs. Why oh why had she so liked the taste of the evil one's phallus?

A shuffling sound from the far end of the table finally caught her attention and freed her from this spiral of terror and self-loathing. She looked up and saw Mother Superior shifting in her sleep. The holy woman had been knocked unconscious by Satan's spell. Sister Dorcas knew she had to wake her. Such an experienced woman of God would surely know exactly how to banish the Devil!

Sister Dorcas began to crawl on all fours towards the chair where Mother Superior dozed. As she crawled she began to feel as though she were somehow outside of her body, and she realised this whole diabolical situation had the perfect makings of a Lifetime TV movie. Who would play her after the story broke? She thought she was definitely a Melissa Joan Hart, but she knew they'd probably get someone like that smug Shannen Doherty bitch. Denise Richards could totally play the part of Mother Superior, the powerful saviour of the Sisters. When Mother Superior died, and maybe even when Sister Dorcas died, they would be canonised. This last thought gave Dorcas the strength to shimmy the rest of the way across the floor to the feet of Mother Superior. She grasped the old nun's ankles, just as Helga's screams of lust and Satan's rant about The Man rose to pandemoniac levels, a crescendo of evil building to something truly apocalyptic. She had to wake Mother Superior before it was too late.

"Mother Superior," she hissed. "Mother Superior! Please, you need to wake up!"

No response from the old woman.

"Mother Superior!" Dorcas screamed. "The convent needs you!" She jerked on the old nun's habit, finally waking her.

+++

"Uh? What?"

Mother Superior looked around. Was she still in a dream? Sweat soaked her shift, and it felt hotter than hell. In her nightmare she had been burning.

"Sister, down here!"

Mother Superior heard the harsh whisper of a voice between her legs. When she caught sight of the demon pig clutching her habit she shrieked and fell backward in her chair.

"No! In Jesus' name!" She crossed herself. This was no dream. The pig whore came at her, its black eyes and gnashing teeth worse than a nightmare.

"Please!" cried Mother Superior. "In the name of God, be gone!"

"What's the trouble, Sister?"

A voice rang down from above. The demonic pig was lifted away. Its grunting and snorting continued as it struggled in a man's arms. He threw the creature aside. Mother Superior watched, paralyzed, as monsters even more wretched ripped the pig apart. When she realised they were eating the beast alive she opened her mouth in a silent scream.

A dishevelled face pale as death looked down upon her, and Mother Superior clutched at her chest. How could God betray her like this? She'd done everything he'd ever asked her to do. And yet he had put her in the damned place. And now? Now he was sending her to hell. She felt the cold, invisible fingers of the reaper wrap around her heart and squeeze.

313

"No," she wheezed. "Not like this! Not like this!"

"Sister?" the man said. But Mother Superior knew he was not a man.

"You will never have my soul!" she cried before going limp.

+++

"Is she dead?" asked Whoreface.

"Yes." Hand of Glory said.

"The religious ecstasy was too grand for her," Sister Blood explained.

"Damn." Jesus looked at the dead Mother Superior, her face twisted in a final expression of agony. His heart sank. Dead bodies meant cops, and the last thing he wanted to do was deal with that shit. He was still way too high.

"I'm going to fetch the authorities!" screamed Sister Dorcas. "The highest authorities! The Pope! You shall all burn for what you have done!" As she spoke she rose from the floor. Blood trickled from the split lip Leper Licker had given her, but she felt no pain. Instead she felt the power of the Lord wash over her. It was her time to stand up against evil.

"Like hell you are," said Whoreface.

"What are you going to do, kill me? Ha! God will never allow it!" Sister Dorcas fled down the hall.

"Should we try to stop her?" asked Jesus.

"Nah," said Leper Licker. "She'll just freeze to death if she goes outside. This place is a three day journey from town, and Dorcas can't drive."

"I'm going to tell everyone! *Everyone*!" Screamed Dorcas. "Demon whores!" Dorcas laughed. Feeling free for the first time, she ripped off her robes, cloaking herself only in God's Glory. They would never find her.

314

They would never stop her. The Lord was guiding her. She was THE CHOSEN ONE!

Soon she was outside the convent. The snow burned her feet and the wind lashed her skin like a hundred whips as she entered the wintery night. And yet she continued to run, following the twinkling eye of God high in the Heavens. The rocks on the embankment were sharp against her bare feet as she attempted to make her way down into the gorge, where her wicked sisters would never find her.

+++

"We should follow her lead and get the hell out of here," Sister Blood said as she rifled through Mother Superior's pockets, removing a silver rosary and a few stray coins. "Get the gold and silver from the altar."

"Wait, what's going on now?" asked Jesus. He felt tired and confused. The drugs were wearing off. He felt vomit rise in his mouth but managed to swallow it back down, so that only a rancid belch escaped his lips. "Man, I think I need to get some sleep."

Sister Blood looked at him. "You cannot sleep, Warrior King. We have your Word to spread. Why do you say such things, after all you have shown us? We cannot rot away in this forsaken place for another moment. You told us so!"

"I did?"

Jesus was beginning to question his life choices. Giving acid to religious fanatics might have been a bad idea. Just look at the results. Sure, there had been some gnarly sex, but now one nun was dead and another was running around naked in the freezing snow, while the four who remained had just started robbing the place. By the time dawn arrived there would be two

315

dead bodies and a lot of missing valuables. What if the cops tried to pin it all on him? Wouldn't Sven love that, to see him in fucking jail! How would he ever compose his great masterpiece of black metal vengeance from prison? All of this shit was just way too heavy to deal with in the middle of a crashing come-down.

"I'm going to go take a nap," said Jesus. "I suggest you all do the same. My head is going to split the fuck open in about two seconds." He staggered off in search of something resembling a bed.

"What a fucking wimp," Leper Licker said.

Hand of Glory slapped her face. "You watch your tongue, Sister! That is our Black Metal Jesus. He has blessed us, given us new names, revealed HIS Word, and broken our chains. Let him rest. His work is done, but ours is just beginning."

The nuns gathered sacks of antique candelabras, savings from a small safe, rosaries, crosses, and a discoloured tapestry of Judas making out with Jesus.

"It is so seductive." Hand of Glory insisted.

Leper Licker and Whoreface trailed behind Blood and Hand of Glory, knocking over candles and dropping lit matches like breadcrumbs on the dry timber flooring.

"Goodbye bondage, you bitch!" Sister Whoreface said.

Soon the four sisters stood on the road watching flames eat their way through the decaying roof of the convent. The morning sun peeked over the edge of the mountains, staining the sky a deep pink.

They loaded their sacks in the back of Jesus' van. Sister Blood got behind the wheel. A twist of the key and the engine turned over without delay. The Sisters let out a sigh.

"It is a true miracle!" Hand of Glory said.

The others agreed. They pulled away, leaving the

inferno behind them. The Messiah of Black Metal had set them free, and now it was their turn to repay the favour.

+++

Fears For Lead Singer/Guitarist of Virgin Raper Still Missing After Months

It has been nearly four months since the singer of the controversial Florida black metal band, Virgin Raper, has gone missing. Jesus Heretic (real name Toby Lee Evans) was last seen parting ways with his bandmates at the Hungarian border town of KisBúkk. He was first reported missing about 1 week after he failed to meet back up with his band in Salgótarján. Rumors of a rift within the band have led some to think that Evans may have committed suicide.

The official missing person's report was filed after his mother and father, Judy and Pastor Ron Evans, flew to Hungary to aid in the search for their only son.

"Over the last few weeks the friends, family, and fans of our dear Toby, known to you all as Jesus Heretic, have been working closely with local authorities to piece together his whereabouts. We hope to come to a positive resolution soon," they said in a statement released earlier this week.

Authorities issued a plea for anyone with information on Evans' whereabouts to please come forward.

+++

317

Church Burners? The Rise Of Christian Black Metal

Black metal has been known as Satan's game for a long time, but the Sisters of Temperance Holocaust are changing all of that with the release of their first single Burn In Ecstasy Sweet Jesus.

The Sisters, despite their gimmick of posing as nuns, have been called "neo-skinheads" and even "unholy terrorists." The radical Sisters have personally claimed to be arsonists, mystics, murderers, and also devoted Christians. Some think this group might be responsible for the bombings across Europe last summer.

The lead singer, Sister Blood Cunt Christ Fucker (real name, Helga Chelovekonenavistnichestvo) denies these allegations and has been quoted as saying "We rage war with our music. Humans are sheep, Bah! Bah! They are stupid followers of the false god! People love evil because it tells them what to do, while the Black Metal Messiah will set you free! We spread His Word like a metal fist to the face with our divine prophecies. We do not need your bombs or guns, we have our machine gun bass. We hate love and peace! It makes me sick! Cower before Black Metal Jesus and be done with it, fools!"

Temperance Holocaust has recently been invited to the Vatican by the Pope himself. It is expected he will bless their upcoming full-length album, Dawning of the Deathgash.

Leave A Review!!

By reading this book you are showing your support for indie authors and small presses like us. For this, we want to say thank you! If you would take a moment to leave a review whether it's on Amazon, Goodreads, or any other social media platform, we would very much appreciate it.

Books don't make themselves. Many countless hours go into creating the work you are about to read. Often times, indie authors you enjoy create these books as a result of raw passion, artistic expression, and pure drive, while also working day jobs. A review is a great tool to help get their books into as many hands as possible plus earn a piece of recognition for writers who truly deserve to have their names read and remembered.

At Swann + Bedlam we began publishing as a way to get wicked awesome books to readers like you. Our mission is to publish the offbeat, the macabre, the problem child, the outcast, and the flat-out weird. No genres, no boundaries, no agenda.

Once again thank you for reading and reviewing this work.

DON'T LET THE MAN BRING YOU DOWN.
Power to the people!

Published by Swann + Bedlam

Copyright © 2024 by BJ Swann + Elizabeth Bedlam

All rights reserved.

No part of this publication may be reproduced, distributed, or transmitted in
any form or by any means, including photocopying, recording, or other
electronic or mechanical methods, without the prior written permission of
the publisher, except as permitted by U.S. copyright law. For permission
requests, contact Swann + Bedlam.

The story, all names, characters, and incidents portrayed in this production
are fictitious. No identification with actual persons (living or deceased),
places, buildings, and products is intended or should be inferred.

Book cover by George "Corpser" Salazar
Interior cover by The Parish Priest
Logo by Rotten Fantom

Formatting by Swann + Bedlam
Editing by Swann + Bedlam
an imprint of Punk AF Publishing
287 Exhibition St,
Melbourne, VIC 3000
Australia

swannbedlam.com

Expanded edition 2024

About the Authors

Elizabeth Bedlam is a writer of satire, dark humor, and low-brow literary fiction. She has been featured in anthologies as well as zines which include *Anti-This/Anti-That, Low Life, Horror Sleaze Trash,* and *Soiled Purity.*

Her most-read works include *Hello Old Friend* and *The Way The Light Falls.* She has been praised for her realistic depictions of neurotic females.

She is a Michigan native but currently lives and writes from Melbourne, AU.

B.J. Swann is the incarnation of a cosmic demon who shall not be named. He has come to earth to usher in the Aeon of Chaos, an age of madness, mayhem, and pleasures undreamed of.

He likes comic books, bubble tea, and boneless fried chicken.

Other Books From

Life and Other Unfortunate Horrors
by Quinn Hernandez

Dead Endings
by Henry Ben Edom

Dog Men
by Gavin Torvik

Doomsday Daytrip
by Rob Ramirez

Cigarette Lemonade
by Connor de Bruler

Psychedelica Satanica
by Sybil Oxblood-Pope

FOR MORE BOOKS CHECK OUT
SWANNBEDLAM.COM

FOLLOW US ON INSTAGRAM
@SWANN.BEDLAM

BECOME AN ARC READER EMAIL US AT
SWANNANDBEDLAM@GMAIL.COM

www.ingramcontent.com/pod-product-compliance
Lightning Source LLC
Chambersburg PA
CBHW010450100726
47904CB00008B/2558